Fit Company for Oneself

By Connie Kronlokken

The author believes that all quotations in this book have been used under the "commentary and criticism" fair use of copyrighted materials.

Published by

Lightly
Held
Books

ISBN-10: 0692451021
ISBN-13: 978-0692451021

DEDICATION

To Solveig, Naomi, Ruth, David, Ann
And in memory of Rebecca and Susan

Also by Connie Kronlokken:

Pleasure's Only Rule
Friends and Magicians
Living in the Flatlands

So Are You to My Thoughts Series:
The Pastor's Kids
Fit Company for Oneself
With One Hand Waving Free
Pulled Into Nazareth
Nature's Stricter Lessons
A Moon Every Night
So Are You to My Thoughts

Fit Company for Oneself

The day Hanna was born, the house was full of black raspberries. Paul, a tow-headed 12-year-old, was the first one home from school. A silver pail of the black, sweet fruit held down a note in Mother's perfect cursive. "We have gone to the hospital. Please go get Kristen at the Sherwood's. Make yourself some scrambled eggs for supper. Love, Mother."

The large frame house at the edge of town in the rolling hills just west of the Mississippi River was very quiet. Usually Paul could hear the sounds of his parents, or his sisters shuffling about on the creaky floors, talking, maybe a radio playing. It was rare that the parsonage was empty.

Paul opened the freezer to make sure there was some ice cream and left the house. He stopped in the yard to unleash Foxy, his mostly golden border collie who was tied up at this time of year so a neighbor wouldn't come after her with a shotgun if she got into his garden, and went through the hedge to the Sherwood house next door.

It was quite warm, the first week in September. Paul could hear John twitching apples off the top of a tree with a long fruit picker, and Kristen, who was only three, crowing as a heavy apple came swishing down. When she heard Paul, Kristen looked up. She has no idea, Paul thought, that she might have a new baby sister or brother by this time. They all hoped the baby would be a boy, as Paul was so far the only son. But God, in his wisdom, would make that decision.

"I'm helping," murmured Kristen softly. Big yellow curls wafted around her head and her pink, chubby arms stuck out of a blue cotton tee-shirt.

Paul smiled up at wizened old John, whose thin face opened like a walnut under his engineer's cap and red bandana. "She's a good little helper," John said.

Foxy snuffled at the squashed, bruised apples at the base of the tree, which smelled sickly sweet. But Paul warned her away with a low-voiced "Foxy, come here." There might be wasps in them.

"Come on, Kristen," said Paul. "Let's go home and have black raspberries and ice cream." His instinct, like that of his parents, was to circle the wagons, collect the family and wait upon events at home.

To John he said, "Do you think I can let Foxy run free soon?"

John stood as straight as his hunched back would let him. "Another couple of weeks," he said. He took off his red bandana and wiped his face. "It'll frost soon and then it will just be the potatoes and the roots left." He leaned down and picked some apples out of the bushel, but Paul could only take a couple.

Paul grasped Kristen's hand firmly. "Thank you for watching Kristen," he called, as his little party turned and headed through the tall hedge that separated the Sherwood's acre of land from that belonging to the parsonage.

Paul scooped a bowl of ice cream for Kristen and himself, and the two of them ate at the table in the big, light-filled kitchen. The thud of a heavy case announced Line's arrival as she dropped her French horn. Books fell on a coffee table.

Line sailed into the kitchen. "How exciting!" she said, as she looked at the note. She was tall, 16, with a pear-shaped body like mother's. Sunny blonde strands in her red-brown hair curled around her face. She wore a green shirtdress, belted around the waist. Paul thought she was pretty, though she wouldn't have said so herself. It wasn't very important to her. "Have you heard anything?"

"Nope, not a thing," said Paul. He held up a spoon of creamy vanilla with blackberries smashed into it. "The food of the angels," he said. He beamed up at his sister's shining face. The natural kinship between them was taken for granted by both. Dad called Line "Sparky," the leader of a gang made up of Paul and Marty. They weren't so much a gang any more, as Paul knew little of what went on in high school, but they still shared deep knowledge of each other, the camaraderie of siblings growing up close in age.

Kristen hardly looked up. She plodded through her dish of ice cream like a little bulldozer, eating one spoon after another.

"I'll go change," Line said, as she turned and left. Paul heard a little chortle as she passed the hall table and dashed upstairs. He too had seen the letter with the exotic stamp from the Philippines on it. Line found writing hard, liked speaking much better, but the idea of foreign pen pals spurred her into spending her small allowance on air-mail stamps.

Marty was the next to arrive, more still, darker and slower than Line. At 15 she was growing up too, but differently. In her, the light was not on the surface, it was buried deep in a thoughtful face.

"Where's Mom?" she asked Paul. She put her stack of schoolbooks carefully on the table and picked up Kristen. Kristen's crib was in Marty's room and Marty rocked her to sleep with a book almost every night. Marty hugged the solid, heavy little body, but then put Kristen down. "You're getting too big and you're sticky, you little rascal!" she said. Sweet cream circled Kristen's lips.

Paul handed Marty the note. A pink flush crept into Marty's pale cheeks. "I guess Dad's going to call us?"

"Yep," said Paul. As he said so the phone rang and they both raced into the study, colliding at the door.

* * *

As the elder, Marty answered the telephone, but it was only Mrs. Nelson, the church organist, calling Dad, the pastor, to ask what the hymns for Sunday would be. Putting down the phone, Marty said, "I better go take off my school clothes. I'll be right back." She blew dark, sweaty bangs off her forehead as she went upstairs in the heat, her hand trailing along the oak banister.

Line stood in her bedroom door. "I guess that wasn't Dad," she said.

"No," said Marty. "We'll just have to wait." What are we going to do with ourselves, she wondered. She was already in waiting mode, unable to do anything until Dad called with news.

"How long ago was it we went berry picking?" asked Line.

"It was Monday, Labor Day, the day before school started," answered Marty. "And today's Friday." She looked hard at Line, knowing what Line was thinking.

"I don't really think the accident could have affected the baby," said Line. "It was supposed to come this week."

"Yes," Marty said hopefully. "She's been fine." They were both wondering about Mother. "We'll just have to wait," she said again.

3

That Monday the family had packed themselves into the Studebaker station wagon, with a paper bag full of sandwiches, empty silver sorghum pails and plastic ice cream tubs, and gone out to a neighboring farm to pick black raspberries.

Dad, wiry and vigorous with a long shaft of dark hair he greased into submission, drove, wearing an old tee-shirt and a pair of khaki slacks. Mother, in the passenger seat, with soft brown curls framing her gentle face, cradled her big stomach under a homemade maternity sundress, a brown and white striped tent dress with straps that tied at the shoulders. The belt at the waist was up around her breast, Marty had noted. But it was a day to be comfortable. No one was there to notice what the pastor and his wife were doing, where they were going, or why. It was what Mother loved about Nature. Under God's heaven, out in the woods, the only prying eyes and clacking tongues were the birds, and they had little judgment.

Marty sat in the middle of the cracked leatherette back seat, hanging onto Kristen's waist, as she stood looking between Mother and Dad. Marty didn't want her to go flying. Line rode with her head and arms out the window, breathing in the warm gusts of air. Paul leaned out the other window. In shorts, Paul's thin, polio leg was a contrast to his powerful leg. Both legs worked though, and Paul himself hardly bothered about them any more.

The gravel road went up and down the ravines and a dusty wake followed the car. Much of northeastern Iowa near the Mississippi was rugged with hills. It was called "The Little Switzerland of Iowa," and farmers made the most of it to grow the corn and soybeans that fed their livestock, plowing in contours around the hills.

A mischievous grin spread across Dad's face as he pushed the accelerator down on the way up a hill. "Hang on, kids!" he yelled.

"Rolly coaster!" shouted Paul. The station wagon sailed over the crest of the hill and Marty's stomach sailed with it.

"Ooooooh!" chortled Kristen. Marty grabbed her and pulled her down into the seat. The kids loved the "rolly coaster hills" and Dad didn't disappoint them.

Mother held on to the dashboard with one hand, but she was smiling. Dad's foot pressed down hard as they rode up the next hill and careened down it. All of a sudden, at the bottom of the hill, the wheels hit something and the car twisted out of Dad's control. The station wagon was in the ditch, still going fast, with tall dry weeds whizzing past the windows.

Dad hung on, gripping the steering wheel and easing the big car to a stop. He looked at Mother, whose face was white. "I'm sorry, dear. That was really foolish," he said. "Are you okay?"

"Yes," Mother said shakily. "I'm glad we didn't roll over."

Dad looked anguished. "Are you sure you're okay?"

But Mother sat there quietly, listening to her body and the new life within it. "Yes, I think so, Carl," she said.

Dad turned around, but he didn't have to ask if the kids were okay. They were beaming, excited by the adventure of landing in the weeds in the ditch. Kristen bounced out of Marty's restraining hands. "Again? Rolly coaster again?"

"Nope," said Dad. "That's enough for one day! I'm not even sure we can get out of the ditch!"

In fact they couldn't. Dad had to walk over to the farm and ask one of the Hansen boys to bring a tractor and a winch to drag the car up onto the road. The old Studebaker was fine, and so was the family, eating their sandwiches as they waited. But they were all a little subdued and careful as they went into the woods with their pails and tubs. Kristen perhaps didn't know how bad an accident could have been, but Marty and the others certainly did.

Black raspberries grew in thickets in the woods full of oaks, hickories and black walnut trees. Marty breathed in the fragrant smell of the woods in the heat, the leaves of the tall trees sun-burnt and drying. It was the smell of fall. Above her, the sky was clear and intensely blue. Later in the year, they would come out to harvest nuts when their drying husks began to fall off the trees.

"Who's taking Kristen?" Mother asked. It was too easy for everyone to assume that someone else took her with them.

"She's with me," said Marty. The two of them headed toward a spray of the black fruit. Marty picked the dark berries into a clear plastic ice cream tub, her hands quickly turning purple. Beside her, Kristen grabbed at the berries with both hands, stuffing them in her mouth. She didn't seem to notice the thorns, so she must have learned to pull the berries off. But she wasn't gentle or dextrous and dark purple berry juice circled her mouth and ran down her tee-shirt.

"Come on, Kristen," said Marty, teasing. "One for you and two for the pot." She ate a few herself, of course. Sun-warmed berries, plump and dark with wild-tasting sweet juice, were so good. The black raspberry branches climbed up over each other, arching toward the sun and hanging down in long sprays. When she reached into the thickets, Marty got scratched, but the best berries were often hiding, growing succulent under the leaves.

Marty and Kristen kept moving, lured by the abundant dark purple berries. Dad said it was a black raspberry year like no other, and he was right! It must depend on the rain, the sun, and pollination, mused Marty. She picked only the best ones. They could never pick them all.

All of a sudden, Marty froze. Someone was calling her. Her tub was half full, but she was worried. Where was everyone else? She looked down at Kristen, oblivious, eating berries like a little bear. Marty could not tell where the call came from.

"Marty," called Line's voice urgently.

Marty started in that direction, taking Kristen by the hand. "Come on," she said quietly. But thickets blocked the way between her and Line's voice.

Dad called too. "Marty, Kristen!" He sounded like he was somewhere else.

Marty turned and stumbled through an open space, tugging Kristen behind her. She mustn't let Kristen feel her panic. "Come on, Kristen," she said.

"Where are you, Marty?" called Paul.

"Here!" said Marty, chagrined. It didn't help much.

"Come this way," called Line.

Marty tried, but the woods were thick. Finally she saw the road, the Studebaker shining in the sun. She headed toward it, dragging grubby little Kristen by the hand. Dad stood by the car, and Mother was already inside, tired.

"Marty's here," called Dad to Line and Paul, who were looking for her. "Let's go!"

Marty didn't say anything. Dad sounded grouchy by this time, and she was just glad to find them. Being lost was what she remembered most from the afternoon, as she stood talking to Line, wondering how Mother was doing at the hospital.

"Dad's a great driver," Line said. She was taking driver's education that year. "Most people would have jerked the wheel or jammed on the brake if they went in the ditch, which can make the car roll over. But Dad didn't. He just hung onto the wheel and eased to a stop."

"Mother said so too," said Marty. "She said it was because he was used to ice and snow and knew how cars behave. He drove as if he were driving on ice." She remembered the weeds whizzing past the window.

"We were lucky," said Line. "Once again."

"Yes," said Marty, retreating into her bedroom.

The two girls rarely knew what each other was thinking any more. They didn't share a bedroom and they were very different. They both took the bus home from the low modern high school, set two miles out in the country between towns, but often they didn't even wait to walk home together.

Marty sat down at the little alcove desk built into the back hall where a maid once crept down the steep stairway to the parsonage kitchen in the mornings. From a library book, she copied phrases supposed to have been written by the Chinese poet Tu Fu: "When a place is so lovely, I walk slow. I long to let loveliness drown in my soul. To the depths of my bones I love old trees and the jade-blue waves of the sea." Marty wished she could feel herself, who she actually was, just for a moment. Her self always slipped away. She couldn't hold it.

* * *

Line went down to the kitchen and scooped herself a bowl of ice cream. She could see Paul pushing Kristen in the swing under the cedar trees. She went out and sat on the back steps watching, letting the cold berries and cream slip down her throat, her mind jumping from thing to thing.

Line's letter had been from her penpal in the Philippines. She imagined going for a year as a foreign exchange student. It must be very hot there, as it was near the equator. No winter! On the globe, the place looked like it was all islands. But Josie's letter didn't tell Line what she wanted to know. Josie wrote about her family and what she was doing in school. It was no different than if she was a boring American! But of course, that couldn't be true.

Line thought about talking to David Berglund, who was sweet on her, about having a real farm animal project for 4-H. She was sick of the projects town girls usually had, baking or furniture projects. And how uninteresting student elections were in contrast with the exciting speeches of John Kennedy, the Democratic candidate for president. He said he would not make promises to Americans, he would set challenges for them. This appealed to Line's hot, young heart. She wanted challenge, change, things to happen!

The phone rang and Line ran to answer it. "Hello?"

The voice wasn't Dad's. It was Ellie, their oldest sister, 19, married and living in Iowa City, where her husband Bruce was studying for a business degree. "Hi, Line," said Ellie. Her voice was cheery, but also impersonal. Line knew Ellie didn't want to talk to her. "Is Mother there?"

"Nope," said Line. "They've gone to the hospital." Marty clattered down the stairs and stood listening, but it obviously wasn't Dad on the phone.

"Wow," said Ellie. "So it's just you guys home? Dad's gone too?"

"Yeah. He'll call us when the baby's born, but it should be soon," said Line. "How are you?"

"We're fine," said Ellie. Line had last seen her when Ellie and Bruce joined the Mikkelsons at the lake for a few days in August. "Bruce started school this week and I just got home from work. But I better not talk long. Please ask Dad to call us when the baby's born, okay?"

"Sure," said Line. Long distance telephone calls were expensive and Ellie never called. She and Mother exchanged letters two or three times a week. Ellie must have been anxious for news. Line replaced the black receiver on the telephone and looked at Marty. "Just Ellie," she said.

Marty sighed. "Dad will never call."

Line laughed. "What are you so worried about?"

"Nothing."

"You're not having a baby," said Line. "Just think. Ellie's almost twenty years older than this baby. Isn't that amazing?"

"It could be Ellie's baby," said Marty. "But I'm glad it's ours!"

"I guess we should make supper," said Line. She felt listless all of a sudden. The sun was slipping behind the hills, but the air was still very warm. Line cut bacon into pieces and fried it. She poured in a scramble of milk and eggs. Kristen stood by the stove, watching, and Marty set the table in the capacious farmhouse kitchen.

It was a strange meal, but Line was used to it. In a big family, you never knew who would be home for supper. A brooding silence hung over them. Line wanted to laugh at Paul and Marty acting like the parents, watching over Kristen.

Line turned on the television after supper for company. There was no homework since it was Friday, and the new shows were beginning. The four of them watched *The Flintstones* and then *77 Sunset Strip* to see what Kookie was up to. It was fun to see him tooling around on his motor scooter. Los Angeles was a long way from Montauk, but Line didn't really want to go there. It wasn't foreign enough and no one there needed her help.

Kristen was falling asleep. "Come on, Kristen," Marty said, dragging her toward the stairs and propelling her up, holding onto the banister, one step at a time. "You're too heavy to carry!"

Line changed the channel. Dinah Shore sang "See the USA in your Chevrolet … America is asking you to come." How often Line had heard this commercial, Dinah's skirt swishing as she strode around, her blonde hair staying perfectly in place.

The phone rang. Line raced to answer it and Marty came careening down the stairs. Dad's warm voice came down the wire. "Congratulations, kids, you have a new baby sister."

"A sister!" said Line. She held the black phone receiver out so Paul and Marty could hear.

"Yes," Dad's voice sounded tired. "Mother and baby are fine. Her name's Hanna May."

"Hanna May," breathed Paul.

"You kids go to bed," said Dad. "I'll be home soon, and tomorrow we'll all take a trip to the hospital so you can see her."

"We're glad Mother's fine," yelled Marty.

"Yes," Dad's voice came. "We're very pleased."

"Don't forget to call Ellie," said Line. "She called, but I didn't have anything to tell her."

"I will," said Dad. "Good night. God be with each of you."

9

"And you, Dad," said Line into the phone. "Thank you for calling us. We were all on pins and needles." The suspense was over. Everything was fine.

"Well, it's over. Mother is resting," Dad said. "Go to bed, now. Good night!"

"Night, Dad," Line put the phone down. "I can't believe it! Another girl!" Paul grinned and Line punched his shoulder. "I guess it's official," she said. "You're my only brother."

"I can't wait to tell, Kristen," said Marty. "She'll be so excited!"

"You're not going to wake her up, are you?" asked Line. No one in the Mikkelson family waked a sleeping child if they could help it.

"No," said Marty. "I'll tell her first thing in the morning."

The sound of crickets chirping came in the screen door from the front porch. "I'm going to go tell Foxy," said Paul as he headed out the door.

"At least there's no school tomorrow," sighed Line as she followed Marty up the stairs.

The town of Montauk was too small to have even a clinic. After lunch the next day the Mikkelsons went to the new blonde brick hospital building spread out near the edge of a nearby town. Dad parked and Line and the others walked into the modern building wearing their school clothes. Kristen was scrubbed and wore a dress which had once been Marty's Christmas dress.

"So these are your other kids," said a sweet-faced nurse to Dad as they stopped at the front desk. Her starched white cap inspired respect and the quiet, sterile-smelling atmosphere meant that people might be suffering near by. Line looked at Paul, who was the only one familiar with hospitals. Paul had lived in a clinic for months at a time during his first polio attack and reconstructive surgeries. Line remembered staying with Paul during his second surgery, when he had been in such pain.

"Yes, this is Line, Marty, Paul and Kristen," said Dad. "How're my girls?"

"They're doin' fine," said the nurse. "Your wife just finished lunch, and I think they're bringing the babies up just now."

Dad knew where to go. Mother looked relaxed and happy, sitting up in bed with a light cover drawn up over her nightgown. She must like being fussed over, Line thought. Mother never got much attention at home. But they didn't have a chance to talk to her before a nurse brought in a bassinette with the new little Hanna May in it.

The nurse handed the bundle wrapped in a white blanket, to Mother and the kids finally had a chance to look at her. Hanna was red-faced, with soft light-colored hair. She had the biggest eyes and an ambivalent look.

"She can't see us yet," said Line. She felt like an old hand with babies, but she was struck by how different Hanna looked from Kristen. Kristen had a stolid little face from the beginning, but Hanna looked ethereal, as if she was uncertain whether she belonged there. It was amazing how much you could see of a person in their face and body.

"No," said Mother. "Not yet. But I bet she can hear you. Talk softly to her." One by one, the older kids leaned over to touch and smell Hanna's soft skull. What did the sweet, milky smell come from, Line wondered.

Dad held Kristen up so she could see. Kristen reached out her hand to the baby's face as if she were a new puppy or kitten. But Hanna's red face screwed up into a scowl and slowly, as they watched, a tiny, raucous screech came out of her. Once it started, it looked like Hanna wasn't going to stop wailing.

Dad laughed, "Little Chief Rain-in-the-Face. Princess Storm Cloud." Kristen looked at him, shocked. "You were that little once," he said. "You cried too. Plenty!"

"If only Ellie could be here," said Mother, lifting the tiny Hanna to her shoulder. "Then we'd all be together."

Those days are over, thought Line, though she didn't say so out loud. Mother would just have to get used to it.

2

The air was crisp and Line could see her breath as she bicycled out of town early in October on her way to David Berglund's farm. David had promised she could share in the pig project his Dad was letting him run.

Marty had answered the phone. "David's on the phone for you," she said coyly.

Line was annoyed. He was just a friend. Why did people have to be so silly?

David's voice sounded excited. "The sows are farrowing! If you want to see them, come as soon as you can in the morning." It was lucky it was Friday night. If it were any other night, Line couldn't have gone, though David could take off a day of school or skipped church. Though he had a general idea when his pigs would give birth, they did it on their own time.

"Are you going to spend the night in the barn?" asked Line. She tried to imagine what it would be like.

"Yup," said David. "I'll be out there." Line knew that the barn was warm from all the animals in it, and that there were heaters. The Berglunds had raised pigs for many years. Pigs needed to be kept warm, especially the new little piglets. So maybe the barn wouldn't be too cold, but Line was glad she would be in her own warm house that night.

Line popped awake early in the morning. Only Dad was up, having a cup of coffee in his study, getting ready for the confirmation classes he taught on Saturday morning for young Lutherans. Line ate a bowl of cornflakes and a piece of toast. Mother knew where she was going so she didn't have tell anyone. She slipped out the door and found the blue bike in the garage. It was an old Schwin Dad bought second hand, a girls bike. But it worked.

Line pushed the blue Schwin up the hills, puffing frosty air out her nostrils as she went. The sun wasn't up yet and the woods were blue in the distance. Black fields rimmed with frost lay on one side of the road, and a cornfield full of dry standing stalks on the other. The hush of the coming winter lay over them. There were sparrows chattering on the telephone lines, but the melodious redwing blackbirds of summer had left.

When she got to the top of a hill, Line had to decide whether it was too steep to ride down. It was wonderful to coast down a gentle decline that curved through woods and fields, but down steep hills Line walked the bike. The gravel was frightening under the thick bike tires and there was nothing to slow the bike down.

As always, Line's thoughts roamed far from home. Maybe I could go to Russia or Cuba as an exchange student, she thought. She wondered what communism was really like. Every day in the news it seemed there was discussion of the Iron Curtain between the western countries and the Soviet bloc. They must just be people, thought Line. I would really like to talk to them. But of course, she would have to learn Russian, and how could she do that?

It was five miles to the Berglund farm. In the summer, when Line helped David walk beans, hoeing weeds out of the rows of soybeans, she rode her bike. But today, in the cold with the wind in her face, it felt much longer. There were hardly any cars on the road. Line could hear them behind her, and see them in the distance as they came around the bends. The sky ahead of her was pink with the coming light behind the almost bare trees.

When Line got to the neat farm, she went straight to the barn. As she went in the side door, Line smelled hay and manure, and something pungent, like cedar. In the dim light, she saw David dozing in an old Army sleeping bag on a pallet of hay bales. Tenderness rose in her and she went and sat beside him. He was Swedish, but his skin was dark from the sun and his short curly hair was burnt and sunny too.

"Good morning," said Line. The thing she liked best about him was that his body spoke more than he did. His thick lips in a long, thin face formed words slowly. She was like this herself, didn't like to speak if she didn't have to.

David raised himself up on a lanky, brown arm. "You're a nice wakeup," he said. He looked over toward the pen where a large sow lay on her side, and then back at Line.

Line leaned down, her nose touching David's. "I'm an Eskimo," she said, softly, rubbing her nose back and forth.

"I like it," David said thickly.

"Where's your Dad?" asked Line quietly, looking around. Her blood was stirred by the bike ride and coming into the hushed atmosphere of the barn heightened Line's senses. Orange-tinted slivers of the rising sun came through crevices along the barn doors, illuminating the heads of cows and pigs, the edges of hay bales. The sounds of the animals moving in the straw and snuffling was peaceful, almost sacred. Better than church, thought Line.

"He's around," said David evasively. "Probably getting some coffee."

"And how's the sow? Is there more than one?" Line looked over. She was going all soft around the edges, being so close to David.

"She's doing fine."

"Am I in time to see her farrow?" Line asked, standing up.

"You missed one of them. See? Over there," David pointed to another pen where piglets lay against a large sow, nuzzling her teats. "But you'll get to see Sweetie," David stretched and yawned.

"Does she need you? Or does she do it all herself," Line wondered, going over to look at the little piglets. They looked so clean and pink lying beside their mother on a fragrant bed of cedar chips.

"She does it herself, on her own good time," said David, "but we have to watch to see that everything is going okay." He stood up and came over to the pen,

"Which one is yours? Or ours?" Line asked, kneeling to look at the small pigs. "Can I hold one? How can you tell them apart?"

"Okay, okay," laughed David. "Hold on there. You're too fast for me this morning!" He knelt down and lifted a pink piglet from the litter of six and placed it in Line's arms.

Line held the little pig with its tummy up as if it were a newborn baby, remembering Hanna, who was born only six weeks ago. The piglet was soft-skinned and felt so alive in her arms. Its small eyes were filmy, and its little body heaved with its breathing. Don't have souls, Line thought to herself, scornfully, remembering what Mother told her. That was ridiculous. Animals must have souls.

"We call this sow Mrs. Bossy, because she's the first to get to the food, and she pushes Sweetie out of the way. Sweetie loves the apples I always give her for treats," said David slowly. "Dad will clip numbers to the feeder pigs' ears, so we know which is which."

"Do I get to help with Sweetie's piglets?"

"Yeah, that's the idea," said David. "We'll wean them in a few weeks, and then fatten them up." David looked at her significantly, as if to tell her she better not get any ideas. Pigs were raised for money. That was all there was to it.

But he didn't have to tell Line. She knew as well as he did that pigs became bacon. Line never turned up her nose at a bacon, lettuce and tomato sandwich. In fact, it was her favorite. She leaned down and kissed the soft skin of the little piglet. "Enjoy your life," she said out loud. She might eat part of him one day, but that would be sacred too.

"Pigs are really intelligent," said David. "They're a lot like people. I think they know." He looked over at Sweetie.

The door opened and Mr. Berglund came in. He was a black shadow with the sun bright behind him, steam rising off him. "Hey, Line," he said. He went over to Sweetie and drew an expert, rough hand over her flank. Like David, he was thin and dark, wearing rough denim clothes. He had the same short haircut as David, but grey showed in the curly, wiry thatch.

"Contractions?" asked David.

"Starting," said Mr. Berglund.

"Come on, Line. Let's go boil up a kettle of water at the house," said David. "We wash the piglets in warm water. I'm hungry too." The two of them went out into the low-angled sunshine and over to the brick farmhouse.

In the kitchen, Mrs. Berglund was having a cup of coffee while David's two younger sisters washed dishes. If she wondered what Line was doing there, Mrs. Berglund didn't say so. David filled a kettle and turned up the gas under it. His mother fried eggs for them.

Line was impatient to get back to the barn, but David slowly and methodically ate toast and eggs and drank coffee while the kettle chortled and steamed. On the way back to the barn, he filled a big pail with cold water from the outdoor trough and poured in the hot water. He collected soap, explaining, "I'll hand you the piglets as I pull them, and you can wash them." He dipped his hand in the pail to check the temperature.

"Okay," said Line, tentatively.

"Just lay them out on the cedar chips when you're done, so they feel close to Sweetie," he said.

"Okay." Line admired his practicality, his sureness in the face of the strangeness, the wonder of new life. She had never seen anything being born before.

"Wash your hands," said David, as he washed his with soap in the pail. "Here's a rag. Just pretend they're like little kids, and wash them all over."

"They are little kids," said Line.

It was an amazing morning. Line watched as the soft little pink piglets emerged from the sow in the holy silence. David pulled them out as soon as there was something to grab onto, a foot or an ear, deftly, gently guiding them. Mr. Berglund stood beside him, swiftly cutting the cords to their mother with a knife, and handed them to Line. She sat in the straw and cleaned amniotic fluid out of the little snouts as the piglets struggled to breathe, and then washed and rubbed them all over with a towel. The little sows had tiny teats and the boars a rudimentary penis. Mr. Berglund looked each of them over to see how healthy they were.

Four piglets emerged, three little girls and a boy, but Mr. Berglund seemed to think there should be more. He started the other morning chores, turning the cows out of their stalls, cleaning them and pitching down new hay.

David and Line waited, watching in silence for over an hour as the piglets crowded close to their mother, David's hand helping them to find her milk. Finally, Mr. Berglund came over.

"Guess you better check her out, David," he said. "See what's going on." He leaned down to watch as David washed his hands in the pail and rolled up his sleeve. He reached a long brown arm into Sweetie's uterus to see whether he could feel any more pigs.

"I don't feel anything, Dad," he said.

"Hmmmmph," said Mr. Berglund. He knelt down and put his own hand in, searching. "Well, maybe you're right." He stood up.

"Want to feel, Line?" asked David.

Line looked at him in surprise. "Really? Me?"

"Sure. But you don't have to unless you want to."

It felt like a challenge. "I want to," said Line. She began washing her hands.

"Do it now," said David, watching Line screwing up her courage. "We've probably bothered her enough."

Line swallowed and let David guide her hand into the opening of the sow's vulva. The sow's muscles contracted, trying to get rid of this unwanted intrusion. "Go ahead," said David. "There's a long way to go." The soft, wet flesh against Line's felt powerful. Line inched her hand in, but then, all of a sudden, she pulled it out, swallowing again as her stomach seemed to rise into her throat.

"It's okay," said David. He looked at her, smiling. "Now you know what a hog feels like inside!"

Line sat back. Life felt intense to her. And good. Birth was wonderful. "Birds do it, bees do it," she said shakily.

"Good girl," said David. But then he became practical. "I better help Dad," he said, standing up and looking around. "I'll choose a couple of these piglets and make them my 4-H project this year. And you can help. Especially in a few weeks when they're weaned."

"Okay," said Line, shyly. "I guess I should go home. Thank you for letting me help." They washed their hands again and made sure Sweetie was comfortable.

Line felt a little limp from the powerful feelings of the morning. But David didn't notice. He measured feed carefully from bags along the wall into two pans. He had watched sows farrow since he was a little boy.

"Bye," David said casually as Line got ready to leave. "I'll see you in school." He went to Dad's country church and Line didn't see him on Sundays unless the Luther Leagues from the two churches got together in the evening.

Bicycling home with the low sun behind her, Line was exhilarated. David was so wonderful. She did wonder if doctors stuck their hands inside women when they had babies. Line doubted it. She knew they sometimes pulled babies out with forceps, which was bad for the baby. Baby's heads were very big. Line shuddered. She knew absolutely that she would have children, that one day she would feel like that sow.

But I won't be a farmer's wife, she said to herself sternly. I won't stay in Iowa. I want to go places, do things, do something great. She was surprised at her own vehemence, and the energy it gave her as she pedaled up a hill.

That week Valley High School held a mock election. Posters of John F. Kennedy were all over the school. Many students wore buttons saying "Vote for Nixon" or "JFK for President." The Mikkelsons, like most people from Iowa, thought Nixon had the needed experience and could handle the problems he would face. He was the Vice President under Eisenhower, and people were happy with Ike. Also they were not anxious to have a Catholic president.

Marty waffled as usual, influenced by Mother and Dad, and others. But Line wanted the young Kennedy and his wife to win the national election. She liked the way he expressed himself. He said, "I don't speak for the Catholic Church on public matters, and the Church doesn't speak for me." There was a new feeling about him. It was the daring kids at school who supported Kennedy, town kids usually, not the farmers. When the votes were in at Valley High School, the Nixon-Lodge ticket won.

Not so in the national elections. Kennedy won by a slim margin and a majority of the electoral college. Three days after the election, Nixon said he would not contest it.

Line and Marty got off the bus together and walked home in a light snow. Nixon's speech had been announced in Line's history class.

"I feel sorry for Mr. Nixon," said Marty. "Losing by a third of a percent! I'm going to write to him and tell him I'm still behind him."

"You are so annoying," said Line vehemently. "Why can't you accept the fact that Kennedy might be a good president?"

"I do like his wife," said Marty, looking wistful. "She's just beautiful."

"I really want to be a foreign exchange student next year," said Line. "We talked about it again in history today. Remember when we used to put our finger on the globe and spin it? Wherever our finger landed, that was where we were going to go? I think I'm going to do that. I don't really care where I go. I just want to go somewhere!"

"But it will be your senior year!" said Marty.

"Who cares!" Line said hotly, as she scuffed along in her snowboots. "Nothing happens here. I can imagine everything that will happen next year. I want to go somewhere that I can't imagine."

"We were reading glimpses of other countries in English today," said Marty. "I liked what this Danish writer said about her coffee plantation in Africa. 'Here I am, where I ought to be.' Isak Dinesen. That's what I want. I want to find the place I ought to be."

"That's good," said Line. "I guess I just know that this is not the place I ought to be! I don't know where I should be. I have to find it."

"Well you're a little young for that, aren't you?" said Marty sensibly.

"Darn!" swore Line daringly. "That's what Mother keeps saying."

"They're worried about all the things they hear about the cousins. You know. Uncle David tells them about his problems with Diana. She's running around with a bad crowd, smoking and drinking, doesn't listen to her folks," said Marty.

"Yeah," said Line. "But I'm not like that. I can take care of myself. And I'm not as wishy-washy as you are. I'm not like the grass leaning whichever way the wind blows."

"I'm not a conformist," Marty insisted. "I just see all the sides of a question, that's all. And it's easy enough to be influenced by the people around you. That's what Mother and Dad are afraid of. You know. Like they still aren't happy about Ellie running off and getting married at 18."

18

"I'm not like Ellie, either!" retorted Line as she leapt up the steps to the porch at home. The snow was wet and light, not settled yet, or icy. But talking to Marty helped. Line didn't feel the need to storm into the house and badger Mother about letting her become a foreign exchange student, again. She would talk to Mother, but she knew that if she let her ardor cool a little, she could make a better case.

At suppertime, Line set the table in the dining room, going back and forth to the kitchen where Mother was stirring a goulash on the stove. Early in the school year Mother tried to make dinners special, giving each of the kids a chance to talk about what happened in school that day. By the holidays, leisurely meals went out the window with the pressure of events, but it was still early November.

Line collected the silverware for six out of the drawer. It was stainless steel, of course, but everyone still called it silverware. "Is there dessert?" asked Line. If there was, they might need spoons.

"I guess so," said Mother. That meant ice cream, Line thought. She counted out the spoons.

"We talked about Israel today in history," began Line reasonably. "Everyone's reading *Exodus*."

"I know," said Mother. "There's a movie coming out about it soon."

"I do think I would learn more about places if I were actually there," said Line. "Books just don't give you as clear a picture."

"That's true," said Mother. "Books usually have a point of view. You kids must learn to distinguish what is true from what isn't. There are so many points of view out there. The election has certainly shown this."

"But I can't read all the books," said Line as she passed Mother with a stack of plates.

"You know, Line," said Mother, with the authoritative voice that meant she was getting exasperated. "I can see where you are going with this. Again. But there is no possibility of your leaving home right now. You must give up the idea of being a foreign exchange student. You are not mature enough to go far from home and live on your own. You must settle down!"

Line looked at Mother, her heart slipping down into her socks. She could tell from Mother's tone that she was putting her foot down. Line had raised the issue so often that Mother was tired of it.

"America is full of its own problems. There's a very good article on Martin Luther King in the *Life* magazine this week," Mother went on. "You might study the campaign Dr. King is making. He sounds like a wonderful man, and a good Christian."

Line felt silenced. She looked at Mother's gentle but firm face. There was no use continuing if Mother was dead set against her plans. Dad wouldn't help her if Mother was against it. She rarely got Dad's sympathy anyway.

"Go tell everyone to wash up for supper," said Mother, turning toward Line. "You have a big life ahead of you, Line. Don't get so impatient. Everything will come in its own good time."

Mother meant well, but it felt like salt in Line's wounds. She slunk off to call the other kids and think about her life. It was hard to find sympathy, that was for sure. She couldn't talk to Marty or Mother about David Berglund without them taking it too seriously, and she couldn't talk to David about her desire to leave Montauk and do something great with her life. There wasn't really anyone she could talk to. Maybe Paul, but he was too young to feel as she did. Line brooded. She didn't say anything during dinner, except to answer laconically when Mother spoke to her. When it was clear she didn't want to talk, Mother, and everyone else, left Line alone.

But Line's emotional weather moved from shadow to sunlight fairly quickly. Not even counting schoolwork, there was so much to do. Basketball games were starting and the girls team was rated best in the state. Line had given up on being on the basketball team, but she played in the band and sang in the chorus. She practiced driving the new forest green Ford Country Sedan Dad bought and she wrote a speech titled "Are you encouraging anti-Semitism?" which Mrs. Tannahill thought was good. Line had never met a Jewish person, but with all the interest in Israel and in Anne Frank, the topic was easy to write about. It was Line's entry in the Radio Speaking category of the county speech contest.

Snow covered the highways and roads and it was too cold to bike out to Berglund's farm. Line couldn't really claim a pig as a 4-H project, she realized. Mother was always telling her she couldn't do everything. But one Saturday David stopped for her in the pickup on his way out from town.

The little pigs had been moved into another shed, far from their mothers. And they were a lot harder to hold on to! Line couldn't tell Sweetie's pigs from Mrs. Bossy's, but David, having worked with them every day, knew a little about each of the surviving thirteen pigs. He spread out food in the pans and pointed out which ones were more aggressive and which ones were shy. He picked up the smallest pig and gave it to Line to feed. The pig protested loudly at being dragged away from the others, struggling, but Line spooned warm mash into the mouth under its little snout and it settled down.

The pig house didn't have the sacred feel of the barn on the day the pigs were born. David was busy, unloading the feed he bought and replacing the straw bedding where the pigs spent most of their time. He went back and forth to the barn with wheelbarrows, his breath steaming as he came into the warm pig house. He walked around adjusting heaters and lights. Line tried to stay out of the way. She rarely saw his thin body at rest, she realized. He didn't usually miss school, but he didn't do extra-curricular activities either.

In the late afternoon, they went into the farmhouse kitchen, where Mrs. Berglund laid out supper a little early, as David wanted to go in to the basketball game. She smiled at Line, but her warmth was limited, Line could tell. Line was known as David's girlfriend, but Mrs. Berglund was protective. She wasn't so sure about Line.

The kitchen was warm and cheerful, surrounding a table in the middle covered with a multi-colored oilcloth. Mr. and Mrs. Bergland sat at either end, and the two younger girls opposite David and Line. After grace, steaming plates of boiled potatoes and cooked green beans were passed, and a plate of beef.

"Some gravy, Line?" asked Mrs. Bergland, passing the old-fashioned china gravy boat. Line spooned gravy onto her potatoes, but she didn't know what to say. The silence was cordial, but it oppressed Line. Perhaps they weren't used to guests.

"How'dya like those feeder pigs?" Mr. Bergland asked Line.

"They're wonderful," said Line, politely. She wondered what Mother would have said in this kind of silence.

"David raises some champions," he said. He and David discussed the weather and the temperature the pigs needed, but the two younger girls said hardly anything and Mrs. Bergland was silent also. It seemed the point of dinner was eating. Dishes were passed around for seconds, but David was in a hurry.

"Come on, Line," he said. "We don't want to miss the pep bus." They put on their coats and boots, wrapping scarves around their necks. David drove the pickup into town with Line sitting in the middle of the front seat next to him, her body touching his. The boys' basketball game was exciting and fun. Line cheered and clapped, jumping up and down on the bleachers next to David. But she was nervous. She could tell that David, who was a year older than she was, was beginning to take life more seriously than she.

When they drove home, David parked the old pickup in front of the parsonage. He wrapped his arms around Line. With the ignition turned off, the pickup quickly got cold, but it was pleasant sitting next to each other in heavy winter clothes, faces nuzzling. They were friends, used to each other and there was no awkwardness. Neither of them spoke.

At last David said, "What am I going to do with you, Line?"

Line looked up at his thin, handsome face so close to hers. She loved his directness, his honesty, but she could hear a painful topic coming.

"I'm 17, and all I want to do is farm, but you don't want to be a wife."

"Not now, anyway," said Line.

"You're a willow-the-wisp," said David. "And our dreams don't match. That's all there is to it."

"I'm glad you understand," said Line, slowly. "I love you. I know I do. But I can't stay here. I want to go to college. I want to do all kinds of things!" Her stomach hurt. She never felt as comfortable with anyone as with him. He knew all about sex, had explained it to her, and yet never took advantage.

David's face grew hard, practical. "Well, no sense worrying about it. You can't get blood out of a stone, and all that. Good night, Line," he said releasing her. He kissed her cheek quickly and Line got out of the pickup and hurried up the snowy walk in the cold air to the house, feeling the sad tug between her mind as sharp as a stone and her heart as soft as feathers.

3

As the Valley High School girls basketball team got closer to being in the state championships, every game became a matter of life and death. Particularly to Marty. She wasn't living in her own skin during the games, but in the bodies of the six girls, some of them her friends, who were down on the court.

The district finals were held in March, in Manchester, an hour and a half away from home. Marty traveled on the pep bus with Cathy, a thin, energetic girl with a ponytail who lived a few blocks away. They entered the gym in the middle of a low-key consolation game, but as soon as the kids from Valley High School arrived, it erupted. Valley school songs flowed from their pep band and the crowd, even though their game hadn't started!

Rival Maquoketa fans had taped a big paper "Beat Valley!!" sign on the concrete gym wall, right above where the Valley fans were sitting. The Valley kids tore it down and put up their own, "Go Valley High Girls!" in blue and red letters.

"They had no business putting that sign up," groused Cathy. Marty agreed. But here came several boys from Maquoketa, tearing down Valley High's long paper banner.

In seconds Valley fans raced to the top of the bleachers to save the banner. There was a big rip along one side, but they taped it back up. Several of Valley's biggest football players, including Jim and Rodney from Marty's class, sat in front of it and it was left alone.

The Valley team was rated first in the state all year. They did not lose a game. But could they hold their lead? Mary Hallborg, a tall, slim forward, the best shooter anyone had ever seen, sparked the team. The year before they had lost the state championship, winning a consolation trophy. This year, all the girls on the first team except for Georgia, one of Marty's best friends, were seniors. They had to win the championship this year. They just had to.

As the game started, Valley surged, making point after point. But Maquoketa had little to lose and their best guard badgered Mary Hallborg, fouling whenever she could. Marty jumped up and down, yelling and almost choking on her gum as Mary Hallborg took her classic left-handed jump shots.

Mary seemed to have the sniffles, but she kept playing, slim and graceful in a silky white suit with blue and red braid. Marty ached to see her leaning over when the ball passed to the Maquoketa side, as if she had a pain in her stomach. Coach Farnsworth stalked the edge of the bleachers in front of his girls, wearing his trademark bow tie and a light colored sport jacket. Georgia, with her dark short hair and pale skin, was guarding carefully, keeping the Maquoketa forwards from getting a shot.

At half time, Valley was still ahead, but Maquoketa kept up and gained the lead in the third quarter. The guard assigned to Mary fouled out, but Mary fouled too as the game got rougher. Coach Farnsworth pulled her onto the bench after her fifth foul. They couldn't afford to lose her.

"We're not going to make it," wailed Marty to Cathy beside her, feeling the hand of fate moving toward them. She twisted the class ring on her finger so much that it fell off and rolled under the bleachers, to Marty's horror.

"Do you want me to go get it?" asked Cathy, calmly eating crackerjack from a box. But a little boy was already scrambling through the iron legs below the bleachers to pick it up.

Disaster averted, Marty looked down on the bench where Mary Hallborg sat between Barbara and Coleen, her sun-streaked hair frizzy, her chest heaving. Mr. Farnsworth walked back and forth beside the team, taciturn, calm. "We want to go to State so bad, we're not going to get to!" Marty said intensely to Cathy.

Cathy looked at her with amusement. "Where's your faith, Marty? Believe! Don't give up yet!"

Three minutes in the game to go. Coach Farnsworth sent Mary back in and she made basket after basket. In very short order, Valley was 14 points ahead. Marty jumped and yelled so much she almost fell head first into a parent's lap!

The buzzer sounded. Valley won. They would go on to the State finals. Marty was beside herself, hugging Cathy as everyone poured down onto the gym floor. How exciting it was to be on a winning team.

On the pep bus going home, wrapped in her coat and scarves and mittens, Marty was sleepy and happy, her imagination replaying the evening. She was in the skins of her friends, smelling the sweat and warm rubber tennis shoes of the locker room as the girls changed into ordinary clothes and came home, heroes.

It wasn't that Marty loved basketball so much. She loved the poignancy with which Mary Hallborg carried the honor of the school on her slim, graceful shoulders, playing whether she felt good or not. She loved the deadpan way Mr. Farnsworth moved along the sidelines, quiet and collected under the pressure of the screaming fans. She loved knowing that Georgia and Barbara, her good friends, were on the team.

Angst and excellence, the elements of heroism were played out right down on the court, where Marty could watch. Mary Hallborg, tall and pretty, was a farm girl who spent the summers shooting baskets, thin and proud. She was never without her sidekick Luann, a guard on team. The whole team was excellent. But they were modest and careful. Everyone knew that pride went before a fall and the stakes were very high.

Line was on the bus too, but strangely, she didn't seem as wild about basketball as Marty did. Something was eating her, Marty thought. She was growing older, was fighting her own battles. She didn't seem to

24

care as much about Mr. Farnsworth, who had once been her hero, either. Marty knew better than to ask Line what was going on. She suspected it had something to do with David Berglund.

When the girls got home, Mother was up, sewing in the warm dark house. She laughed at Marty, all riled up from the game and talking a mile a minute. Marty explained about the gold and onyx class ring, which Mother had given her so she didn't have to spend money on one.

"It's okay, Marty," said Mother. "I don't care a fig for that class ring. I hardly know anyone from high school any more, and none of it was as important to me as college."

"But this is a once in a lifetime experience! It isn't every day that your team becomes a contender for state champion!" crowed Marty.

"Well, maybe you're right," said Mother quietly, smiling as she stuffed pieces of cloth under the thread gate and put down the presser foot. She and Line exchanged glances, as if they had discussed Marty. "Go to bed now girls. Tomorrow is another day, you know."

Marty felt Mother's mocking amusement keenly. Why did Mother have to laugh at her, trying to curb her enthusiasm as if she knew better. Line even joined her! Marty added it to the store of bitterness she held against those who tried to take her down a peg.

In school, the basketball players stuck together, walking back and forth to classes and their lockers like lambs to the slaughter. Marty felt compassion for Mary Hallborg as she walked through the halls, her frizzy blonde head taller than most of the other kids. She was beautiful and delicate, the star, with people's expectations resting on her. Could she go the distance without crumbling, the heat turned up?

A new golden District champion trophy was added to the long glass trophy case in the front of the school, but the team hardly celebrated. Marty didn't learn much from Georgia and Barbara. They were resting, conserving their grit for the coming fight. Excitement mounted as everyone made plans for the coming week.

Carloads of kids drove down to Des Moines to the tournament, but Marty and Line didn't even think of asking if they could go. There simply wasn't money for such gallivanting. Kids would pile up in hotel rooms, sharing expenses, but Mother and Dad didn't like that idea either.

The week of the tournament, school was a ghost town and Marty wandered around, distracted. No one could concentrate. Lost Nation High School, a hundred miles south, was now considered the top team. They had won the championship the year before and they hadn't lost any of their star forwards. In a game between Lost Nation and Valley at the beginning of the year, Valley won by only one point.

Valley High won their two bracket games, though, and on Thursday afternoon a huge snowstorm blew in, with snow flurries so thick that no one could see where they were going. The school bus lumbered back to Montauk, and Line and Marty walked home in the twilight world of a low grey sky, wet flakes falling and snow piling up in the roads.

"I hope the snow doesn't affect the games," said Marty.

"Everyone's used to it," said Line. "There will be plows out. It's such a wet snow it won't last long."

"I feel so sorry for Mary," said Marty. "Everyone's depending on her."

"Oh Marty, you're just star-struck. There was a newspaper article today about how good the defense is. They're playing pretty well and Mary isn't, according to Mr. Farnsworth," said Line.

"Really?"

"Mr. Farnsworth is kind of mean, talking that way in the newspaper. He said, 'Defense won it for us again. Hallborg scored a lot, but she missed shots she doesn't usually miss. She can play a better game than that.'" Line recited as if she were reading. "Now how do you suppose that makes Mary feel?"

"Wow," said Marty. "Did he really say that? That is kind of mean." Perhaps all wasn't as rosy in the locker room as it looked on the surface. "Is that why you quit basketball?"

"Well, Mr. Farnsworth was nice to me, because I wasn't that great. But I could see how he treated the good players, manipulating them. I didn't like it."

"He's a good coach with a winning team. No bad thoughts, Line. Don't jinx it!"

In the morning they woke to drifts of clean whiteness piled high everywhere, hiding the ugly aspects of life. The dark green cedars looked like they were sugar-frosted and heavy snow outlining their branches bowed the bushes down. The roofs on the shed and the garage were outlined in a thick layer of snow. School was called off until the roads could be plowed and everyone settled in to a day of doing as they pleased.

Dad swept off the bird feeder, put out a dried sunflower from the garden and nailed on a big lump of suet. The blue jays and downy woodpeckers were quick to find it, flashes of color against the snow. Chickadees and nuthatches swept in when no one was looking to have a bite. Brilliant cardinals were attracted by the sunflower seeds. When Paul and Foxy went out in the yard, Foxy floundered in the deep snow. Marty could see their footprints and wallowing marks from the big windows.

Big lazy flakes wafted down and Marty tried to help Paul look at them on his new microscope. Paul brought in a dish of snow, but every time, before they could transfer a flake to the slide, it warmed up and became a puddle of water. Every snowflake was known to have a different, frosty and delicate shape, but they could see them better with their naked eyes. Especially Marty, very near-sighted without her glasses.

"We have to take the microscope out where it can get cold," said Marty. "Maybe that will work."

But even when they put it in the freezing entry, the effort of moving the snow onto the slide warmed it, and it was a pool of water before they could look at it. Paul was disappointed, but he kept trying things, putting the slides in the freezer, looking at snow collected from different places. His interest persisted long after Marty's waned and she wandered off.

Six-month old Hanna was another matter. Marty could play with her for hours, just watching her quirky face, letting her roll and play on the floor, holding her so she could stand and talking to her. Hanna wanted to be part of everything. She waved and talked baby talk and smiled at everyone who came near. She wanted to touch everything and see what it felt like, and taste whatever she could get close to her mouth. Kristen was still in Marty's room and Hanna slept in a crib in Mother and Dad's room, but Marty liked to put them together, watching to see how different they were.

Kristen played and talked with small dolls and toys. She liked to be around everyone else, of course, and tried to involve the rest of them in the small farms she set up. She was interested in Hanna, the baby, but it was quite clear that she was "a big girl now." No one was going to hold her in their laps as often as they held Hanna.

Kristen was stolid and heavy, lots of weight in her bottom. Hanna was lithe, rolling over and over on the rug, and thinner. Her face was responsive, whereas Kristen focused on the games she was playing. Perhaps it was just a matter of age, thought Marty. Kristen was three. But watching the "little kids" as they were called was her favorite chore.

In the afternoon while the little kids napped, the grey light turned to sunshine, purpling the shadows and melting the heavy snow. Dad stayed in the study, tuning in to conversations on his ham radio. Line was in her room, reading and brooding as usual and Paul shoveled sidewalks, since it seemed to have stopped snowing. He loved being outdoors.

Mother asked Marty to bake cookies, so Marty got the mixer going, creamed butter and sugar and mixed up a batch of ginger crinkles. Waiting while they baked, she watched Mother patiently filling a notebook with Spanish vocabulary and verbs, as directed by the Spanish correspondence course she was taking.

But Mother felt bothered by Marty hanging over her shoulder and said, "You should practice the piano. Mrs. Jorgenson will be back from southern California soon and you will be sorry you haven't practiced all year!" Mrs. Jorgenson, Marty's piano teacher, spent the winters at her home in California, returning to Montauk in the spring to teach.

But Marty was restless. She didn't want to do anything. She sat at the kitchen table, dipping cookies in milk, loving the taste of the spicy ginger with the cool milk. Soon Kristen wandered downstairs and the house was no longer quiet.

That evening the championship game of Valley against Lost Nation was televised. The whole family watched. Mother held Hanna, who stood up and bounced in her lap, as sprightly a baby as one could imagine. Kristen made a farm on the floor, not very interested. Paul and Line sat beside each other on the couch, a bowl of popcorn between them. Even Dad went back and forth to his study, keeping tabs on the action.

Marty could not sit down or sit still. She stood at the back of the room, watching the tiny screen with the black and white figures of her friends rushing back and forth down the court two hundred miles away.

The Valley girls got a big lead early in the game, but Marty could feel the adrenaline surge through her body. Could they hold it? It wasn't quite like being at a live game, but almost.

All of the girls played brilliantly. Lost Nation failed to rally and the game wasn't actually very exciting. The built-up tension was released. They did it. The Valley High girls basketball team won the state championship, the top team in the state. Mary Hallborg scored 60 points, tying for a third place all-time record in individual scoring for one game. She made the all-tournament team and so did her friend Luann.

After the game, an interviewer with a microphone stood out on the floor as the trophy was presented. The golden trophy with basketball players atop tall columns looked as if it was taller than Kristen! Mr.

Farnsworth, who barely came up to Mary's shoulders, lifted it high. The interviewer thrust a microphone at each of the girls.

Mary Hallborg was sweet and grateful. "Last year we got the child," she said, referring to the trophy. "This year we got the mother."

"Great playing," said the interviewer. "How do you feel now that this long season is over? You've won every game!"

"We're all very happy," said Mary. "It's a dream come true."

"Lot's of hard work making that dream come true, wasn't it?" said the man with the microphone.

"You aren't just a foolin'!" said Mary, smiling and stretching her long torso.

"This is your last game, isn't it, Mary? This is a great win to cap off your career! I guess you'll be hanging up your suit for good?"

"Yes," said Mary. "Everything's gone so well. Maybe I'll play in college. Haven't figured that out yet." It was the most relaxed Marty had ever seen her. She was the reigning queen, the star, stepping down with honor.

When the interviewer saw Georgia rubbing clammy hands on her suit, he asked, "Are you nervous?"

"Yes!"

"What do you want to say to the folks back home?"

"Just want to thank them for their support. We're a team and we all work together, and you're part of our team too!" She was afraid to look at the camera.

"So how do you feel about the game?"

"I thought this game was actually easier than the others. I was surprised."

"So do you think you'll be bringing your teammates back to this championship arena next year?" Georgia was the only one of the first team not graduating.

"Well, I'm not sure," said Georgia. "We'll have to see what kind of team we can put together." She grinned nervously, throwing a quick glance at the camera.

Marty found it odd to see Georgia's face close up, so far away yet so near. Georgia, who sat beside her in English and was her main competition for the best grades in their class. Georgia, on television as if it were the most natural thing in the world.

On Sunday afternoon, Marty, Line, Paul and Dad went down to watch the victory caravan of cars come in to town. The sun was brilliant, the snow was melting and slushy and the air was quite warm. A banner saying "Welcome Home Valley Girls" hung over the main street between the brick department store and the tiny grocery where the Mikkelsons did their shopping. Nothing was open on a Sunday, of course, but lots of people were downtown, milling about in the spring air. Everyone was smiling.

When the caravan of cars drove under the banner, most of them parked right in the street. Six guys from the football team got out of one car, including Marty's friends, the genial Rodney and big Jim. They wore red, white and blue letter jackets and carried the noisemakers they used at the game.

The pep band full of cornets and trombones formed up in their winter coats and scarves and played "Hold That Tiger," the Valley fight song, over and over while they waited for the station wagons with the basketball players to arrive.

When the girls got out of their cars, people erupted into cheers. There was short Mr. Farnsworth, who emerged from a station wagon, pulling with him the huge golden trophy. He held it up with both hands, and then Mary Hallborg and Luann came over and took both sides of it. It was clearly heavy!

The mayor tried to speak to Mr. Farnsworth, but there was no loudspeaker, so the hundred or more people standing around in the middle of the snowy street on a Sunday afternoon couldn't hear. Marty and Line stood as close as possible, but they didn't even get to greet their friends. The public gathering of congratulation broke up quickly, the caravan was moving on to the other towns in the consolidated school district. There was to be a program out at the high school, but Mother wanted them to come home. "Enough excitement," she said. So the Mikkelsons didn't go.

When they got home, Marty didn't want to go indoors as the sun lowered and the purple shadows got longer on the shining snow which lay almost golden all around them. She and Paul walked around the block, watching Foxy who was free to ramble at this time of year sniffing around the telephone poles. The bare canes of the raspberries pushed up out of the snow in the garden and the little apple trees Dad planted stood, leafless and ready for springtime. The Sherwoods' big orchard also stood waiting, and flocks of little birds careened through the trees, settling on one and then rising in a cloud, twittering and settling on another.

But as soon as the sun sank behind the bare branches of the trees on the hills, the chill came up and Paul and Marty and Foxy went back to the cozy parsonage where Mother was making toasted cheese sandwiches and cocoa for supper.

Marty's excitement rose again as she got ready for school in the morning. Dad had cut her hair and she curled it with plastic rollers around the front. She surveyed herself in the mirror. It was well known that boys didn't make passes at girls who wore glasses, but she didn't look half bad otherwise. She wore a new dirndl skirt she made from cotton on which the printed pattern was different around the bottom. She couldn't wait to get to school and find out all the news.

School buzzed with stories and references to things that happened during the tournament week in Des Moines. But it sounded as if they were speaking a foreign language to Marty. Everyone else already knew the stories about what had happened in which hotel room late at night. About which couple sneaked out of the game and weren't seen for a day.

Marty didn't even dare ask what they were talking about. She felt stupid, like someone from another planet who showed up in the middle of something everyone else knew all about. No one noticed her new skirt or her carefully curled hair.

Marty stumbled through classes. Noisy kids giggled and told jokes. Marty sat miserable on the edges, unable to quite hear what they were talking about, not part of the group. How could this happen to her? She had been so excited, had shared the excitement of the championships with everyone. But now it was as if she were invisible. Her shocked silence didn't help.

At the end of the day Marty went home, rushed up to her little desk and wrote in her diary, "I need a shoulder to cry on, Anne." Her imaginary correspondent Anne Frank could certainly provide her with a sympathetic shoulder. The flood of her feelings was so hard to explain, her superfluous sympathy for people and her confusion.

Hanna, little Hanna whose silent body Marty could hold close to her, and Kristen, who hardly talked but welcomed any sisterly embrace, also helped. Marty gathered the two little girls to her. With Kristen sitting on one side of her on the couch and tiny Hanna propped up on the other, Marty opened the big dog book that Kristen loved. Kristen looked up at her, trusting and sweet. Who knew if Hanna was listening or not as they discussed the various dogs, especially the tiny dog which was photographed in a tea cup. Marty's bitterness dripped away in the presence of the two little girls.

Finally Marty sat down at the piano and opened the piece of music dotted with notes on the treble and bass clefs of the page. It was Mozart's "Fantasie in D Minor" that was to be her piano solo that year. Her fingers, curled in the little curved barns Mrs. Jorgenson recommended, felt strong and powerful as she practiced. Rolling chords climbed up the keyboard and back down into Marty's favorite dark, crashing chords. Lighter Mozartian clavichord melodies in the middle also soothed her.

No one bothered Marty as she sat at the small blonde spinet, practicing. She played the Grieg "Nocturne" she had learned the year before and played so badly at the Dorian festival. It was getting better, stronger. Her right hand found the bird trills, but the best part was the continuing dark chords of the left hand. By the time the melody meandered up and settled back down into silence, Marty felt much better. She held the richness of the music close to her chest. If she couldn't share in the euphoria of the winning team's week in Des Moines, she vowed she would find her own, hard-won happiness.

4

"Alan Shepard has just returned from space," said Mr. Johnson, Paul's young, thoughtful history teacher, on a bright morning in May. Paul heaved a sigh of relief at the dramatic announcement. Everyone knew he was going up. Paul watched the agonizing preparations on television that morning as he ate his breakfast cereal. When the countdown was halted to see if visibility would increase, Paul had to leave for school. It wasn't a sure thing. No one knew whether Shepard would get off the ground, or get back to earth safely.

The United States was behind in the space race and Paul so wanted them to catch up. But also, he worried about Mr. Shepard, sitting in that tiny capsule. Lots of things could go wrong, but they apparently didn't! "Okay, class," Mr. Johnson said as the buzz of student conversation settled down. "Let's get back to World War I."

Paul exchanged a look with his friend Ernie Regan, who was just as excited as he was about Alan Shepard going up in a rocket. Ernie, with dark hair, pale skin and freckles, wanted to be an engineer. He was always tinkering, much better than Paul at mechanics. Paul liked biology best, but all kinds of science were needed to conquer space.

Like Paul, Ernie wanted to know more about the space launch too, right now! World War I was interesting. Airplanes were used in World War I, but conquering space was now! On television! In Paul's living room!

After class the boys commiserated as they walked down the hall to their next class. "Why can't we take off school to watch something like this," Ernie voiced what they were both thinking. "It's much more important."

"Yeah," said Paul. "It's more exciting if you get to see it when it's happening. My Dad is home watching."

"I hated going to school this morning," said Ernie, "but my Mom made me." Ernie lived at the opposite end of town and walked to school like Paul. His Dad ran the feed and fertilizer store.

"Yeah," said Paul. "The countdown stopped and we didn't even know if he would go up. So I went to school. I guess they'll replay it tonight."

"Yeah," said Ernie, mournfully, "but it won't be the same."

In English, Mr. Potratz, droned on about diagramming sentences, drawing them on the board with his old-fashioned ornate handwriting. Mr. Potratz wore expensive pin-stripe woolen suits, with starched white shirts and ties, as a compensation for his short, hunchbacked body. Beside Paul in the crowded seats, Ernie drew diagrams of the Redstone rocket which launched Freedom 7 into space. His head down, his pencil moving on the wide, note-taking arm of the wooden chairs, it looked like he was paying attention.

But no one was. When Mr. Potratz turned around, the class struggled to return from whatever daydream occupied them. Paul tried to listen as he felt sorry for Mr. Potratz, who was earnest and well-intentioned. But learning to diagram sentences was not what he wanted to be doing.

School went very slowly that day. Finally the last bell rang and Paul rushed home. When he got there, the television was off. With the success of the mission, the television networks thought people would rather watch game shows than more about the space program! Paul asked Dad if he saw the whole thing.

"Yup. Pretty short trip, but it means the next one will be longer!"

"The next one!" said Paul. "I wonder who'll get to go up on that one." Paul had followed the astronauts since they were first chosen. He couldn't pick a favorite, but now he decided it was Alan Shepard.

Space, to Dad's amusement, was defined during the International Geophysical Year as 62 miles, or 100 kilometers up, at a line named after Ted von Karman. Apparently, heaven, as seen by their ancestors, must have been higher! But Dad and Paul were both dedicated to science. Alan Shepard went up 116.5 miles and, like a missile, sank back down. But he was definitely in space. And he briefly took control of his ship, unlike the Russian Yuri Gagarin, who orbited the earth in an automatically piloted space capsule a few weeks earlier.

That evening, Paul listened to the replay of the launch broadcast. Merrill Mueller, the broadcaster who talked through the launch said, "He looks so lonely up there," and then fell silent. Shepard was a symbol of what every man in America wanted to do, fly higher, faster and farther than anyone else. He placed himself in danger, remained simple, practical and determined, and he did it for all of them, taking a step into space that didn't put America equal to the Russians, but at least showed she could be in the future.

Paul would have watched any amount of television about the space race. There was never enough to satisfy him. He was making a Heathkit transistor radio with Dad. Dad sent for it and the pieces came in packets, together with step-by-step instructions and diagrams on how to do it. Paul didn't quite understand the schematics or why the radio worked, but he loved picking out the transistors, their tiny colored stripes showing which one was which. He soldered them into place, first one piece, then another. He was thrilled that he could do it.

By May, however, the outdoors was so sweet it called to him. The sun returned and the new green grass forced its way out of the dry mats of old grass that covered the ground. The smell of sap running in the trees was strong on warm days and new leaves and seedpods popped out of dead, dormant branches. It was hard to stay in soldering transistors, though the project was almost done.

Other things pushed Paul outdoors. Like Marty and Line fighting. Not yelling so much or hitting each other. They were getting too old for that. On Saturday, when Paul heard them arguing and Marty's bedroom door slamming, he left the house and went outdoors, where he climbed the pine tree in the front yard.

He couldn't hide because Foxy sat at the base of the tree, patiently waiting for him. But no one seemed to notice. Paul climbed up the closely grown branches, avoiding the sticky pine pitch near the trunk. The branches were scratchy and sharp, trying to prevent him from climbing. But Paul's stomach wanted to get away. He just didn't like conflict, didn't think there was any reason for it. He climbed quickly, his strong leg first, pulling up the skinny leg after him.

He knew what the girls were arguing about. How could he not? Line was going to the prom that night and she begged Marty to borrow a new pair of nylons, as hers were all full of runs. Marty didn't want to give them to her. New nylons, still in the package, were precious. Neither of them wanted to ask Mother and Dad for money to buy them.

Paul knew that Marty was jealous. She wanted to go to a prom, but no one asked her to either the junior or senior proms. Line could go to both, as her boyfriend, David, was a senior. In the end, Marty threw the package of nylons at Line and slammed her bedroom door.

Girls, thought Paul, up in his tree. He was glad he wasn't a girl and didn't have to worry about curling his hair, what his clothes looked like or wearing high heels and stockings. He wished he were Ernie Regan. Ernie wasn't surrounded by a family of girls. He only had a younger brother. He could study and do things and no one bothered him.

Paul loved his sisters, but they could be a pain in the neck. He was sensitive, wanted them all to be happy. But they weren't and he couldn't help. The best thing to do was to put them out of his mind. Paul tried.

He imagined himself in the Freedom 7 capsule at the top of a huge rocket, waiting for it to be launched. The gantry pulls away. He is now alone, tons of explosive rocket fuel beneath him. Slowly, the countdown continues. He can hear it on the radio in his headphones. At last the final counts, 5, 4, 3, 2, liftoff. The G-forces increase. His facial muscles tense, he feels light-headed, weight pressing on his chest. Shepard felt 6.3 Gs during the launch and 11.6 Gs during re-entry into the earth's atmosphere. Paul could not imagine that.

Then Paul decided the project was a moon shot, and that once he landed he would be able to get out and walk along the surface of the moon in his special space suit. What would it be like to be all alone up there, the only person? There must be mountains, valleys that they saw on the moon's face. God would be there, of course. He made the solar system, the planets, the sun around which they revolved. What would it be like to be alone with God?

Actually, Paul thought, he was alone with God up in the pine tree.

A car pulled up in front of the house and David Berglund, in a suit and tie, carrying a white box, went up the walk in the afternoon sunshine. Paul sat quietly in the tree, still as a mouse, but Foxy arffed at David, following him up the steps to the porch, wagging his tail.

Pretty soon, here came David and Line. Line wore a gardenia pinned to a flowered dress gathered in at the waist. She looked pretty, her red-brown hair fluffed out around her head in a cloud of waves. Usually her hair was held tight to her head by a rubberband. Paul thought she was ever so pretty, as she went quickly down the walk in black spike heels. He was proud of her.

David held the car door for Line as she awkwardly got in and settled herself in the passenger seat of the Chevrolet. And then they were gone.

Paul tried to get back to the story he was telling himself about walking on the moon with God. "And He walks with me and He talks with me and He tells me I am His own," he sang to himself in the voice of Tennessee Ernie Ford. The moon was empty right now, pure, not sullied by the sins of man. Could it be kept as a place of peace? Even after the Americans and the Russians competed in the space race?

The evening light was long in the early summer and Paul could have sat longer in the tree. But Foxy was getting impatient. She got up, walked around the tree, and then arffed at Paul. "Well, bless my pea-pickin' heart," said Paul out loud in Tennessee Ernie's slow drawl. He climbed down the tree. "I do believe you want to go for a walk."

On Memorial Day, the Mikkelsons, even Dad, took off a whole day for a picnic at the creek. Mother called it a double picnic, as they could stay for both lunch and dinner. The creek was so close they could walk to it. Willows along it made for shady places, but the shallow creek itself lay shining in the sun. The perfectly clear water flowed over sand and pebbles, fast and bubbling as it ran through a narrow part and then slow and placid in the wide, shallow places. Late in the summer it almost dried up, and in the winter it iced over and the Mikkelsons skated on it. At the moment, it was full of the clear water running off the hills from spring rains and snow-melt.

It was astonishing to Paul that no one else was there. It seemed to be the private province of their family. Mother put Hanna down on a blanket beside her in the shade of a willow and settled down with a pair of binoculars to watch birds.

Paul didn't want to get out of the creek. He scrunched his toes down in the clean sand and looked at his feet, scarred by the cutting and splicing of tendons after his polio. They looked like real feet, scarred but working. One of them was thin and hard, and the other was more fleshed out under the powerful calf which often bore more weight. But they were real feet! No open sores or stitches. It was a miracle. Paul felt the sand surging up around his feet, burying them with a sucking and grinding sound as he moved.

Kristen was entranced by the shining pebbles. Paul helped her collect them, looking especially for anything that looked precious. Maybe jasper or jade. Flecks of mica showed in the granite pieces. They were always more beautiful when they were wet than when they got dry and lost their sparkle. There were a few small shells, from snails and tiny mollusks, but the creek supported more insect life than anything else.

Paul found dark shale and split it into pieces. He skipped the flat rocks across the deep part of the water, trying to see how many times he could make it glance off the surface and spin up into the air before sinking.

After lunch, Dad, Paul, Line and Marty hiked up the meadow on the far side of the creek, looking at the way it lay along the pastures. Foxy followed them, overjoyed to be exploring. A creek had a mind of its own as it came out of the hills, gathered tributaries and ran down toward the Turkey River.

When they got back Mother told Paul to tie Foxy and pointed silently to a low willow where they could look into a cardinal's nest, with two bald babies in it, all mouth. Mother said she had seen at least 15 bird varieties, including an indigo bunting up close.

Marty said she had a terrible headache because of the sun beating down on her thin scalp. She walked home by herself to go to bed. The rest of them took their time, gathering up the wooden picnic basket, blankets, everything they brought, and walking slowly home in the lowering sun.

Tragedy had struck while they were gone, however. A message left at the house said that one of the parishioners, old Oscar Wheeler, hung himself in the shed attached to his house. Paul was shocked. Dad left immediately to see what he could do to help and comfort Sophie Wheeler. Only the week before, Mr. Wheeler was joking with Paul, up on a ladder at the house, helping Dad take the storm windows off and replace them with screens.

Paul and Foxy walked out to the garden in the twilight, past the hated asparagus bed which was finally going to seed. Paul lay in the grass in the tiny space under the apple tree thinking, his arm around Foxy's white ruff of fur, his head cradled on his other arm.

Death was so sudden. And why? What made someone kill themselves in this beautiful world. Was Mr. Wheeler sick? Was he tired of living in an old house and sitting across the table from his wife every day, though she made sweet jams and jellies?

Mr. Wheeler was thin, his face lined and his eyebrows bushy under a white painter's cap. He reminded Paul of a pickle, with his thin body and sweet and sour facial expressions. He didn't talk much, but he liked kids, Paul could tell. He did house painting and odd jobs, helping people all over town. Maybe he was sad because he didn't have any kids. Paul remembered a joke he made.

"Where do you send puppies when they don't have a mommy or a daddy?" Mr. Wheeler asked Paul.

Paul remembered shaking his head and looking at Foxy.

"The Arffanage!" sang out Mr. Wheeler with a wry smile.

His wife, Sophie Wheeler, was an ugly woman with a dark, sharp face a witch would envy. The two of them came to church, of course, but Paul saw Sophie mostly in her garden. She knelt, weeding, a big straw hat on her head. Paul kept Foxy close to him when he walked by the place, because Sophie was sure Foxy would root around in her precious flower and vegetable beds. She made wonderful jam, though. Raspberry, rhubarb and strawberry jam. Paul could almost taste them.

Paul wondered how Dad felt about it. What Dad knew about other people's troubles, he didn't tell his kids. Dad was a counselor, a comforter, a leader and shepherd of his flock. He listened to people, told them they had sinned and that Jesus forgave them. They were saved by His grace. Dad relied on the Bible, on his long training and the power vested in him by the Church, but he must surely be moved by the lives of his parishioners.

Paul did not think he could do what Dad did. Paul hardened himself to his own pain, but he was so sensitive he hated to see anyone else suffering, whether they be person or animal. Foxy being tied up to keep her out of people's gardens, was enough to make Paul miserable. He imagined a collar around his own neck as he strained to get closer to the action all around him. Aaargh! It was terrible. But Foxy was smart. And there was some chance they would be going to the lake that summer, where both he and Foxy were free.

Montauk was a little town, built at the bottom of a bowl. Hills surrounded it and the Turkey River ran through it. A sawmill was the first thing built along the river, but a brick works insured that many of the buildings were brick. Yankees, Swiss, Irish, Swedes, and Norwegians settled there. Farmers brought their crops in and shipped them off on the Rock Island Line. They bought feed and groceries, and put their kids in school. Several churches served the little town, including Dad's parish full of Scandinavians.

"Come on, Foxy," Paul said. Twilight was growing and the June bugs were out. The bright evening star, which Paul knew was Venus, hung in the luminous western sky. Lights were on in the parsonage and in the little frame house where the Sherwoods lived next door. Paul wondered what Mr. Sherwood thought of Mr. Wheeler hanging himself. He would have liked to go ask him, but he wasn't sure he should.

Paul ducked through the hedge and knocked at the open screen door.

"Hello, Paul," Mr. Sherwood said in his ancient, cracked voice. "The Missus has gone to bed, but come on in. I'm having a nightcap." The two of them sat at the formica table in the tiny, perfectly clean kitchen, Foxy outside the screen door listening.

A nightcap turned out to be a small bowl of ice cream. "Want some, Paul?"

"Sure," he said. Mr. Sherwood scooped ice cream into a tiny cut glass bowl and handed it to Paul. At Paul's house, a scoop of ice cream would have been three times bigger, but maybe that was why the Sherwoods were so thin.

"What have you been doing today," asked John Sherwood. His wrinkled, brown face opened like a walnut when he talked. The top of his head was pale, however, as he wasn't wearing the engineer's cap and red neckerchief Paul usually saw him in, and whisps of white hair floated below his balding pate.

"We went to the creek, had a picnic and saw lots of birds. Mother showed us a cardinal's nest."

"Cardinal! How did she know?"

"The cardinal came back. She's much duller than the male, but she has that crest and a brilliant beak. Mother knows everything about birds," said Paul.

"Yes, I know."

"And then, when we got back, we heard that Mr. Wheeler hung himself, so Dad went over there." Sophie Wheeler had found him in the morning in the shed, hanging from a leather strap. Paul didn't try to imagine how he looked.

"Yes," said John Sherwood. "I was over at the mill, cleaning it up for the summer, and someone came and told us." Mr. Sherwood helped at the sorghum mill in the next block at the edge of town.

39

Paul waited, spooning his strawberry ice cream slowly to make it last. He wondered whether Mr. Sherwood would say anything else. Surely the two men had known each other forever.

Mr. Sherwood seemed to be musing. "He was in the war, you know. The first war. Never quite the same after that. He got gassed. Told me he took off his mask to get a breath of air. Wished he hadn't. He was in the hospital a long time, only 24. That stuff comes back to you when you're old. Those memories get bigger than what happened the day before."

Paul listened, mesmerized.

"But that's a tough way to go. Hard on everybody," said Mr. Sherwood. "They outlawed gas after that war. Didn't use it in the second war."

Paul breathed in, listening. "My Dad's brother got killed in France."

"A bloody century," said Mr. Sherwood. "I'm Swiss, of course. Don't understand it. I managed to stay out of it, being on the railroad. I'm almost 90, you know, Paul. I was born in 1872, same as Fritz Larrabee, son of the governor. Too old by the time the wars came." He got up and took the dishes to the sink, switching off the little electric light over it. "No, the railroad was enough excitement for me!"

Paul knew many of the railroad stories, but he could tell John wanted to go to bed. There wouldn't be any more stories tonight. He stood up, still full of questions.

"Did you see Alan Shepard go up in space?" he wondered.

"No, read about it in the newspaper," said Mr. Sherwood. The Sherwoods didn't have a television. In the evening Mr. Sherwood read the books on his shelf and Mrs. Sherwood pieced together quilts or braided rag rugs. They led a quiet, frugal existence without worrying what the world was up to. But how could you not care about the first man in space?!

"It's so exciting!"

"I don't know," said Mr. Sherwood. "Gettin' a little big for our britches here. You would think God's green earth would be enough for us."

"But if we don't go, Russia will be up there before us!"

"Yup," said Mr. Sherwood, laconically. "Might be."

Paul knew it was time to leave. "Good night, Mr. Sherwood. Thank you for the ice cream."

"Good night, Paul. God be with you."

Mother was up when Paul got home, watching a television program. She turned it off when Paul arrived. Like a hen fluffing her feathers around her chicks at night, she invited Paul to sit by her on the couch.

"What are you thinking about, Paul?" she asked.

"Just wandering and wondering," Paul said. "Mr. Sherwood said Mr. Wheeler was gassed in the first world war."

But Mother didn't seem to want to dwell on this topic. "Have you finished soldering all those transistors?" she asked, putting her arms around Paul.

"We've done all the soldering. We're just about to put the cabinet on it." The radio was about as big as a large book standing on end; the cabinet was beige plastic.

"Does it work?" asked Mother.

"Yes!" Paul replied. "Dad said he listened to Paul Harvey on it."

"Wonderful," said Mother. "So are you going to have science projects this summer when we go to the lake?"

"Are we going for sure?" Paul looked anxiously at Mother. He hadn't dared hope. Uncle Herb's family was moving to the East Coast, too far away to have a cabin on Lake Michigami in Minnesota. Aunt Rose had agreed to buy it and Dad would put what he could into the cabin, including his own sweat equity, becoming half owner over time. The cabin was no more than a wooden frame shell at the moment. Letters and phone calls were flying back and forth between the aunts and uncles, plotting and planning.

"In a couple of weeks, Paul. After Bible school. For sure."

Paul smiled up at Mother. "I can't wait!" he said. "I can't wait to go swimming, and boating! I can't wait to smell the forest."

"You're a boy after my own heart," said Mother, hugging Paul's broadening shoulders. He was 13 now, but it looked as though he wouldn't be tall. More wiry and short, like Dad. Mother grew solemn. "You must realize, Paul, that we can't take Foxy this year though."

Paul looked at her. Both he and Kristen had struggled with poison ivy for weeks last year as Foxy's long fur got in it, and neither of them would stop putting their arms around her. Burning red bumps, itching. Kristen wouldn't stop itching hers no matter how much calamine lotion

Mother put on it. Paul knew Mother was right, but what would happen to Foxy?

"We should take her back to the farm," said Mother. "She wouldn't have to be tied up there and you could get her back at the end of the summer."

It was inevitable, Paul knew. Dogs could be sacrificed to the needs of the family. But it was hard for him to imagine life without Foxy. Slowly he said, "I guess she'd probably like it out there."

"I know you will miss her, but it will work out for the best for both of you. And I don't want you to be worrying about Mr. Wheeler. Only God can see into a person's deepest thoughts. We must let him rest in peace," she said softly.

Paul rested his blonde head on Mother's shoulder. It was a lot to think about, but he didn't want to go to sleep with the image of a man hanging from a rafter in his head. It would be better to think of the coming summer, the beautiful lake and all there was to be done. He and Foxy would have to start getting used to the idea of being apart. "OK, Mom," he said. "I will."

5

Paul sat very still in a little dried up bog in the woods near the cabin on Lake Michigami in northern Minnesota. It was his bog, the place he felt most himself in the world. Two soft grey mice played around his feet. They had never known a human. Predators could find them, of course, but they weren't worried about people. Paul concentrated, looking at their pinkish ears and their tails to see what he could see. Tiny mammals just out of the nest.

That summer Dad cut paths through the woods, exploring. In the middle of the woods in front of the cabin, open to the sky was a bog, a low place of fallen, moss-covered logs. Paul sat, literally a "bump on a log." He had to admit, the mice wouldn't be playing around his feet if Foxy were with him.

It was midsummer and the ground was just barely dry. The birches and poplars above shook their leaves in a light, constant vibrating patter. The sun beat down through the trees, its intense heat shimmering through the leaves. At the edge of the circle where the ground had been soaked, stood a few low blueberry bushes and a young maple tree with perfectly shaped small leaves. Stiff iris stalks in clumps rose, one directly from a decayed log, though there were no flowers. A few mosquitoes found Paul by his smell. But it was very pleasant.

When a butterfly showed up, Paul watched its flight. Erratic, as if it were looking for something, it kept returning to him. It was small, with light colored wings, and it cut the space around it with its seemingly aimless fluttering. Paul wondered what it was looking for in the sunlight at the bottom of the forest. He followed the bright wings as they flew up, down and back, the tiny insect holding his attention until it finally flew deeper into the woods. Paul sat on and on, feeling that he was part of the forest, a small mammal in harmony with the light and the breeze.

The Mikkelson family had driven up to the cabin a few days before, pulling a trailer full of boxes and furniture behind the Country Sedan Ford station wagon. Sheets of rain poured out of the sky as they drove. They had to ignore the open trailer, protected only by a few rugs.

When they unpacked the trailer, everything was soaked. Wet clothes and rugs hung from every rafter dampening the glory of their arrival at the lovely cabin smelling of pine boards. Mother was horrified. Aunt Rose and Grandma Bakken were coming the next day. Aunt Rose wanted the cabin, the first home she ever owned, to be perfect.

Luckily the sun came out the next day. Dad hung a clothes line, and with a burst of energy, Line and Marty helped Mother stuff the raggedy Mikkelson possessions out of sight.

Aunt Rose had paid for partitions to be built for bedrooms for the grownups upstairs. Dad brought up the old gas stove and refrigerator they once owned in North Dakota. A long table came from the Mikkelsons and a sofa and chairs were handed down from Aunt Rose's apartment. New army cots were placed in a row in the cement-floored basement for the Mikkelson kids.

The first thing Aunt Rose did when she arrived was put yellow and white gingham curtains in the bedrooms, and darker woven cotton curtains at the long row of windows looking down on the lake.

"I probably wouldn't even bother with curtains," said Mother. "The woods comes right up to the house, and who could possibly look in?" But Grandma Bakken and Aunt Rose were used to having curtains.

"We should have some bookshelves along this wall," said Aunt Rose. "It's too bad there isn't a window here to the west." The cabin was a simple frame shell, built by Uncle Herb for his family.

"We'll just have to go down to the lake when we want to see the sunset," said Mother. "Doesn't it look nice!" Mother was used to moving into new houses and making them hospitable, making the best of what was there.

"Yes," said Aunt Rose. "I think we're in business."

Dad put a pot-bellied wood-burning stove in the bottom of the split-level building. It was cold on June mornings, and a fire helped dry out the damp cement basement. Paul and his sisters called it Old George, and they all made fires in it. Whoever was up first made the fire while the others stayed cozy under the covers. The empty room did look like an army barracks with its row of beds for Paul, Line, Marty and Kristen against the wall, their cardboard boxes of clothes and books tucked underneath.

Paul loved making the fire, but he was slow to get up. He learned to lay the fire the night before, with paper and dry kindling in a little tent under the logs, so he could hop out of bed and light it first thing. There was no shortage of wood in the northern forests, but it was wet from the winter and smoked. Paul spent lots of time that summer chopping kindling and bringing in logs from the woodpile to fill the hungry belly of Old George.

Paul had little time to himself at his bog. The lake teemed with activity. The Bach Lumber Company was finishing a custom log cabin on Uncle David's property next door to the Bakken/Mikkelson cabin. It was beautiful, made of symmetrical logs peeled and planed on specially built machines and notched together on the property. A stone chimney along one wall serviced a great fireplace, and inside were a bedroom for the grownups, a tiny kitchen and a loft where the cousins would sleep. Paul was impressed with this cabin, which rose out of the woods like a piece of art. It was a real log cabin.

But no one worried about what they didn't have at the lake. The lake was a blessing, a clean, clear space of water and sky lying at the foot of the hill below the cabins, ringed by forest and wilderness. Minnesota was known as the land of 10,000 lakes, and this one was now, with unexplainable luck, the Mikkelsons' summer home.

Dad was in his element. His father had been a carpenter and Dad helped him as a young man. Dad was full of ideas and didn't stop working all day. Even when he was in the lake in his swimming trunks, he picked rocks and threw them into organized piles to make a jetty for the aluminum boat Uncle David bought.

Paul followed Dad around, watching and learning. With Aunt Rose's agreement, Dad planned to build a new dock on the western side of the shoreline, sheltered under three tall Norway pines. He had other ideas about a boathouse and studio, but they would have to wait!

Paul went with Dad into town to buy the lumber to build the platform above the dock. The town of Walker had only a few businesses on both sides of a road which practically closed down in the winter for lack of activity. Here, no one knew Dad.

"Kind of nice not to be the pastor up here," Dad said. "I guess that's what vacation is all about." Properties along Lake Michigami were being bought up by Lutheran pastors and their families beginning with the Landes, whose cabin the Mikkelsons stayed in years ago. But all of them were on vacation.

"It doesn't seem any different to me," said Paul.

"No," said Dad. "I'm not doing anything I wouldn't do at home. It just feels different." Dad drove through town, looking for the hardware store. Paul thought of Foxy. He was taking a vacation from Foxy too, and that felt different.

Paul remembered what Dad always said about being a pastor. If you could avoid becoming a pastor, you weren't called to it. For Dad, it was a vocation he was called to, as Jesus called the apostles. No one could refuse a genuine vocation.

Dad had brought his carpenter's tools up to the lake. All they needed was nails and lumber. Paul followed him through the hardware store, smelling the new pine boards.

"Pine won't last forever. Especially for the platform we're going to tuck in to the soil bank," Dad said to Paul. "But it doesn't hurt to rebuild once in a while. It would be nice to build with birch, but you see how expensive it is."

"Birch fires are the best," said Paul, thinking of the way wood burned in Old George. Birches were thin, but beautiful, with papery white bark. They didn't grow into big thick trees. Everyone hated to cut down a birch. Most of what was in the woodpile was poplar, cut from the trees cleared to build the cabin. Poplar was relatively hard, but it decomposed quickly. Pine did also. It was soft wood that didn't even give off much heat when it burned. But pines were beautiful. No one would cut down a pine either, if they could help it.

When the man who rang up the wood and nails at the cash register heard Dad was living over on Lake Michigami, he asked, "So are you catching any Northerns out there?"

45

"Nope," said Dad. "Too much to do this year. I didn't even get a fishing license!"

"Yep. It's a good fishing lake. We heard a fellow caught a 20-pound Northern out in the middle of that lake the other week. Ask over at the Benedict Store. They'll tell you."

Behind him, on the wall hung a Muskalunge which looked to be up to Paul's shoulders. "Quite a Muskie you've got there," Dad said.

"Yeah, Mike over there pulled that out of Leech a couple of years ago. So proud of it he had it mounted," the hardware man snickered wryly as if he wouldn't have done it himself, or maybe was just jealous.

Walker lay at the edge of Leech, one of the biggest lakes in northern Minnesota. The Mikkelsons had walked the long pier going out into the water. Mail boats went out from it to remote homes around the lake, and a few bigger boats were moored along it. Paul couldn't even see to the other side of Leech Lake. Dark grey, cold water went on forever, whipped by the wind into whitecaps the day they saw it. It was said to be full of finger bays, islands and coves. Lake Michigami was tiny by comparison, but it was theirs. There was no need to explore other lakes.

When they got home, Dad mixed cement into some sand and water and took it down to the edge of the lake. The platform site was very irregular, sloping steeply down. Just above it was the path everyone used which ran along the edge of the lake. Dad's idea was not to change anything, but to use ingenuity to make a level platform where people could sit and watch swimmers, with a few steps going down onto a dock that would stick out into the water.

He picked out and laid rocks in the spots he planned to build, setting rock upon rock, making them as stable as possible. Anchoring a few two by fours on the rocks, Dad poured a little concrete around them.

Paul was nonplussed. "But what if things shift?" he asked. "Like the soil, or something. Those rocks might move!"

"Well, for one thing," said Dad, "the weight we put on top of them will keep them stable. And for another, we're working with nature, not against her. See? I'm going to snug boards up into the soil right there. Everything stabilizes each other. Before I'm done, the platform will be part of the lake edge."

"Wow," said Paul. He looked out across the lake. Fluffy clouds banked against each other high in the sky in the middle of the day, and the wind whipped up a little, making troughs in the water, but not quite whitecaps. "I'd love to see this place in the winter."

"Not so fast," said Dad. "Let's enjoy the summer while we've got it! Now Paul, hand me a couple of those big flat rocks." The knees on Dad's khakis were dirty and his work boots were worn out. Paul loved standing next to him.

Dad was right, thought Paul. He watched as Dad set another two by four on rocks almost at the edge of the lake.

"We're building high enough above the water line," Dad said. "I doubt if the lake has ever been this high. Ice won't hurt it." Docks were pulled in off the lake in the winter. It froze hard and the powerful breakup of the ice in the spring crushed anything left in the water. "And look at these trees! They're not going anywhere, roots right at the edge of the lake." Tall Norway pines spread above their heads. They craned their necks up to see the branches.

"The roots might help," said Paul. A chipmunk ran up the tree beside them with a "churrrr" of warning, its thin tail flicking. Black and white stripes ran along its back, but its tail was like an afterthought, nothing like the beautiful, expressive brush a squirrel had. Paul liked how the chipmunk moved, its loose fur bunched up into pockets. The chipmunk wasn't used to people either. How wonderful it was to be in a wilderness! Hardly any farming was done up here, as the soil was too poor. Much of northern Minnesota was unsettled national park. There were also large areas of Indian reservation.

All of a sudden a bell sounded clearly above them. Someone up at the cabin was banging on the rusty old cowbell Dad hung near the door, calling everyone to lunch. Dad and Paul left the tools down at the lake and took the path which zigzagged up the hill. Dad put his arm around Paul. They weren't wrestling so much any more, as Paul found ways to exercise his legs by himself, but they were still very close. Being the only men in the family helped. They had to defend themselves after all!

But Dad and Mother didn't treat any of the kids differently from the others. Fairness was the rule and all of them knew how to divide things equally. Equality was especially true among the older three, Line, Marty and Paul. Kristen was only four and Hanna a baby, so things were different for them.

After lunch Hanna napped and Kristen sometimes did too. Everyone else laid low. Paul usually snuck off to the bog, hoping no one would notice and he could feel life around him without interference, but today Line asked him if he wanted to take the boat out.

The two of them went down to the water's edge. Line carried her drawing pads, books and pencils. Aunt Rose, who painted herself, had given Line a book on drawing animals and Line was absorbed by it. The Danish relatives, Aunt Rose said, had all been artistic. She hoped the love of art would continue in her nieces and nephews.

Paul collected life jackets and the paddle Dad bought in hopes of some day having a canoe. Line brought the oars. The boat was snugged up to a tree with a rope on a bed of old tires Dad laid in the water to protect its sides. It didn't belong to the Mikkelsons, but to Uncle David. His family wasn't here yet, as their cabin wasn't ready to be lived in, but it would be soon.

Paul pushed the boat out into the water, stepping carefully on the rocks and then hopped in, maneuvering the rocking boat over to the tiny dock where Line waited. Until the boat was safely past the rocks and on the water, only one person could be in it, as Dad taught them.

Paul rowed out into the sunshine, using two oars in the oarlocks and keeping the boat perpendicular to the troughs. The hot sun felt good on his back, but his skin was red from being sunburned. Paul was proud of his upper body, the muscles in his arms and his broad shoulders. They compensated for his skinny leg. Both he and Line wore shorts and limp, much-washed tee-shirts.

"This is a good place," said Line. They were very close to shore and the breeze was strong enough to keep the mosquitoes off them, but not so strong it made whitecaps. On the hill behind them were the cabins hidden in the trees.

While Line sketched, Paul hung over the prow, peering into the shallow clear water, looking at the sand which the waves made into ridges of light and shadow. Seaweed grew in some places, small clam shells lay on the sand and occasionally the snakelike movements of a brown spotted leech moved through the underwater sunshine. Not so many fish. Minnows glistened in shoals along the shore, especially in the early morning, and small perch hid in the shade under the old dock, but it was rare that you saw fish swimming in the afternoon.

The boat didn't stay in one place, however. They had no anchor, and the boat kept being pushed by the waves towards shore, towards the old Lande cabin where they once stayed. Just beyond it was the forest where the trolley car still stood at the top of the hill, though it was long abandoned. Line, concentrating in the stern, drew stubbornly, ignoring the rocking boat.

All of a sudden Paul saw that rocks instead of sand lay below them. Sitting in the prow, he took the canoe paddle and began to pretend that the wide, lumbering aluminum boat was a canoe as he had seen Dad do. First he paddled on one side, then on the other, steering by the amount of water he drew with his paddle. Dad could maneuver the boat paddling on only one side, by "feathering" his paddle, lifting it and twisting it at just the right moment so the boat didn't go in circles.

But Paul wasn't that good. He paddled hard on both sides, the boat slowly moving out from shore, the stern where Line sat becoming the front as he paddled directly against the waves coming toward him.

"Dad must really want a canoe," said Paul to Line. "This doesn't work very well!" Dad explained that in a canoe they could glide along noiselessly as the Indians did, so that birds and animals scarcely knew you were there. A canoe would be effortless compared to the heavy boat.

"Keep it out of the trough," yelled Line over the noise of the wind as the boat wavered, rolling in the waves. "My papers are getting wet!"

Paul quit trying to "praddle," climbed into the rowing seat and "roared" the boat back to a place a hundred yards out from the cabin. "Roaring" was the word Marty came up with for rowing conventionally with the oars. "Struddering" was when someone sat in the stern using the canoe paddle as a rudder, while someone else rowed. Dad and Mother trusted them on the water. As long as they kept life jackets in the boat and told their parents where they were going, they could go wherever they wanted, even out to the Bucket lakes, which was a day long trip.

Paul lay back on the long middle seat of the boat, squinting at the edges of the sky. He loved the uninterrupted expanse of sky on the lake and the way the lake reflected its color. The sun was high and washed over him with its afternoon light. It would have been too hot, if it weren't for the breeze. He dreamed of a belling sail above him. He had only seen sails in photos; never up close.

His own main project this summer was looking at lake water specimens, plant parts, bugs and whatever else he could find under his microscope. He had given up collecting things, as there was no end to it. Specimens were everywhere. But he kept a notebook and sketched what he saw under the microscope. He and Mother kept lists of the birds they saw. They looked at small Audubon guides of plants and birds, trying to identify them. Aunt Rose too loved trying to help Paul figure out the names of plants he found in the woods. Truth, it seemed to Paul, was a matter of observation.

Paul found a kind of berry that grew on trees that were usually as high as his shoulder. They looked like blueberries, but were darker, bigger. Blue colored berries in nature were often poisonous, so he must be careful.

But the purple dark berries Paul finally identified as serviceberries were delicious.

The treehouse Paul had built so laboriously with his cousins the year before, tying it to several poplars, was still there. But it was no longer attractive. It was too close to the cabin and the twine was disintegrating. Kristen was too little for it and he was too big. Wandering in the woods like a bear eating berries, and collecting specimens to observe and record was much more appealing.

The boat drifted in toward shore again. Interspersed with dreaming, Paul was kept busy, rowing the boat back out to safety.

Finally, Line got restless. "Let's go back," she said. "I think we should go for a swim."

"Sure," said Paul. He was never the one to want to leave first. He could always count on someone else to think of food or sleep or other bothers to take them away from what they were doing. "Want to roar?" he asked.

"No, go ahead," said Line. Her red gold hair wafted freely around her face. She was four years older than Paul, but they still had a lot in common. They liked listening to baseball games on the radio together, as they did back when Paul was in the hospital and Line stayed with him. Neither of them liked to read as much as Marty, whose nose was always in a book.

"Can I see your drawing?" Paul asked as he let Line off at the dock. It was just a length of wooden slats nailed together and anchored by poles in the water. The new dock on the far side of the property would be much grander.

"Sure," said Line nonchalantly.

Paul pulled the boat up on its tires and cinched the rope to a tree. Line waited for him and opened her sketchbook. Paul was surprised by the line drawing of himself leaning back and rowing with both hands on the oars, looking toward the shore. It was really quite good. He smiled up at Line, appreciatively, but Line said, breezily, "It's just attention, like Aunt Rose says. Just pay attention and draw what you see."

Paul turned the pages of the big sketchbook. There was a drawing of the chipmunks and one of loons. Each was detailed, showing every patch of light and dark she could see. Paul was impressed. He hadn't known Line could concentrate so well.

As they walked up the hill to the cabin, they heard shouts and giggles. Marty was playing monkey in the middle with two friends they didn't know, and a volleyball. They stopped and introduced themselves, a girl who was babysitting for a family down the lakeshore, and her friend.

Paul recoiled a little. He liked it best when it was just their own family, but the lake was an unusual place. Everyone came and went. There were no time constraints to the long days and not much that must be done. Time and space contracted and expanded to its own measure.

On the porch steps outside the cabin, Kristen ran her little cars through a stone village she had made with Aunt Rose's help on a piece of plywood. Line sat down beside her. "Here are the churches," Kristen said, pointing to the big stones, "and here are the stores." The stores ran down a little main street in an orderly row. "And this is where we live," said Kristen with her soft, lisping voice. Small stones for houses littered the board, with pine cones for trees in the yards. "My cars go down the road."

"That's great," said Line. "Can I have the blue car? I'll live over here, and then I'll come to visit you." She took the tiny blue car from Kristen and drove it purposefully down the "road."

But Paul was hungry. The smell of coffee brewing wafted out the screen door. Paul pushed open the door and heard Aunt Rose say, "But he told me she doesn't listen. She's 20 now, and she thinks she is grown up and can do as she pleases."

Talk stopped abruptly when Paul and Line entered. In the spacious room which served as living and dining room, with the kitchen along one end, Mother, Grandma Bakken, Aunt Rose and Dad sat at a long table. They were drinking their afternoon coffee and eating sweet bars of oatmeal and chocolate Aunt Rose mixed up from a recipe in the *Betty Crocker Cookbook*.

Paul knew they were talking about Diana, Uncle David's oldest daughter, who smoked and drank and wouldn't listen to her parents. She was an art student at Wittenberg College, where Mother and Dad met, and Line was planning to go in a year. Stories about her dark clothes and beatnik ways circulated at the edges of the grownup's talk often lately.

Paul cut sweet crunchy bars for himself and Line. Bars were devised to bake quickly, unlike cookies, which took a lot of time. A layer of sugar, butter and cereal, a layer of chocolate, and then another layer of cereal to top it off.

"What are you kids up to?" asked Aunt Rose. She had never married and looked upon the Mikkelson children, the children of her sister, as her own. Mother was only seven when their father died, but Aunt Rose was 21. She taught school and made a home for Mother and Grandma Bakken, never showing a moment of unhappiness that she had sacrificed her young life to theirs.

"We went out in the boat," said Line politely. "Paul rowed, and I was drawing."

"Oh!" said Aunt Rose, excited. "Can I see!?" Line handed over her sketchbook.

Baby Hanna sat in Grandma Bakken's lap. Hanna was an energetic baby, but for the time being she sat quietly, perhaps knowing that Grandma Bakken, who was growing old and trembly, would have to put her down if Hanna became too much for her.

"Well," said Dad to Paul, standing up and putting his coffee cup in the sink. "Want to get back to building that platform? I'm afraid I have less time than I hoped."

"Sure," said Paul.

"Dad's going to go home tomorrow for a funeral," said Mother. "Old Mr. Fjelstad died. Someone came over from the Benedict store to give us the message. Line, would you go in and help me get groceries tomorrow morning? We have to stock up." When Dad made the long drive back to Iowa, they wouldn't have a car until he got back.

"Yup, we'll do as much as we can on that platform this afternoon," said Dad. It wasn't all free and easy at the lake, thought Paul. At least not for Mother and Dad. He wondered how Foxy was doing out on the farm. Paul figured she loved it, running with the other dogs. He was just fine himself.

6

On New Year's Eve, like most people, Line took stock. A cold grey sky lent a white light through the many windows of her room. Between picking up Kristen's toys and her own clothes off the floor, she looked out the window at the snowy cedar trees and the slush-covered road below. Kristen, almost five, had moved in with Line, since baby Hanna's crib was now in the small back room with Marty. Kristen was easy, placid and happy, going to bed early and playing downstairs most of the time. But she didn't bother to pick anything up off the floor.

Line put clothes into Kristen's dresser drawer and toys and books into the wooden orange crate shelves along the wall. She picked up her own old doll. Sophia had a lovely molded face with blue eyes and lustrous black hair growing out of roots in her head. Line planned to save it for her kids, as she herself never played with dolls. "Unless it gets contaminated first," she thought. Radiation was much on her mind.

Everyone said the world was closer to war than it had been in a long time because of confrontations between the United States and the U.S.S.R. over Cuba and the U2 spy flights. Dad was collecting things they needed for a fall-out shelter in the basement, where the family could stay until the radiation after a nuclear attack was deemed safe. That is, if it ever was. Radiation did not go away. It stayed in the air forever, killing those who lived after an attack slowly, if not quickly.

Dad was the Civil Defense director for Montauk, based on his ham radio communication skills. He often told the story of the two little girls who were late to school. One said, "Let's stop and pray and maybe the Lord will help us." But the other said "We better run for all we're worth, and pray on the way!" Protecting themselves did not mean they didn't trust in the Lord.

Sophia sat on top of the row of orange crates, dusty but pure. War seemed inevitable in Line's lifetime. She was terribly anxious to get out and do things! So much was stirring and fomenting in her mind, but she was still stuck in Montauk, at least until she went to Wittenberg next fall. College was certain, but it was still a long way off.

At Wittenberg, someone exhorted demonstrating against the House Un-American Activities Commission after seeing *Operation Abolition*, the movie HUAC made to try to convince people that communists were stirring up riots against them. Not much came of it, but Line was surprised by the stance the Lutheran church took. Articles in Lutheran magazines advocated shutting down HUAC. When Line finally saw the movie, she didn't believe what it was trying to tell her either. Even she, small town girl that she was, could see that it was biased.

It was all very confusing. Line was just as anti-communist as the next person. Dad belonged to the Christian Anti-Communist League and she listened with him to their speeches. According to the League, the U.S.S.R. was afraid of Red China and thus could not disarm. The communists might say they wanted peace through disarmament, but no one should believe them. The League insisted that communists intended to take over the world one step at a time. The Philippines would be next. Line meant to write to her pen-pal in the Philippines and find out what Josie thought of this.

Line arranged her school books on a shelf and folded her clothes. There was no closet in this room, but she hung clean blouses and skirts on hooks along the wall, and put sweaters away in a drawer. Next year at Wittenberg she would have a beautiful room like the one Ellie was given when she went to Wittenberg for a semester. She would share with other girls, of course. If the war would just hold off long enough for her to get through college, perhaps she could become the foreign diplomat who surprised everyone with her remarkable, intelligent ideas about how to prevent it. Young people like her were the hope of the world, Line was certain.

In fact, she and Marty had written to Khrushchev, the human face of communism who held up his fist and shouted, "We will bury you." But he was also photographed in Iowa, holding up a cob of corn. The letter was Marty's idea, written in her best penmanship, and posted at the end of November, but Line signed it too. In it they asked Khrushchev whether he wouldn't rather stand for love than hate. They described their faith in Christ and asked him whether he actually memorized the first four gospels of the New Testament, as they had heard, and whether it affected him at all. Marty was much more of a goody-goody Christian than Line.

Line giggled to herself, imagining the letter being opened in the faraway Kremlin in Moscow. They apologized for the fact they had to write in English, but no doubt it could be translated, as President Kennedy's discussions with Khrushchev were. Marty was just as hot-blooded as Line was, in her way. They both loved the exciting discussions of politics and the news that went on in school and on Sunday afternoon television.

Line looked out the window, leaning over the steaming radiators. Across the street Mr. Brookhaven came out of his house and got into his car, the only thing moving. Light snow was falling and it looked very cold. Line knew she must go downstairs and bake the cake for Marty's 16th birthday. Mother gave her the responsibility, as she and Dad were invited to a progressive dinner that night. Appetizers would be served in one house, the main course at a second house and dessert at a third. It sounded like fun, but kids weren't invited. And Line was still, for a few more months, a kid.

She would be 18 in May. And what did that mean? She would graduate from high school and then sit out the summer, waiting to go to college. There were no jobs in Montauk. Summer would move very slowly. Maybe she could make a few dollars walking beans, as she did at the Berglund's farm in previous years. But she didn't especially want to see

David and she knew he didn't want to see her. He was studying at the agricultural college in Ames, Iowa.

Line was glad she didn't have a boyfriend at the moment. She felt free and easy. No one cared what she thought or how outspoken she might be. She missed David and his prize piglets, but she shuddered when she remembered David's mother and sisters, silent, dumpy creatures who lived in the kitchen and the garden. "I won't be like them," Line thought. "I want to do things!"

Downstairs, Marty and Paul were playing chess and Kristen milled about, pretending to play the piano and sing. When Line went out to the kitchen and rummaged through the cupboard looking for a cake mix, Kristen followed.

"Chocolate?" asked Line.

"Oooooh, chocolate!" replied Kristen. "I like chocolate!"

Line poured the mix and some water into the mixer and turned it on. Kristen dragged a chair over to the counter and climbed up on it.

"Do you want to put in the eggs?" Line asked.

"I can do it," said Kristen.

"You know who the cake is for?" Line handed her the eggs and a bowl to break them into, so the cake wouldn't be full of shells.

"Marty," said Kristen firmly. "It's her birthday." At breakfast that morning Marty was given a seed pearl purse with sixteen sugar cubes tied to ribbons, just like the one Mother received at 16. Line helped her tie the ribbons around the sugar cubes. At 16, Line had received the same present. She sighed as she stuck a rubber spatula into the cake mix, making sure the edges were mixed. She had tried fasting that week.

She and Sylvia, a friend from school, agreed to fast during Christmas vacation. They wanted to find out how it felt to be hungry, as the small children with bellies distended from famine in the photographs must feel. Mother did not forbid it. The plan was to do it for three days. Line tried, skipping breakfast and lunch. She called Sylvia to find out how she felt, but Sylvia hadn't done it at all because she couldn't break training for basketball.

The project seemed useless. At supper Line came down and ate with the family. She would never know how it felt to be really hungry. No one laughed at her for going back on her word. They just ignored her and passed her the tomato goulash. Everyone was absorbed in their own lives.

Ellie and Bruce were coming New Year's day for dinner and Mother wanted to make sure there was enough cake left for dessert. Line frosted two layers and dressed the cake with 16 candles. Mother and Dad weren't there though, and the New Year's eve celebration was rather subdued. Chess and ping pong on the new green-netted tabletop Dad and Mother gave them for Christmas, and putting the little girls to bed. That was it.

Line felt sluggish and didn't even care when midnight came, but Marty insisted they play ping pong at least once after midnight. One year slipped into another with very little fanfare. Paul beat them both, one after the other, and that, thought Line unhappily, was probably what would happen for the next year.

Ellie and Bruce arrived the next morning. They took off their snowy wraps and hung them under the oak stairway in the front hall. They were staying in Elk Creek at Bruce's parents, where there was more room. They came at Christmas a few days before, but Mother was overjoyed to see them again.

Ellie's cheeks were plump and pretty. She wore her blonde hair up in a little chignon with a red ribbon around it. Bruce, young and vigorous in a wool sweater, was solicitous, and Line saw that she loved it. Perhaps no one ever loved Ellie as much as Bruce did. But does she have to dress as if she were 40? Line wondered uncharitably to herself.

Mother pulled out all the stops for a celebratory dinner in the middle of the day. The antique lace cloth, the vine-encircled dishes, the Fostoria glasses, pretty paper Christmas napkins and the silver. In the centerpiece little wax candle figures of choir boys and angels with wicks coming out of their heads which were never lighted stood on a bed of snowy cotton batting. The Christmas tree and the manger scene were still up, and greeting cards were taped to the woodwork around the windows and doors.

Line wrote people's names on the glass name cards painted with flowers and put them at each place. The frosted part of the glass allowed you to write a name in pencil and erase it to use again later. Dad was at the head of the table, of course, and Mother at the other end, with all of their kids, plus Bruce, their new son-in-law. Eight places at the table and Hanna in a high chair. No wonder Mother was happy.

In the living room, the television screen displayed the Pasadena Rose Parade. It was incredible that in California girls could ride on floats full of roses with bare arms and lacy dresses. In Montauk, a snowy world surrounded them though it was cozy and warm in the parsonage. The café curtains in the dining room were pushed back to let in the bright white light reflected off the snow. The smells of meat cooking came from the kitchen and steam fogged the windows while the vegetables cooked. Mother made gravy and Marty mashed the potatoes.

Dad had brushed off the bird feeder and made sure there was suet and seeds for the bright cardinals, bluejays, juncos, chickadees and woodpeckers. The birds were so used to the feeder that even the activity of everyone sitting down to dinner didn't bother them. They flew back and forth, colorful against the brilliant snow.

"So you're graduating in May?" asked Dad, passing the meatloaf to Bruce. "And are those plans of yours panning out?" Bruce hoped to go to Minneapolis and work at the big Minnesota Mining and Manufacturing Company, where his uncle worked. During all of his studying and working at the university, this plan hadn't changed one bit since he explained it to the Mikkelsons at his high school graduation!

"I'm going up to the Twin Cities for a few days in February, between semesters," said Bruce. "My uncle writes that it is looking good. They are busy and taking men on. I just have to do well in the interview. My grades are pretty good and I can get my professors to recommend me."

"Sounds wonderful," said Mother. "I'm so proud of you two!" Line helped Hanna cut her meat into little pieces, but she could feed herself with a spoon. Her face was thin, for a baby, her eyes serious.

"Bird," said Hanna, waving her hands at a bluejay grasping a sunflower seed in its sharp beak at the feeder.

"A bluejay!" said Mother, turning to her. "Yes! You know what it is."

Line watched Ellie turn around and look out the window, her bangs curling around her face and the red ribbon bobbing. But Ellie was too docile. Letting Bruce talk for them. Beside her, plump little Kristen plowed through her mashed potatoes and gravy, oblivious to the talk around her.

Bruce put a protective arm around Ellie's shoulder all of a sudden. "You know, we just can't keep our news secret any longer," he smiled. "We're having a baby!"

Mother put her hand on her heart, but Dad spoke for them all. "Congratulations! How wonderful! When is it coming?"

"In June, just when I'm graduating! It's all going to happen at once!"

"You're right about that," said Mother. "That's a lot on your plate!"

Line could see Mother mentally counting backwards nine months, as she was herself. Ellie was almost three months pregnant. Come to think of it, she did look a little plump around the middle, or was Line imagining it now that she knew.

"We wanted to ask whether Line could come down and help us this summer," Bruce continued. "We could pay her some pin money, though not much. We really do need someone to help. I might be gone a lot, and we'll be moving up to Minneapolis. I don't think Ellie can do all of it with a new baby." Bruce was pleading, looking at Line.

Line felt something click into place in her life. Iowa City, then moving to Minneapolis. Yes. The big city. That was it. She felt her face grow hot. Everyone was looking at her.

"What do you think, Line?" asked Mother.

"Are you kidding?" crowed Line, her voice louder than she expected. "I can't think of anything I'd rather do!"

"Great!" said Bruce. "That is a load off my mind!" He smiled at Line.

"Your baby is going to have a two-year-old aunt!" said Marty. Everyone looked at Hanna, who banged her spoon on the high chair as she felt the attention turning toward her. What an odd thing that would be!

With the momentous news crackling around them, dinner conversation loosened. Marty and Paul described to Bruce what they were doing in school and Mother and Ellie discussed how Ellie was feeling and whether she suffered morning sickness. But Line was far away. In her mental picture, she walked through a park by a lake, pushing a baby carriage, passing sophisticated city people. Women wearing hats and gloves. Men in suits with ties and briefcases going to important jobs. She had only gone to Minneapolis once, shopping for Christmas dresses with Mother. What would it be like in the summer? By herself?!

Line was thrilled. Marty was known to love babies and probably would have liked to go. But Line was older and clearly the right choice. She and Ellie didn't get along perfectly, but it would be okay, and all of a sudden, Line decided Bruce was great. She didn't know him very well, but she would, she thought. She would make him an ally.

"Are you going to watch the football game with us?" Line asked Bruce. Line wasn't that interested, but Paul would watch it with her and

Bruce probably wanted to too. After cake and ice cream, stuffed and happy, it was fun to relax in front of the television, and the cheerleaders were good, if football wasn't Line's favorite game.

With plans for the summer in front of her, Line grew less morbid. She stopped worrying about nuclear war and communism so much and poured herself completely into the senior play, *The Family Upstairs*.

"I think you're the best actress in your class," said Mrs. Tannahill, a big woman with frizzled hair in a dark print dress. "I know the Mother is unattractive, but I think you could have fun with it."

"The mother sounds like a terrible old battle-ax," said Line. She stood at Mrs. Tannahill's desk after speech class.

"Actresses like parts like this," said Mrs. Tannahill. "It gives them a chance to show what they can do. Think about it, Line. I need someone good in the part."

Line read the play and agreed to play the mother. She knew Marty would never have done it, but Line would be leaving high school soon. Who would remember her as a loud, abrasive mother wearing old-fashioned clothes covered with a big sloppy apron? Probably no one.

The play involved a family whose daughter worked and educated herself, but wasn't too quick to find a husband. When she does bring a young man she likes home, he is put off by the manners and misbehavior of her family. Finally, with the help of her father, the young man realizes Louise isn't like the rest of her family, and they are united.

When Mrs. Tannahill posted the names of the people who would be in the play, Line was delighted to find that Melvin would be playing her "husband." He was big and easy-going and they often kidded around. He stood his crew cut up with lots of grease. But the father in the play would never have had a haircut like that.

"Imagine that you live in an apartment in a city," said Mrs. Tannahill at the first practice on the stage at the edge of the gym. "Imagine that it is back in the 1920's. Everyone around you is having a good time. It's between the wars. Everyone in your lower middle class family would like to better themselves, but most of them just talk about it. Louise, our heroine," here she indicated Linda Anderson, a bright-faced cheerleader with a short blonde pageboy, "actually goes to work in the mornings in an office. She seems a bit more refined than the rest of her family."

Everyone giggled. Mrs. Tannahill chose according to type. There was nothing of the actress about Linda. She was persnickety, sure that she was better than the rest of them already, and convinced she was the heroine of any drama around her. It wasn't Line's idea of Louise, but it might work.

"Louise's family, come on, over here," Mrs. Tannahill drew Line, Melvin and the boy and girl playing the snotty little sister and mean brother together. They stood in a row, apprising each other. Melvin leered humorously at Line who grimaced back. Their classmates imagined Line and Melvin as a mother and father, having this batch of kids! Line was a little taller than the "children" and a little bit bigger-boned.

"Okay," said Mrs. Tannahill, when everyone's parts were introduced and the sniggers subsided. "This is a dark comedy, which speaks to American ideals. We're here to entertain the public, but also, I think this play will make them think. I trust you each to learn your lines well and project yourselves into your role!"

The students walked through the parts, reading their lines from the little grey booklets that were copies of the script. The stage was dark, lit only by garish overhead lights, but it was relatively new and big enough for a simple living room set. The play was full of jokes and slapstick and yelling. Line could see how, if it was done well, it could be funny. She vowed to do her best, and see what happened.

The senior class had fun with it. Not one of them heard the word "darling" used in their homes and Line felt odd berating her "daughter" about working. The mother felt that the daughter was too good to work for a living. She should get a husband. Line could also tell it was from the 1920's because the father couldn't retire until the son started bringing in money. None of them could imagine what an apartment in a city would be like, but otherwise the family didn't seem so strange.

Line's best turned out to be pretty good. She was on stage all the time, coaxing and complaining. Melvin was grouchy about his "son," solicitous of his "daughter." Between them, they were the life of the play. The daughter simpered too much for Line's taste. Mrs. Tannahill tried to get her to act naturally, but she was terribly self-conscious and wanting to seem perfect, ended up rather lifeless. Her young man, Charles, had the least difficulty. He could just play himself.

Play practice was endless fun, a way to goof around with other kids. The whole class helped with the sets, constructing doors and windows and painting flats. Line stayed after school every night for a month. Costumes turned out to be fun too. Mrs. Tannahill came up with an old dress for Line, and a pair of ancient shoes. Her "daughter" was dressed in a 1920's frock and the men wore snappy suits with vests. When they came into the "living room" on the set, they doffed ancient hats that Mrs. Tannahill dug out of an attic.

At dress rehearsal, Line was sad because she realized the play would soon be over. It was the middle of April and spring rains and wind cleared the ground of snow and blew the seed pods off the trees.

Mrs. Tannahill sat Line down and powdered her hair and face so that Line would look older. She used eye shadow, rouge, lipstick and painted tiny red dots under Line's eyes which was supposed to make them look brighter. Waiting in the wings to enter, Line felt larger than life. It was only dress rehearsal, so she didn't feel nervous. In fact the boy's basketball coach was still shooting jump shots in the gym.

When the curtain went up, Annabelle, the younger daughter, practiced the piano on stage. Line came out in the light in her apron, carrying a pot which she stirred more furiously as she grew angrier, counting the time for Annabelle, who didn't want to practice. Line fussed and fumed.

By this time everyone knew their lines and was chiming in almost fast enough to make it funny. Melvin raged against his son and Louise was quiet and mock-heroic. But in the end she got her guy.

Afterwards Mrs. Tannahill said, "Well this scares me! If the dress rehearsal goes well, something is bound to go wrong on the night of the play! You are all doing well! Remember to project your voices, so people in the audience can hear every word you say. Don't just say your lines. Project them!"

Line whispered to Melvin, who was standing next to her. "She says this every single day! She's like a broken record."

"We probably need to hear it every day," said Melvin, grimly. "There's a lot of dialog in this play. And tomorrow everyone will be nervous!"

"Not me," said Line bravely. "I don't care what anyone thinks."

"If I take off my glasses I'm not nervous," said Melvin. "I can't see a thing!"

"That doesn't help me," said Line. "I'm farsighted. But I really don't care. I'm just an old battle-axe in this play anyway."

"I'm depending on you, Line," said Melvin. "If you give it all you've got, then I will too."

The night of the play most of the senior class stayed after school. The home economics classes made sandwiches at Mrs. Tannahill's request, but they ate them early, so they wouldn't mess up their makeup. Melvin got talcum powder in his hair and a powdered face also.

"Yuk," he said, standing stiffly in the wings next to Line. "I don't know how you girls stand it." His hair was slicked down with a side part for the role. No crew cuts were seen in the 1920's!

"We don't," said Line. "Or at least I don't. I hate makeup." They could hear people in the auditorium behind the curtain. In rows of folding chairs lined up on the gym floor people in coats and sweaters talked behind their programs, coughed, sneezed.

The curtain rose on Annabelle playing the piano. Line stood in her sagging dress, tucked behind a big apron, her bowl and spoon in her hand.

"Break a leg," whispered Melvin, as Line began calling to Annabelle from offstage.

Halfway into the play, Line noticed the Mikkelsons in the third row on the left in the audience. She avoided looking at them, as she knew if she wondered what they were thinking she would forget everything she was supposed to say.

Mrs. Tannahill's fears turned out to be unfounded. With only a few muffs in dialog, the play went off without a hitch. Afterwards the actors all came onstage and bowed, back in their own real selves, though dressed in ridiculous getups. The lights were hot and sweat drizzled down into the powder on Line's face. But it was over, the applause was long and loud. Line looked out toward the Mikkelsons, where Paul and Marty, with Hanna on her hip, stood, applauding, big smiles on their faces.

When the curtain dropped for the final time, the disheveled actors appeared among their families and friends.

"I'm very proud of you," said Dad, and Mother gave Line a hug.

"You look funny," said Kristen, looking up at her.

"You were the only one I could hear! Everyone else muffled their words," said Paul.

"I think it was a tragedy," said Marty, thoughtfully. "The parents loved their children so much they pushed them too far. No one ever got a chance to be alone. They were always nagging at each other."

"It's just a play," said Line, dismissively. She mentally counted up the weeks until she would be out of school and off to the city!

Marty, in a pair of Levi cutoffs and a blouse, held up a piece of dark crepe paper covered with silver stars while Rodney tacked it into place. Rodney, a genial farmer's son in a plaid shirt and jeans which had seen better days, was the social glue of the junior class. Marty liked working with him. Everyone did. It was his idea to make the low star-studded ceiling, so the dance floor area of the gym would be more intimate for the junior prom.

"Just think how different we will look tonight," Marty laughed, looking around. She got down off her chair and moved it so she could unroll the next sheet of crepe paper and hold it while Rodney tacked. Students all over the gym hammered and tacked, or laid out tables and folding chairs. Georgia and Barbara, whose hair was in plastic rollers tied up in a red bandana handkerchief, tacked crepe paper roses onto a painted white trellis one of the boys borrowed from a hardware store. The trellis separated the banquet tables from the dance floor.

"Hope so," Rodney said. "I'm worried about the band. I hope they all come!" The local jazz band was hired with money the class raised by car washes and bake sales. The music stands and chairs for them stood in one corner of the dance floor.

"Don't worry," said Marty. "We're paying them, and they said they'd come." They weren't being paid much, but she hoped they wanted to play together.

"Well, it's going to sound stupid if one of them is missing, like the drummer."

"We could have had a record player," Marty said, her stomach tensing. "But I'm glad we have a real band. They can play 'Moonlight and Roses' can't they?" It was the theme for the prom. A thousand things could still go wrong. And it would be her fault. She was responsible, the class president that year. Not, she knew, because she was the most popular girl in her class, but because her classmates thought she could organize the prom.

"Yup," said Rodney. "I made sure of that."

In the corner, Jim, Marty's date for the evening, stood on a ladder attaching the aluminum foil moon with its silver rays to the basketball hoop, trying to hide it. He was a big guy, with a wide shy smile. Marty was avoiding him. She didn't want to see him until he arrived at the door to pick her up. She felt silly around him and couldn't talk naturally. He was one of the smartest boys in class and Marty loved arguing with him about politics and ideas. In one memorable argument Marty insisted the foreign aid it provided to other nations didn't impoverish the United States, while Jim took the opposing side.

As the leader of the prom committee, Jim worked well with Marty all year. Tonight he would be the Master of Ceremonies. But when he finally awkwardly asked Marty to be his date at the dance, it got difficult. Marty hoped he would ask her, but she was shy and anxious. She wanted to see him and even wrote down what he said to her in her journal, but all of a sudden it was no longer easy to talk.

Since moving to Montauk, Marty didn't have any boy she felt as close to as she did Michael back in North Dakota. They still wrote to each other at Christmas, and Marty liked wearing the tiny Lucite heart with a rose in it he had given her. It had the word "Love" printed on the back in gold letters. But she would never see Michael again. He was too far away. It was odd that there had been no special boy for five years. Marty figured college was soon enough to have a boyfriend, but she thought about boys a lot. Maybe Jim was becoming that special boy.

By noon the gym was as nice as the students could make it. The banquet was in the hands of the school cafeteria workers and the rest of the evening in the hands of God. Marty caught a ride home to spend the afternoon getting washed and dressed.

It was a warm Saturday afternoon in mid-May. The rest of the Mikkelsons were energetically planting the half-acre garden at the back of the house. The plot was tilled and Dad raked it smooth and laid out rows with Line's help. Sticks at either end of the rows were tied with strings stretched straight to mark the row. Kristen followed Paul's hoe, counting the right number of corn kernels out of the package to put in each hill of corn. Marty looked longingly at them, barefoot in the soft black dirt, and then went in to bathe.

When Jim arrived that night in his father's car, Marty's hair was carefully washed and rolled into soft curls framing her face. She hated her glasses and wished she were far-sighted like Line, but that couldn't be helped. She wore black heels and carried her tiny seed pearl purse. In it were Kleenex, a comb and the words to the welcome and prayer she would give that night at the banquet.

No one in the family was surprised at Jim's arrival, and most of them made themselves scarce. Only Mother and Hanna were in the living room to greet him. Jim was tall and affable, a football player in a white shirt, bow tie and sports jacket, his short crew cut waxed straight up and stiff. It was his first visit to the parsonage.

"Nice to meet you," said Jim, to Mother. "And this is Hanna? Marty's talked about you," he said solemnly, bending down to Hanna's level. He handed Marty a white box.

"Oh, you brought carnations!" Marty said, touching the sweet-smelling blooms to her nose. "I have one for you too!" She held up the white boutonnière the busy florist had made, with its pearl stick pin.

"Mother, can you help me?" asked Marty. Mother carefully pinned the red and white corsage to Marty's dress. Her Christmas dress that year was chosen so she could wear it to the prom. It was a sleeveless princess dress printed with blue and grey roses. Under it Marty wore the infamous crinoline she had fought so hard to get.

Dad stepped out of his study at that moment and greeted Jim. "Here, I can help with that," he said, deftly pinning Jim's boutonniere into his lapel. "Well," he said. "Can't think of a thing new to say! I'm sure you'll take good care of our girl."

"Yes, sir," said Jim. "We won't stay out too late, but we are going to a drive-in movie afterwards with a couple of friends."

This was news to Marty. She held her breath.

"Okay," said Dad. "Take it easy!" Mother held up Hanna, who waved her little hand as they left the house in the late afternoon sunshine.

Alone with Jim, driving down the road, it was easier to talk. "Are you nervous about being Master of Ceremonies?" she asked.

"No," said Jim, smiling. "Doesn't bother me."

"It does me," said Marty. "I hate to talk in front of groups! Or play the piano or do anything by myself. I don't mind if there's a big group, like chorus." She sat stiffly on her side of the seat, her net skirts billowing up underneath her dress. She did feel a little dreamlike, as if she were Cinderella, whisked away by a dashing prince in a crew cut and bow tie as the sun went down.

The dream continued when they entered the gym, looking as they never saw it. Lit only with candles, darkness hid the awkward parts of the room. Their classmates were seated at tables covered with white cloths, wearing flowers and light dresses. When it seemed that everyone was settled, Jim stood up and introduced Marty.

Still in the dream that protected her, Marty's voice sounded shrill to her, but it was loud enough. "I'd like to welcome you all to the junior prom and thank everyone who worked so hard to make this a festive night." She asked them to bow their heads in prayer. "Oh Lord, we thank you for your bounty spread before us. We ask your blessings upon us as we enjoy this evening together. Amen." Marty sat down. She wasn't going to worry about another thing. She was just going to have fun.

After dinner they walked through the rose-covered trellis and stood along the wall under the silvery moon. Jim went to get Marty a glass of punch as the band played. "Moonlight and roses bring wonderful memories of you." It was a slow, romantic song and the words crept into Marty's head, even though no one was singing them. She looked over at Rodney, who stood near his date, Cheryl, a girl Marty didn't know very well. When Jim came back with fizzy fruit punch, they joined them.

"The band sounds fine to me," said Marty.

"Me too," said Rodney. "They sound great!" All of a sudden they broke into a rollicking song Marty thought she knew. How did she know it? "That'll be the day, when you say goodbye."

Rodney grabbed Cheryl and swung her out on the dance floor. He moved smoothly and Cheryl was pretty with her hair teased into a bouffant do and a lacy dress with a big skirt. Marty looked on enviously. She had never learned to dance, but it looked like so much fun! "You say you're gonna leave, you know it's a lie." Cheryl stepped, bobbed and Rodney spun her around.

"It's much too fast for me," she said, looking up at Jim.

"It's okay," said Jim. "I'm not very good either. We'll try a slower one." They stood looking out at their braver classmates dancing.

Marty could feel her body dying to move with the music, but it was nice standing still with Jim. She could feel his closeness, even though they weren't touching. When he put his hand on the small of her back, tendrils of heat licked about her. Marty had never felt like this before.

At last the band played the slow, romantic song that was unavoidable the last year. There was a moon in it, too. Jim took Marty's hand and they drifted out onto the dance floor, stepping slowly, Marty trying hard to match Jim's feet and not step on them. "Two drifters, off to see the world. There's such a lot of world to see."

They stepped slowly, swaying together a little awkwardly, trying not to knock into each other. "My huckleberry friend," thought Marty. "Moon River and me."

"Oh, I love that song!" said Marty as it finally ended. She hardly knew where it came from. It might have been old or new, but it was so ubiquitous as to be conventional. Marty didn't care. She just wanted to keep floating. Jim held her hand as they eased off the dance floor.

The night was long and lovely. When people finally started to leave, Jim and Marty went with Rodney and Cheryl to Rodney's car. "So," said Rodney. "Olwein?"

"Sure," said Jim. "Let's go." He and Marty got in the back seat, sitting close to each other. Marty put her glasses in her little seeded bag and lay back in the curve of Jim's big shoulder. Whatever she was feeling was new and lovely.

At the drive-in, Rodney parked the car next to a speaker stand. He unhooked the speakers and hung them on the car window. Not too far away, on a big outdoor screen, the movie *From Here to Eternity* unfurled in front of them. Marty could not pay attention. It was about some soldiers on a base in Hawaii, and the women who loved them. She recognized the handsome stars, but whatever was going on up there was much less important than what was going on in the back seat of Rodney's car!

Marty lay against Jim's shoulder, his left arm encircling her and his right hand on her waist. This is it, she was thinking. This is the real thing. Up on the screen, Burt Lancaster and Debra Kerr lay on the beach, the surf washing up around them as they kissed. Yes, thought Marty. This is the grandeur of life!

Later the young soldiers fought each other, dying on the eve of Pearl Harbor. "What a waste," said Rodney, turning back to look at Jim. "It's crazy to fight like that."

"Switchblades, no less," said Jim. "I've never even seen one."

"Well," said Rodney to Cheryl. "Hope you girls didn't mind that too much. Let's go have something to eat!"

Olwein's drive-in restaurant was still open. Root beers, hamburgers, fries. Marty lost all sense of reality. She ate in a dream, letting the others talk. From reading magazines, Marty knew that teenagers did all the things they were doing. But it was all new to her.

At last, Jim drove Marty home. The stars were bright above them and the moon had gone down.

"Such a nice night," Marty said softly when they got to the parsonage. "Thank you so much! It was wonderful." It was late, and neither of them were inclined to talk much. Jim got out of the car and walked Marty up to her porch. He leaned down and kissed her on the cheek, as propriety required, went down the steps and drove away. Marty slipped up to her bedroom where Hanna slept in a crib, and lay down, tired but wide awake, stars in her eyes.

After church and Sunday dinner the next day, Marty took Hanna and escaped. She wanted to think about everything by herself. Hanna toddled slowly, and Marty followed her, ambling along the road to the Catholic cemetery. They turned down the lane to the creek in the lengthening afternoon light. The weather was warm, the sun strong, tiny new leaves on the trees and grass burgeoning. Marty picked up wood chips and put them in the creek so Hanna could watch them slide down stream on the quick spring current.

Marty had been taught about sex. Mother and Dad read them a book called *Little Acorns* showing the organs of the male and female body and how the egg came down and met the sperm to form a baby. But she did not understand that a man must invade her body for sex to happen.

In one of her favorite books, *The Queen's Grace*, the story of Katherine Parr, the last wife of Henry the VIII, the words "thoroughly compromised" represented sex between Katherine and her lover. The lovers hoped Katherine would become pregnant and not have to marry Henry. Marty wondered what the words actually meant physically. It wasn't until she read the sexual parts of *1984* that winter that she understood a male put part of himself into the female. She was nauseous for weeks afterwards whenever she thought about it. She couldn't finish the book.

But now, after experiencing the sweetness and heat between men and women for the first time, she understood why women let men come into them. It was a revelation. Now she could see why a woman would let herself be "thoroughly compromised." It was Jim, she thought, who made her feel that way. She didn't feel that way with other boys. But something was drawing her toward Jim, making him feel special to her. It must be love, Marty thought shyly.

Line must know about sex. But Marty and Line never talked about their feelings for boys or sex. Gossip about boys made friendships with her school friends, Georgia and Barbara, sweet, but no one talked about sex. Marty did wonder whether, because she was the Lutheran pastor's daughter, there were things no one would say in front of her. But her new knowledge was secret, precious. Marty carried it inside of her like a jewel.

Hanna was a safe little creature, happily picking up stones and throwing them into the creek in the light and shade under the willows. She looked up at Marty, pointing to a leaf she threw into the water as it skittered away on the current. Toddling, but still in diapers, how delightful Hanna was, Marty thought. She gathered Hanna up and hugged the sweet-smelling, spirited little body to her.

Too quickly, though, the spell the prom cast lifted. The dreamy atmosphere of the night and her sweet new knowledge evaporated in the harsh daylight and familiar corridors of high school. Marty was even less able to talk to Jim than before the prom. She wanted to say something special to him before school got out, but the time just didn't come up. Before she knew it, summer vacation was upon them. Marty knew she would hardly see her friends until school started again in the fall.

Marty felt depressed and sorry for herself. The day school ended she came home and crashed out the dark chords of Mozart's "Fantasie in D Minor" on the bass end of the piano. The piece had both darkness and light, but the dark passion was the thing that helped.

The other thing that helped was a wild storm that blew out of the east at the end of May. Marty stood on the front porch, watching its approach with Foxy beside her. In the west, fluffy clouds looked like the Tibetan mountains shown in the television movie *Shangri-La* in the clearest blue sky. Toward the north and east, ominous dark clouds rolled in. Looking east, the hills and trees lay in sunshine, but above them the sky was dark and forbidding. The birds, wheeling and circling above the hill, seemed to feel something was about to happen. It gave Marty an eerie feeling, as if a great misfortune were spreading dreadful clouds across a happy world. Foxy was still, looking out across the world with Marty, entranced by the storm.

Soon the wind lashed out in all its fury. Rain began to fall, but the sun was still shining. The wind became more and more wild. The beauty of it chilled Marty. Finally, grey clouds passed over the sun and the world became dark. A bird perched on the willow, but there was little protection among the budding leaves. All of a sudden, the western horizon was on fire. Something was burning over there, thought Marty, too big for her to imagine. The entire sky grew black, deadening the world. Marty buried her arms in the long, warm fur of Foxy's white ruff, glad to share the beauty with someone.

Summer brought heat and long evenings. The Mikkelsons put Line on a bus to Iowa City to help Bruce and Ellie pack. They couldn't move until the baby came at the end of June, but Ellie was resting and needed the help. Marty felt her leaving like a big rip in the family fabric. It didn't help that Line was so anxious to leave.

As they drove home from dropping Line off, Marty and Paul looked at each other. Line was the meat in the sandwich, the two of them flanking her in their adventures. Line would never be home again for very long. The gang of three they had made up since they were born so close together would never be the same. They weren't close lately, didn't confide in each other. In fact they each sought secret refuges for their budding thoughts and feelings in the big, rambling parsonage and its grounds. But Line buffered the chilliness of the world for Marty and Paul, leaving Marty to its beauty and Paul to his observations.

Marty struggled with the loss of Line and the summer's freedom, not knowing exactly what to do with herself. She spent lots of time with Hanna and Kristen, and collected books around her in which to lose herself. They would go to the lake in a few weeks, but otherwise the summer stretched, empty and lonely in front of her.

One thing Marty planned did come to fruition the week Line left, however. Above Montauk on the hill was the Larrabee mansion in which the last of the Larrabee daughters, Miss Anna, lived. She was in her 90's, a relative of the Mikkelson's neighbor, Mrs. Appelman. The Appelmans ran the sorghum mill which perfumed the air with boiling sorghum sap in the late summer and fall. Marty asked Mrs. Appelman whether she could go see Miss Larrabee and Mrs. Appelman told her she would take Marty with her the next time she went to visit.

What Marty wanted most was to see the house. Its brick façade was slightly visible through the tops of the trees as you climbed the hill out of town, but that was all Marty ever saw. The marks of the Larrabees were all over Montauk, statues and buildings and even in a few stories old Mr. Sherwood told. Marty was terribly curious about them and the mansion in which they lived.

Mrs. Appelman called to say she was going for a visit and she would pick up Marty in her car. "There's a beautiful grand piano up there," said Mrs. Appelman as she drove up the hill. She was young and vigorous, though white hair curled around her face. "Miss Larrabee might like to hear you play." Marty was glad she had worked enough on her Mozart to be able to play it without music.

The house was classically beautiful, imposing at the top of the hill with no trees in front of it. Sunshine and a clipped green lawn surrounded the brick building with its bright white columns and painted arched woodwork at the windows. Below the house was a woods and beyond it the town of Montauk stretched to the river and beyond. Behind the well-kept mansion were the farm buildings and more woods.

Miss Larrabee greeted them. She was very short and thin, with sharp eyes in her wizened face. She wore a dark dress and a shawl pinned

70

with a cameo brooch around her shoulders. From the front hall a staircase went up to the second floor, just as at the Mikkelsons, except theirs wasn't carpeted.

Miss Larrabee showed them into a big sunny drawing room. Thin wooden blinds filtered the light that came in through the tall windows. Marty sat at the edge of her chair, hands folded in her lap, her feet together. On a marble-topped table next to her stood a lamp with a shade of colored glass.

"The Mikkelsons are well known for their sunflowers," said Mrs. Appelman. "They plant lots of them to feed the birds in the winter."

"How nice!" said Miss Larrabee. "Which birds like them?"

"Cardinals," said Marty, "and bluejays, and of course woodpeckers, but they really prefer suet."

Miss Larrabee turned to Mrs. Appelman, "What did she say?"

Mrs. Appelman asked Marty to repeat what she said. Miss Larrabee leaned in, but she couldn't understand Marty at all.

The two ladies conversed, while Marty looked around. Statues of children and paintings stood against the walls and in every corner. Through a door Marty saw a rich library lined with shelves of leather books.

Miss Larrabee turned to Marty, sweetly and gestured toward a room down the hall. "Now, dear, you just go into the music room and play the piano, and forget about us."

A luxurious black baby grand stood in the painting-lined music room. Marty sat down and tentatively touched the keys of the ancient instrument. The tone was beautiful and the instrument was in perfect tune. She began Mozart's "Fantasie," moving up and down the keys and allowing her fingers to pound out the chords. It sounded wonderful. She played it again. At the moment it was the only piece she could play without music in front of her. She kept playing until Mrs. Appelman stood in the doorway.

"We mustn't tire Miss Anna out," she said.

Marty moved toward the front door where Miss Larrabee stood waiting. "I would love to come up and see you again," she said, taking the hand Miss Anna extended.

Miss Larrabee turned to Mrs. Appelman, who repeated what Marty said.

"Isn't that nice," said Miss Larrabee. "I asked some of the girls if they wanted to come up and practice on the piano, but they never came."

"I will come, thank you," said Marty. "It has a beautiful sound." She wished she could tell Miss Larrabee that she wanted to see the rest of the house, but perhaps, if she became a good guest, that might happen some day.

"Thank you for the visit," said Miss Larrabee.

"Thank you so much for having me," said Marty, slipping out the door behind Mrs. Appelman.

Driving back she thanked Mrs. Appelman for introducing her. "You can go by yourself now," said Mrs. Appelman. "It's only a mile out of town. I think she likes hearing that piano."

"Does she play herself?" asked Marty.

"Of course! She studied music at Julliard in New York. Her mother was quite the woman! But she's been gone thirty years now. Anna is the last of those children after Fredric died. Those two never married. The farm is kept up, though. There's a couple who live up there with Anna. They do the farming."

"It's a beautiful piano," said Marty. It was funny to think of Miss Anna, a 90-year old woman, as a child! "I could walk up the hill. It's not so far. Line and I walk home from high school sometimes. That's two miles." A pang shot through her. Line would never do that with her again. Line would be at Wittenberg College next year.

No Line and no Jim, for the whole summer, unless Jim came to a summer band concert. It will go as slow as molasses in January, thought Marty. She got out of the car.

No one seemed to notice that Marty had been gone. Kristen played in the sandbox under the cedar trees with Hanna beside her. Paul was thumbing through a book nearby, keeping an eye on them. "Life will go on," thought Marty, melodramatically, in the words of Edna St. Vincent Millay. "I forget just why."

8

Line turned out the light in the tiny kitchen after doing the dishes, and found Ellie, big with child, prone on the couch. Humidity hung in the warm air and made it difficult to move. No breezes blew in the apartment where Bruce and Ellie lived.

"Come on, Ellie," Line said. "Come outside and sit on the porch with me and I'll read to you from Dr. Spock." The days since Bruce left to look for an apartment in Minneapolis were the slowest Line ever experienced. He had been gone five days, during which Ellie became a slug, silent and heavy.

But Line was good in crises, and this felt like one to her. She sat down beside Ellie. "Come on, we need some air," she said. Ellie got up, smiled wanly and the two of them went out to sit on rusty metal chairs on the long porch which lined the front of the aging university housing for married people.

It was rather public, sitting out under the electric light, but many people were out that night as the hot, clammy air filled their apartments. "Okay," said Line, "I'm going to read the part about crying." Line began, "'Few things are more upsetting to a parent than a little baby who cries and cannot be comforted. It's important to remember that excessive crying in the early weeks is usually temporary, not a sign of anything serious.'"

When Mother had a baby, she said little about it, simply leaving for the hospital with Dad and returning home after a few days with a newborn. All of the Mikkelsons were trained in how to handle a baby, how to bottle-feed and burp it and support its head, and Line knew about bathing and diapering as well. But Line was shocked to find herself in the presence of a young mother, her sister, terrified that her husband wouldn't be home in time for her baby's birth, and unprepared for what was happening to her body.

The Dr. Spock book didn't say much about what to expect at the hospital and Line would have liked to know more. Most likely, Bruce would be back when Ellie's time came, and Line would again be an unnecessary third thumb. Meanwhile Line was sure Ellie resented her cheerfulness, while at the same time was trying to be a grateful Christian.

The girls sat on the porch late into the evening, reading and watching the June bugs fizz and spin in the yellow light. Eventually they went in and lay, sweaty in their beds, Line's the couch made up with sheets. Line went to sleep, but in the middle of the night, Ellie stood over her, touching her shoulder.

"Could you help me?" Ellie said. "My bed's all wet and I think I should go to the hospital." Ellie's eyes looked wide and scared.

"Okay," said Line, standing up quickly and pulling on her clothes. There was no way to call Bruce to find out where he was. "I'll call Wayne and ask if he can take us." Line's fingers shook as she dialed the number that was posted over the telephone. She could hear Ellie putting on her dressing gown.

"Wayne, this is Line, Ellie Morland's sister..." She waited for Wayne, Bruce's friend, to figure out what was going on. "Yes, we think she should go to the hospital... Okay. Thank you," said Line. It was all very difficult. Ellie had enough of Mother's sense of propriety that she didn't want anyone else involved in the intimacy of her family. But it couldn't be helped. Circumstances were taking over.

Line thanked Wayne as he dropped them off at the university hospital, and assured him that he didn't need to wait. The air was still moist and warm. Line carried Ellie's suitcase as the two girls walked in the front door. Ellie looked uncomfortable, and the nurses whisked her away, leaving Line standing at the registration desk. It was 4 a.m.

"Don't worry," a stiff night nurse told Line. "It will be a while. We'll take care of your sister. And where's her husband?"

"We hope he is on his way," said Line. "He had to go out of town."

The nurse's lip curled. What sort of husband left when his wife was about to have a baby? "Well, maybe you could try to call him?"

Line thought a moment. "Can I make a collect phone call from here?"

"I guess that would be allowed," the night nurse said. She turned the phone around and listened as Line dialed, praying Dad and Mother would wake up and pick up the telephone.

Line was overjoyed to hear Dad's sleepy voice accepting the call. "Y'ello."

"Dad, this is Line. We're at the hospital and Bruce isn't home yet. Have you heard from him?"

"No," said Dad. "But if he calls us, we will certainly tell him to hurry home." There was silence as they both considered. Bruce was reluctant to give any of them the phone number of his new boss at 3M Corporation, even though the man was very helpful. "You know, Line, the doctors will take care of everything. I'm sure Ellie is in good hands."

"Yes," said Line. "But she's been so sad without him."

"I know," said Dad. "We will say a prayer for both of you. And please call again when you know something. Your Mother is very worried about all this."

"Yes," said Line. "I wish she was here."

"We can come down," said Dad. Again they both considered. Mother and Dad felt Ellie's baby's birth was the province of her own new family and they didn't plan to come and see them until after the baby was born.

Line knew, too, that the only person who could really help Ellie was Bruce. "Bruce calls sometimes," she said. "Why don't you wait a little. I will call you again this afternoon to let you know how we're doing." Minneapolis was only about five hours away. Bruce was trying to do so many things at once, start a new job, have a baby, move his family 300 miles to a new city. He would be miserable to miss his first baby's birth, Line knew.

"Okay," said Dad. "Call us as soon as you know anything. Oh wait, here's Mother," he said.

"Thank you, Line. I'm so glad you are there with Ellie," said Mother's dignified voice. Line could hear the sympathy in it. Once again, Ellie seemed to be getting the short end of the stick.

"Me too," said Line. "I never knew having a baby could be so exciting!" But the nurse at the registration desk was getting impatient. "I've got to go," said Line. "Don't worry. I'll call you." She hung up the phone and the nurse grabbed it from her.

"This is a hospital," said the nurse, stiffly. "We have to keep the phone lines open."

"Yes, thank you," agreed Line with exaggerated courtesy. She went back and sat down on one of the leatherette chairs in the waiting room. Out the window to the east, the sky was lightening a little. There was nothing more Line could do. She put her head down on her arm and fell asleep.

When she woke a few hours later, nothing was changed, except that big patches of full sun lay on the floor of the waiting room. The air was sticky. A few people came and went.

Line went up to the registration desk and asked about Ellie, explaining that she was her sister. This nurse was younger and more sympathetic.

"I'll go find out," said the young nurse, her soft rubber heels squishing as she walked down the cool green and white corridor.

When she came back she said, "Ellie's fine. Her contractions are coming about five minutes apart and she's starting to dilate. It might be a few hours yet, though."

Line's stomach was giving her pangs, but she had forgotten to bring money to buy food.

"Mr. Morland called this morning," the nurse added. "He said he would be here by noon."

"Noon!" said Line. That was wonderful. It was nearly noon now. "Thank you! I'm so glad!"

A little while later Line watched Bruce Morland rush into the hospital in a wrinkled white shirt, his handsome face animated. He spoke to the nurse who gestured to Line, and then came over.

"I broke the speed limit getting here," he said. "I called the house and when no one answered, I knew I better step on it!"

"Do you think they told Ellie you were coming?" Line asked. "Maybe that young nurse would go tell her you're here. I don't suppose they would let you go see her. She's been wanting you so."

Bruce's face reddened. "Yup! I'll go see what I can do."

They didn't let Bruce go see Ellie, of course, but surely it made things easier for her, knowing he was in the hospital. Bruce drove Line back to the apartment and grabbed some lunch. That night, when Ellie delivered a baby girl, Bruce was the proverbial anxious father, pacing the waiting room at the hospital.

Ellie and the baby, Brenda, were in the hospital for a week. Line found this week slow too. The Morlands didn't want to move until the baby was at least a few weeks old, so there wasn't much she could pack. Line wandered the grounds of the university, stopping to sit under trees and sketch. Aunt Rose had given her a book of photographs called *The Family of Man* in which people of all races and ages danced, played, worked or looked pensive. She carried it around with her, marveling at the many different sorts of people there were in the world.

Bruce and Ellie's family was exotic enough. The main difference from Line's own family was the part that Bruce seemed to play in household economics. Unlike the large, loose Mikkelson household, Bruce knew every piece of toast that Line ate and how much margarine she put on it. Bruce allowed Line to shop, but she must bring home the receipts and put them on his desk so he could see them. He told her ahead of time the things he wasn't willing to spend money on and provided her with coupons for things he noticed were on sale.

"I know that your mother didn't pay much attention to expenses," Bruce said to Line, "But I have a lot of goals that can only be accomplished by discipline. And discipline begins at home." The Morlands drank skim milk, from which the milk fats were removed, as they didn't want too much fat in their diet. It was all very odd to Line. She was wary around Bruce, though she got along with him better than she did Ellie.

When Ellie and Brenda came home, Line found much more to do. Bruce made a frantic trip to Minneapolis. He had rented an apartment and took winter clothes and anything else he thought they could get along without. In a couple of weeks, they would put everything else in a truck and move! Line couldn't wait. In the Twin Cities there would be more to explore and Bruce and Ellie could begin to put down roots.

Ellie was listless and quiet, recovering from the birth and her hospital stay. Line shopped, cooked, cleaned, and bathed the baby. She sterilized bottles and made formula. At meal times she nagged Ellie to come and sit in the tiny dinette at the formica table and eat whatever Line put in front of her. Line was shocked that she was still so wan and disconnected.

But on Friday Ellie did smile when Line put the tiny, freshly bathed Brenda in bed with her. Brenda's skin was now soft and pink, her eyes were sunken in fat cheeks and rolls of skin surrounded her tiny limbs. "Isn't she just the sweetest thing?" Line asked.

"Yes, she is," Ellie's finger traced the little face, smiling.

Line looked at her. "You look better today," she said. "How are you doing?"

"I am better," said Ellie. "Look at you," she said to the baby. "So sweet smelling and soft."

Line's heart leapt up. "I'll get you her bottle," she said, stealthily. She was afraid to crow or get excited. The house was so still and quiet; if she rushed Ellie, Line was sure she would sink back down into lethargy. But Bruce was due home that night and Line could see that things might soon begin to right themselves.

When he arrived, Bruce too was delighted with little Brenda. He held her and stroked her little hairless head when she opened her big eyes and looked at him.

Line did her best about supper, baking chicken parts smothered with a can of Campbell's mushroom soup over minute rice, and cooking frozen broccoli as the vegetable on the side. Little Brenda slept in her bassinette nearby, while Bruce waxed enthusiastic at the crowded table and Ellie, propped upright beside him in a summer dress, listened.

"It's right near a park," said Bruce, describing the apartment. "They were built in the 1920's, solid, you know. And the city is full of lakes. I walked half a mile from our apartment the other evening and found a little lake and a park." Line knew the city was full of lakes. She remembered the imagined picture of herself, pushing a pram around a lake in the city.

"'Course it's just temporary," said Bruce. "We'll have a house in the suburbs before long, before Brenda here goes to school. They like me at 3M! An international company!"

Bruce was also happy that Ellie was a little more herself. "You're going to love it, my lovely wife," he said. "There are Lutheran churches everywhere." Line was surprised to find that Ellie relied heavily on religion to get her through the days. She knew Ellie insisted at their marriage that Bruce become a Lutheran, the one thing she made any fuss about. In everything else, Ellie let Bruce rule. Surrounded by it as she was, Line took her own Christianity for granted.

With Bruce at home, Line felt like a fifth wheel again. Ellie assumed the role of wife, and neither she, nor Line, told Bruce that she had spent the week he was gone in bed. Line left the little family by themselves after the dishes were done, walking across campus in the long summer evening light, wondering what to do with herself. She didn't know anyone in Iowa City, but there wasn't any point anyway.

Bruce decided that they would move to Minneapolis the following weekend. So finally that week, Line packed dishes and clothes. Bruce came home early to supervise. He packed his precious record player and his long-playing records himself. No one else was allowed to touch them. A moving van arrived on Friday and the furniture and boxes were piled into it, to be unloaded Saturday.

Line looked longingly towards the town of Montauk as they passed it on their way north. She was homesick and longed to be free of the complex responsibilities she had taken on, if even for a moment. But the Mikkelsons were at Lake Michigami. They hoped to stop by the new apartment in Minneapolis when they drove back south. Line hardened herself as she watched the green landscape of farms, cornfields and trees unrolling beside her. The weather was warm and lovely, Bruce and Ellie needed her, and she was headed toward the new.

Dinner was a stop at an A&W Root-beer stand for hamburgers and French fries. Arriving in Minneapolis, Bruce unlocked the door to the clean, echo-y apartment. There were several freshly-painted spacious rooms with hardwood floors, but no furniture. Bruce slept there on an air mattress, and there was a bit of food in the refrigerator.

"We'll be camping out for the night," Bruce said. "Until things arrive tomorrow. But it's home!" He put down the little bassinette they brought in which Brenda lay peacefully sleeping.

Ellie and Line walked around the rooms. Green ceramic tiles were fixed to the walls of the bathroom and the tub was white porcelain. Glass was inset in the doors on the painted kitchen cabinets. In the living room long windows went almost down to the floor. "French windows," said Bruce, enthusiastically. Yellow evening light spilled in between the trees whose branches came up to meet them on the second floor.

"Ellie, you take the air mattress," Bruce said. "I'll go out and get milk for breakfast." Line wanted to go with Bruce, to explore the neighborhood as soon as possible. It was exciting! But her duty lay with Ellie and the baby, helping to make them comfortable. Bruce and Line, the healthy, strong ones, were treating Ellie and the baby with care.

The next day when the moving truck came, Bruce and Ellie organized their simple possessions while Line took Brenda across the street to sit in the shade of the great oaks of a little park. While Brenda slept, she tried to draw the streets as they drew away from the green oasis. But she was better at people, things up close. She drew the tiny sleeper, nestled in her blankets.

The next morning, Sunday, Bruce took his little family to the nearest Lutheran church. He was anxious, wanting them to make a good impression. Ellie curled her blonde hair for the first time in weeks and wore high heels. Her pretty face was pale against Bruce's dark suit. Line wore a cotton print dress she had made from a well-used pattern. A cummerbund wrapped her waist in a solid color as was the current fashion. But she didn't bring nylons or high heels with her. She just wore black flats, the best she could do. She sturdily carried the baby, while Ellie clung to Bruce's arm.

The church was much bigger and grander than what Line was used to. Four rows of pews spread out across the room leading to a large altar. The sun shone in through richly-colored stained glass windows. But it used the new red hymn books, the same liturgy and the altar wore the same green altar cloths as her home church. Ellie smiled at Line and reached for the baby in its blanket. This would be Ellie's home, Line could tell, as she handed Brenda over. Ellie would join the church ladies and make friends.

As the organist played the opening prelude, Line looked around at the people in the pews. It was a varied crowd, more like the people in *The Family of Man* than in her home town of Montauk. There were several Negro men, and one whole Negro family. Perhaps they were Africans, come to the United States to study, or perhaps they lived in the city.

A large choir sang an opening hymn as they filed down the aisle and into the choir stalls. Behind them, processed two acolytes to light candles, read the lesson and pass collection plates. Finally the pastor came, wearing a white surplice, a green stole around his neck. The pastor was inviting, but he spoke the liturgy rather than singing it, as Dad did in his warm tenor. The sermon was on the Prodigal Son.

When they filed out after the service, Bruce was proud to introduce his family as they shook Pastor Daniels' hand.

"And this little one?" asked Pastor Daniels, whose dark wavy hair was slicked back from his face. "She must be new to this world." Brenda wore a little pink cotton garment, evidence that she was a girl.

"Born June 21," said Bruce. "We just moved here. My wife is anxious to have the baby baptized. Her father is Pastor Carl Mikkelson. He suggested we have Brenda baptized here, with our new congregation."

"Oh, I think I've met Carl," said Pastor Daniels. "That's very good of him. We will offer this little girl the blessings of the sacrament!" He held out his hand to Line.

"I'm Line Mikkelson, Ellie's sister," Line shook the pastor's hand.

"Oh, good!" said the pastor. "Now, all of you, go over to the parish hall and have some coffee. The ladies serve cookies after the service every morning. Go over and get to know people."

Line wondered how all of these people ever got to know each other. There were so many of them. She was attracted to those who looked different, as though they might come from somewhere other than America. She took a cookie, but ignored the coffee as she needed both hands to carry Brenda. Plucking up her courage, Brenda on her shoulder, she went over and said to a dark young man, "I'm new here. Where are you from?"

"I'm from Southern Rhodesia," he said in a British accent. He smiled widely, his white teeth perfect. "I'm studying medicine at the university. My name is Paul, after the apostle. Pleased to meet you." He made a little bow.

"Oh!" said Line. "That's my brother's name! I'm Line. What part of medicine do you plan to go into?"

"I shall be a general practitioner," said Paul, smiling. "In my country there are not so many physicians just now."

"I'm sure they need you," said Line. But Bruce was tugging at her arm. She bobbed her head awkwardly. "Pleased to meet you," she said as she left with Bruce. It wasn't much, but it was a start. She had met someone in the big city.

In the few weeks of summer that were left, the days took on the regularity of Bruce's job. He left early in the morning driving to the big campus of the corporation where he worked. Once he was gone, Ellie and Line did little but care for tiny Brenda. They explored the neighborhood while doing the grocery shopping, but not together, as they didn't want to carry around the heavy bassinette with Brenda in it. The park across the street, in the shade of its big leafy trees was far enough!

Bruce wanted to buy something for them to wheel Brenda in, but he felt she wouldn't be little long, and didn't need a baby carriage. He would have used one handed down from the Mikkelson family, but their ancient carriage had been given away. He thought they should buy a stroller, which would last a lot longer. But Brenda wouldn't be able to sit in a stroller for some time. Bruce and Ellie discussed the problem until Line was sick of hearing them. On the third night of discussion, she said she would be back soon and slipped out of the house.

Just before the sun set, the evening was warm and breezy. Line crossed Clinton Avenue and looked back at the apartment building before going into the park. She sat on a park bench, watching people passing, her mind blank and open. She loved the fact that no one knew who she was. In the whole city! People were walking dogs, little children. Two lovers sat on a bench near her, their arms around each other. Birds were making the soft twittering noises they made in the evening. Line couldn't hear them without thinking of Mother, who knew and loved birds.

Lights began to come on in the apartments, but Line didn't want to go in. What do I want? she wondered. College, yes. She wanted badly to go to college. But after that? What? It was a shocking question. Until now, little of Line's life had been up to her.

Line imagined her own husband and her own house. He would not be domineering like Bruce, or work in a big corporation. And he wouldn't be a farmer, deep in the country with fields and animals. Did she even know what her husband would be like? Line imagined travel, going to a foreign country, learning another language, a modern house with a garden, like she saw in magazines. Would she be allowed to choose what she wanted? So far, most things seemed to be a matter of economic necessity. But "building castles in the air is fine," Thoreau had said. "Now put foundations under them."

Only when everyone but the lovers and a man who looked a little drunk left, did Line get up to leave. She walked into the drugstore which stayed open late. She spent five cents of her weekly pay, which was supposed to help buy her college textbooks, on a Snickers bar and ate it standing in front of the magazine rack. Even such a small act was a courageous act of choice.

Line felt the boy behind the lunch counter watching her. She could tell he wanted to talk to her. But with a young wide open face and a lower lip that stuck out, he didn't look interesting. He looked too much like herself. Line didn't want to talk to him.

Line had little choice; that was for certain. There wasn't much to do but go home. She walked slowly along Clinton Avenue, through the pools of light below the street lamps. They illuminated the trees above them and the big dark blocks of buildings. In lighted apartment windows, Line caught glimpses of people, lamps, television sets flickering. Cars came toward her and then rushed past, windows open, radios playing, tires whispering on the road. A black cat walked along the sidewalk and looked up at her before making its way along a fence toward darkness. So many people and things happening.

As she climbed the stairs to the Morland apartment, Line heard faint strains of jazz. Bruce was playing something she had never heard before. The carpeted hallway was dank and airless. Line opened the door with her key. Bruce smiled at her from where he sat in front of a pile of papers spread out at the kitchen table, his briefcase open beside him.

"Nice night?" he asked. Ellie sat beside him, reading a magazine.

"Beautiful," said Line. "It isn't too hot or sultry. It's just perfect. Who is that playing?"

"Dave Brubeck," said Bruce. "Like him?"

"Yes! I do," said Line. She sat in the dark of the living room, her shoulders moving to the music of the intrepid saxophone, and then the drums playing against the light piano accompaniment. The music rolled on and on out of the speakers, no one singing except the instruments. Not caring, light, excited, like the city. At last the saxophone fluttered out, but the music hung in the air.

Bruce came over and carefully took the record off the player, placing it in its paper sleeve and then in the album cover. "I just bought it," Bruce said. "Isn't it great?!"

"It sounds like I feel right now," said Line. "Like who I am."

"Me too!" said Bruce. "Like it's all starting! But I guess we better go bed if we're going to be worth anything in the morning! Come on, my dear," he said to Ellie, taking her hand. "You need to sleep until the baby wakes up at least. Good night, Line." He neatly packed his papers into his briefcase and put it beside the door so it would be ready in the morning.

Line pulled her bedding out of its pile in the corner and made up the couch, but she could not go to sleep. The drums, the saxophone, the piano of the city played through her like choices, like love, like the future coming to meet her from far away.

9

Clouds of steam rose from the boiler chimneys at the sorghum mill, perfuming the air with its sweet, syrupy smell as Marty and Paul left for school on a September morning. Mists hung in the distance over the hills and fields as they walked out through the bottom of town, crossing the Turkey River on an iron bridge. Once they left town, behind the hills the sky was clear from horizon to horizon, open and infinite.

It was two miles on a flat gravel road out to Valley High School. Marty liked being with Paul because his quiet observation didn't get in the way of her own thinking. She didn't have to bend toward him to find out how he felt about things, or away from his moods.

"I think I might go out for wrestling," said Paul, tentatively, the sounds of his feet crunching a little unevenly on the road.

"Good idea!" said Marty. "You've got the upper arm strength, that's for sure." She knew how badly Paul wanted to be a well-rounded person. His polio prohibited running sports, but he might be good at wrestling. It was his first year in high school, Marty's last. "I've never even been to a wrestling match. If you went out for it, I'd go!"

"Yeah," said Paul. "I'll see." They both wore jackets and carried piles of books in their arms. As they walked, the sun came out from behind the hill, warming their faces. The early morning air was crisp and tangy. The leaves turning brown and drying on the trees smelled faintly burnt, though they hadn't fallen yet. It was almost autumn, not quite.

"I can't wait until you have Mrs. Grove for English," Marty said. "Last spring, when I walked to school I kept saying to myself: 'the world is mud-luscious and puddle-wonderful, and the little lame balloon man whistles far and wee.' It's from an e.e. cummings poem." She switched her armload of books from one hand to the other. "And now I'm thinking of the one about autumn."

"Autumn?" said Paul, returning from his reverie.

"Four words," said Marty. "'A leaf falls, loneliness.' Except it is printed all funny with parenthesis around the word 'one' in the middle of the word loneliness. He's an American author. You'll get him when you're a junior."

"A leaf falls," said Paul. "Loneliness. I wonder if Line's lonely, up at school."

All of a sudden Marty felt lonely. But she said, "Nah. She's surrounded by new things. I doubt if she even thinks about us."

"She said she was lonely this summer," said Paul.

"Well, that was different. She was stuck in someone else's life. This is her life she's in now," said Marty. Line didn't write. But Wittenberg College was close. The family would go up and visit her soon.

When Line wasn't around, people actually noticed Marty. Line's bright face and outgoing manner took up all the space when she was there. Marty was the shadow, darker, somewhere in the background. She liked it when Line deflected unwanted attention, but she also resented it. At school, in her own class, Marty had her own friends. None of them really knew Line.

The walk was lovely and took about an hour. The mists dissipated and the sky was a clear blue. Marty didn't want it to end, but the long, low newly-built school building began to appear in the distance. Walking to school seemed to get the day going in the right direction, a day which would soon dissolve into the flurry of social interactions which Marty both loved and hated.

Marty and Paul were greeted by Barbara in the entrance hall, dressed perfectly as usual, in a skirt and sweater with a small gold circle pin on her left shoulder. The low sun bounced off the glass trophy case full of gold statuettes of people engaged in all kinds of sports, the first thing anyone saw when they came to the high school. The biggest one of all was the Iowa State Championship trophy the girls basketball team had won the year before.

Barbara taped posters for her bid for Student Council president on the wall next to the case. She was a smiley, gracious presence, and Marty's class representative for the past two years. Marty thought she would be an excellent president, but Rodney was also running. It would be a close election.

"Don't forget to vote for me, Paul," she called cheerily.

"I won't," Paul reddened, flustered at her attention. He hurried off toward his locker.

"Do you want some help with that?" Marty asked. She wanted to be like Barbara, the true queen of their class. But Barbara never talked about her feelings. Marty felt Georgia or Maureen, with whom she shared secrets and gossip, were more her friends. They were safer too, didn't live in her town or go to her church.

"No, thank you, I'm almost done," said Barbara. "I made these last night and just wanted to put them up." The posters were simple requests in black magic marker on white poster paper to "Vote for Barbara Odegaard, Student Council President." Student council was the most prestigious group in high school, with the possible exception of the girls' basketball team. But Barbara was on the basketball team too. She was really the girl who had everything.

Marty felt exhilarated all day. Between classes she hummed a song they were singing in chorus from *West Side Story* which seemed to apply to her life. "Somethin's coming, something good, if I can waaaaiiit," she dragged out the word as they did in the musical. "Around the corner, or whistling down the river. Come on, deliver."

She managed to talk to Jim that day in physics. "I'm so excited about the science club," she said. Mr. Gordon, the amiable physics teacher, proposed it. Marty, surprisingly, liked science. Or maybe she just liked the idea of being in a club with lots of boys!

"Yeah, it'll be fun," said Jim. He was a natural at science, didn't have any trouble with math or physics problems.

"I spent almost an hour on one physics problem last night," Marty said.

"Really? Which one?" asked Jim.

Marty showed him the page and the problem. Even after all her work, she wasn't sure her answer was right. Jim was happy to help and Marty was thrilled to find any reason to talk to him. It wasn't easy. By this time, every interaction with him felt serious. Once during the summer he had asked her out. With his Elk Creek church group, they went on a launch which floated down the Mississippi River. It was a romantic, moon-lit night and they sat together in the warm night on seats open to the sky.

Marty told Jim the names of the constellations she knew from studying them with Paul. She loved sitting beside him and having thrilling feelings spilling through her. But she hardly knew what to say. She wanted to keep their relations on a lofty plane, and she succeeded at that by being pretty silent! She couldn't think of much to talk to him about. But conversation on a date was clearly her responsibility. She knew that from *Seventeen* magazine.

"Have a good game tonight," she managed to say, as they both veered down the hall toward other classes. "… The air is hummin' and somethin' great is coming, who knows." The words with their exciting syncopation thrummed through Marty's head.

Marty went with Georgia, Maureen and Marlene on the pep bus to a nearby town for the football game. Marlene, who was a cheerleader and could talk the paint off the side of a car, always knew what to say to boys. Marty was shocked to hear her say "If we don't win tonight, I'll strangle every one of those guys."

They lost though, by one point. Marty was sad and deflated. She wondered how Jim would take it. According to him, Mr. Farnsworth, who coached the winning girls basketball team and also football, liked to win. When they didn't, Mr. Farnsworth took it out on them, sometimes being actually mean.

On Monday Rodney came up to Marty in the hubbub between classes and said conspiratorially, "Now, you're going to vote for me for student council president, aren't you?"

"Rodney!" wailed Marty. "How can I vote for you? Barbara's been my friend forever! And she goes to my church." She had only gotten to know Rodney in the last year. It was actually surprising that he was so popular all of a sudden. But Marty could see why. He just had a way with words, was smart and sociable. Not like most of the boys. Marty hardly knew what boys thought, as they didn't talk to girls. But Rodney was good at it.

Out of the corner of her eye, Marty saw Jim watching them talk in the hall. She hadn't talked to him about the game yet. Didn't know what to say.

"Think about it," said Rodney as he walked Marty down the hall smiling, freckles crinkling on his cheeks. "I'd appreciate your vote!"

Horrors, thought Marty, Jim will think I like Rodney better than him. Rodney played the field if anyone ever did, teasing Maureen, Marty, anyone he liked. Aloud she said, "I wish you the best, Rodney. As they say, may the best man win!" But she was loyal. She would vote for Barbara. She ducked into her next classroom, wishing Jim hadn't seen Rodney talking with her as if they were sharing a secret.

When the votes were counted, Rodney won! It was amazing. Marty knew Barbara was hurt. That evening, while she dried the dishes Mother was washing, she told Mother about the election.

"She's never lost a thing she wanted before," said Marty. "I'm sure she minds."

Mother knew that Marty envied Barbara. At the moment, Marty was saving up her allowance and babysitting money to buy a gold circle pin like Barbara's, the current epitome of style. "Put it in perspective," said Mother. "It doesn't hurt you girls to lose once in a while."

"I'm not sure what student council even does," said Marty. "I think they get to represent the students to the faculty, though."

"She's already Luther League president, isn't she?" asked Mother. Mother knew Barbara's family well. They were one of the most important farm families in their church.

"Yes," said Marty. Marty was nominated, but she refused, as Pastor Carl's daughter. "She is always so pretty, so perfect. I feel stupid, like a hick next to her."

"You know, Marty," said Mother. "Barbara has several older brothers and sisters who have paved the way for her. It is probably easier to be the youngest in the family, you know. And their family is well off."

Marty pondered this. "I know I'm smart," said Marty. She and Georgia were usually paired at the top of their class, and Marty got the top score on the National Merit Scholarship test, though it wasn't high enough to be in the running for a full scholarship. Mother said she was proud of her, told her it was probably because Marty read so much. "But I'd rather be pretty! I'll always have to wear glasses!" She would never be pretty.

"Take them off when you're talking to someone important!" said Mother disgustedly. She was farsighted and didn't need them. "But, Marty, remember, you have many years yet to be interested in boys. I'm so glad Line hasn't spoiled her chances at an education."

Marty flushed. She knew Mother was thinking of David Berglund, who had loved Line. Marty felt again their competition. Line forged ahead, not caring what people thought, following her instincts. Marty did care what people thought, wanted to be like the other girls or the perfect photographs in *Seventeen* magazine.

Marty agreed with Mother about waiting to be interested in boys. It was just that she was having so much fun! As she watched a melancholy Jim walk around school with the lost honor of the Valley High football team heavy on his shoulders, she felt they had a certain lonely companionship. Like her, he didn't exactly know how to get what he wanted or to be popular.

That week, Mother and Dad drove up to Lake Michigami to close up the cabin for the winter, leaving Paul and Marty to take care of the little girls for three days. Marty took two days off school, to stay with Hanna and be home when Kristen got back from kindergarten at noon.

Being given the responsibility was exhilarating for Marty. It wasn't difficult. It was just a matter of fixing meals and spending time with Kristen and Hanna. There were many known dangers, like handling the gas stove and the furnace, but Paul knew how to bank the coal in the furnace and keep it going, and Marty already did a lot of cooking.

Everything went well the first day, but by that evening Hanna had a raging fever. She whimpered and couldn't fall asleep. Marty was awake a lot that night, picking up Hanna and carrying her, comforting the hot little body, until she could fall asleep for a little while. When she woke crying, Marty got up and took her in her arms, rocking back and forth as she stood silent in the house, which felt big and empty without Mother and Dad in it.

After Paul and Kristen left for school the next morning, Marty placed a long distance call to the cabin where there was now a telephone. Mother and Dad were concerned, but they were hours and hours away and didn't want to come back that day. They would stay one more day, coming back Saturday evening as they planned.

"Call Mrs. Omundson and ask her to come over. She can tell you whether Hanna needs antibiotics," said Mother.

"Okay," said Marty. She was sleepy and couldn't put Hanna down even for a minute without her whimpering.

Mrs. Omundson, a nurse who lived down the street and was a member of their church, came over with a bottle of pink antibiotic liquid. Between them they tried to spoon it into Hanna's mouth, but Hanna wasn't having it. Fever raged in her hot little body. Marty put on records and stood in front of the hi-fi speakers, rocking Hanna back and forth in her arms. The little girl was already two and heavy. Marty's arms ached. But she spent the day that way, putting Hanna down seldom except to sit with her in the big rocker.

When Kristen came home, she played by herself and read her books. Paul made scrambled eggs for supper for all of them, fed Foxy and put Kristen to bed. Mrs. Omundson came over and again she and Marty tried to get the antibiotics into Hanna. She even stayed the night, sleeping on the couch and trying to help Marty keep Hanna comfortable.

Early in the morning Hanna's fever broke, and she was able to sleep, drenched in sweat under her blankets. Mrs. Omundson went home and Marty slept beside Hanna's crib, exhausted.

When Hanna woke up, Marty got up too. They were both hungry.

Downstairs, Paul and Kristen were watching Saturday morning cartoons. Mighty Mouse flew across the screen to save the day once again and Kristen sat rapt, watching.

"How is Hanna doing?" asked Paul. They were both still in their pajamas.

"Much better," said Marty. "She's not so feverish. Mother and Dad will be home tonight. I think the worst is over."

The house was warm and cozy, even though clouds hung over the house and it looked as if it might snow.

"I wonder if there was snow up at the lake," said Paul. The cabin didn't have any heat and Dad had to turn off the water so the pipes wouldn't freeze over the winter. He must also take in the dock so it wouldn't be smashed when the ice on the lake broke up in the spring. "It's probably much colder up there. I'm sure this is the last weekend they could go before winter. Wouldn't you love to see it in the winter?"

Marty sighed. She was very tired and didn't care what happened. "Sure," she said. "But right now I just want them to come home."

That day too, Saturday, Paul did the cooking and chores, getting Kristen to help him, while Marty played music on the record player to calm the sleepy Hanna. Three times a day she tried to spoon the pink antibiotic syrup into Hanna's mouth. It was a quiet day and Marty was woozy from lack of sleep.

Finally that evening, Foxy began barking and the kids saw the green Country Sedan roll into the garage. In a minute, Mother and Dad were in the warm kitchen, enveloping Marty, Paul, Kristen and Hanna in their arms.

Marty relinquished Hanna to Mother, who shooed her off. "You go and take care of the things you haven't had a chance to do," Mother said.

Marty wanted to tell the whole story of the three days they were gone, starting with day one. "Mrs. Omundson really helped," she blurted.

"She stayed here last night and Hanna's fever broke this morning. She's been sleeping some today."

Mother made a face, as if Marty shouldn't have asked for so much support. "Well, we're here now and everything's fine. Hanna seems quite well!"

Marty felt hurt. Her abilities were strained to the limit and Mother didn't even thank her. She slunk off to her bedroom, rebuffed.

Later she came back down to the kitchen, where Mother, Dad, Paul, Kristen and Hanna were having ice cream.

"It's good to be home," Dad said. "But it certainly is beautiful up there. The lake was frigid. Snow flurries were starting as we left. I'm sure that by now the two-lane track into the cabin is all snowed in."

Paul sat listening. "Sure wish I could have gone with you," he said.

"Someday," said Dad. "Someday maybe we'll get a furnace up there, so we can keep the place warm during the winter."

"Don't you remember how we used to get antibiotics into the kids?" Mother asked Marty. "Put it on ice cream like a sauce!" Hanna was eagerly spooning up the thick pink antibiotic liquid on her ice cream.

Once again, Marty felt flustered. She was so proud that she could take care of Hanna during her fever. She was a hero, but no one was going to listen to her story or accord her that status. Marty realized Mother felt guilty that she had been away, that her feelings too were strained with worry. Paul was a hero too, keeping the furnace going and the house warm. But Mother and Dad were home now. There was nothing to do but step back, get some sleep and get back to normal life.

Unbeknownst to Marty, even greater evils than a sick child lurked that week. By the end of the month, everyone knew that the United States and Russia had come closer to nuclear war than ever before during what was called the Cuban Missile Crisis. Marty was glad she didn't know much about it. What could she have done. Nothing. She never received a reply to her letter to Khrushchev and she had given up on politics. Her interests lay closer to home.

The last football game was on the Valley field, the homecoming game. The team was having a dismal season, but it would all be over soon. At half time, a float carrying Barbara Odegaard, homecoming queen, was pulled out onto the field by a John Deere tractor. It was fitting, thought Marty, waiting in her uniform to go out on the field with the rest of the band. Barbara was the queen of their class.

Barbara made a beautiful queen, a flashing silver tiara on her head and a blue cape trailing behind her. She was probably cold, Marty thought, in her sleeveless dress. John Reilly, her squire, was last year's football hero, a burly red-headed Irishman, now out of school. Marty helped make the floats by stuffing hundreds of white napkins into chicken wire. The homecoming princesses, mostly girls on the basketball team, with Georgia among them, rode other floats in formal dresses without much warmth.

Marty marched in the half-time routines the band prepared for the honor of the queen and her court, playing the Valley fight songs on her piccolo. She was a background player, she felt sadly. Marching was fun, but it didn't assuage the ache in her heart. She had hoped Jim would ask her to the dance after the game, but he hadn't said a word. At least Maureen was in the band, playing piccolo and marching into place beside Marty.

Even after the team lost the game, as the band members frantically changed out of their uniforms and into their clothes in the big locker room, Marty harbored a secret hope that Jim would still ask her. People were rushing in every direction, getting together to have something to eat before coming back to the dance. But oddly, no one talked to Marty. She saw Jim hurry off with some of the football players. She hung up her uniform in her locker and ignominiously took a school bus back to Montauk, walking home through town alone in the cold October moonlight.

It was her own fault, thought Marty. She didn't know how to talk to boys. Perhaps she would never learn, would never have a boyfriend or get married. It was a terrible thought. Sadness crushed Marty. No one talked to her! It was as if she didn't exist, or as if they knew something she didn't. Probably everyone knew why Jim didn't ask her to the dance except her!

When Marty got home, Kristen and Hanna were still up, toddling around in their pajamas, getting ready for bed. Paul was up in his room. Mother didn't say anything when she saw Marty's face, which, whether she wanted it to or not, always revealed her feelings. Marty offered to take Hanna up to bed.

Hanna was completely mended. Marty found it comforting to sit in the big rocker with the little soft body beside her. She read their favorite book about Winnie the Pooh, and the enchanted places at the top of the forest until Hanna fell asleep and she could lift her into her crib.

Marty turned off the light. The moon climbed high in the sky, leaving a patch of moonlight on the floor beside her. She opened the door to the attic, letting the cold air rush over her and smelling the sweet tang of the bushel of newly-picked Jonathan apples stored on the steps. Marty felt in the dark for one and curled up in the darkness in the rocker.

Homecoming during your senior year was the pinnacle of dating, cementing couples into those who were going steady, getting serious. Marty remembered the dreamy night of last year's prom when she was the star, giving a speech at the banquet, accompanied by Jim, the master of ceremonies. They had gone off to a drive-in movie and eaten hamburgers just as teenagers did in the magazines.

But tonight was not Marty's night. She wasn't going to be Jim's girlfriend. She must accept her failure. She sat for a long time in the moonlight, rocking.

"Somethin's coming, I don't know, what it is, but it is gonna be great," she sang to herself softly in syncopated rhythm. When one door closed, another opened, Marty knew, though she couldn't imagine it at the moment.

10

Line carried a heavy tub of dishes from the hatch window in the college cafeteria where students dropped them off after eating. Lukas, a burly man with an eastern European accent who managed the night cleanup crew, smiled at her and gave her a "thumbs up." He wore white from head to toe, with a big rubber apron over his clothes. Line wore a rubber apron too, and rubber gloves.

The big machines where the dishes were inserted in huge racks, washed and dried, made the dish room loud and steamy. Line stood next to Gary Gee, an exchange student from China, companionably scraping the leftover food off plates, separating the glasses, cups and silver into the right compartments for washing. There was no need to talk, in English or any language, as tasks in the dish room were clear and simple. Physical work, clearly laid out, in the lean, new student union with interesting companions suited Line well.

In the next room Line could see Tommie Walker mixing up a batch of pancake batter. Tommie didn't work in the dish room, but did food preparation. Line was in awe of her. A Negro woman, thin and pretty with big eyes and a bouffant hairdo, Tommie was a junior and two years older than Line. As an exchange student from Berea College in Kentucky who would be at Wittenberg for only a semester, she was almost as green as Line. She gave Line a friendly glance.

Lukas washed a big pot in the huge stainless steel sink, spraying hot water from high faucets to rinse them. He sang "Somewhere over the rainbow ..." in the protection of the noisy room. Line's laughing eyes met his. He had a family, two small children, and no need for anything, no need to fly over the rainbow.

Line was given the job in the dish room as part of her student financial package. She didn't have the skills to work in an office, as Ellie had when she started Wittenberg College. Several of the other student workers in the dish room were exchange students and it turned out to be a wonderful way to get to know them.

Gary was silent, a physics student who cared little for anything but science. But he was also droll in a way that surprised Line. "Please speak carefully to me," he begged Line. "I need to learn the English." He was from Taiwan and exactly Line's age. His well-off family fled Shanghai during the upheavals there in the 1940's and now owned a factory which made venetian blinds in Tai-Chung City. They were connected to a Lutheran ministry in Taiwan and thus Gary made his way to Wittenberg.

"You must come to International Relations Club," Gary said. "We study world situation, make speakers. You would like, Line."

"Yes," said Line. "I would. Tell me when the next meeting is, will you?"

"Every month," said Gary. "I will tell you."

Line was interested in how Gary was as a person, how he acted and thought. She noticed, for instance, that he didn't like Lukas telling him what to do. He listened, then moved abruptly off without replying, going about his tasks as if he were a secret aristocrat. Line sympathized. Doing cleanup work was low on anyone's totem pole, but it was fun! Line didn't care anyway.

When her shift was over, Line put on her coat and walked out on the wide balcony which looked west over the river valley below the new student union. A low building, set into the hillside, there were views of the valley from each of its three levels. The building was full of conference rooms, student lounges and the large, lovely dining room, a replacement for the temporary buildings which housed the food services in the past. The older students could not stop exclaiming on how wonderful it was.

It was a clear, cold night with a little sickle moon hanging in the sky next to the evening star. The first snow had come a few days ago, and lay reflective of any light. Line was happy. As always, Line learned from people, and the people at Wittenberg came from all kinds of backgrounds. They were like walking books, she thought, imagining that Marty would be shut up with real books if she were here, content to learn from them.

"I thought I saw you come out here," came Tommie's slow southern voice.

Line turned around. She was thrilled to see Tommie coming toward her. "Doesn't it get this cold in Kentucky?" asked Line. "Does it snow there?"

"It gets cold," said Tommie. She too leaned on the frozen iron railing and looked out over the snow-lit valley. "But it doesn't snow much. Or when it does, it doesn't last long. Gets icy though."

"I like snow," said Line. "Can't imagine not having it." Line was wracking her brain for all the questions she wanted to ask Tommie. "Did you cook at Berea?"

"Everyone at Berea works," said Tommie. "They have a big farm and I work in the gardens. They grow their own food, so it isn't so expensive."

"That's amazing," said Line. "Do you want to be a farmer?"

Tommie laughed. "Not this girl! When I get out of college, you won't find this girl out in the dirt! I want to be a journalist."

"A journalist!" said Line.

"So what are you studying, Miss Norwegian dishwasher?" asked Tommie, teasing.

"Sociology," said Line. "Either that or I'd like to be a forest ranger." She loved Tommie already. "We could go in, so it wasn't so cold," she said.

"Brrrrrr," Tommie shivered, turning up the collar of her woolen coat. "Are you Norwegian?" she asked. "I never met one until I got here, and now I'm surrounded!"

"Three quarters," said Line. "I have a Danish grandfather. And I've always been surrounded by Scandinavians! But then, we're even. I don't know anyone like you either." Line looked apologetic, as if it were her fault. The two girls headed toward the glass doors beyond which were warmth and big soft turquoise couches where students could be seen in all kinds of relaxed poses.

"Looks inviting," said Tommie as they pushed open the doors. "But I think the library is still open. I need to go have a look at the newspapers."

"The newspapers?" asked Line.

"James Meredith," said Tommie. "He's at the University of Mississippi. I think of him every day."

Line looked quizzical. She didn't bother with the newspapers, did not really know what was going on in the world unless someone mentioned it. She knew the Russians were moving missiles into Cuba because everyone talked of it.

"It's in the newspaper," said Tommie. "The riots. The whites are trying to keep him out. I pray for him every day. Can't imagine how it would be to be surrounded by troops going to class, shunned at meals." Tommie's voice was warm and intense.

"Can I come with you?" asked Line. She was struck by the importance of the struggle Tommie was involved with.

"Sure," said Tommie. They hurried over to the library. The *New York Times* came by mail, a few days after its publication. The thin sheets of the *Christian Science Monitor* did also. The only current wire service news was in the *Des Moines Register*. Tommie lifted the stick with the newspaper on it out onto a table and she and Line turned the pages quietly. A few students studied at the long tables in the big reading room, so they didn't talk.

There was no news that day about Meredith. Tommie explained what she knew to the ignorant Line as the two of them went down the stone steps and out into the cold. Troops and National Guardsmen from several states were called out by President Kennedy to support Meredith at the University.

"He knows what he's doing," said Tommie. "He was in the army, he's older than most students. But I'm sure it isn't easy."

Line was seared by these revelations, the knowledge that a friend could be moved every day by what was going on miles from where they sat talking and that you could read about it in the newspapers.

"Thanks for showing me," said Line, shyly, as their paths diverged. There was little movement across the big grassy campus, lit by pools of street light and snow.

As she headed to the dorm, Line thought of her roommate Phyllis, who was homesick for her family in Wisconsin. Why was Line so much more moved by Tommie's imaginative empathy than by Phyllis' whining?

In the brightly lit entry porch of the old brick Larson Hall, girls stood about in the arms of their boyfriends, saying good night before they must go in. The doors were locked at 10 p.m. and all the girls must be inside. Line snaked her way between the couples and ran up the stairs. She went down the creaky wooden floor of the corridor to the room she shared. Phyllis sat at a small desk in her pajamas, her hair rolled in big plastic rollers, hunched under the light with her books spread before her.

"Are you reading *The Odyssey*?" asked Line.

"Trying to," said Phyllis. Phyllis was not a stellar student. She attacked her work with great energy, but a literalness that surprised Line. Phyllis wanted to teach elementary school. She was short, dark and she reminded Line of Marty a little. But Marty's way of thinking was deeper.

Wittenberg turned out many teachers every year, but the broad background it gave in history, literature and religion was more than Phyllis had bargained for. Line, given the delight her parents took in stories and books, found she was much better prepared for a liberal arts college than Phyllis. Phyllis lived for letters from home, went home on weekends if she could and talked about the store, her family and the people in her Wisconsin town constantly.

With more than 600 students in her class, Line was still sorting out her place among them several months after school started. She knew the girls on her corridor, of course, and the college provided mixers and events for freshmen. She liked Phyllis, but it was clear that Line was considerably more adventurous.

Given her concerns about fairness, Line was always watching out for underdogs. Phyllis was something of an underdog. But, if you were at Wittenberg College, you had done something right. Line could see that the kids from the larger cities had better wardrobes and were better educated. Many had been in college preparatory classes where they studied classics Line had not read.

But students separated along lines of interest, not into richer and poorer. Those interested in music tried out for the famed Nordic Choir or the college symphony. If they didn't get in, there were other choral and instrumental groups in which they could participate. People interested in math and science had an entire hall of science to explore. The art department had a studio, with places to do sculpture, drawing and even a kiln to fire pottery. The library had more books than Line could even imagine reading, and, though the gymnasium had burned down the year before, a new one was being planned and the athletic teams were well-supported.

Line found herself distinguishing between those who acted like sheep and those who were like goats. All of the freshmen were away from home for the first time, entreated to pursue what called to them. Sheep were content to follow established traditions, making the most of their opportunities, hoping to parlay their college education into a career which would allow them to have comfortable lives. The goats, among whom Line numbered herself, were more adventurous, climbing every little precipice they saw to find out what lay on the other side, and if the grass that grew there was for them.

"We're supposed to finish by tomorrow, aren't we? I guess I better get going," said Line, yawning. Phyllis would go to bed soon. Line would have to go to the study hall, where lights were never out. She loved studying late at night when everyone else was asleep. Line changed into her pajamas and wrapped a blanket around her shoulders.

"I'll see you tomorrow," Line said, as she gathered up her books and left the room.

"Good luck!" said Phyllis. "Remember there's a folk singer in chapel tomorrow. You shouldn't miss it." Chapel was required for freshmen, but it was impossible for anyone to know if you were there. Chapel requirements were always being discussed, pro and con, by the student senate and the professors.

"Yeah," said Line. "Just rattle my cage. I'll get up. Don't worry."

"Good night," said Phyllis as Line left.

The two girls were considerate of each other and didn't mind spending time together. But they weren't best friends. Phyllis was definitely a sheep. She made friends on another corridor with more patience for her than Line had. Phyllis spent most of her time with these girls, while Line was still going up to new people, exploring ideas and ways of being.

Line had discovered she liked coffee and was experimenting with how little sleep she could get along on. In the small study hall a coffee brewer sat on a hot plate. Three other girls were already there, but no one looked up when Line took a chair and spread her book and notebook in front of her. She poured herself a cup of coffee and began.

What Line liked about *The Odyssey* was the story of Penelope, weaving and re-weaving her tapestry, holding off the suitors with the help of her son, waiting for her husband to come home. A brave woman, thought Line, a match for the wayward Odysseus.

Line read, wrapped in her blanket, until the room emptied and her eyelids were hard to prop up. She read as fast as she could, skipping through the difficult words to get to the end. Penelope's rugged faith in her husband did not let her down Line was pleased to see.

Line went back to her room and slipped into bed. In the morning, she was sleepy, but she dutifully followed Phyllis to chapel.

The folk singer, Dave Thompson, was introduced by the campus pastor after the usual early morning prayers. With his shock of blonde hair, he reminded Line of her brother. He gave a brief talk about a song, "Michael Row the Boat Ashore," which was sung by slaves during the Civil War. The guitar, which he wore on a wide strap over his shoulder, punctuated everything he said. He could hardly speak without touching it, dark melodic chords rippling outward.

"The song's about faith," the young man said. "There are many lyrics people have made up over the years, but all of them come back to the issue of faith." He touched his guitar and sang, "River Jordan is chilly and cold," he strummed. "Chills the body but not the soul. Sing with me! Hallelujah! They nailed our Jesus to the Cross, but his faith was never lost." He strummed the simple chords.

He paused again, stepping out from behind the podium. "People are singing new lyrics in the South, showing their faith in civil rights. And the 'Hallelujah' at the end of each chorus is praise for the faith we share and the action that faith generates."

"Okay!" he said, lifting his hands to get everyone to stand up. "Stand up and sing with me. I'll say the verse over the microphone and you sing it, followed by the chorus."

Line stood, sleepily, but soon the room echoed, "Joshua at Jericho, Hallelujah. Alabama's next to go." Her voice raised with those beside her, Line felt chills ripple through her spine. "So Mississippi kneel and pray, Hallelujah! Some more buses on the way, Hallelujah." Excitement flowed all around her, wakened and loosened by the singing. She didn't need sleep. She needed singing!

"Thank you, thank you," Pastor Michaelson said. "What a wonderful song. I feel it in particular, the invocation to the Archangel Michael, my name saint. So may we join our voices with all the saints, asking equality for all. May the Lord's blessings rain down upon us. Hallelujah!"

Line looked around, wondering if Tommie was singing. The song surged through her. She couldn't imagine needing civil rights herself. In the world she grew up in, farming brought in money and schools and churches created social life. Exclusions and slights were personal, often imagined, while sour old prejudices against Catholics seemed laughable in comparison with what Negroes were fighting for.

Tommie empathized with her fellow student James Meredith, whose courageous challenge to the bitter exclusion of Negroes from white schools was part of the civil rights movement. Perhaps a powerful song playing in your head could help you stand up to taunting, hateful crowds. It was hard for Line to actually feel what was happening in the South.

Line walked thoughtfully back to the dorm beside Phyllis and her friend Sonya in the frosty morning air. She looked askance as Sonya chattered about how "cute" David Thompson was. Of course he was "cute." He was doing something important.

Line took a shower and then rushed to an English discussion group. Her bright eyes followed the strange-looking Mr. Hirsch as he stood at the front of the class, asking what the class thought about the end of Homer's *Odyssey*. He looked like an owl, young, but almost bald with a huge forehead and a few whisps of dark hair around his ears.

"Do you see any Christian themes in the book?" Mr. Hirsch asked.

"Odysseus is a person who learns from his mistakes," said Mark, a well-dressed student always quick to answer. "Earlier in the book, he can't control himself, but when he finally gets home, he can. Such as when he doesn't kill the servant Melanthios because doing it would bring attention to himself, reveal who he is."

"His longing for home," said another. "It's so strong that it leads Odysseus to forsake easy pleasure and keep pursuing his goal of reaching home. As we might pursue a Christian life."

"Longing for home is like a longing for God?" asked Mr. Hirsch.

"Yes," said Mark.

"For Aristotle, happiness is 'the virtuous activity of the soul in accordance with reason.' So would we say that Odysseus is happy, Line?"

Line wasn't sure why Mr. Hirsch spoke to her directly, asking her questions. But she always paid attention, tried to express what she was thinking as clearly as possible. "Odysseus is human," she said. "He does what is natural to humans, exploring, adventuring and then coming home to his family. I think in the end, he is virtuous in that he is acting naturally."

"In accordance with natural law, that is, reason," said Mr. Hirsch. Reason led straight to Thomas Aquinas and the Medieval Synthesis. The Greek and Judaeo-Christian cultures were knit together by Aquinas into a supple structure, the basis of Western Civilization, just as core courses at Wittenberg were knit together. The core course had discussion groups in religion, history and literature, which were tied together with overarching lectures by Dr. Rolfe Magnusson.

After class, Line filed out with the others, but Mr. Hirsch stopped her.

"Don't be afraid to talk in class," he said. "I can see your thoughts going on behind your face!"

"Really?" asked Line. She was rarely singled out by teachers.

"Really," he said. "It isn't just a game to you, I can tell."

Line thought about this as she headed off toward a drawing class. It was true that nothing was a game to her. She acted naturally herself, exploring. There must be a reason for discussing the Medieval Synthesis and seeing what lay beyond it. The attention made Line glow. She could feel the tingle of Mr. Hirsch's words rippling up her spine.

Flushed and thoughtful as she was, she almost slid into her infamous cousin Diana and Jack Kjome on the snowy walk down the hill to the art studio.

Diana looked tired and there were circles under her eyes. A new haircut showed that she could be pretty, however. Line had hardly ever seen her, knew her by what the grownups said of her. When Line first met her, she looked unkempt and scattered. Now, she barely looked at Line, but Jack stopped her.

"Hey there, Line," he said. He was a big guy with earmuffs over his shaggy hair and a big red muffler around his throat. Jack came from Montauk. A fatherless young man several years older than Line, he often stopped by the parsonage to argue with Dad. Line didn't know what their discussions were about, but it seemed Jack wanted to talk philosophy.

"Hi," said Line, shyly.

Diana looked unenthusiastic but waited while Jack said, "Why don't you come out tonight. We have some great talks."

"Maybe I could," said Line tentatively.

"Just come down to the studio after dinner. We'll be here," Jack said heartily.

Diana and Jack's crowd was the influence Mother and Dad feared at Wittenberg College. Line was surprised at the vehemence of a letter Dad sent begging her not to become involved in this "artsy" group. Diana and her friends reputedly smoked, drank and did as they pleased, rebels with some cause of their own. They weren't sheep, in Line's terms, but Dad needn't worry. Line didn't want to waste time drinking.

Loving drawing as she did, it was natural that Line took a drawing class. Mother and Dad knew that Line's ideas would unfold as she went. Her path wasn't clear even to her. Girls were apt to hedge their academic bets with teacher training. But Line did not want to be a teacher. She saw herself doing social work of some kind, even though she didn't know anyone who did it.

The Mikkelsons wanted a liberal arts college education for each of their kids, an education for their lives. They didn't see it as a luxury. Mother and Dad were anxious to counsel and share Line's experience. But she must follow her own natural bent, make her own living. Because Ellie quit and got married, Line thought Mother and Dad were being as gentle as possible with their advice. Line wasn't as biddable, or as gullible, as Marty was in any case. Mother always said she counted on Line's common sense.

In the art department building, in a big, airy studio, Mr. Widness set up interesting still life collections. Students put up an easel and spent the hours drawing with pencils, charcoal or pastels, while Mr. Widness walked around, pointing out things about composition or color. Sometimes he collected the class around him to show them a technique or a way to draw light and shading. It was a quiet couple of hours.

Line found herself watching other students drawing. Some attacked the paper, intense and desperate. Some were very relaxed, holding pencils in ways that surprised Line. Everything each one did, including how they sat in front of their drawings, went into the idiosyncratic details of the finished drawings.

In the last few minutes of the class, everyone put their drawing on the table in front of Mr. Widness. It was thrilling to see each one completed, fifteen different perspectives of the still life arranged in front of them. Line looked from each drawing to the person who made it. Hands, eyes, limbs correlated to penciled lines. Her own was simple, as faithful a reproduction of reality as was in her power.

"What are you doing here, Line?" asked Mr. Widness. "Is there anything you want to tell us?"

Line looked at him, wide-eyed. "No," she said.

"Good!" said Mr. Widness. "That's a fine answer. Do any of you know the Italian painter Morandi? Intensity of observation and contemplation allowed him to stay with simple groupings of bottles, vases and bowls throughout much of his life. Stay with it, Line. Draw exactly what you see."

Line was having a good day. Recognition! It was again a surprise. Praise from family didn't mean much. Of course they loved you! But praise from people she barely knew? That was something else again. She breathed in and looked down at her drawing as Mr. Widness moved on to the next one.

Drawing was a joy, but Line wasn't interested in art in and of itself. Her true interest was in service to people. And what a wealth of interesting people college opened up! Line looked at her drawing. A coffee can with a plant in it, a book of poems, a mug, a sea shell. Would she come back tonight to listen to the artsy crowd talk? She probably should, just to find out what all the fuss was about, but talk wasn't interesting to Line. She wanted action.

11

Paul and Foxy set off as soon as the Sunday dinner dishes were cleared. Walking down to the frozen creek with Foxy was one of Paul's favorite things to do. Days were short in January, but very beautiful. They must make the most of the daylight.

Paul stumped along the road beside Foxy in falling snow being blown by a fairly strong wind. Cars churned up the gravel and dirt along the road, but when he and Foxy slipped down the path to the creek, human noise and movement ceased. Snow lay everywhere and obscured the sky as it fell. Bare willows looked like a kind of tall pale grass with snowy fronds hanging over the creek bed. On the banks the lacy branches of leafless oaks were outlined by fallen snow.

The ice on the creek itself was windswept, different colors where it had marbled, freezing and then thawing and freezing again into a thick opaque plate. It was solid. Line and Marty skated on it at Christmas. In the places where the water pooled, Paul knew bloodless fish swam slowly below the ice through the dark, freezing months. The ice was too thick to see them.

Ahead of Paul, the creek meandered frozen through the fields. In the winter he could cover more ground. In the summer, all sorts of rocks and vegetation impeded travel, but when the creek froze, it was a long, smooth icy pathway. Paul could see different things in the winter. He and

Foxy pushed on up the creek into the wind. Coming home the wind would be behind them, though without any sun, the world was directionless.

The only tracks Paul could see in the falling snow were those of a recent rabbit, crossing from one side of the creek to the other. Foxy followed them, snuffling along the banks. She loved being out in the wind also. The winter birds Paul could see were those which came to the parsonage feeder, small nuthatches, chickadees and raucous jays, but their tracks were obscured.

At one point along the bank, water falling off a hillside had made an ice waterfall. Paul looked closely at its structure. Winter beauty was all due to water, the steam in the air, the frozen water of the creek, the falling crystalline snow, and the light on these things, or the lack of it. Not much sky light today. Foxy in her thick fur overcoat and Paul in his woolen one, followed the line of the creek in the bitter wind.

All of a sudden, Foxy emitted a low growl, surprising Paul.

"What is it girl?" he said, loudly. Foxy stopped, then headed toward the edge of the creek. Paul looked for tracks but could see none. Foxy started yipping, but Paul couldn't see anything unusual. He hiked along the edge of the creek. All of a sudden his leg went down, almost to his hip, in some kind of hole or burrow. His leg was caught in roots and branches. Paul struggled to pull it out as his ankle throbbed with pain. He got it out with some effort, wallowing in the snow on his hands and knees.

Foxy stood beside Paul, growling and then whining. Paul tried to stand up, but the injured leg was his good one and there was nothing to hang on to. He did manage to stand, but pain ripped upward along his good leg. Not broken, he didn't think, but certainly sprained. Paul looked back down the creek. They had come a good way.

Paul considered. He could try to cut a willow stick and walk back using it to prop himself up, except that his weak leg wasn't used to his weight. Or he could crawl back. Paul tried it. He made some progress, but there was a long way to go. Nothing to do but get to it, he thought. It felt funny, like he was an animal for sure now, making weird plowing motions with his hands and knees in the snow on the creek. Foxy watched him.

"I know you think I'll never make it," Paul said to her. "But I will." He plodded on, his mittened hands wet, dragging his feet behind him.

After a hundred yards or so, Paul crawled to the edge of the creek and, finding his knife in his pocket, cut a willow stick just thick enough, he thought, to hold him. He pulled himself up and tried standing. Every step was painful as he put weight on his good foot. He couldn't tell how far he was from home, but it was surely too far.

"What are you looking at," he said annoyed, to Foxy. "Go home and get Dad!" He pointed forcefully in the direction of home. The wind was gusting behind him. Foxy whimpered. Paul pointed again, "Go home!" And Foxy did go. Paul began plodding slowly along, dragging himself on his ill-mannered feet.

"Go home! Go home!" Paul shouted. When Foxy was gone, Paul got down on his hands and knees again. He crawled forward, dragging his stick, inching along, the bitter wind at his back. His hands felt like cakes of ice in their wet mittens. He had no idea how far he must go, but he would keep going. After a while he stood up again with his willow stick and painfully stepped forward. Slowly, slowly. Was it getting darker? Paul couldn't think. He just kept going. Snow was falling on his cap, on his arms.

After a while he saw a dark figure up ahead and Foxy came running toward him, arffing loudly. Dad was coming toward him and was soon upon him. Paul shivered, falling sleepily into his arms.

"Come on, son," said Dad. "We have to get you home!" Dad wrapped him in the blanket he brought. "Sit on this," he commanded in a voice Paul had never heard him use before.

Paul sat down on the green fiberglass saucer. Turning it around with Paul's legs splayed out behind him, Dad pulled the saucer on a rope as if Paul was a little kid. Foxy ran along beside them. In what seemed to Paul like minutes, they were out in the lane that led to the road. Dad had parked the car there and pulled Paul into it, turning up the heat full blast as they drove the short distance home.

"So glad you came," said Paul sleepily, taking off his wet mitts. He couldn't stop his teeth from chattering. He shivered and shook. "Good girl," he said to Foxy at his feet. "Good girl." He put his hands next to the warm body, under her fur.

When they got home, Dad commanded Paul to take off all his clothes. Mother brought down Paul's pajamas and some blankets, while Marty followed her with more quilts. Paul lay on the sofa, the heavy pile of warmth on top of him.

"I'm less worried about your foot than about hypothermia," said Dad. "Mother's making you something hot."

Mother thrust a mug of hot cocoa into Paul's hands and he sat up to drink it. He was still shivering. But relief was all around him. Kristen and

Hanna on her little legs stood at the edge of the couch, uncertain what had happened. "Okay Paul?" asked Kristen.

"Yup, okay!" Paul said. "Foxy came and got Dad to help me!"

Dad sat down beside Paul and held the offending foot in his hands. "I'm not going to put ice packs on this!" he said, wryly, relief in his voice. But the ankle was very swollen. Marty stood beside him looking helpless.

Mother was so worried she hadn't said anything, but Dad now seemed to think everything was fine. "This is going to take a while to heal," he said. "Weeks, in fact. We'll have to get out those crutches again. But it will heal. And you are home safe and warm. That's the important thing."

Paul felt blessed. The fear that he had not felt while he crawled along the creek in the chilly wind rose up only to remind him that all was well. He was home, warm and safe, not lost in the snow trying desperately to get home. The radiators hissed beside him and lamp light illumined his small sisters, standing beside the couch in their little corduroy pants and sweatshirts. As for Foxy, Mother was so grateful to her, she let Dad bring Foxy's bed up from the basement and put it in the hall.

Paul also felt vaguely ashamed. Perhaps it wasn't his fault that he had stepped in a hole while out on a walk he often did, both winter and summer, but perhaps there was something he could have done to prevent it? Been better prepared? Paul didn't feel that anyone was going to scold him. He was just ashamed that he had not been a better woodsman and naturalist, unable to get home by himself.

Gradually Paul warmed up. "Will you read to us?" asked Kristen.

"Sure," said Paul. "Bring me *Wind in the Willows* and I'll read it." He was thinking about Ratty rescuing Mole in winter in the Wild Wood. He identified with Ratty. He wondered whether it was a muskrat hole he stuck his foot into. Softly, to himself, he sang Toad's little song, "When the Toad came home …" He was celebrating, but, like Toad, under his breath.

When Kristen brought the book, he turned to the pictures of winter. "Here," he said. "This is a little like what happened to me." He began to read to the two little girls, who sat on either side of him. In the kitchen, he could hear the sounds of Mother and Marty making supper.

School was an effort that winter. Paul struggled around on his crutches as his foot healed, but at home he stuck his foot up on a chair and let Marty wait on him. She seemed to enjoy it! She was also willing to play chess with him during the long, dark evenings.

Months before, Dad had noticed Paul's rapt attention to Ricky Nelson playing a guitar and singing on television. Dad bought a guitar for the family at Christmas and no one was surprised when Paul took to it, especially now when he was having a hard time getting around.

The folk music phenomenon was beginning to reach into the more remote areas of the country and for once, Mother and Dad supported this popular music. Paul played the Kingston Trio album over and over. Some of the songs were wry and comic and touched the Norwegian funny bone, like the story of Charlie on the MTA who couldn't get off for lack of a nickel. Others came from history, ballads showing what happened to someone or work songs shared by whole communities.

Paul lay on the couch one afternoon before dinner, his foot up and the guitar on top of him, strumming chords and humming "Where Have All the Flowers Gone." His fingers were strong. He liked the sound of the guitar much better than the sound of his trumpet.

"Gone to graveyards every one," he sang. The guitar strings were a little out of tune. He twisted the tuning pegs to try to get the chords to sound better. He liked everything about the guitar, holding its golden wood in his arms, listening to the strings vibrate as he played. The song was about soldiers, but Paul knew people with polio didn't go into the army. That was one thing he did not have to worry about. Like Dad, he was expected to finish college and go to the seminary, becoming a Lutheran pastor.

"You sound really good," said Marty as she strode through the room. The two of them sang together some, now that Line was gone. "Is there any harmony to that?" Marty loved to sing alto, the lower parts.

But Paul didn't have a book, he was just sounding out chords, trying to figure out which were the right ones for the song. Marty stood beside Paul, singing the well known words. "When will they ever learn? When will they eh-eh-ver learn?"

"Supper!" sang out Kristen's six-year-old voice from the kitchen where she was laying the table.

When Paul's sprained ankle was somewhat healed, Dad made an appointment with Dr. Cousins, who looked at Paul's legs every once in a while. The clinic was only a couple of hours away and Cardinal, the town where Line was going to college, was on the way. They must go on a week day, though, when Dr. Cousins had office hours.

Early in the morning, the whole family got up and packed themselves into the car even before Marty left for school. She wanted to go with them badly, but the senior class play was coming up and she couldn't miss school and play practice. Three-year-old Hanna in her red snow clothes trailed after brown-haired Kristen, who trailed after Mother out to the station wagon. Paul said goodbye to Foxy in the dog house where she spent the day. Dad was the last to come out to the garage, where Mother and everyone else were waiting in the car.

The misty early morning twilight gave way to sun as they drove north. The car was warm and winter clothes felt excessive. Paul unbuttoned his coat. The highways were clear and dirty snow was thawing in humps along the road.

Paul was apprehensive. He could walk on both legs now, though twinges of pain bothered him now and then. Going to the clinic was scary, memories of the painful reconstructive surgeries and the long months in physical therapy surfacing. But he was feeling strong and was sure, as Dr. Cousins once said, that it was up to him now. The surgeons had done all they could with his legs.

The nurse weighed Paul and measured him and made him sit on a thin mattress on the examining table. He felt vulnerable waiting, dressed only in his shorts with his scarred legs sticking out, one thick and one thin. Paul swallowed, his throat dry. The shiny steel bars overhead reminded him of the day two doctors with pliers had pulled the stitches out of his legs after his last surgery. He had almost bent bars like those with his hands, holding on and shrieking against his will, as the two young doctors bent over his legs, ignoring him, talking to each other.

But when Dr. Cousins came in, he was warm and approving.

"Your weight and height look good, Paul," he said. "Quite normal." He flexed Paul's legs and measured them. "Good muscle too. Yes, you've been doing well. Walk to school do you?"

"The high school is out of town and my sister and I walk sometimes, two miles," said Paul. "But not in the winter. We walk to the bus every day, though."

"Two miles!" said Dr. Cousins. "You're a toughie for sure. And how about this sprained ankle? When did that happen?"

Paul recounted the story of his winter adventure. Dr. Cousins probed the ankle a bit and asked Paul to walk around the room for him and do some knee bends. Then he told Paul to put his clothes back on and called Mother and Dad in to hear his verdict. Kristen and Hanna must stay in the waiting room.

"Paul is doing very well," said Dr. Cousins. "Everything we could hope for. His right leg is compensating quite a bit, of course, which puts the spine off balance. But there isn't much we can do about that. I would advise Paul to continue with as full a physical life as he feels he can. Even a little more than you think you can, Paul. Use of both legs ensures circulation and muscle development. Stretching is essential to get blood and oxygen to all of those cells." He looked significantly at Mother and Dad.

"Doesn't hurt any of us," said Dad. "The winter makes us all constricted. I really feel the need to limber up now in the spring myself."

"Sometimes people who have been through what Paul has, actually become more physically fit than those who haven't," said Dr. Cousins. "He was lucky, really. The disease didn't get to his spine or his lungs."

"Thank you for your encouragement, Doctor," said Mother. She stood with her hands folded over her purse, looking on with her intelligent eyes.

"Yes, I don't think I need to see you for a couple of years," Dr. Cousins said, smiling. "I'm sure that's the news you want to hear!"

Paul smiled widely, exhilaration filling his body. He was right! He was his own man!

"We're very proud of him," said Dad, the warmth in his eyes visible to Paul and everyone else. "It was a tough row to hoe, but he's got a life in front of him." He put an arm around Paul and squeezed his shoulders.

Hands were extended in every direction. Goodbyes were said. Paul felt as if a weight was taken off him. He walked through the door of the clinic as if it were the last time he would ever have to come.

In the evening, the Mikkelsons stopped to see if Line could have supper with them. Mother had sent a postcard, but she did not receive a reply. It was dark, but the little girls quivered with excitement. Paul took Kristen and Hanna up the steps to Larson Hall to find her, while Mother and Dad waited in the car. If they had been his own kids, Paul couldn't have been prouder, holding them by their little hands.

At the desk, a young woman buzzed Line's room and, all of a sudden, there she was, coming through the double doors into the front lounge. Her face shone with excitement at seeing her siblings. She wore her winter coat, boots and a muffler. So she had gotten the postcard. She punched Paul on the shoulder, Peanuts style, and grabbed Hanna, lifting her up.

"You little sweetheart!" Line said. Hanna had a solemn little face and big eyes. She looked almost like a little boy, which people found mysterious and attractive.

Paul and Kristen stood, waiting for Line's attention, which was entirely enveloped in Hanna. At last, Line put Hanna down and kneeled to hug Kristen. Kristen was stolid and uncomplaining, as usual, but she smiled widely when Line hugged her.

"Do you want to see my room?" Line asked the little girls. "Come on, it'll only take a minute." To Paul she said, "We'll be right back."

Paul couldn't go, of course. Only girls could go behind the swinging doors into the dorm. He stood beside the desk in the public lounge. A few people sat waiting on the couches in the big room, lit by lamps. A girl in a bathrobe wandered in and went to the Coke machine in the back of the room, put her quarter in and took the resulting can of Coke. Paul did like Cokes. But he doubted that he would have any extra quarters when he went to college.

At last his sisters came back. In the car Dad asked Line where they should go for supper, and Line said with no hesitation, "Mabel's Pizza!" There was no pizza in Montauk, but Paul occasionally had it with friends in other towns. He loved the idea.

"Okay," Dad said. "We're celebrating, I guess."

"What are we celebrating?" asked Line.

"Lots of things!" said Mother. "Let's get settled and I'll tell you then."

Mabel's had black and white tiles on the floor, and booths with red leatherette benches in which the Mikkelsons just fit. It was warm and inviting inside after being out in the chilly night. Mother sat between Kristen and Line on one side of the booth, and Paul and Dad, with Hanna between them, sat on the other. Paul wished Marty were there. She was definitely missing out. The family hardly ever went out to eat.

The other booths were full and a colorful jukebox in the corner was playing a pop song. "Well, I'm the type of guy," sang Dion in a sort of sing-song rhythm to a loud guitar, "that likes to roam around, I roam around and around and around."

A waitress popped up as they settled themselves. "I don't think I've ever ordered pizza," said Dad loudly so she could hear him over the din.

She was a college girl, probably, with a little cap to match the red trim on her dress. She wore an apron with pockets from which she took out her pencil and a little tablet to write down the order. "We have small, medium and large. And you can have one with everything, or you can order the toppings you want," she explained.

"Toppings?" said Dad.

"Pepperoni," said the waitress. "Or sausage, mushrooms, peppers, olives."

"We'll just get one with everything," said Dad.

"That's a large for all of you? And to drink?"

"Water is fine," said Mother. Just as Paul thought, Cokes were more expensive than what Dad and Mother wanted to pay.

Once they ordered, Line begged. "Okay, Mom. We can't wait any longer. What all are we celebrating?"

Mother laughed. "Well, to start with, Paul has a clean bill of health. No more surgeries scheduled."

"Yay!" said Line. "That's wonderful, Paul! I heard about your sprained ankle. Is that okay now?"

"Pretty good," said Paul. "I can walk on it. The doctor said it would twinge for a couple more months as it heals, but it's fine." He beamed at Line, recalling how she stayed with him at the hospital, finding baseball games on the radio and reading to him.

"Great!" said Line, her eyes meeting Paul's as if she were thinking the same thing. "Anything else? Surprises?"

"Oh yes," said Mother conspiratorially. "This is about you, Line. I hope you haven't any plans for the summer, yet. Your sister Ellie is pregnant again. She's hoping you will come and stay with her this summer. The baby isn't due until September, but she's hoping you could help take care of Brenda."

"Another baby!" said Line. "We're all aunts and uncles again!" she said. "Even you, Kristen," she said, stroking Kristen's face beside her.

"Big families," said Mother. "It happens."

"Well, that's a surprise," said Line. "And I'd love to go back to the Cities. Any others?"

"Just one," said Dad. "Your mother has gotten a job at the high school as a librarian. She has to take summer classes though, to get her certification. She's going to be at a teachers' college at Mason City, so Paul and Marty will be keeping house during the summer."

"Whew!" said Paul. "I didn't know that!"

Mother looked a little embarrassed. As the backbone of the family, attention rarely turned in her direction. But Dad said, "It's wonderful. We need the income with all of you kids going to college!" Paul could almost feel his warmth, beaming across the table at Mother.

"Does Marty know about this?" asked Paul. He wished she were there even more.

"Yes," said Mother. "It just got finalized this week. We've been planning this for a while. I told Marty last night. She'll enjoy it, I think."

"That is a big change," said Line. "I'm proud of you, Mother." But she looked a little chagrined as well. "I'm sorry we are costing so much money," she said.

"Now, don't you worry," Dad said. "You're helping work your way through college and you've got loans which you'll have to pay off later. We're all doing our best. But next year there will be two of you in school and we are pleased that Mother found a job which is right for her."

"Yes," said Line. "It's amazing. There just aren't many jobs in small towns, are there."

"Nope," said Dad.

"I'm glad Bruce and Ellie want me," said Line. "I like being in Minneapolis. And it will be easier this year, now that I know it."

"My good girl," said Mother. "I know you will start having other ideas, but Bruce and Ellie do need you this year."

"Yes," said Line. "I'd really like to do one of the exchange programs that Wittenberg has with Negro colleges. But it wouldn't be next year. You usually go in your junior year. I'm getting to know this girl from Berea College in Kentucky. But her school is half white and half Negro. She thinks I should get the full experience of being a minority. She thinks I should go to Spelman or Fiske."

Paul watched Mother and Dad looking at each other. But Line was her own person now and must make her own decisions.

"It sounds interesting," said Mother.

"How do you keep 'em down on the farm, after they've seen Paree?" asked Dad. "Sounds like you've been thinking about your future too."

To Paul, Line looked like a grownup all of a sudden. Television news was full of demonstrations in southern states, about integration of schools, restaurants, and buses, about voting.

"I do want to see what it's like to be in a minority," said Line. "To actually be there. Tommie says she's never seen so many Norwegians in her life!"

"Norwegians are a minority," said Dad, "in some respects."

"Yes," said Line. "But we look just like Germans, English people, Irish, Swiss. We could be anything. We can pass!"

Paul tried to imagine Line at a Negro college, but he couldn't.

"I want to go to college," sang out Hanna all of a sudden. "I want to sleep in Line's room."

"Someday," said Dad, putting his hand on her little blonde head. "Someday, but not for a while yet."

"Thank goodness!" said Mother.

The pizza was delicious. It came, hot and spicy, on a big round tray, with the pieces cut in wedges, like a pie. Paul put one on his plate, but Line picked one up in her hands. "You eat it like this," she said, biting off the point. "Sometimes our counselors order one for all of us, if we're having a party."

"And it comes to your dorm?" asked Mother.

"Of course!" said Line. "We all love Mabe's pizza."

All was right with the world, thought Paul. He was in the middle of a bright, busy family, his legs were fine and he didn't need Coke. The pizza on a cold night was a hot, warm treat. It felt like the world was expanding. And he would not be left behind.

12

On a June morning, Marty stayed home to make bread while Paul took Kristen and Hanna down to the creek. She softened the yeast with some salt in lukewarm water, adding powdered milk and butter, and then threw in honey, and Brewer's yeast to add to its vitamin content. The big kitchen was bright and airy in the warm weather. Screens on the windows kept flies out of the house. As Marty beat many cups of flour into the liquid with a wooden spoon in a big stainless steel bowl, the dough got stiff and sticky.

Marty was barefoot, in shorts and a tee-shirt. She loved the warmth of summer. Everyone was free to come and go. No one worried about getting up in the morning or what time it was, or even what the little kids were up to. No one told them what to do. They had to figure that out for themselves.

Marty did miss Mother. Mother had always, always been at home. Whenever Marty came home from school, the first thing she did was figure out who else was at home in the spacious parsonage. Mother's quiet, strong presence was always easy to find. She would be sewing, reading magazines, or studying for her Spanish correspondence course. But when Marty arrived, Mother put her work down and listened, putting in her own strong opinions, guiding Marty without her knowing.

Marty sighed. She spread a bunch of flour on the table and turned the bread dough out on it. Gathering the sticky edges in and turning it as she punched and handled it, the dough became smooth and heavy. Marty punched and turned, kneading the bread as Mother taught her. She was 17 and high school was over. She had nothing to keep her from moving on to college in the fall. No best friends or boyfriends who would miss her deeply. She had shared the top of her graduating class with Georgia as usual. The girls she knew were either going on to college or taking jobs and getting married. The boys would go to school and then take up the reins on their family farms and businesses. Marty had no idea what direction her life would take.

Marty put the kneaded bread back in its bowl and put a towel over it. She put it in a patch of sunlight to warm. She went looking for the *Life* magazine that arrived the day before. Dad was out somewhere on visits. It was a rare thing to be alone in the house.

In the magazine, the photographer Margaret Bourke-White described how she took up her profession, photographing steel mills the way no one had before. "I had a feeling of rightness with a camera in my hand," she said.

"Do I like photographs or writing better?" Marty mused to herself. She couldn't tell. Photographs told stories, taking you straight to a place with an atmosphere. She loved magazines because photographs accompanied the words. Photographs filled her eyes and were unequivocal. No one could quarrel with a photograph. They were indeed worth 10,000 words.

But words took Marty places faster, and went deeper. Books with characters in them showed her things she had no way of knowing. And here was a photographer talking about what was behind the photos she had taken. They didn't exactly stand on their own. A photo Bourke-White took at Buchenwald was shown in the magazine. You could see in the people's eyes how they felt, but you might also want to know more, in words.

When Paul and the little girls came back from the creek, Marty was on the front porch steps waiting for them with the little black Kodak camera Aunt Mabel had given her. "Don't do anything different," she called to Paul, who trailed behind Kristen and Hanna, Foxy beside them. "Just stop, so I can get you in focus."

Marty looked down. In the camera, she saw a boy with powerful shoulders, jeans rolled up at the bottom and short-sleeved plaid shirt, stopped mid-step and carrying a brown paper grocery bag. A stocky little six-year-old girl in shorts and a sleeveless buttoned top, and a three-year-old with her hands in Foxy's ruff of fur. They were coming up the walk between two tall cedar trees, silent, after a day of sunshine, their faces drunk with the wild contentedness of little animals. Marty pressed the lever. No one needed to know what they were thinking, she decided.

She took other photos: Kristen pushing Hanna in the tire swing in the corner of the yard with the dark cedars behind them. Paul kneeling in the garden, pulling weeds around the hills of corn. She didn't want to take the sort of photos where people stood there, looking at the camera. She wanted to photograph people doing things, making a record of a moment which could not be refuted.

The trouble was, photos cost money. Marty didn't have enough to buy film and then develop it once she took pictures. Dad would support such a hobby, of course. But writing or drawing was almost free. The parsonage was full of paper and pencils, colored pencils, even. Marty could write or draw to her heart's content. Marty wound the button which rolled the negatives back onto the reel. She put the camera in the study, where Dad would see it.

Four loaves of the rich, sweet-smelling brown bread sat on racks in the kitchen. Two of them would go into the freezer, and one had already been attacked. Paul was cutting slices of the fresh bread for the little girls to have with milk. Marty laughed. "Bread and milk and blackberries for dinner, I guess," she said.

"Blackberries?" asked Kristen.

"I was just kidding," said Marty. "You know. Peter Rabbit couldn't have any, but the other rabbits did."

"I want blackberries," said Hanna.

"It's too early," said Marty. "Blackberries come at the end of the summer. Right now we can have strawberries, asparagus. Maybe peas. Are there any peas we could eat, Paul?"

"Peas porridge hot, peas porridge cold," said Paul. "I'll go see." He took the last half of his thick peanut butter sandwich and went out the back door.

Marty made deviled eggs for dinner. While she mashed the hard-cooked egg yolks, she realized she was trying to make a supper Dad would like, trying to please him, as Mother would have effortlessly. But Dad, eating the few peas Paul brought in, the asparagus and deviled eggs with thick slices of the fragrant new bread, was uncomplaining. He ate whatever was put in front of him.

On Sunday evening the Mikkelsons, including Mother who was home for the weekend, went out to Dad's country church for an ice cream social. The Luther Leaguers were to put on a play, but they must wait until it got dark, almost 9 p.m. at this time of year.

Long tables were laid out in the parking lot in front of the brick church which stood on a hill with fields spread in every direction, a cemetery alongside it. The crowd around the tables laid out with pies was gay on a summer evening. At the end of the table, two men dug into five-gallon brown paper cartons of vanilla ice cream with aluminum scoops.

Many people filled their plates with two or three kinds of pie, but Marty went straight for the rhubarb pies she had made herself. She was persnickety and didn't like the lard piecrust most people used. Hers was made from Betty Crocker piecrust sticks. Many of the pies were made with canned fruit, topped with questionable cream. Who knew whether the meringue pies were fresh? The Mikkelson pies were filled with fresh cut rhubarb and sugar, which baked into a luscious juice, sweet and tangy at the same time.

Marty cut a piece for Kristen as well, who stood beside her looking up expectantly. Marty held up their plates and one of the men put a scoop of vanilla ice cream on each of them. "That's not much," said Mr. Olson. "Only one piece? Well I guess you want to keep your girlish figure."

Marty smiled at him. "Come on, Kristen." The two of them walked toward the cemetery with their plates. Several high school kids Marty knew were sitting on the tombstones. In the evening sun, they were just markers, smooth granite stones carved with names and the dates the person was born and when they died, giving off long shadows. In the distance Marty saw a recent grave, a rectangle heaped with fresh dirt and a few flowers. She remembered that Dad held a funeral service at this church recently, but she did not know who had died.

The cemetery with its tombstones sloped down the hillside towards the fields. The setting sun lit the people's faces obliquely. David Berglund's voice sang out as Marty came near, "Hey, Marty!"

Marty hadn't seen him in years. "David?" she asked. She settled Kristen on the grass with her plate of pie and ice cream in her lap.

David pulled a girl toward him, saying cheerfully, "Marty, this is my fiancé Greta. Greta, this is Marty. Remember, I told you about our pastor's family. Line was the oldest, and then Marty here."

Marty smiled at him, reaching out her hand to Greta. "You're forgetting my oldest sister Ellie," she said. "Line's living up in Minneapolis with Ellie's family this summer."

"Great!" said David. "City girl, that Line."

Marty sat down beside them. Greta was as blonde as anyone Marty had ever seen. She was pale, but with healthy color in her skin.

"Greta goes to school with me," said David. "We're getting married next year. I'm showing her our farm, getting her used to things here. Greta's from Germany."

"Germany!" said Marty. No wonder David liked Line, she thought. He might be a farmer, but he was adventurous.

Greta inclined her head. "It's beautiful here," she said. A foreign lilt in her voice betrayed that English was not her first language.

"They don't call it the Little Switzerland of Iowa for nothing," said David.

"So I guess you're Lutheran?" asked Marty.

"Sort of," said Greta. "We don't go to church much in Germany. I like it here. It feels like everyone knows each other." She looked admiringly at David's long sun-browned face.

Marty noticed that ice cream was about to drip off the plate onto Kristen's dress. White cream encircled her lips. Marty grabbed the plate and wiped Kristen's face with a napkin.

"I'll tell Line I met you," said Marty. "We don't hear from her much. She's not much of a letter writer. Even when she's at college."

"Wittenberg?" asked David. Marty nodded.

"Oh!" said Greta. "I've been to Wittenberg, Germany. That's where Martin Luther lived."

David looked out over the fields and pointed, his arm making a long shadow across the gravestones. "Our farm is over there, behind that wooded hill." Below them the fields were plowed in contours around the hills, rows of soybeans and corn planted sideways against the hill to keep the soil from running off. To Marty he said, "It's flat as a pancake over near Ames. I never knew how hilly our farm was until I got there."

"Do you like Ames?" asked Marty. All of a sudden the sparkling sun went behind a thick stand of trees, leaving the graves, the people sitting in the grass in shadow.

"It's okay," said David. "I'm anxious to get home. I'd much rather farm than study. Another year, maybe. We'll see how Dad's doing. And what Greta wants!" He tugged this very blonde girl toward him, putting his arm around her waist.

"I want to live on your farm!" said Greta. Marty could see the happiness between them. She was thrilled to learn another piece of David's story.

Marty stood up. Kristen had wandered over to a tiny gravestone on which the date of death was only a few days after the date of birth. The parents of the child lay in graves beside her, their deaths long ago. Twilight rose up and the unmistakable dark shape of Paul with his slightly lop-sided gait came toward them.

"Come on you guys," Paul said to everyone in general. "The play's about to start!"

In the parking lot, the tables were cleared of pies and the ice cream put away. Big stainless steel coffee urns stood beside rows of ceramic cups and saucers. The folding chairs were now arranged to face a makeshift stage. A sheet hung down like a curtain in front of it. Marty could see Dad manipulating a light on one side of the stage.

Marty, Paul and Kristen found chairs next to Mother, with Hanna in her lap. Hanna had not let go of Mother the whole evening. Or perhaps it was Mother who didn't want to let her youngest daughter get away from her.

One of the Luther Leaguers came out and stood in front of the white bedsheet. He announced that the play they were about to see was fiction and should not alarm anyone. "But cover the eyes of your children if you need to," he said warningly. He looked as if he would burst with excitement!

117

Bright lights were turned on behind the sheet. As the cast came out, speaking their lines, no one could see anything but their shadows, falling on the pale sheet. Someone was gravely ill. The "doctor" held his stethoscope to the "patient's" chest. "You need an operation, no doubt about it!" the doctor said. He made the patient lie down on an operating table and began surgery, joking all the while. Soon he held a large skill saw above the patient and the shadows showed he was slicing into the patient's stomach.

The patient groaned loudly and the doctor began to pull things out of his stomach. "Oh, these must be the intestines," he said, pulling what looked like sausages from the patient. "You probably don't need them." He threw them away. The shadows of coils of wire, a spoon, a hammer appeared on the sheet. "What's this?!" shouted the doctor, as he pulled a large frog from the patient. "Owwww!" howled the patient. The audience laughed.

Marty looked down at Kristen. She could see Mother holding a sleeping Hanna. "It's just pretend," Marty said to Kristen, whose eyes were drooping anyway. On stage, the doctor stuffed everything back in the patient and sewed him shut with a gigantic needle. Marty was glad Mother was there.

Afterwards the Mikkelsons didn't stay to help cleanup. Dad and Mother must get up at 5 a.m. to take Mother back to school. Mother hated being away from home, didn't want to leave until the last minute. There were still five weeks before she could come home for good and the family would go up to Lake Michigami for a short vacation.

Dad brought home the photographs Marty had taken a few weeks later. The negatives had been left at the dry goods store, sent to another town and came back in two weeks, a packet of black and white photos set in white paper frames with crinkled edges, the date in the corner.

Marty was mesmerized by the photos. There they stood for all time: Kristen with white limbs sticking out of her shorts and top, Hanna with her hands in Foxy's ruff of white fur, and Paul with a peaceful face, carrying a grocery bag. The photograph was grey-looking and a little fuzzy, but the day Paul took Kristen and Hanna to the creek was fixed, exactly as the photograph showed. Shadows lay on the grass beside the kids and their dog.

In other photos, the evening sun's rays could be seen coming through the trees. Kristen pushed Hanna in the tire swing, their white skins glowing against the dark cedars. And in the evening sun, Paul knelt beside rows of corn, pulling weeds around the hills, his long shadow beside him.

Marty wanted to send the thrilling photos to Line, so she could see what they were doing. But, if she sent them, Marty might never see them again. She wanted them for herself, to put in an album like the beautiful one Mother had, with photos glued to black pages.

How was Line liking her second summer in the city, Marty wondered. She wrote to Line, but she couldn't bear to send the photos. She told about meeting David Berglund's fiancé. Line would feel less guilty if she knew that David was happy, Marty thought.

Mother often told Line and Marty when they were fighting with each other that they would be each other's best friends. Marty thought of this now when the summer days were long and she was lonely for all the friends she had seen daily in high school. Mother's own friends were scattered. She had moved several times, had no hometown and was closest to her own family members.

Paul was a good friend though. Many nights Paul played the tapes Dad made of *Hootenanny* shows with a big reel to reel tape recorder attached to the television, while Marty rocked Hanna to sleep. Paul sat on the sofa, trying chords on the guitar, and writing them down in his notebook. "I would love to photograph him," thought Marty. "But it's too dark." She loved to see him concentrating on the music in the twilight, the guitar spread across his stomach.

There were hours of tape. Paul stopped and started them as he wrote down words. Marty sang along. Many of the songs were easy to learn and Marty loved the singers, especially Ian and Sylvia, who were from Canada, and Judy Collins, who sang by herself with a guitar.

"I know where I'm goin', and I know who's goin' with me. I know who I love but the dear knows who I'll marry." Melodies rose up in the evening and Hanna slept in Marty's arms. Quiet songs which spoke of intimate feelings. There wasn't a song Marty didn't love and some spoke to her directly.

"If this train runs me right, I'll be home Saturday night." The longing spoke to Marty of the distances they were all traveling. She hadn't missed Ellie so much, but Mother and Line were far away, and next year, she herself would go off to college. The New Christy Minstrels, a big group with many guitars, banjos, bass violins, sang "I'm nine hundred miles from my home. And I hate to hear that lonesome whistle blow."

Hanna was heavy, but Marty could still carry her upstairs. Kristen was easy to settle, sleepy and sweet. But when Mother wasn't around, Hanna didn't go down without Marty holding her, rocking her or reading to her. Hanna and Kristen shared the big room now that Line was gone. In the morning, they took care of themselves, dressing themselves and going downstairs to find bowls of cereal for breakfast. Marty loved the easiness when it was just family around, even as she missed the ones who weren't there.

At the last summer band concert scheduled in Montauk, Marty was delighted to see high school friends. She and Maureen set up their music stands in the crowded little pavilion in the park near the parsonage. The band rarely played there because it was so small. The park was dense with trees and felt dark all around the old pavilion, which was strung with electric lights. Most people just sat in their cars to listen, so it felt like the band was playing for themselves, but Dad, Paul and the little girls were sitting somewhere in the darkness.

Marty didn't expect to see Jim or Rodney, as they weren't in the band. But all of a sudden they appeared while she and Maureen were pulling their oboes out of cases and sucking on their reeds to get them to the right degree of dampness. The girls hung over the rickety painted railing of the pavilion, talking to them. Marty was shy, but Maureen asked them what they were doing.

"Just hanging around," said Rodney. "Looking for trouble. Guess it's here!"

"Maybe," said Maureen dubiously.

Jim smiled at them. He usually let Rodney do the talking. All of them would be leaving for different schools soon.

"Are you going to Iowa City after all?" asked Rodney.

"Yes," said Maureen. "They've got a good music program. I think I'll like it."

"Me too," said Rodney. "I'll see you there! But it's an awfully big campus." They were talking about the University of Iowa, where Ellie's husband Bruce had gotten his degree. Marty knew what some of her classmates were doing, but not all. Barbara was going to nursing school, and Georgia would be at the same community college in Mason City where Mother was taking classes to upgrade her credential.

"How about you, Jim?" asked Maureen. She looked at Marty, who was helplessly silent.

"Oh, I'm off to Grinnell," said Jim. "My mother went there, and I like its liberal political ideas. I'm thinking of joining the Peace Corps, but I think they'd like you to have a little education first!"

"That's great!" said Marty, all of a sudden bursting into speech. "How exciting!"

"Are you going to play football?" asked Maureen.

"Nope!" said Jim. "At least I hope not!" He turned toward Marty. "I guess you're going to Wittenberg?" Everyone knew she was following Line off to school.

"Yes," said Marty. "It scares me. But I guess it will be fine."

"Fine! She got into the honors program!" said Maureen, speaking for Marty. "But of course she wouldn't tell you that. She already knows which books she's going to be reading!"

Marty moved as if to slap Maureen's hand. "Oh, you. I'm excited, of course. But I'm scared too."

"We're all scared," said Rodney. "It's a big step. Leaving home and all."

But Mr. Greenway was tapping his music stand, calling the band to their seats. "See you!" said Rodney. They waved as they walked away into the darkness. Marty hoped they might be around after the concert.

When Mr. Greenway raised his baton, Marty and Maureen followed his arms, lifting their instruments and playing the popular show tunes, marches and other old favorites. Mr. Greenway felt free to talk to the band between the numbers, as there was no amplification and few people sat in the seats near the pavilion.

"Okay," he said after they had played for an hour. "Now let's do 'The Stars and Stripes.' Marty and Maureen come up here with your piccolos, and you all know what to do when I start singing!"

Marty followed Maureen to the front just below Mr. Greenway. They raised a music stand high enough to see the notes, as the piccolo solo was difficult. Marty could play it, but it was much better when they both did.

Mr. Greenway raised his baton. No matter how much he tried to speed up the band's playing to lighten the march, it was always a little ponderous. The horns and trombones just weren't good enough to be spritely.

Maureen and Marty must be the sprites! They played the piccolo solo as quickly and carefully as they could, together. When Maureen missed a note, Marty caught it, and when Marty missed a phrase, Maureen was there!

When the whole band joined in after the solo, Mr. Greenway began singing. No one else could hear him over the band, but it helped them know what to do!

"Be kind to your web-footed friends, for a duck may be somebody's mother," he sang. "Be kind to your friends in the swamp, where the weather is very, very damp. Now you may think that this is the end, well it is!" He put his arms down and the band stopped all together. The silence was deafening! Even the drums stopped the vibration of the snares and cymbals.

Everyone laughed, people clapped and car horns began tooting. Marty heard shouts of "More! More!" but it was the end. The very end. The band began packing their instruments away.

Marty sang to herself as she put away the piccolo and carefully packed up the oboe and its reeds. "Now you may think that this is the end. Well it is!"

13

Marty and Ann, her Wittenberg College roommate, dressed carefully in skirts, sweaters and nylon stockings for the honors banquet, just as if they were going to church. Only twelve freshmen were invited, as well as several faculty members.

Marty minded that Ann, who seemed to pay no attention to her looks, always looked wonderful with her hair curling naturally into a smooth brown pageboy. Marty slept on rollers every night, but her hair seldom looked the way she wanted it to. Ann didn't even need to wear glasses! Her clear brown eyes shone, though she didn't smile much. They were probably put together because they were both bright, but they had little in common. Ann spent her days at Valders Hall of Science, taking all the science classes she was allowed, though she also took the core history, religion and literature courses all freshmen must.

Carrying their copies of the assigned book, Camus' *The Stranger*, in their purses, Marty and Ann made their way across the campus on a clear, cold October night and entered the sleek glass doors of the student union. The cool teal-colored upholstery made the special dining room look as if they were in a gracious modern home, unlike the functional cafeteria below. Prints and paintings on the wall were lit from below with small lamps. Otherwise, the only light came from candles on the long table.

The table was laid with beautiful Scandinavian china and cutlery. The plates were simple and the glassware severe, but the effect was very elegant. Marty had attended few elegant dinners. Most of the social life she knew was church-related, and celebratory family dinners took place on Mother's old-fashioned lace cloth with her ivory china and Fostoria goblets with indented patterns. Marty felt shy in this lovely modern setting, where the light glinted off the china with an understated grace.

The faces of faculty members and students alike glowed in the lively, flickering candlelight. Places were designated so students sat interspersed with faculty members. On Marty's left was Mr. Hirsch, the English teacher Line liked, and on her right, Miss Borge, professor of German language and literature. Ann was at the other end of the table. Erik Lehman, a tall thin philosophy major with spectacles on his nose, and David Stensrud, also thin and dark, with bad skin and deep-set dark eyes, sat across the table. Marty was marooned, surrounded by people whose intellects were certainly more powerful than her own.

The dinner began with people eating the small lettuce and tomato salad in front of them. Baskets of dinner rolls were passed, and butter, which each person kept on a bread plate beside their place. When the salad cups were finished, they were whisked away by student servers and a large plate laden with a slice of ham, a bit of pineapple, and rice with carrots and peas was placed in front of each of them. The portions on the plates were the same for everyone. Marty labored to finish hers, but she managed.

While they ate, people chatted, but not about the book, as that would come when they were finished. Mr. Hirsch wanted to know about Line, who interested him.

"We were very close, growing up," Marty murmured. "My Dad called Line Sparky, and my brother Paul and myself were her 'gang.'"

Mr. Hirsch laughed. "She's very interested in the rest of the world, I find."

"We all were," said Marty. "We read all the *National Geographics* and would play with the globe, putting our finger on it and whirling it until it stopped to find out which country we would end up in."

"Hmmmmm. *National Geographic.* Somehow, I don't think everyone at this school is anxious to learn about other countries."

"What are they interested in, then?"" asked Marty, surprised.

"Good question," said Mr. Hirsch. "What are you interested in?" he fired across the table at David.

David smiled a dark smile, which invariably made one think of nefarious plots just because of his coloring! Marty didn't know him at all, except that he seemed to be well-read and spoke well in her history class. "Pretty much everything," he said. "It would be easier for me to think of what I'm not interested in. Sports, maybe."

Marty laughed. "Me too! I wish I were more interested in sports."

At her elbow was a student server asking Marty whether she would like coffee with her dessert. "No thank you," said Marty. She tried to imagine Line serving this group, but she couldn't. She felt guilty to be included, to have such formality lavished upon her. She sometimes glimpsed Line in the dish room, horsing around with her friends as she worked. Marty's job was in the library, a refuge from all the newness around her.

Dessert was a slice of lemon cake with a small scoop of vanilla ice cream. Marty spooned up everything in front of her. At the end of the table, young Dr. Nesset, a sparely-built Norwegian with a long, dour face, stood up to speak. He led Marty's religion class. Clinking his coffee cup with a spoon, he got the attention of the quiet, self-conscious conversations going on around the room.

"We welcome all of you honor students, selected from your high school classes. We want you to get the chance to explore the world of the intellect in a more relaxed setting," said Dr. Nesset. "We teachers are looking forward to it as much as you are! We tried to keep this group small enough that discussion works. So I'll throw out the first question. Why do you think we chose this book, Camus' *The Stranger*?"

Marty sighed. She wondered the same thing herself. The story was completely foreign to her. A young Algerian man kills someone, almost randomly, and then discusses his fate with various people as he sits in prison, awaiting sentencing. The judge feels the young man, Merseault, has no remorse because he didn't cry when he learned that his mother had died. He is sentenced to death, which he welcomes in the end.

Miss Borge, an energetic middle-aged woman, began, "Camus wrote it in Paris, during the war. He was born in Algeria, so I believe he felt alienated in Paris, and the war could not have helped this."

"So are you saying it is a treatise on alienation, and we should read it as such?" asked Dr. Nesset.

"The character Merseault is very honest," said David. "He can't find meaning in life and he simply doesn't feel a need to disguise his opinions. At least not in the novel."

"He tells the priest 'Nothing, nothing had the least importance,'" said Ann from her end of the table. "This is a nihilist position. We might meet it in our friends. It doesn't hurt to know how they feel." Marty was impressed that Ann spoke. Ann was from a big school in the Twin Cities, more sophisticated than Marty, but not very interested in literature. She wanted to be a biologist, or a doctor. She seemed guarded in her statement. Marty knew she was questioning her beliefs, just as Merseault did. Ann thought Marty gullible, her beliefs coming directly from her parents.

"Life itself bears the highest value for Merseault," put in Dr. Magnusson, the charismatic young professor who had put together much of Wittenberg's new core course. He had long dark hair, a mustache, wore a clerical collar, and spoke with the dramatic flair of a European professor. Marty found his lectures mesmerizing. "But the universe is silent. He cannot find meaning anywhere."

"Merseault finds the world absurd for sure," said David. "He has no normal responses to it. That is why he is condemned."

"I think Camus must have been reading Dostoyevsky during the war," piped up Mr. Hirsch from beside Marty. "This was his first book. It follows the form of *Crime and Punishment*, with a different outcome. A person condemned, who doesn't recant his nihilistic beliefs."

"Merseault's viewpoint dominates our modern day," said Dr. Magnusson. "Man is alone in his subjective state, his existence at the moment is the only reality. He lives in the shadow of death and nothing mitigates this."

"But it's so extreme!" burst out Marty. She was surprised to hear herself speak. She wanted to ask why read something you can't identify with at all, but, as that would expose her own ignorance, she quickly stopped. She wondered if Line would have said this out loud.

"I suppose it is something of an allegory," said Dr. Magnusson mildly. "It's a philosophical work. The state of mind of the fictional character Merseault is used to express ideas. We're looking at characters as exemplars of certain ways of thinking. Camus wrote *The Stranger* in the light of several different philosophies prevalent during his time, and ours."

Marty considered. She felt confused. She could imagine nothing of Merseault's state of mind. But she hadn't been in the war, nor close to anyone ambivalent about life.

Dr. Nesset sat down. The discussion was going well, but he let Dr. Magnusson talk, Marty noticed.

"I think what makes it literature," said Mr. Solberg, one of the handsome young English professors, eager to put in his oar, "is that it cannot be reduced to one philosophy. Merseault is a realistic person. His thoughts and expressions are contradictory."

Marty looked around at all the animated faces shining in the candlelight, their minds active and listening. The students spoke tentatively and the professors vividly. They were courteous to each other, but some were more anxious to speak than others. Marty tried to be open, to hear what they were saying.

Dr. Magnusson summed up the discussion. "It's true. Camus said several times that he was not an existentialist. Philosophical works may be contradictory, but you can see the winds of the times blowing through them. To have value, life must have meaning. Merseault sits in this contradiction."

"I kept thinking of Brecht's *Mahagonny*," said Miss Borge. She sang in something of a monotone: "Oh show us the way to the next whiskey bar. Oh don't ask why. Oh don't ask why. I tell you we must die." Everyone laughed at the wry face she made.

Marty went to bed that night stimulated as much by the heightened elegance and beauty of the dinner as by the discussion. The dinner had shown her something of what life could be like, a worldly life spanning continents where people discussed the ideas of the day.

Luckily, the dinner was on a Friday night, which gave Marty the weekend to study, especially her Latin, which was not going well. Beginning Latin class was bright and early on Monday morning.

"Sunt ne quaestiones?" Dr. Haatvedt's piercing eyes bored into Marty. He reached up his hand and scratched his fine, almost hairless, head. A venerable professor of the classical languages, Latin and Greek, Dr. Haatvedt had been associated with the school for more than forty years and taught both Mother and Dad in their day. He paged through the book on the table in front of him.

Marty had no questions. The vocabulary wasn't hard. It was the declensions, the tenses, the masculine and feminine endings of words which must be memorized that were not easy for Marty. She was sure her open face looked as empty as her head.

"You look sleepy," said Dr. Haatvedt to one of the boys. "Come on. Stand up. Touch your toes." Dr. Haatvedt leaned over and touched his toes, bobbing his short, powerful body. The young man, whom Marty didn't know, stood up sleepily, but he could not reach his toes with his fingers!

"Mens sana in corpore sano!" said Dr. Haatvedt. "You must get your sleep or you'll never learn!"

Marty sat still, eyes wide, frightened she would be asked to stand up and touch her toes. Dr. Haatvedt scared most of his students. All pre-seminary students must get a start on their Latin and Greek from Dr. Haatvedt in order to study the New Testament and church fathers. There were few girls in his classes.

But Mother was a Latin student. She and Dad reserved their academic expectations for Marty, who had always loved books. Line was a good student, but she learned from people and Mother and Dad recognized she was more interested in social ideas and art. Marty was smart and biddable, happy to do as Mother and Dad suggested.

Dr. Haatvedt's kindliness was clear to Marty. His piercing eyes might terrify you when you were searching your brain for an answer to his questions, but he understood and cared for his students as well. Just the other morning, walking down the hall with him, Marty mispronounced the word "comparable," and Dr. Haatvedt gently corrected her. Mother laughed at her when she mispronounced words she had read, but not Dr. Haatvedt.

By the time Dr. Haatvedt called again for questions, class was over. Marty stood up and collected her books, brains tingling, braced for the day. She walked out into the October sunlight. The sun was warm, but the moment a tree shadow fell on her the air was chilly. Marty crossed the wide central campus, being careful not to walk on the grass. As a freshman, she was not allowed.

Marty felt small, not the only pebble on the campus beach. She was one of hundreds of new students, wearing blue beanies on their heads, walking every day from class to dormitory to the student union where people ate and got their mail. Line was here, but she lived in a different building and they were unable to meet after 10 p.m. each night when the girls' dormitories were locked. They rarely saw each other. But Marty was adjusting. She was thrilled to be at college.

Biology was her next class. She couldn't wait to tell Paul that they were pithing frogs, i.e. destroying the nerves in the brain so they could watch the frog's reflexes while it, presumably dead, felt no pain. She wondered whether Paul would like this kind of research. Marty worked with a partner, and she had to admit, she hung back. If her partner Diane wanted to do the dirty deed, Marty was perfectly happy to let her. Biology was even tougher than Latin, full of vocabulary and things to memorize, none of which came naturally.

After class Marty walked over to the student union, where the mail must surely have come. There was a letter from Maureen, her fellow high school oboe player, which delighted Marty. She read it standing by the mailbox. Maureen wrote that she was overwhelmed by college and homesick. Could Marty please send her a letter to cheer her up?

Marty tucked the letter in her books and got a tray for the cafeteria line. She filled her plate and hovered near the tables, looking to see which one she might join. This was a tense moment for Marty. Did she see a table full of freshmen girls where it would be safe to put down her tray? Girls not too pretentious, sporty or popular?

Finally, against the window, Marty saw her roommate Ann with two friends. She greeted them and sat down, saved once again.

"So Marty," said Ann. "Is Line going to pledge?" The sophomores were to be chosen by upperclassmen to join Greek societies which had social implications. The sophomores pledged the group they wanted, but not all of them would be chosen.

"I don't know," said Marty. "I hardly ever see her." Line never worried about being popular, but if Greek societies did useful things, she might join.

"Well, ask her when you see her," said Ann. "I want to know what happens to you if you don't pledge."

"Study more?" said Karen, who sat beside Ann. Everyone laughed. Marty admired the dark sweater she wore with the crisp white collar of her blouse showing beneath it. Karen wanted to be a chemist. For scientists, even more than for everyone else, knowledge had no limit. You could never learn enough.

"Ice cream?" asked Ann, standing up as she finished her lunch.

Marty winced. Paper cartons of ice cream with dollops of chocolate in them were available every day. "Yes, please," she said. Ice cream was too good to pass up, though Marty noticed that her waist was thickening under the belt of the favorite blue shirtwaist dress she was wearing.

Ann came back with four small cartons of ice cream and dished them out to the girls. Little wooden paddles were neatly glued onto their bottoms. Ice cream after a meal was a seductive, dangerous ritual.

"I need some coffee to keep me awake in Magnusson's lecture," said Karen.

"Boy, I don't see how you have a problem with that!" said Marty. "He's so dramatic, and he makes such interesting connections!"

Magnusson's lectures were the glue that held the core courses in history, literature and religion together. Each freshman was also in discussion groups for each discipline, but the course was laid out so that the same time period, the Middle Ages for instance, was studied in all of them.

Karen stood up to go get a cup of coffee. "He's good, but not everyone thinks like you," she said.

"That's certainly the case," said Ann. "None of us think alike, and a good thing too! But I think Magnusson's lectures are great. They might not help my career, but I'm sure they contribute to my understanding."

"I think that's the point," said Marty, ignominiously hunting for the chocolate in the delicious vanilla ice cream. "That's what we're here for." The smell of Karen's coffee preceded her back to the table. The black, acrid liquid did not appeal to Marty, but she loved the smell.

The four girls turned in their lunch trays and headed to the biggest lecture room on campus. The auditorium in the new hall of science was full of pale blue metal, upholstered seats sloping down to a lab desk with faucets and a sink at the base. At the top of the room, the lights were dimmer, and you could conceivably be present without paying much attention. But the girls sat in seats assigned so that if one of the 600 freshmen were missing, someone would know. The teachers attended the lectures as well, so everyone knew what was being said.

Marty, hemmed in by people on either side, tucked her books underneath her and pulled out the little wooden, note-taking arm of her seat. She opened the blue, fabric-covered notebook with its green-ruled paper that she had designated for Magnusson's lectures, uncapped a cartridge pen with blue ink in it and sat poised to write down as much of what Magnusson said as she could.

When Dr. Rolfe Magnusson entered, he did not disappoint. A more dashing figure Marty could not imagine. He walked back and forth at the bottom of the lecture hall, gesturing and speaking in long, perfect sentences.

Dr. Magnusson described St. Augustine's progress, how his Christian theology was based on his reading of scripture, but influenced by the Greek philosophers. "Augustine developed his understanding of original sin and the need for redeeming grace in the context of his struggle with the Pelagians."

Dr. Magnusson swept up a piece of long hair that was falling in his face and strode to the other side of the room. "The Pelagians believed that persons are free to act righteously or not. But Augustine pointed to Adam and Eve's disobedience of God, the disobedience of the flesh to the spirit. The notion of original sin and our need for divine grace was St. Augustine's great contribution to theology." He paused, putting his hands on the silver pipe which drew water into the lab sink.

Marty sighed, her pen racing across the page. She had dutifully read *The Confessions of St. Augustine*, but it didn't live in her imagination. She could not have pulled from it the conclusions Dr. Magnusson reached.

"St. Augustine was born into a world in which the classical certainties were disintegrating. Rome fell to the Goths in 410 A.D., twenty years before his death. The range of solutions Augustine offered, including monasticism, and the rule of the state by the moral authority of the church, would carry some light through the Dark Ages and be revived by Charlemagne in the eighth century. We'll take up the thread of understanding preserved in the monasteries in our next lecture, for which your reading will be, as you know, *Mont-Saint-Michel and Chartres*."

Marty sat back, her mind spent in a different way than it was after class with Dr. Haatvedt. All around her, people collected their books and scurried out of the hall. At the front of the room, Dr. Magnusson was also putting his things into his briefcase. He hardly needed notes. It seemed his life was there in front of Marty, given as a gift in the form of brilliant sentences which made perfectly whole systems.

Marty was slow to pack up. She loved the feeling of being carried away into the extraordinary reality of the past, where people were just as human as she was. Where, incredibly, they solved their problems with ideas. Marty had no problems. Life was serene and she was very lucky to be at college.

Until the next morning, that is, when she stepped out of bed and heard a pop. A spike of fear surged through her. She had stepped on one of the lenses of her glasses! Usually she tucked them just under her bed so she could put them on first thing in the morning. But this time they were too far out, she got up before she remembered and with her bare heel stepped squarely on the lens.

"What was that?" asked Ann from her bed.

"My glasses," said Marty. "What am I going to do now?" Marty picked them up and put them on. The right lens was cracked in many pieces. It held together in the frame, but it was broken. "What a stupid thing to do!" Marty said aloud. She was deeply ashamed.

Marty looked in the mirror, assessing the damage. She could sort of wear them, but they looked ridiculous. When she called home, it turned out Dad had just shot a deer with his bow and arrow and was basking in the excitement of this unlikely event. Dad had made a new friend, Archie LeBlanc, who didn't go to church. Dad spent time with him, discussed his beliefs and learned from him how to make arrows. In the process, Archie came to church, and Dad bought a powerful bow and went hunting.

"I'll send you the photograph they put in the paper. You can show it to Line," Dad said. "It was beginner's luck. It isn't easy to get a deer with arrows."

All of the implications of this were surprising to Marty. She knew about Archie LeBlanc, and that Dad was interested in archery. But hunting? She wondered what Paul thought of this new development.

"Don't worry about the lens," Dad said. "Take your glasses down to an optometrist and order a new one. Do you still have check blanks?"

"Yes," said Marty. "I do. I'm sorry Dad. I just about had heart failure when I heard that pop and felt the lens under my foot."

"Don't worry about it," said Dad. "Accidents happen."

Marty felt lucky to have caught Dad in a good mood. "Dad," she said, stricken all of a sudden with longing, "I miss Hanna! Is everything okay? How is Mother?"

"Don't worry, Marty," said Dad. "We're all fine. We'll see you when we come for homecoming in a couple of weeks."

That weekend, Marty tried to get around without her glasses. She used them for studying, perching the broken glasses on her nose, but she went to meals without them. Ann laughed at her. Marty tried to walk through glass doors, couldn't recognize people unless they were very close and couldn't find her coat. She tried to find it funny, and of course it was. She was surprised she could see at all!

But in a week, things were back to normal. A perfect new lens was made for Marty's glasses and homecoming was coming up. At the homecoming football game, Queen Lorna would allow the freshmen to become full members of the school. They could stop wearing their beanies and walk on the grass! And Marty would see her beloved little sisters. Oh, how lonely she was for them.

In the religion discussion group for Marty's core course, Dr. Nesset pushed the students further. He asked, "Do you believe in the 'three-storied' concept of the universe, with God up above, the earth in the middle and hell down below?"

He paused, letting the question sink in. "If you do not, what happens when men die and do not go 'up' to Heaven? Does the soul merely sleep?"

No one in the class seemed to have an answer, so Dr. Nesset continued, "The idea that the body is separate from the soul was a product of Plato's picture of the invisible ideal world, a world of unchanging forms which make up what he saw as 'the real'.

"Augustine was an unrepentant Platonist in this regard. He liked to describe the relationship of body and soul to marriage. Initially they were in harmony, but after the Fall, they came into conflict."

He looked down at the class from the lectern behind which he stood. "So the question is, are you Platonists?"

Marty finally responded to his stern gaze. "Why does it matter?"

Dr. Nesset walked across the room, gesturing with long fingers. "We live in the modern world. We don't want science and psychology to think for us theologically, but at the same time, we must take them seriously."

Marty felt lost. She certainly hadn't thought her way through to a theology. Ideas floated around in her head, but she didn't really feel the conflict. Did it really matter? Must every Christian have a theology?

Dr. Nesset continued, "Heaven is a state of being rather than a place. Man is a unity, not an immortal soul using a mortal body, though much of our Christian liturgy and church practices may sound as if this were true."

Dr. Nesset sat on the desk at the front of the room, his long legs dangling. "Some of us have a sneaking suspicion that most religious people are Platonists when thinking theologically. This is inconsistent with modern science and psychology. Is it possible to develop a more consistent way of life? Magnusson and I believe the Church is still in need of reformation!"

Marty wrote all these ideas down in her current notebook. They weren't something she wanted to think about right now. The suggestion that people went up to heaven or down to hell was certainly all around her, but Dad never made much of it. Heaven and hell were old-fashioned concepts. Dad loved science. In his estimation, heaven was being with God, hell being without him. And God in his infinite mercy granted salvation to all who confessed Christ to be their Savior. This was all the consistency Marty needed.

Marty packed up her books, put on her jacket and headed off into the cold gathering twilight. Lights shone in the windows of buildings all around the dark circle of campus. She might be a ventriloquist's dummy, mouthing the words of the people around her, as her roommate Ann pointed out. But some day she would figure out what she thought on her own.

14

For Paul, the only one of the older Mikkelson kids left at home, the fact that Mother left every day to work as the high school librarian changed everything. That fall Paul and Dad took over more household duties and everyone had to get used to it! But it didn't stop anyone from having plans and projects.

One October day Paul came home from school to find Dad had purchased a 44-pound recurved bow. That meant it took 44 pounds of strength to pull it. Dad put the bow in Paul's hands. It was smooth and powerful, made of beautiful laminated and polished wood. Paul pulled on it, but he could barely extend it fully. "Whew! This would take some practice!" he said.

"It's such a great thing," said Dad. "Human power. If I can't get a deer with this, I shouldn't get one."

"Where'd you get it?" asked Paul.

"I got it second-hand from a guy who wanted a better one. Got a license too. Archie wants to go out; hunting season has started. You'd probably like to come out too," said Dad.

"You bet!" said Paul.

The blonde heads of the little girls, Kristen and Hanna, bobbed into the kitchen, listening and watching as Dad pulled on the bow, extending the bowstring the full width of his chest. Kristen was home from first grade, and Hanna from staying with Mrs. Boyce, who watched her in the mornings.

"Can I come?" asked Kristen.

"Have to get up pretty early!" said Dad. "Way before the sun comes up. I think you will still be asleep when I go."

Archie LeBlanc, Dad's new hunting friend, had a house at the edge of town and was an odd duck. Archie said he was descended from French metis people, the original French explorers and trappers who had married Native American women. He made his living as a "chiropractor," but his work had a shady character in that no one knew if he was really a doctor. He placed his hands on people (mostly women) when they came to him, and many felt healed.

Archie was a game hunter, using only a bow and arrows he had made himself. As Archie put it, since the wolves were long gone, deer had become a problem in northeastern Iowa. They were like big rats, feeding on the bushes and forest seedlings, eating the farmer's corn, defoliating trees and proliferating. Iowa gave out licenses to hunt deer, but most used shotguns. Of the hunters who took out licenses every year to hunt with bow and arrow, only a few would get a buck.

"No one sees hunters," Archie had said, describing his own hunting etiquette. "What they do in the wild is on their own conscience."

"Sounds good to me," Dad told Paul. It did to Paul too. Being out in the woods, watching and tracking were his idea of heaven.

"You girls go pick up the living room," Dad said to the little girls. "I'm going to go get Mother. She'll want to sit down for a moment before she makes dinner." Dad had waited until Paul could get home and watch the girls. Paul hadn't even taken off his coat.

The radiators were hot, beginning to steam, as the weather was cold and the furnace was lighted. The storm windows were up too, helping insulate the house. Paul went out to the living room and picked up his guitar while Kristen and Hanna mumbled about, pretending to pick up, but not doing much. Kristen was slow, but careful and liked to help. Hanna was fractious and unpredictable. Mother not being home all day was hardest on her.

"Come here, Hanna," said Paul, his hands moving on the wire strings. "Let's sing the spider song."

Hanna did not need persuading. She came over to Paul and began, "The itsy bitsy spider went up the water spout," sang Hanna, her little fingers making climbing motions. She giggled, and Paul and Kristen joined her. "Down came the rain and washed the spider out."

"I want it," said Hanna, climbing up on the sofa and picking at the guitar strings. Paul put the big guitar in her tiny lap. It was almost as big as she was! "Ahhh-hhhh-hhh," she sang as she picked randomly at the strings with tiny fingers.

When Mother arrived home from school, she was very organized. She made dinner and Paul and Kristen cleaned up, putting the dishes in a newly-arrived dishwasher. The routine had acquired an odd normalcy. Mother made sure Paul did all the extra-curricular activities he wanted to, which wasn't much! Marching band with his trumpet, which meant football games, was about it. In the winter there would be wrestling.

That evening, Mother and Dad went over to the church for a meeting and Paul helped the little girls to bed. He played romantic gypsy music, dancing around wildly with them, swooping, gliding, twirling. He picked them up and swung them around until they were dizzy.

"More, more!" shouted Hanna, reaching up her arms to be picked up and twirled again.

Paul obligingly twirled her around in the center of the room, her little legs splayed out behind her.

"Dance, dance," he said to Kristen. They all circled and swooped, laughing. When the record was over, Paul fell on the floor as if he'd been hit. He wouldn't move, even when Kristen and Hanna took his arms and tugged at him.

"He's dead," said Kristen. "A dead man." She tried to drag him by his leg. But Paul made his body heavy and still.

Finally Paul pretended to wake up. "Okay," he said. "Who wants to swan dive?"

"Me, me!" shouted Hanna. She stood at Paul's feet and he took her hands. She was so little and delicate, but he put his stockinged feet at her hips and raised her up so she could look like a swan.

"Put your legs up," commanded Kristen. "Here, I'll show you."

Paul lifted Hanna down and raised Kristen above him. She stuck her legs in the air. If she had come down it would have been squarely on her belly!

"See," Kristen said. "You have to hold your legs up." Paul let her down easy.

"Swan dive! Swan dive!" shouted Hanna.

Paul tried again, and the little girl raised her legs behind her, holding his extended hands. "Perfect, Hanna," said Paul. He stood up and brushed himself off. "Okay, now we'll play soldier," he said. "Follow me!"

Paul stood straight, as if he were a sergeant with his tiny corps behind him. "March, march," he said. "Halt!" He stopped, stiff legged. He looked behind him to see if the little girls were following. "Left, left!" he began to march again, thinking of marching band exercises at school.

Paul stopped. The two little soldiers stood straight behind him, but Hanna was giggling, as usual. "No giggling," said Paul sternly. "This is serious!" He gruffly shouted. "Left, left! Halt! About face!" Kristen marched and Hanna followed her, but neither of them knew what 'about face' meant.

"'About face' means turn around," said Paul. "Okay, I'm the sergeant. You can be corporal, Kristen, and Hanna will be a private. Salute!" He put his fingers to an imaginary hat. "When I say 'about face' you turn around. But don't lose your discipline, men!" He marched the little girls through the dining room out to the kitchen and then back.

"Left, left," said Paul, the little girls following. "Right face!" He turned to the right and marched into the hall and up the stairs. "Left, left," he shouted. "March, march!" He didn't turn around but could hear Kristen coming up the stairs behind him. Hanna could barely take the stairs with her little legs.

At the top of the stairs, Paul said, "Good work, troops! Fall out! Last one in their pajamas is a rotten egg. I'll read a story when everyone is in bed." The little girls clambered into their room, competing to get ready first. Paul retreated into his room, listening for noises in the bathroom, and then the sounds of bare feet scampering back to the girls' shared bedroom.

Before bed, Hanna needed to hear where everyone was. She didn't remember Ellie, but Mother constantly reminded her when they went through the bedtime litany. Paul sat on her bed while she ticked off on tiny fingers, "Dad and Mother are at church, Ellie and Bruce and Brenda and the new baby live in Minne-Minne," she struggled over the word.

"In Minneapolis," said Kristen sleepily from her bed. "The baby's name is Rhonda," she said firmly. Ellie's new baby was only a month old and none of them had seen her yet. Ellie's family would come at Thanksgiving.

"Minneapolis," said Hanna. "Line and Marty are at college," she looked up at Paul sadly.

"And we're here," Paul finished, "Paul, Kristen and Hanna. And Foxy sleeping down in the basement. Let's say a prayer for everyone." He began, "Now I lay me down to sleep."

"I pray the Lord my soul to keep," said Hanna. "If I die before I wake, I pray the Lord my soul to take."

It was the same prayer Paul had prayed as a little kid. He could already hear the placid Kristen's heavy sleep breathing. "Do you want a story?" he asked Hanna. "Or shall I sing to you?"

"Story," Hanna's active little mind went through the books beside the bed. "*Good night moon*," she said.

But Paul was trying to learn the words and chords to a song. "Story song," he said. He began to sing softly. "Puff the magic dragon, lived by the sea, and frolicked in the autumn mist in a land called Honalee." He tried to remember the words, which went on and on. "Noble kings and princes loved that rascal Puff. Pirate ships would lower their flags when Puff roared out his name!" And was Hanna asleep? He began again, being as repetitive as possible. He looked. Yes, maybe. He tiptoed out of the room.

Dad went out hunting many mornings with Archie that week, staking out the deer in the area most accessible. Paul was itching to go, but Mother wouldn't let him. School was more important and he needed his sleep. On Thursday night she finally agreed that he could go with the hunters the next morning. He could make up sleep on the weekend.

Way before the sun was up, Dad and Paul picked up Archie. Dad already owned a camouflage jacket and Paul wore his dark winter jacket. They liked to go to a swampy area along the river where a creek joined it. It was pasture land and cornfields, owned by a farmer Archie knew. When they got out of the car, Dad and Archie went in different directions as they usually did. Paul trailed Dad.

"Rut season has just begun," Dad said softly. "The deer are showing more now. They often come through here." He hiked a short distance to a rock pile, which he tried to hide below.

The rocks were freezing, and the coarse weed stalks didn't offer much of a blind to the two of them. The light was coming on stronger too, but cloud cover kept it from being very bright. Dad gestured toward dark shapes moving through the cornfield and lifted his binoculars.

When he had looked, Dad handed the binoculars to Paul so he could watch the many-point buck who was watching them.

"They certainly know we're here," Dad said softly. The buck plodded back and forth a couple of times, letting his does move farther away. "I think he's trying to decoy us."

Paul and Dad walked back to the station-wagon. With Archie they drove a ways, moving with the deer. The deer seemed to be totally unperturbed by the car, but as soon as anyone put a foot out of it, they spooked and ran and all you could see were their upturned white tails.

"Living with people around them, these Iowa deer are pretty wily," said Archie. "Joe says that as long as he's on a tractor or a piece of machinery, the deer are unafraid, but if he gets off or leaves the machinery, it's bye bye. They take off!"

As Dad drove, the men passed the binoculars, watching several does and a younger spike buck circling the swampy area. The older buck was up on the ridge in the withered cornstalks.

They drove on. Dad had to take Mother and Paul to school and it was almost time to leave. But up from the creek bed, came the group of deer, as if they meant to cross the road. All of a sudden the big buck bounded up on the grassy bank with his head held high, a brave gesture to lead them off the other deer. Dad screeched on the brakes and the buck made a stately and beautiful dash across the road and stood still, 100 yards off up the road, as if he were trying to lead them on. Archie jumped out and lobbed a couple of arrows his way, but the buck loped off as the bow was released.

"I didn't hear him laugh," said Archie, "but I'm sure he was!"

"He's beautiful!" said Paul, in awe.

"It's a moment I won't soon forget," said Dad.

At school that day, Paul thought of the younger buck, and the brave older one heading the herd off, the beautiful rack of antlers carried proudly on his head. He loved being out in the early morning emptiness with the men, and could understand why the wily deer were so exciting to track. But he was totally unprepared for what happened next.

When he got off the bus after school, there was Dad in the green Country Sedan with Kristen and Hanna in the back seat. "Come on, Paul," said Dad, heading him off before he started walking home. "I got that buck! It's down at the locker; want to show it to you."

"You got that buck?" asked Paul, incredulous.

"Yup," said Dad. "The guys didn't believe me either when I tried to get them to come and help me! I had to ask them three times!"

Dad drove over to the meat locker and told the little girls to stay in the car. He didn't want their dreams full of dead deer. But he and Paul went in and were shown into the freezer room. Lying on a table was the intact head of the buck with its antlers, five points cn one side of the big rack and six on the other. Its large eyes looked up at the ceiling and its tongue hung out. At the back, hanging on a hook in the ceiling, was the skinned body of the buck, waiting to be butchered. Paul felt sad.

"250 pounds," said Dad softly. "He didn't really see me coming. I went back along the road after I dropped you and Mother off at school. I saw him in the cornfield, pursuing a doe. My approach was masked by a noisy pickup pulling a disk, and the buck was standing there! I got him broadside at 15 yards. Couldn't have been a better shot. I didn't expect it, but I acted quick and took it. The wind was right too."

Paul looked into the brave, dead eyes, the thick pink tongue lolling out from the mouth. How could Dad have killed this wild and beautiful thing?

"He charged by me, but I saw the fletching sticking out of his side and I followed the blood stains. He was down. I didn't have a knife with me, but I put an arrow in his rib cage and forced on it. Stupidly. Didn't know exactly what I was doing. Then I went back to town to get Archie to help me." Dad spoke softly, recalling the moment in the sacred presence of the dead.

Paul was astonished, listening. Was this Dad? Who never even wanted to fish? Behaving like Davy Crocket on the wild frontier? It sounded so intimate.

"It took four of us to lift him into the station wagon. It's going to make a lot of venison!" said Dad, inviting Paul to share his adventure. "I still don't believe it. I got my buck!" He moved toward the door. "We better get back," he said. "Those little kids are waiting and I have to go get Mother."

"What happened?" asked Kristen, as she and Hanna and Paul went up the steps to the house and Dad swooped off in the station wagon. "Dad killed a deer?" Dad had told them, but she was still trying to figure out what it meant.

"Yep," said Paul. "With his bow and arrow. Not often that happens."

"What happened to the deer?"

"He's going to be butchered and we're going to eat him," said Paul. "Like we eat chickens or beef or pigs."

"Dad said he was going to get a deer hide jacket," said Kristen. "It sounds nice."

"We'll see," said Paul. He was thrilled to have been drawn into the company of men who hunted. He knew Dad wanted to show him the deer's head because Paul had seen him alive that very morning. Paul could see that beyond the sadness was the thrill of possession, of participation in the chain of life living on life.

The freezer at home was soon full to brimming with deer steaks, deer sausage and venison hamburger. Mother minded it less than when the Mikkelsons were given whole pheasants or ducks to put in the freezer. She didn't want to pluck the feathers off them and would rather have served tv dinners! But she could deal with venison hamburger. A packet of Lipton's Onion Soup mix made it hardly any different than beef.

For Dad, the euphoria was long-lived. A photograph Archie took of the buck lying in the back of the station wagon with Dad and his bow standing beside it appeared in the paper. Dad bought extra copies and sent them to his daughters in Minneapolis and Cardinal, and his parents in Renville.

The story got into his sermon that Sunday, as much of his life did. The sermons took the text prescribed by the church for a particular Sunday, but to the discerning listener, such as Paul, much of what Dad was thinking about crept in. If it didn't go in the sermon, Dad put it in the announcements.

"As many of you know, I shot a deer this week. The first shot I ever got at one with my bow and arrow," Dad said, standing in front of the congregation in his white surplice with a silk stole wrapped around his shoulders. "It was simply beginner's luck, of course, which makes me very humble. But it has given me much to think about with regard to the Lord and His creatures. All of us, His creatures, knit together by the grace of His great love."

Paul admired him. No matter what Dad said, his warmth and love for all of life shone forth. Paul could hear it especially in the in the words of the liturgy, which he sang in his mellow tenor.

By the time Dad finished the second of his Sunday services, his voice was tired and gravelly when he held up his hand to bless the congregation. Paul stood up beside Mother, with Kristen and Hanna in their Sunday dresses beside her. "May the Lord bless you and keep you; the Lord make his face shine upon you and be gracious unto you, the Lord lift up his countenance upon you and give you peace." Paul lifted up his face, feeling warmth and peace washing over him.

Just before Thanksgiving, the nation was shocked to its core by the death of President Kennedy, killed by a sniper as he rode in an open car in a parade in Texas. Days of mourning and a large ceremonial funeral followed. No one was untouched by the event, which dominated television.

Paul was surprised at how deeply he felt the loss of someone he didn't even know. No one spoke of it in his family, because the event was so thoroughly discussed on television and the radio, and what was there to say, anyway? Because the two events happened so close together, for Paul, President Kennedy and the beautiful buck raring up and trying to draw the hunters off his herd of deer became the same brave head. He could not think of one without the image of the other passing in front of his mind's eye.

Thanksgiving that year found the adults subdued, watching a house full of youngsters. Ellie and Bruce came with their new baby and tiny Brenda who was just walking. Grandma Bakken and Aunt Rose came, and Line and Marty were down from college.

"It's so nice to have everyone home!" Mother said, again, when Line and Marty arrived. "All of my chickens under my wing!"

The house bustled with activity, people in the kitchen cooking, others watching the babies and little kids playing together in the living room. Mother had limited the amount of television they watched to the morning news, as she didn't want the national tragedy to affect the little girls.

Paul, as usual, found so many people in the house at once overwhelming. He slipped out the door for a walk, taking Foxy with him. He was fighting the anxiousness in his stomach. "Come on, Foxy," he said. "Nobody needs us here."

A thin white blanket of snow lay over the land, dressing the cedars and other, leafless trees. The sorghum mill lay still, though a sweetish odor hung near it as they passed on the road. The silence under the overcast sky was refreshing. The sky and the air felt so much more alive over Paul's head than interior rooms. He slushed through the snow in his overshoes, Foxy bright and dancing behind him on tiny white feet.

They began to climb the hill, crunching through the dead leaves under the thin crust of snow. It was hard to go up the hill, as there was no path, but Paul wanted to look down on the town from above.

Soon they were up under the trees where Mother and Dad hunted for morels in the spring. Paul turned around and looked down at the little town spread below him. No one was on the roads. Their garden was empty, snow-covered, the apple trees bare and dormant. Smoke rose from the chimney on the Sherwoods' tiny house. He could see the tree line where the Turkey River ran through town.

Foxy investigated a burrow under some nearby bushes. Paul saw rabbit tracks. A more peaceful view could hardly be imagined, but Paul could not feel the peace that passeth understanding. He thought about all that was happening in his family.

Marty had little to say about college, but she had a big pile of books with her. She was thrilled by the little kids, and Hanna wouldn't let her out of her sight. Line did have things to say. Her International Relations Club had learned something about Oswald, Kennedy's killer. She told Paul he was a communist sympathizer who had lived in Russia and married a Russian girl. He was angry that the FBI was checking on his wife to find out if she was a Soviet agent.

Line's application to be an exchange student the following year had been accepted. "I'm not sure where I'm going yet," she told Paul. "I want to go to one of the colleges where most of the students are Negro."

Paul stood up in the snow, looking down on the little town of Montauk. Line coming home always riled him up. She had so much to say about the outside world. She actually liked living in the city in the summer, she said. She liked the fact that no one knew she was a pastor's kid, that people on the street didn't know each other at all. "Ellie likes it too," she told Paul. "Ellie likes just being ordinary."

Paul liked being ordinary too. He liked being among trees and fields, though. He did not think he would like living in a city. He liked people, but he was happier when there weren't too many at a time. Ellie felt quite foreign to Paul. It had been so long since she lived with the Mikkelsons. And even then, the seven years between them meant he didn't know her well.

The phrase from Luther's catechism about loving your neighbor ran through Paul's head. "We should fear and love God that we may not deceitfully belie, betray, slander, or defame our neighbor, but defend him, speak well of him, and put the best possible construction on all that he does."

Oswald was not there to tell his story. He was shot by Jack Ruby. What he had thought, no one would ever know. There was a new president, Lyndon Johnson. Mrs. Kennedy, with her two young children, behaved with great dignity. Paul had liked President Kennedy. He was young and boyish, a good speaker. "Ask not what your country can do for you. Ask what you can do for your country," he had said.

Paul thought of the buck. There would surely be some form of venison at their Thanksgiving dinner, with prayers of gratitude for it. Mother was also roasting a turkey and making Paul's favorite cracker crumb and sage dressing that she learned from Grandma Bakken, who would share it with them. Paul's world was secure, no matter what might be going on in the great world.

Paul looked out across the snowy bowl full of houses and roads below him. He was too far away to smell them, but he knew that turkeys were being roasted all across town. He wondered whether the Sherwoods would have one. They were so old now, and they didn't eat much. Paul could feel a bit of gnawing at his stomach, thinking about turkey. And pie, he remembered. He started down the hill. "Come on, Foxy," he called.

15

Late one night just after Christmas Paul and Marty played a game of chess. The house was warm and silent, the café curtains drawn, with just enough light to see the wooden pieces. Lights blinked on the Christmas tree, sending colored shadows against the wall. Christmas cards were still taped to the moldings between the living and dining rooms, and on the piano was the manger scene with its dolls dressed as wise men, shepherds, Mary and Joseph, and the Christ child in the manager. But none of these things held the expectancy and magic they had a few days ago, before the big day.

As Paul waited for Marty to move, he saw Line creeping down the stairs in an old sweatshirt and jeans, trying not to wake Mother and Dad and the little girls. He smiled. Just the three of them awake together. How rare that was these days.

"Cocoa?" asked Line softly as she passed them on her way to the kitchen.

"Oh yes!" said Marty. She had moved, Paul noticed.

"Paul?" asked Line.

"Yes, me too," Paul said. "Thank you." He was worried about his rook, but he had made a daring move, and his knight was more important. He decided to save the knight and let the rook go. Moving the black knight, he looked over at Marty, who looked back significantly as if to say, "Oh ho! I see what you're up to."

Marty did as expected, taking Paul's rook. In a few minutes, Line returned with mugs which she set in front of them. At the top of Paul's mug floated three miniature marshmallows.

Line sat on the sofa in the dark, drinking cocoa and coolly waiting for the game to be over. But Paul didn't care any more. Let Marty win for once, he thought.

"Check," said Marty.

Paul sighed. "It's all yours, Marty," he said. "I'd rather hear you guys talk."

"Me too," said Marty. "We hardly ever get to talk at school."

"Why?" asked Paul.

"It's so fast," said Marty, sadly. "We rush from one thing to the other, and Line lives in a different dorm."

"Marty typed a paper for me," said Line. "Learn to type, Paul. You'll be sorry if you don't!"

"Yeah, in the laundry room after every one else was in bed!" said Marty, ruefully.

"What was it about?" asked Paul. The idea of a "paper" interested him. He sometimes wrote an essay, but never a "paper."

"The beginnings of the Peace Corps, for my sociology class," said Line off-handedly. "They've been going for two years now. I really want to go."

The shadow of President Kennedy's death fell across Paul's thoughts. Kennedy would be forever associated with the Peace Corps.

"But what about the exchange program?" asked Marty. "Aren't you signed up to go Spelman next year?"

"Of course," said Line. "The Peace Corps is after school is over. Actually, did I tell you, I'm rooming with a girl from Spelman next semester! I'm so excited! Ruthann is going to Spelman this year and a girl from there is going to room with us!"

Paul felt confused. He knew Ruthann was one of Line's roommates, but what was Spelman? He listened to see whether his question would get resolved.

"And where is Spelman, again?" asked Marty. "I always forget."

"Atlanta, Georgia," said Line. "It's a Negro women's college. I want to go down South. It would be so different."

"Snow?" asked Paul, trying to imagine a place without it.

"Hardly ever," said Line. "They have winter, but it's just cold and rainy. Apparently there's no snow."

"You keep getting farther and farther away!" said Marty.

"This is the time for it," replied Line. "Aren't you going to go to summer school, finishing school in three years and all that?"

It was the first Paul heard of this. Dad had bought a canoe that Christmas, and Paul was already dreaming about Lake Michigami. How could Marty give up the lake?

"That's the idea," said Marty. "Mother doesn't have to go to summer school. She can take a correspondence course and that is all she needs." She turned to Paul, "You guys will get to spend the whole summer up at the lake! You'll be in that canoe every day!"

"Can't wait," said Paul, an image of the canoe hovering in front of his eyes. It was blue, fiberglass, with two seats, another triumph of human power. No use for it in the winter. It hung in the frozen garage at the moment, but come spring, Paul knew he and Dad would be out in the slough. He turned to Line. "But how about you? Will you be there?"

Line stretched her legs and her arms like a cat, yawning. "I'm not sure yet. But I'll be working somewhere. I'm sure Bruce and Ellie don't need me, but I can't just stay home! There's so much going on! Have you guys read *The Other America*? It shows pretty clearly that poverty is the real problem in America."

"Poverty?" asked Paul. The word called up images of people in the Dust Bowl, wearing rags, standing in front of derelict farmhouses without a stick of vegetation around them. Certainly nothing he could imagine in the lush Iowa and Minnesota summers.

"Yes! Real, grinding poverty in the inner cities," said Line. "Negroes can't get anywhere, and there are poor whites struggling too."

"All the city girls I know at Wittenberg have more nice clothes than we do," said Marty. "And money for music lessons," she said ruefully.

"Of course!" said Line in a scornful voice. "You're not going to find poor people at Wittenberg!"

Paul looked at Line, who was no longer sleepy after reminding herself of the injustices she had been reading about. It made Paul uneasy.

Were Marty and Line going to fight? What was wrong with staying home and enjoying the lake in the summer?

But Marty was conciliatory. "I really like just our family together," she said. "It's so nice to be here with you guys. There's so much pressure at school to be one thing or the other, but at home I can just be me!"

Paul relaxed. "Me too! I like it when it's just us. And I miss you guys. It's odd now, as if I'm a grownup. The whole house is focused on Kristen and Hanna!"

"I bet Hanna likes it! Kristen too," said Marty. "When we were around, Kristen didn't have anyone of her own."

"Anyway, I'll miss you guys if you don't come to the lake," said Paul.

"I'll be there in August," said Marty. "At least a little. I want to try out that canoe myself!"

"I'll try to get there," said Line.

"I was afraid I'd miss so much of Christmas, being at school this year," said Marty. "But it was actually like having two Christmases! We had lovely decorations all over the dorm," she said to Paul. "And I wish you could have heard *The Messiah*. It was so wonderful."

"You got to sing in it?" asked Paul.

"Yes," said Marty. "Anyone can sing in the chorus. We went downtown to practice, and then came home in the snow. It was so Christmasy, coming home with those songs in my head!"

"Did you go?" Paul asked Line.

"Yup," said Line. She smiled widely. "I loved it too. One night we went caroling on the way home, to some of the faculty houses. It was fun!"

"Jesus our brother, kind and good," began Marty, singing. When Paul, Marty and Line sang the song about "The Friendly Beasts" at church, Marty liked being the dove, while Line was perfectly happy to be the shaggy brown donkey. But Paul was too sleepy to keep going, singing the verse in which he, the sheep, gave his wool for a blanket warm. He closed his eyes, listening.

Pictures of early morning on the azure lake, a few loons calling and the sun making a shining path to wherever you stood passed through Paul's head. When he opened his eyes, he was surprised to find that Marty and Line were gone! He had fallen asleep and they had left him lying on the sofa in a darkened house. Someone had put a blanket over him.

Paul stretched, feeling his legs and his powerful arms. He was going out for wrestling, the only high school sport he could manage, and he quite enjoyed the sweaty sport. But how great it would be to get his hands on a canoe paddle. He agreed with Marty that the best times were when he was at home. He liked being the oldest kid. He could get Mother or Dad's attention whenever he wanted it. But it was even better when Line and Marty were there. He didn't have any friends as close as they were.

Musing and tired in the middle of the night, Paul turned over, rolling off the sofa onto the floor. He got himself a glass of very cold water from the tap and crept off up the stairs to bed.

In the morning, while people were sitting around, eating toast and talking companionably, the phone rang.

Kristen ran and grabbed it, still in her flannel pajamas. "It's for you, Paul," she said.

"Por moi?" Paul said. He never got phone calls.

"Paul!" Kristen shouted at him as if he hadn't heard her, holding out the black receiver with its long curly chord.

Paul took the phone. "Good morning."

"Paul, this is Dennis Dugan. I heard you play the guitar. And that you sing with your sisters."

Paul considered. Dennis was a junior in high school, a nice kid, but assertive and a trifle obnoxious with long, slicked down hair. Paul had hardly ever talked to him, but he knew he could be a malicious tease. "Yeah," said Paul. "That's right."

"Me and Michael are trying to make a group for a talent show and we're wondering if you would come over and try practicing with us."

Paul was thunderstruck. He didn't know what to say.

"It's no big deal," said Dennis' voice on the line, trying to be persuasive. "We just want to try it out. Sort of like the Kingston trio."

"Okay," said Paul. It didn't sound so bad. It scared him, but that shouldn't stop him.

"You know where I live, don't you?" asked Dennis. "Could you come today? If you're not doing anything."

Paul was still flabbergasted. He looked around at his sisters' faces, but Line was nodding at him. "I guess so," he said.

"Don't forget to bring your guitar," said Dennis. "Michael's here. Come as soon as you can."

When he hung up the phone, Paul felt chagrined. Hardly knowing what he was doing he had agreed to give up a vacation day with the family to go over and sing with two guys he didn't know, and wasn't at all sure about.

Line encouraged him when he explained. "Just try it," said Line. "You don't have to agree to anything. It sounds like fun! You know how much you love singing. Do you want me to come with you?"

"No," said Paul. "I can manage." Everyone knew how shy he was, but he had said he would go. Dennis surprised him, and he had agreed.

When he went down the snow-covered roads to Dennis' house that day, he carried the guitar in its case. Paul knew where the Dugans lived, but not much about them. Mr. Dugan was a postman who loaded up a truck with mail and covered the rural routes in all weathers. Dennis, his only son, sometimes went with him, placing mail in the farm mailboxes stuck on posts along the roads, and taking in mail if the red flag was lifted.

Mrs. Dugan greeted Paul. The red brick house seemed a little more old-fashioned than Paul's own, but cheerful and warm. The Christmas tree stood in the big kitchen! Mrs. Dugan laughed at Paul's surprise. "We like it better here where we can see it!"

Dennis took Paul down into the basement of the house, where he had set up a den. It was a big room, carpeted with odds and ends Dennis managed to find, with Dennis' phonograph, shelves of junk and his bed in the corner. A few windows high up along the walls brought in light and an old oil-heater gave off blasts of heat in one corner. Clippings and photographs of popular singers were taped to the walls.

"Guess you know Michael," said Dennis, gesturing.

Michael Anderson was lounging on Dennis' bed, bent over a banjo. Paul had never actually seen one. He shook Michael's hand and looked at the big instrument, tight skin stretched over a wooden rim, with strings like a guitar.

"Where'd you get that?" Paul asked.

"Friend of my Dad's." Michael held out the instrument. "Want to try it?"

Paul took the banjo and drew his fingers across it. The resonance was different than guitar sounds, a bit of a twang, but not as long-lasting. The notes were crisp, higher-pitched. The banjo was beautiful.

"Can I see your guitar?" said Dennis. Paul opened the case and handed the guitar, which he knew to be cheap, from Sears and Roebuck, to Dennis. Dennis' own guitar leaned against the wall. Paul walked over and took a look. It was older, a little banged up, but when he picked it up, Paul liked the sound better than his own.

"We tried to sing with another guy," Michael said, "but he didn't really click."

Dennis made a face. "He didn't take us seriously. We really want a good group!"

"Dennis here has this idea he wants to sing," said Michael, his lips curling into a smirk. "Wants us to back him up, I think."

"Mr. Greenway said you sang with your sisters," said Dennis.

"Yeah, we've been doing it forever," said Paul. "But they're not around much any more."

"Well, let's give it a try!" said Dennis. "I got this music for 'Hang Down Your Head Tom Dooley.' There's only about two chords on it. You got any music, Paul?"

"Some," said Paul. "We have a folk songbook. I brought it. I've tried to learn some songs from tapes of *Hootenanny* too. I listen for the chords and try to figure 'em out."

Dennis gave Michael a significant look. "You know, you just might be the man we're looking for!" said Dennis. "Okay! Let's stand here in a row. So, it's D and A7. Got it Paul? I'll take the verses and you guys come in on the chorus. I'll say, 1, 2, 3 to get us started."

Paul ducked under his guitar strap and stood beside Dennis, with Michael on the other side. He knew the two chords, and the song was so well-known, at least the chorus, that he didn't have to do much. His voice was strong and he was never shy about singing if it was in a group. "Hang down your head, Tom Dooley, hang down your head and cry. Hang down your head, Tom Dooley. Poor boy, you're bound to die."

At the end, Dennis said, "One more chorus," and they kept going, following his lead.

When they stopped, Dennis and Michael looked pleased. A small ripple of excitement crept up Paul's spine. It sounded good! Dennis' voice was dramatic, a true, rich tenor. He looked at the other two.

"You know, boys?" said Dennis. "I think we might have something here. I kind of liked it." He turned one way and then the other.

"Me, too!" said Michael. He tuned his strings, thwanging up a few notes.

"Let's try it again," said Dennis. "I can hear you, Paul," he said. "You can be even stronger, though, if you want to be. Try some harmony, if you've a mind."

The voices and instruments sounded loud in the basement room, reverberating off the old concrete walls. When they finished doing the song again, Paul's fingers hurt, but he ignored them. He wanted them to get calluses from strumming.

"You know, Mr. Greenway might be right," Dennis said. "I asked him who I could get to sing with me, and he said 'Paul Mikkelson'. 'Course, we'll have to see," he hedged. "But this is for the talent show. I just really want to put something good together!"

"What do you think, Paul?" asked Michael.

"I'd like to sing with you," said Paul, shyly. "Your playing sounds great."

"Any other songs we should practice?" Michael asked Dennis, acknowledging him as leader. "Picking is harder. I have to learn the songs. All you guys have to do is find the chords."

"Well, they won't let us do more than one or two for the talent show. But let's get a couple more ready," Dennis walked over to a shelf and pulled off a songbook. "I'll pick some and tell you this week at school."

Walking home, Paul felt pleased with himself. Mr. Greenway, the band teacher, had recommended him. He dragged his feet on the slushy road, glad to be out in the air, but also excited.

Foxy came toward him as he got close to home. "I did it!" he yelled. "They liked me!" Foxy didn't seem to know what the guitar case was. It looked like Paul wasn't available. Paul put it down in the snow and knelt down to speak to her. "Good girl," he said, as he brushed her back and scratched the warm fur around her ears. "I'll come back and we can go for a walk."

The night of the talent show came much too quickly for Paul's taste. Mother, Dad, Kristen and Hanna were all in the audience, as well as the whole rest of the high school. Paul's stomach flip-flopped as he waited in the wings with Dennis and Michael. He hadn't been able to eat supper.

As the audience clapped for the previous group, Paul, Dennis and Michael stood waiting in their sport coats and ties, their instruments on straps over their shoulders. Paul collected his inner resources, humming a note to himself to warm up his voice. Dennis' face was pink and sweaty, all keyed up.

"And now, please welcome Dennis and the Dots!" shouted a young announcer, one of the seniors.

Paul's stomach turned over and he marched out onto the stage with the others. Dennis had wanted them to run out on stage, but after one look at Paul running he changed his mind. Paul ran like a lopsided hound dog.

Under the bright lights, Paul was blinded. All he could see were Dennis walking up to the microphone, and Michael standing, his banjo sparkling in the light. Below the stage was a dark sea, where the audience must be. "It's just like playing in the basement," Paul convinced himself.

But for Dennis it was different. Paul saw that he was glowing. He took the microphone as if he did it every day of his life, relaxed and smiling. "Thank you, thank you! We'd like to start off with a Kingston Trio favorite for you. I think you'll all recognize it." He stepped back and looked over to Michael, who picked out the melody on the banjo to get them started. Once again, as they had over and over, the three boys exhorted Tom Dooley to hang down his head. Then Dennis went back to being the poor boy. "This time tomorrow, reckon where I'll be, down in some lonesome valley, hanging from an old oak tree," he sang.

Paul strummed, trying to keep his down stroke and his up stroke even. Dennis was singing his heart out, the light shining down on him. The guitars sounded good together, Dennis playing a darker lower chord than Paul. Paul came in on the chorus, in harmony with Dennis and Michael, who took the bass. "Hang down your head Tom Dooley! Poor boy you're bound to die."

When Dennis gestured, they stopped and there was a moment of silence before the audience broke into excited applause. It was electric. Paul could feel it on stage. This wasn't some tepid response. They loved Dennis and the Dots! Shivers of excitement rippled up and down Paul's spine, but also a bit of chagrin. What had he gotten himself into?

Dennis took the applause gratefully, as if it were his due; as if he had known all his life that people would love him. He stepped up to the microphone again, all smiles. "Thank you! Thank you! We've got one more, an old Woody Guthrie tune for you. Woody rambled the railroads during the Depression and I'm sure some of you know this one."

"The Hobo's Lullabye" Dennis sang as a tearjerker, drawing out the words like a country singer. "Go to sleep my weary hobos, let the towns

151

drift slowly by. Can't you hear the steel rails humming? That's the hobo's lullaby."

Paul found the harmony, shifting into a quieter, slower place in the music. He found it easy to imagine himself in a boxcar, cold, shivering and wondering where he was going to end up. He remembered playing hobos with Line, and wished she could hear them singing. It was a great song.

Dennis sang alone. "Now don't you worry about tomorrow. Let tomorrow come and go. Tonight you're in a nice warm boxcar, Safe from all that wind and snow." Paul doubted if the boxcar were that warm, but he came in on the chorus strongly.

When they finished, the audience again clapped and clapped. Some of them even stood up! Dennis and the Dots bowed, as they had practiced, and walked off stage.

Other acts followed, but in Paul, euphoria rose as relief washed through him. It was over. It wasn't so hard, he told himself, as the three boys stood off stage, quietly putting their guitars away.

"Nice work, boys!" whispered Dennis. "Just like I hoped. I think they liked us," he grinned. "And I hope it's not the last time we do this!"

After the show, as everyone congratulated him, Paul realized it was easy to be in a group. He didn't really want to be a Dot, but it protected him. He could be modest, hide behind Dennis. Dennis wanted an audience, he wanted to shine. And he was nice to Paul.

Mother hugged Paul. "You looked great up there," she said. "I didn't know you had it in you!"

"He's his father's son," said Dad. "Not that you're as much of a ham as Dennis, but I've got a little of that in me too." He smiled at Paul, stooping down to pick up Hanna, who was half asleep in her little wool coat.

"I loved the songs you picked," said Mother.

The experience influenced Paul to pick up the guitar more frequently. He was more attentive to his notebook of songs, copying down the words and whatever chords he could deduce from listening to or watching groups on television. And he looked closely to see how guitar players moved their hands when strumming.

Dennis insisted that the Dots come over to his house once a week and practice, but they didn't know what they were practicing for. Dennis kept talking about performing, but he didn't know where. One day he called Paul to make sure he was watching *The Ed Sullivan Show*.

"There's these guys from England coming on," Dennis said. "You've got to see them for sure!"

The Mikkelsons watched, as four mop-headed young men came out and played electric guitars, a song called "I want to hold your hand!" Paul wasn't too impressed. "It's just pop," he told Dennis at their next meeting. "They're not saying much with their lyrics." He couldn't see what the big deal was.

But Dennis liked it. "I wish I could get an electric guitar," Dennis lamented.

An electric guitar was the last thing Paul wanted. Human power, he thought. Like shooting a deer with a bow and arrow, or paddling a canoe instead of having a motor boat. If you couldn't make music on your own power, what good was it?

Luckily, none of them could afford electric guitars. Folk songs were everywhere. And Dennis began to find places for them to play. Paul, seduced into being a Dot, accepted it and began to enjoy himself.

16

When the new term started at Wittenberg in late January, Line's roommate Ruthann went as an exchange student to Berea College in Kentucky, and Mae Winkler came from Spelman College to live with Line and Joan in their three-person room in Brandt Hall. Line was terribly excited, but Joan advised her to go softly. It might be hard for Mae, a young Negro woman, to adjust to being around so many white people.

Mae turned out to be much like her new roommates. She slept in soft rollers and brushed her wiry black hair into a pleasing bouffant in the morning, liked pizza and ice cream more than she should and had fallen deeply in love with a guy from Morehouse, the Negro men's college next to Spelman, just before she arrived.

"I didn't mean to fall in love with him," Mae told Line and Joan late one night when she had been with them for a week. She was weeping and Joan and Line couldn't help noticing. "It happened all of a sudden. We've been friends for a while, but before I left, he asked me to go walking with him and he kissed me. Sorry," she apologized.

Line had noticed Mae's excessive interest in the mail. "Isn't that just the way!" she said. "Things are never what we expect. I guess it will make you even more homesick!"

"It would be okay," said Mae, "but he isn't a very good letter writer. It's hard on me because I write a letter every day, but I don't know what he's thinking. He hasn't written me one."

"Did he tell you he wasn't going to write?" asked Joan, sitting on her bed in a chenille bathrobe, bare-legged, clipping her nails under the lamp.

"No. He said he wanted me to think of him while I was away," Mae wiped her nose with a tissue. "I've got to settle down. I have to study!"

"It'll be okay," said Line, smiling at Mae encouragingly. "He's not going anywhere, is he? You'll go back in the spring and it will be just the right time for love!" She sat at her desk, books and notebooks spread out in front of her in the usual disorder.

"You don't understand!" said Mae. "Mason's in the Movement. He might get arrested or hurt any time."

Line sat back, brought face to face with the courage Negro students must have as they fought for their civil rights. She looked at Joan. The two of them knew each other well. Neither of them had expected a lovesick roommate.

Line went over to Mae and put her arms around her. "You can talk to us any time you need to," she said softly. "It's all we can do."

"Sorry," said Mae. "I have to get ahold of myself. I'll be okay." She sniffed.

"Maybe one of your friends at home can spy on him, and write to you," said Joan, the practical one. "Do they know about it?"

"No," said Mae. "But I could tell Vinnie. She's a friend of his. She'll write me, I guess." Mae stood up. "You girls are so nice. I didn't mean to fall apart like this. Sorry."

"Like I said," said Line. "Talk to us any time. And don't apologize! We've all got the same problems!" Not exactly, she thought. She had a friend, Henry, who was interested in the same things she was, but he wasn't really a boyfriend. Line didn't love him the way she had loved David Berglund. David was long gone, probably married to his German girlfriend by now.

"It's just so long until I can see him," said Mae, her big brown eyes soft and wet.

"Let us know if we can help," said Joan. "We want you to like it here."

"I will," said Mae, wiping her nose with a Kleenex. "Don't mind me."

In the days that followed, Line asked Mae what being in the "Movement" was like. Mostly it sounded like the girls from Spelman left their walled college grounds and went to downtown Atlanta to picket segregated restaurants. Just before Mae came to Wittenberg, there were mass arrests and lots of people were in jail. Mae herself was a little scared to get involved with the Student Non-violent Coordinating Committee which planned the protests. Her family lived in a small town in Georgia and wanted her to get an education. They didn't want her to go anywhere the Klan might be.

But Mason told Mae that, even though they were sometimes scared out of their wits, it was very compelling. Once when the Klan showed up, one of the Negro SNCC people put on a white sheet and marched behind them, making fun. It was very brave of the person and also hilarious. There were so many people involved in the protests that the city jails could hardly handle them all. In jail, the protesters banded together, singing and talking and raising a ruckus if need be.

Mae explained that two white professors at Spelman made a big impact on her. Staughnton Lynd held non-violence seminars and Howard Zinn talked about history as if it weren't just about white imperialism, otherwise known as Western civilization. SNCC was planning a voter registration project in Mississippi for the summer and Professor Lynd was organizing "freedom schools" which would educate Negroes about their voting rights.

"The Movement is all around me," Mae said. "I can't ignore it. Especially now that I love Mason. There are so many great people involved. But I have to study. I want to be a teacher. It isn't easy for my folks, now that I'm in school." The two girls were having breakfast in the cafeteria in the garish fluorescent light of an early winter morning.

"I know what you mean," said Line. "I have a big family too, and my mother went to work so she could help put us through college." Line buttered her toast. "I really want to go to Spelman the more I hear about it," she said. "I'm applying for next semester."

"It's a lot like here," said Mae, stirring sugar and milk into her coffee. "We get locked in at night too, and have to go to chapel." She sucked the hot liquid in carefully and looked out the floor-to-ceiling window beside her. "I never saw snow before. It's so pretty!" The wrap-around glass windows looked out on the icy river in the wide valley below the student union. Lazy flakes drifted down as the sky grew lighter.

"But the people in the Movement sound so great!" said Line. "It sounds important."

"I can tell that you will probably get whatever you want, Line," said Mae, leaning toward Line with a warm smile. She seemed in better spirits since she had told Line and Joan her troubles.

"I hope so," said Line. "It helps to know what you want, I guess." Line yawned and looked over toward the dish room where she did shifts some evenings. "Glad I don't have to work tonight," she said.

Line did know what she wanted. But her passions radiated out in many directions. That evening she joined her sister Marty for an Audubon "screen tour" in the big auditorium in Valders Hall of Science. Both of them knew they were there as proxies for their parents who had instilled a love of nature in all of the Mikkelson kids. The room was full of older townspeople.

Line and Marty sat in the upholstered seats, talking quietly as they waited for the presentation to begin. Line noticed that Marty kept circling back to home and family, holding her arms around the people she loved. Line was pleased that Marty kept reminding her of people at home, that her direction wasn't as relentlessly outward as Line's was.

"I can't believe that Paul is singing on stage with that Dennis Dugan," Marty said.

"I can see it," said Line. "There's more to Paul than meets the eye, you know."

"I know," said Marty. "I wish I could have seen him. But Dennis?"

"Some people are happier up on stage," said Line, amiably. "It sounds like Dennis is nicer now that he's got a group together."

Behind them a voice questioned, "Line?"

Line turned around. There was Mr. Hirsch, her favorite English teacher, with his wife. She stood up and turned around to greet the Hirsches, whose seats were a step above her. "This is my sister Marty," Line said.

"Yes, I know Marty from the Honors Seminar," said Mr. Hirsch. "I figured you girls were related. There just aren't that many Mikkelsons." He looked around the room full of people who were sitting on their heavy winter coats, if they hadn't hung them at the back of the lecture hall. "What are you girls doing here? I don't see many other students."

"We just like nature!" said Line. "Our mother is a birdwatcher, and I guess she's rubbed off on us." Beside her Marty stood up too, listening.

"I don't see you taking many English courses this year, Line," Mr. Hirsch said, "though I suspect Marty of being an English major."

"I'd really like to be either a forest ranger or a social worker," said Line. "Not much chance of being a forest ranger. And I'm finding I'll have to do statistics next year, if I want to be a social worker." Line sighed. "What use are statistics anyway?"

Mr. Hirsch laughed. "I wouldn't know, certainly." He turned toward Marty. "How is everything with you, Marty?"

"Good," said Marty. "I do want to get an English major. But I can't wait until we get to more contemporary literature. I'm not much for ancient English."

"Even Shakespeare?" asked Mr. Hirsch.

Marty looked rueful. "Even Shakespeare," she said. Mr. Hirsch's specialty was Victorian literature.

By this time the lights were dimming. "Nice to talk to you girls," said Mr. Hirsch as everyone reorganized themselves back into their seats.

The screen tour featured footage of the fauna and foliage deep in the Amazon forest in South America. Loud, colorful birds, huge insects and wide, dirty-looking rivers looked so exotic and strange to Line that it took her far away from the snowy winter scenes around them. Line leaned back and dreamed.

What did she want? She wanted to stand up against injustice and prejudice. She wanted to travel in other countries and meet diverse peoples, like those in the photographs in *The Family of Man*. She wanted to do some good in the world. That was it, in a nutshell. She wasn't so anxious to meet men unless they were also interested in saving the world. But she already knew a few who felt strongly about it.

When the lights went up, Line and Marty scampered back out into the snow, sliding playfully on the ice on the paths. Lights lit odd-shaped buildings across campus, throwing dark blue shadows on the snowy paths. The air was fresh, with a crisp bite to it. Line wound her scarf around her mouth.

"That was fun!" said Marty. "I'll let Mom and Dad know we went." It was understood that, while Line wasn't much of a letter writer, Marty was.

"Okay," said Line. "Tell them I've got plans for the summer."

"You do?" asked Marty.

"Yes. There's a group going to Chicago. Part of a Listening Witness to the inner cities program sponsored by the church. Joan's going. I'll tell you more about it the next time I see you." Line and Marty were making tracks. It was getting late.

"Ok," said Marty. "I better run for it."

"Yup. Me too," said Line. They rushed back to their dorms before the doors were locked.

The next night was an International Relations Club meeting. Joan laughed at Line because Line found all kinds of things more important than studying. Joan was serious about her work. She was quite capable of studying incomprehensible political and sociology texts and blocking out everything around her. Joan was also a good writer. She and Mae were a team. Mae wanted to study too. But Line was bent on dragging Mae to an IRC meeting, the highlight of Line's month.

"Joan thinks you don't study enough," said Mae, as Line and Mae headed to the student union meeting room.

"I do study," Line protested. "I'm doing okay in all my classes. But the world is calling! Urgently!"

"I suppose so," said Mae. "I'm hoping it can wait a little for me. School is so important. I don't want to rush it."

"I didn't pledge a sorority," said Line. "That's the time I use for studying. I know you are an honorary member of Lambda Chi, but those groups are just social. I don't waste my time on that. Like that Delt Bridal Show that they're having tonight! Sorry. You'd probably enjoy it."

"It's all interesting to me," said Mae. "A lot like home. There are those girls who just want to get their Mrs. degree, and those who want to study and get good jobs and people like you who want to change the world, and then there's me. I want to teach," she smiled shyly. "But I am beginning to think about that Mrs. degree!"

"You heard from Mason!" said Line.

"Yes!" Mae beamed at Line. "Just a little letter, but it meant a lot to me. He's fine."

Line was excited. "What's he doing? What did he say?" She knew he was studying music and wanted to direct a choir, probably in high school.

"Not so much," said Mae. "He just told me he's understanding the power of group singing more and more. And that he hoped I wasn't getting too interested in life up North! He doesn't need to worry. You can have your old snow!"

Line laughed. "Yeah. It is getting kind of old. You wait. It'll start melting any day now. And then the world will be mud-luscious and puddle-wonderful. As my sister Marty used to say."

Mae sighed. "It's still a long time until June."

The two girls walked into the warmth of the student union and found the meeting in a room where tables were set up in a U-shape. The president of the group, Josiah Ogude, an African with a British accent, greeted Line as she introduced Mae and explained where she was from.

"You should find common cause with us," said Josiah, in sentences which came out quite formally. "All of us foreign students are a little bewildered to be in such a homogenous community, with the exception of ourselves. It can be quite daunting."

"We are all Christians, though," said Mae. "No doubt about that. I haven't encountered the kind of hatred here that I do in Atlanta in public. If I walked around with a white friend in Atlanta, we would both be called names."

Josiah looked surprised and saddened. "The legacy of slavery," he said. But the room was filling up. He turned back toward the podium and his duties.

Line spotted Henry rushing in and patted a seat next to her. Looking at him from the point of view of her new roommate, Line saw an ordinary sporty-looking guy with an open face and his hair greased into an inviting curl. Line turned toward Mae. "This is Henry," she said in an uncertainly possessive way. "Henry is interested in the civil rights movement too."

Mae held out her hand to him, but Line could tell she understood Line's ambivalent feelings about Henry right away. Mae was no slouch in the relationship department.

The three of them found seats around the table. Joan, with a pile of papers in front of her, sat on the far side, having come straight from the library.

"That's Professor Sheldrake, our advisor," whispered Line to Mae, nodding her head toward an older man with longish, fly-away hair who was seated in the corner. "He lectures in history." Sheldrake had helped set up the core courses in history and was academically respected, though it was said that he drank, an idle rumor which his rumpled appearance did little to discourage.

The hands on the big white wall clock showed it was 8 p.m. and about 15 people were present. Josiah called the meeting to order.

He welcomed Mae and asked her to describe Spelman College in Atlanta and the protests organized by SNCC and the Southern Christian Leadership Conference (Martin Luther King's group), both headquartered in Atlanta. Lots of people asked questions because there was nothing like being present in a hot spot, though Mae said she didn't know about a lot of things.

"I don't usually go to meetings," said Mae shyly. "It was Line here, who wanted me to come."

Line felt protective. "Yes, I thought Mae should know that there are some serious students on campus who are trying to make a difference." She smiled.

Josiah rescued them both. "Thank you Mae," said Josiah. "We don't mean to grill you. But events going on in Atlanta right now have international import."

Line looked around. She remembered that she had first come to IRC because her co-worker in the dish-room told her about the group. Gary was gone now, studying in a university. But IRC was Line's favorite group, full of interesting, exotic people. There were two students from Africa, several serious history and economics students, one student from Spain and one from Norway. Henry also loved IRC. He and Line were thrown together as a committee to find speakers and they had become close friends.

"The mission of this group is to educate ourselves about world affairs," said Josiah, "and to present programs on campus which will acquaint students with foreign affairs and culture. Tonight, Don Clayborne is going to give us his thoughts on Southeast Asia, which he has been preparing for the Wittenberg College debate team. I, for one, am looking forward to it!"

Don, a large guy with thick black plastic-framed glasses and a broad, complacent face, stood up, shuffled a bunch of papers together and came up to the front of the room. Line watched him, thinking that the cliché of the absent-minded professor was certainly true. She was sure Don would some day become one. And who would take care of him, she wondered. But she was impressed with the clarity of his thinking.

"The general consensus of authorities seems to be that the war in South Vietnam is making little progress and may even be getting worse. In response to the failure of U.S. aid in South Vietnam, President Johnson is thought to be considering changes in the U.S. role in the Vietnam conflict," began Don, his face down as he read from his paper.

Don said that the U.S. was being hypocritical in not supporting elections in South VietNam because its government was afraid the communists would win. His paper concluded that the U.S. should either withdraw its support for the conflict or support a governing committee under the auspices of the United Nations.

"Any student of history must realize that war as an instrument of foreign policy in the end benefits no one. It is the duty of informed citizens to pursue peaceful coexistence. It is the present generation which must accept the fact that expediency in foreign policy must no longer be the rule. This is not merely unexamined liberalism. However, the conscientious student is not expected to accept this view uncritically. I welcome your comments," said Don, raising his head to look at his fellow students.

"What exactly IS the U.S. involvement in South VietNam," asked Sofia Baja. "It isn't something I've been paying attention to." She was from Spain. Line didn't know exactly how she ended up at Wittenberg, but she was always an interesting presence, questioning everything around her, often showing her disdain for the U.S.

"We currently have 15,000 'military advisors' in the country," said Don.

Line listened. She knew nothing about Asia. Most of her attention was directed back toward her own ancestors and their surroundings in northern Europe, not toward the millions, maybe billions of people who lived on the Asian side of the world.

"Wow," said Henry when Don was finished and the students were putting on their coats. "I totally agree with him! That was a great presentation!"

"The present generation," said Line. "That's us, I guess."

"No doubt about it!" said Henry.

"Did you enjoy it?" Line asked Mae.

"Sure," said Mae. "It was interesting." She turned toward Line, "Are you guys going somewhere?"

Line and Henry looked at each other. "Actually," said Henry, "I need to catch up with Sheldrake to ask him about an assignment. But I really want to talk to you some time, Mae. I'll catch you guys at dinner one night, okay?" he looked at Line.

"Great!" said Line. "We'll see you later. Good night!"

As they slipped out the door together, Mae said conspiratorially, "You know what, Line? Let's sneak over to Valders and see if they're still having that bridal show. We don't have to go in. We can watch it from outdoors!"

Line laughed. "Okay, I'm with you. If we don't have to go in."

The two girls put on their gloves and buttoned up their winter coats, heading toward Valders. "So that's Henry!" said Mae. "Looks pretty cute to me!"

"He's nice," said Line, "but there isn't much more to say. There's nothing between us to write home about."

Valders Hall of Science was new. In the big open area at the front, two concrete sloping walkways to the second floor floated in space. They made a flattened X visible through the glass wall at the front of the building as they crossed each other. It was called the concourse and it was used for events such as recitals, when a piano might be tucked under one of the walkways.

As Line and Marty approached the building, they could see lights shining on girls drifting down the concourse in long white dresses. The audience sat in chairs set up on the first floor. Line couldn't hear the music, or what the announcer was saying, but it was much preferable to being inside!

"Do you want a white dress for your wedding?" Line's voice was muffled talking to the wide-eyed Mae as they stood watching, scarves wrapped around their heads and gloves holding up the collars on their winter coats.

"Of course," said Mae. "What's wrong with that? Don't you want a white dress?"

"It just seems kind of egotistical," said Line. "When so many people live in poverty, how can I presume to spend lots of money on a dress I'd only wear one day?"

"I'm just an ordinary person, Line," said Mae, serious all of a sudden. "A white wedding would be an achievement for me. It's a symbol, showing that I value tradition and the family I'm about to create. I don't think there's anything wrong with marking this high point in your life with a very special ceremony."

"You're right, Mae," soothed Line. "My Mother and Dad had a big formal wedding. I don't know how they managed it during the war. Mother wore a white satin dress with a sweetheart neckline. I've seen the dress. Maybe I could wear it at my own wedding."

"The wedding photo of my parents shows them in their church clothes," said Mae. "They were married in the war too, and they had a small, quick wedding. They were both very young and my Dad was going away. He got back okay, though. He always says he was a lucky man."

As Line and Mae watched, the clothes on the girls walking down the concourse changed from the long dresses of brides and bridesmaids to the casual clothes one might wear on a honeymoon, Bermuda shorts and sun dresses. Line laughed. "I hope it's warm in there! Sashaying around in hardly any clothes. Serves those girls right."

The girls who were modeling were from the sorority putting on the fashion show. Line didn't really begrudge them time to parade around in new clothes. She just thought it strange that anyone would want to. But she also realized she should tone down her contempt in front of Mae, who might, under other circumstances, have been one of them.

People inside the concourse appeared to be clapping. The show was wrapping up. Line and Mae moved off toward the dorm.

"I'm glad you heard from Mason," Line said. "You're going to look lovely in a white wedding dress."

"Whoa there, Nelly!" said Mae. "Don't let me get ahead of myself! No one's talking about a wedding. But, you know, I'm a girl! I'm just interested!"

"Yes, I suppose girls are," said Line. But she herself wasn't so conventional as to think about weddings very much. It was a measure of how different everyone was. She might want to drag her friends off to hear about conflicts in far away countries, but it was also fine if they were more interested in their own lives and futures. Line knew she must become more tolerant. It was funny to think that she, who thought of herself as utterly unprejudiced, must be taught this by her Negro roommate!

Line and Mae ran the gauntlet of couples kissing on the steps of the dorm. They giggled and stamped their feet on the mat at the door to get the snow off.

"Maybe Henry isn't your prince," whispered Mae as the hot breath of heated interior air enveloped them, "but someday he will come, and you won't sneer at romance!"

"Maybe," said Line. Hopefully it wouldn't be too soon. She liked not having to worry about anyone else but herself.

17

Marty found the Wittenberg campus completely different during summer school, so empty it was almost eerie. Buildings were open and the year-round staff was there, but students were few and far between.

Brandishing the required paperback book, E. M. Forster's *Aspects of the Novel,* Marty walked into her first class and was thrilled to find a teacher so young she might have been a student. Miss Martin, a visiting faculty member from the University of Minnesota, was slim with a soft brown pageboy, dressed in a shirtwaist with a cardigan over her shoulders. Before her was an informal row of chairs, no more than ten or so.

Marty sat at one end of the row. Several of the other students were older people, taking classes to help a teaching credential or for their own amusement. But at the other end of the row, Marty noticed an exotic young woman she had never seen before. She was beautiful, with short dark hair waving around her face and perfect olive-colored skin.

"We're going to begin with the Forster," said Miss Martin, "and then read a novel each week. By the end of the course, you will each pick a second novel by one of our authors and write a paper discussing it in light of Forster." At last, thought Marty. Contemporary novels. It was what she wanted most to study. "You can get some of the novels out of the library, or perhaps share them. Here's the list," she said, passing out sheets of Xeroxed paper.

Marty felt tremors of excitement. A novel a week sounded formidable, but, as with all her other classes, she would somehow get through them. She looked at the list. Some of the American authors were familiar, Faulkner, Hemingway and Fitzgerald, but she did not know E.M. Forster. Virginia Woolf was famous for her stream of consciousness novels and D.H. Lawrence's were infamous. Marty drank in the intellectual seriousness the list represented.

When she heard the name of her young classmate, Marty pricked up her ears. April Anselmino. "Are you staying in Brandt Hall?" asked April after class.

"Yes," said Marty. The rooms in Brandt were set up for three people, but Marty only had one roommate. Linda, an older girl she didn't know well yet.

"Good," said April. "Maybe we can share books."

"Okay," said Marty, a little timidly, dazzled by the freshness of April's face and the simple, dark cotton sheath on her slim body. Marty felt keenly the soft roundness of her own arms, the tight waist of her dress where the extra flesh from too many ice creams the last winter was sitting.

"I've transferred in from the University for the summer. I really love Miss Martin," said April. "Are you going over to the student union?"

"I work at the library," said Marty. "I'm headed there now."

"Oh, all right," said April, acting a little disappointed, but with no lack of the confidence with which she seemed blessed. "I'll see you around."

As she walked across campus toward the library, Marty mused on how much she preferred to be with nice looking people. Linda was pasty-faced and pudgy, with short, curly hair which she didn't pay much attention to. She was a competent person, a good student, and would perhaps make a great teacher or mother, but she wasn't attractive.

April, by contrast, was breathtaking. Marty rarely saw people whose bones were so regular, and who found the discipline to let them dominate face and body. Taller than Marty, she had a long neck and a lean body. She looked slightly foreign, with her fresh olive skin and heart-shaped face, which increased her attractiveness. Marty looked forward to talking to her about sharing novels.

Marty pulled open the doors of the compact brick, Carnegie-style library and went up the wide marble staircase where she worked 20 hours a week. "Hello, Miss Axelsen," she said. Miss Axelsen, a reference librarian, was seated at the top of the stairs on the far side of the large blonde wood cabinets which housed the card catalog.

Miss Axelsen adjusted her cardigan over her ample chest, and stood up. "Good morning, Marty," she said. "We've saved some shelving for you." She smiled and pointed to a metal cart laden with books in two rows.

Solid in appearance, but not unattractive, Miss Axelsen was a contrast to the more ethereal Miss Hageman. the other reference librarian, who dressed as if she were beautiful and wore her grey-gold hair in an attractive flip. Both of them were perhaps 50 and single. In Marty's world, they were virginal old maids, no one to emulate. But Miss Hageman was very liberal, politically. And Miss Axelsen schooled Marty to a courteous professionalism.

Marty nodded. She liked nothing better than to disappear into the stacks with a cartful of books. But it was a lovely summer day and it was hard to go into the dark stacks. She glanced longingly into the reading room to the left of Miss Axelsen's desk. Quiet all day for study and research, the room ran the length of the building. It felt holy to Marty, the soft light from the large, arched windows falling on maps, reference materials, lamps and long tables. The light was moderated by long shades pulled up from rolls at the bottom of each window. It sometimes fell to Marty to pull these shades in the afternoon as the sun moved into the western sky.

Marty wheeled the book cart into the open stacks. There were three floors of stacks, with stone slab floors between them. At the end of each row were carrels built against the thin windows, where a person could spread their work and study for as long as they wanted. The morning light shone in through the thin windows, illuminating the dust motes which hung over the tall shelves of books.

One part of Marty wanted to set up a place for herself at one of these carrels, spread out the books she wanted and never look up. But most of her liked being forced to have a regular life, of classes, meals, being outdoors and going to bed.

Marty organized the books by the Library of Congress number on the spine so she could shelve them quickly. Her cart held the P's, her favorites, English literature under PR and American literature under PS. Marty thought the Library of Congress system infinitely superior to the Dewey Decimal system used by high school libraries. All the books by and about an author, whether biography, fiction or essays, were collected in one place. In Dewey, books were collected by genre and one author's books were in several places. How could you study an author if you must hunt them down all over the library?

As she shelved, Marty opened the books and looked through them quickly, noting who wrote what, whose biographies were being written and what books were borrowed. Her hands moved quickly. She climbed on a stool to get to the top shelves, ducked down to get to the ones on the bottom.

The stacks had an atmosphere of order, no matter how dusty they might be. They were crowded, as the library was begun when there were only 300 students and there were now more than six times that number, but Marty pushed and shoved, making room. The library was well-used, and there were always new books coming in. How she loved books. It was clear that she would never want for things to read. In fact, in her lifetime she could never read everything she wanted.

After her hours of shelving, Marty walked back toward the student union for lunch. In June, the air was humid and hot while grass and vegetation grew quickly under the blazing sun, giving off a lush, wet smell. When the grass was cut on the wide swath of lawn in the middle of campus, great matted chunks lay in rows made by the tractor mower, sending up a sweet green fragrance.

The sun was settling into an afternoon angle as Marty collected a pillow, her books and a light blanket. She wanted to be outdoors in the short-lived nice weather, but she must read many pages in the next few days. She settled down under a tree on a grassy bank, in full view of the dorm's windows. Since most of the rooms were empty, she didn't mind.

Reading, her page in the sun, Marty's eyes quickly got tired. She moved into the shade and it was easier. But she kept twisting and turning, trying to find a place where her body didn't complain and she could get lost in the book. It wasn't fiction. It was about E.M. Forster's concepts, the roundness or flatness of characters, story, plot, pattern, rhythm. Marty's eyes read, but her heart wasn't registering. Ants traveled across the blanket and headed across her soft, white arms and legs. Dappled shadows of leaves fell on the page, inviting drowsiness.

After supper the light was long, but there was still nothing to do but read. The air-conditioned student lounge was almost empty with the evening sun shining through the glass walls at the west. Marty curled up on a sofa and found the page in her book, but mentally she was weighing the moments. She was afraid she couldn't stand so much stillness. Only one class tomorrow, a few hours at the library and nothing else on the horizon for days. What could possibly happen in the emptiness of time in front of her, she wondered.

Marty looked up when she saw the silhouette of someone walking across the carpet toward her. It was April. Marty sat up quickly. The emptiness of the room had encouraged her to lounge with her bare feet on the cushions, but that was not how she wanted to receive a visitor she admired and barely knew.

Nevertheless April quickly fell into a relaxed mode as well. "This is a good place to read," she said, sinking into a soft, teal-covered chair near Marty. She slipped off her thongs and tucked her brown, shapely legs under her.

"Yes," said Marty. "Campus is so empty in the summer. It's like having a huge old place of your own!"

"It's much less crowded than the University," said April. "You could never get this far from people there."

"What are you studying at the U?" asked Marty.

"Music," said April. "Actually I'm studying dance, but I sprained my ankle this winter, and my teacher thought I should just relax this summer. So I came down here because I like Miss Martin."

"Wow," blurted Marty. "What kind of dance?"

"Ballet," said April. "I have a really good teacher, but she thinks I need to go to a bigger city soon, to study. My mom would have to move with me and get a job. So we haven't figured it out yet. We're taking a break!"

Marty thought of her own ordinary circumstances. Her life didn't seem nearly as interesting. "I do like Miss Martin," said Marty. "I was afraid I would never get to read anything contemporary. There's so much old literature to plow through."

"How long have you been here?" asked April, quickly. "Am I disturbing you? Aren't you trying to read?"

"I've been at Wittenberg for a year almost. I want to finish school in three years. And I am trying to study," said Marty. "But there's so much time and so little going on that I welcome the break!"

"So you know the town," established April. "I don't know my way around. Maybe you can show me."

"There are nice places to walk everywhere," said Marty. "It would be fun!"

"Maybe we can take a picnic this weekend!" said April. "We could take some extra food at breakfast and just go for the day!"

"Good idea!" said Marty. Prospects were improving! It wasn't much fun to wander around by yourself, but with a friend a long summer's day could be wonderful.

That summer the two girls became inseparable. Marty no longer worried about who she would have meals with. April was usually at the cafeteria waiting for her. Marty could hardly believe the beautiful April had chosen her for a friend and wanted to spend so much time with her. They did things with other friends too, but, in the small group of summer school students, it became clear that if you wanted to find one of them, you must look for the other.

"I don't think I like the life of the mind," said April, throwing down her book. The two girls lay on a blanket under a tree, as usual reading. April stood up and walked in a circle in her bare feet around the tree. She and Marty were camped out for the day at a natural springs which coursed down the rocks at the edge of steep cliffs overlooking a park. It was only a mile and a half from campus, and they had made the place their own.

April stood at the edge of the blanket in what she had told Marty was fifth position with her knees and toes turned out toward her sides, raising and lowering her circled hands. Her plaid Bermuda shorts gave a comic look to a ballet position, but April's long bare arms moved slowly, with great grace.

"If I could do that," said Marty, looking up, "I probably wouldn't care about the life of the mind either!"

"This is the tip of the iceberg," sighed April. "I must give everything, everything, if I want to be a dancer." She stood there, raising and lowering her hands as if they were the wings of a butterfly.

"It's so beautiful," said Marty. She felt soggy and thick in the hot weather, though the sound of water rolling off the rocks behind them was cooling. She had managed to curb her bad eating habits being with April, but she didn't feel that her own body was anything but a vehicle for carrying around her soul and a lively intelligence.

"I'm not even sure why I love dancing so much. Up until this summer, I've been all discipline. Every moment was regimented. Being able to dance made it all worth it," she said, breaking off her artful fluttering. She did the splits on the blanket, again raising and lowering her arms, bending forward and back like a willow.

April jumped up. "It's so hot!" She ran over to the springs and taking water in her hands, splashed it on her arms and legs. Carrying water in her cupped palms toward Marty, she lifted it in the air and threw it.

Marty ducked under the cold shower, giggling. She stood up and went over to the springs, putting her feet gingerly in the bubbling stream at the bottom. The stream bed was full of sharp rocks. There was nowhere to walk on them. Close to the noisy spring, she couldn't hear anything else. She turned back toward April.

"I said, 'do you want to have lunch?'" said April emphatically. She was sitting on the blanket beside the basket she brought, a perfect picture of summer. Marty could never understand how she managed to both be lovely, and do everything perfectly. When they took picnics, April brought her basket for the food, and Marty carried a thin bedspread they used for a blanket on the grass.

"Yes, sorry," said Marty. "I couldn't hear you." She sat down on the blanket.

April began to lift things out of the basket. Both of them saved bits and pieces from meals to make up their picnics. Marty brought hard-boiled eggs, a banana, a cookie and a buttered bun, while April had managed to scavenge some carrot and celery sticks and half of a tuna sandwich. With water from the spring, it looked like a feast and the two girls fell upon the food.

"So have you decided which author to choose for your paper?" asked Marty, breaking the cookie in half and holding half out toward April.

"Virginia," said April. "I like her the best. She's the only woman, after all!"

"Of course," said Marty. "What novel?"

"*Orlando*," said April. "I found it in the library. It's quite fantastical, but so much fun to read! It's like eating candy. I don't want it to end!"

"How fantastical?" asked Marty.

"The main character, an aristocrat who lives in the time of Queen Elizabeth, wakes up one morning to find himself in a woman's body! Such a silly idea," said April, brandishing a celery stick. "But the writing is so good!"

"I don't really like fantasy," said Marty.

April laughed. "Are you afraid of Virignia Woolf?"

"No, of course not," said Marty, blushing, she wasn't sure why. "But I like Hemingway."

"Ugh," said April, looking irritated. "You and your Hemingway."

"He's down to earth," said Marty. "He writes about woods and plants and fishing. I can find myself in his stories."

"Spare me," said April. She lay down next to Marty, who sat cross-legged on the blanket. "Come on," she said, patting the blanket beside her.

Marty lay down and closed her eyes in the dappled shade under the tree, letting the hot air blow over her and listening to the sound of the water splashing over the rocks. The skin on her bare left arm tingled with pleasure as she felt April's presence on her left side. Deep contentment surged through her. She did not want to be anywhere else, she thought. This was the best, companionship, peace. She felt April's arm touch hers and opened her eyes.

"I like being close to you," said April apologetically. She rolled onto her side, her big eyes looking into Marty's.

"I like it too," said Marty quietly.

"Do you think it means we are fairies?" asked April, her anguished eyes showing this thought was bothering her.

"No, I don't think so," said Marty. "We just like being together." But she did feel guilty, knowing how happy her body was in the presence of this lovely girl.

"I worry that it's wrong," said April, sadly. "But it feels so good." She boldly came closer and put her arm around Marty's waist. "It feels good to talk about it too."

Marty felt confused, but she could not believe it was wrong for her to have such a friend. "Don't worry," she said, from the depths of her small understanding of life. "There's nothing wrong with friendship."

At last April sat up and so did Marty. The shadows were lengthening around them. The long summer day was coming to an end. Tomorrow would be Monday and the week's round would start again, classes, library, meals. Marty knew they could not lie near each other forever, or even for very long. "Come on," she said sadly. "We'd better get back."

And Marty knew, all of a sudden, what she had that the beautiful April didn't. It was the assurance of her tight-knit family and the balance they gave her. She had been given permission by her family both to live and to know where the limits of right were. She was more secure in herself than April.

That week Marty decided she would write her paper on Hemingway. She thought she was responding to the realism of his prose, but was also drawn by the stoicism of the characters, engendered by the war and reminiscent of people she knew. She found all the books she could in the library on Hemingway and checked them out, piling them on her desk and flipping through them. The novel she chose to report on was another long one, *For Whom the Bell Tolls*.

That week also, for the first time, Marty was able to resist April's invitations to spend time together. On a damp afternoon Marty escaped with her book to the historic wooden Norwegian cabins collected in a group under the pine trees above Brandt Hall. Two of them were partly furnished, but locked. The simple wooden pioneer furniture was visible through the glass-paned windows. Around the cabins was lawn, mowed as part of the expanse of woodsy campus.

A third wooden building had been a mill with two giant millstones for grinding grain into flour lying flat at its center. Big eaves protected the cabin. Inside it were shelves on either side of the door. Marty didn't know how the mill worked, or what the shelves were used for. She used them for a seat inside the cabin where she was protected from the rain and people. No one came up to the cabins, and no one could see Marty hidden just inside the open door to the mill, reading.

Marty read through the long afternoon, trying to imagine that she was in Spain, with a group of rebels during the Spanish war. She was the hero, trying to do his duty, and she was Maria, his love. The descriptions were beautiful and again she was struck by the stoic character of the rebels, all of whom faced death daily. Marty knew nothing of death and little of danger. But Hemingway's prose enlarged her life a little, allowing her to get perspective.

Soft rain fell lightly outside the mill, straight down. Summer school was almost over. Marty must finish the paper based on Hemingway. What a lot of reading it was! But then she would get to have a few weeks at Lake Michigami with the Mikkelsons who were already there. April's mother was coming to get her and Marty would ride with them to the Twin Cities. Dad would pick her up and take her the rest of the way.

When the rain stopped, Marty collected her books and ran toward the dorm, crouching over her books to protect them from the wet drops falling out of the pine trees.

The end of the summer term happened very quickly. Papers were finished, turned in and bags were packed. For Marty, the mystery of April Anselmino deepened when her mother came to get them. Mrs. Anselmino was a tall, blonde woman who must have married an Italian. She arrived in a blue Chevrolet, was authoritative and plain-speaking. Though she had regular features, she was quite ordinary-looking.

April insisted on sitting in the back seat with Marty. Marty wondered what made it possible for April to get her own way around her mother. Perhaps it had something to do with the divorce her mother had long ago gotten from April's father. Divorce was unusual and April never talked about it. Marty didn't know anyone else whose parents were divorced. She didn't dare ask about it either.

The drive in the hot August sunshine was heightened by Marty's consciousness of April lounging at her side. Mrs. Anselmino threw questions out into the back seat, loudly and off-handedly, about things Marty thought April might have preferred to discuss in a quieter setting. "Are you ready to go back to dancing?" she asked.

April was equally off-hand, shouting "Yes, Mother," as the landscape circled by them, fields of ripe corn, grain, soybeans. April looked at Marty and edged closer on the seat. "I'm ready. I'm glad to get back to the city! Too quiet in the summer in that little college town. I've got too much energy!"

Marty looked out the window, happy, knowing the poignancy of the fact that she must say goodbye soon. A small farm with barns and silos went by, surrounded by a windbreak of trees. The windows were open and the heat shimmered on the highway ahead of them. Mrs. Anselmino drove through little towns where the car slowed down and stopped at the one stop sign at a crossroads with a few shops on it.

Marty's skin tingled with bittersweet pleasure. The drive felt poetic, laced with the poignancy of endings. She tried making up words for it in her head. "If I never drive through such a warm, lush afternoon again with such a friend by my side, I will have done it once," she thought to herself. It felt as if she were going off to blow up a bridge and die with the Spanish rebels.

They arrived on Friday evening in the lush hot city. Tree bows met above the suburban street where April and her mother lived, in a house April's mother had scrimped and saved to buy, working as the secretary to an attorney. Dad was due to pick up Marty after his church services on Sunday when he headed back north to the lake.

April's room looked out onto a small backyard lawn with peony beds and chairs set out under an elm tree. The sky was opalescent in the west where the sun had set. "It's so beautiful," said Marty, pulling back the curtain. "I can't believe your mother would really leave this and move to New York to help you study ballet!"

April sighed. "I don't know if she will. She's adventurous, and she said she would if I wanted it enough. It also depends on my ballet teacher, who would have to find a place for me. It would be difficult, but we don't know how else to do it."

"You need a rich uncle," said Marty. "Like in the story books. There's always a rich uncle lurking somewhere, isn't there?"

"Not in my life," said April, standing behind Marty and putting her arms around her. "Aunts, but no uncles. And no one's rich. But Marty, I don't want to think about it while you're here." She gave an anguished sigh. "Our paths may never cross again. I want us to just have fun. I'll think about all that when you're gone and I'm lonely. I've never loved anyone like you before."

Marty wondered what she meant by "like you." What on earth was she, Marty, like, anyway? But she replied quietly and truthfully, "I've never met anyone like you either. I'm very happy I did."

Perhaps because the likelihood of her ever seeing April again was so slim, Marty allowed April to drag her into her own bed that night. It was a sleepless night for Marty, but she liked being petted and kissed. Saturday passed in a dream and Saturday night the girls were so tired they slept as sound as little animals.

Sunday morning light fell through the trees in dappled patterns on the walls. Marty felt April's hands tracing her eyebrows. "'You open always petal by petal myself as Spring opens (touching skillfully, mysteriously) her first rose,'" said April softly, quoting e. e. cummings. It was their favorite poem.

Marty kissed the lovely, expressive brown hands. "'The voice of your eyes is deeper than all roses) nobody, not even the rain, has such small hands,'" she finished. It wasn't quite true. April had long, thin fingers.

"Let's never get up," said April, wrapping her legs around Marty. They were in their nightgowns, in a tangle of sheets, the hot humid air weighing on their skins.

"I can't say goodbye to you in front of Dad," Marty whispered. "I want to say it now."

"Okay," said April. "As soon as we've said goodbye, we will act like public people."

"You've shown me something new," said Marty. "Something I didn't expect."

"Me too," said April. "You've made me happy, you Hemingway-loving silly."

"I'll never think of Virginia Woolf without thinking of you," whispered Marty. She passed her hand over April's beautiful, olive-complexioned face. "Goodbye, my darling month of April."

April and her mother didn't say anything about going to church. Instead they had a relaxed breakfast. Toast and scrambled eggs in the kitchen dining nook. April's mother made cups of coffee laced with lots of milk and sugar which the three of them took outside to drink in the back yard. It felt very adult and civilized.

Dad found them on the back porch in the early afternoon, reclining on the webbed lawn furniture. Marty introduced him, but everyone could see that Dad was in a hurry! The lake was calling. He was in no mood to stop for lunch or sit around having coffee. He collected Marty's suitcase from the front hall and they went out to the car.

"April's a nice looking girl," said Dad as the car rolled off down the street.

"She's studying ballet," said Marty shyly. "Thank you for coming to get me," she said. She knew Dad didn't like getting bogged down in city traffic.

"Won't be long now!" Dad said. He looked boyish, his foot on the accelerator, almost straining to get up to his beloved North Woods and the rest of the family.

Marty looked out the window, watching Dad negotiate the city streets and paying attention to her complicated feelings. She was terribly glad to see Dad and couldn't wait to get up to the lake and see everyone. But April's world, lovely, sensual and enticing, did not let go of her. Inner and outer landscapes weren't matching. Marty kept quiet, allowing it to happen.

18

Early in the morning, Paul quietly put a blonde wooden paddle into the canoe and slipped it off the v-shaped mooring of old rubber tires which protected it. In the huge space of sky and water, every sound resonated. Paul felt his own movements very consciously. He tried to be noiseless, to be like an Indian who lived in harmony with the birds and animals around him.

The lake lay like glass, still as milk in a pan. The long, eerie cry of a loon echoed across the still lake. Paul stepped into the blue-painted fiberglass canoe and pushed off into the shallow water. The water undulated only a little under the overcast sky. Light gave pink edges to the pearly grey puffs overhead.

Paul sat in the stern of the canoe, its full weight in front of him, paddling on the right side and twisting his stroke at the end to keep the canoe moving in the direction he wanted. Sometimes he quietly lifted the paddle, watching the drops of water slide off its end, and then stroked on the other side. But mostly he could control the canoe by paddling on one side using the technique called "feathering" Dad had taught him.

Paul was pleased with how his shoulders were developing. His legs were sad, one thin and one thick, unbalancing his body when he walked. But in a canoe, none of his problems were even visible. It was almost like being a merman and having a fish tail. On water he was powerful, able to move through lots of space.

Paul stayed close to the shore, paddling to the little inlet which gurgled into the lake, red with iron ore. Farther offshore a solitary loon was fishing, swimming along and then suddenly disappearing under water. Paul could see better, he thought, in the grey cloud cover. Pine trees came all the way down to the shore here, and a thick carpet of needles lay beneath them, preventing any other vegetation. A family of ducks swam by, the mother trailed by five motley-looking bits of brown fluff. They would look better later.

There were more cabins on the lake every year. When Paul got to Preacher's Point he cut across the bay and into the reeds where the lake opened into a thin channel which led to more lakes. He was far from the Mikkelson cabin now, and he wished he'd eaten more breakfast, or brought lunch. The overcast sky egged him on. The air was humid and warm and it was nicer to be out under the sky than to be indoors. He would just have to go hungry, as he imagined Indian braves did.

As Paul pushed the canoe through the reeds, the clouds began to dissipate and the sun came out. On the far side of the reeds, a narrow, clear channel ran between sandy banks lined with pines. Sun shone through the water onto the sandy bottom, making a green-gold world. Algae-covered logs beneath the surface criss-crossed the shallow stream. Small striped bass and perch swam in their shadows. Water striders moved along the surface of the water with their pod-shaped feet, leaving their odd shadows.

Paul reveled in the watery world, letting the canoe drift. Only one thing would have made it better, if Line and Marty were there. He thought of Foxy too, who had been his companion so long, but Mother insisted Foxy was better off at the farm in the summers and Paul had to admit that without her, there was more wildlife around to study.

The canoe sailed right over the logs with only Paul in it, but in one place he hopped out on the sandy bank and dragged it around a recently-fallen tree. A turtle sat on the log, basking in the sun. Paul let the canoe idle beside it, looking at the beautiful gold markings on its shell. Delicate, shining spider webs hung in the branches above the water.

The air was still, muggy, and the sun was getting high. Paul's tummy began to feel quite hollow. He turned the canoe around and headed back to the cabin.

Mother had three months off from teaching school in the summer and she wanted to spend her vacation at the lake. Dad had bought an old Studebaker Lark for $300. At the end of June the Mikkelsons drove up in caravan, Dad driving the Country Sedan with the canoe lashed to the top, pulling a trailer, and Paul driving the Lark.

Paul didn't like it. He hadn't been driving long, and the eight-hour drive was nerve-wracking. It wasn't hard to see Dad's car because of the canoe on top, but it was hard to stick with him in the traffic. Mother rode with Dad to keep an eye on Kristen and Hanna. So Paul was on his own. But if it helped them stay at the lake all summer, he was willing. Now, when Dad went down to Iowa to take care of his churches, they had a car for getting groceries and possible emergencies.

When Paul got back to the cabin, Bruce, Ellie and their two little girls had arrived. They were having coffee and cornflake bars at the long table at the kitchen end of the big room, with Mother and Aunt Rose. Mother held the plump, rosy little Rhonda, now almost a year old. Grandma Bakken, in a big rocker in the middle of the room, watched Paul's own sisters, Kristen and Hanna, trying to play Parcheesi on the floor with little Brenda, who was three.

"How's it going there, partner?" Bruce welcomed Paul heartily. He stood up to shake Paul's hand and Ellie gave him a hug.

Paul, who had been silenced by the beauty of his early morning canoe trip, had some trouble immediately fitting into this domestic scene. But as the only resident male, he tried to take on Dad's warmth and play the good host. "Great!" he said. "Are you up for the weekend?"

"Just for the day," said Bruce. "We like sleeping in our own beds! And it isn't that far. We started out at 6 a.m., and here we are, 9 a.m. It's not too far to drive." Bruce and Ellie lived in St. Paul, where Bruce was a rising star in his company. Paul noticed that he spoke for Ellie, who, Paul suspected, might have wanted to stay longer.

"We're expecting Dad and Marty tomorrow," said Mother. "It'll be a shame to miss them."

"Well," said Bruce, brushing this off. "You know how it is. Everyone is going in six directions. Ellie doesn't want to miss choir tomorrow, and I'm barely taking a vacation this year. They're thinking of sending me to Europe!" He was bursting with the news.

"To Europe?" asked Mother.

"Yup. 3M is expanding in many directions. They might just send us all to Italy for a year or two." He seemed very proud of this development.

"All of you?" asked Mother, looking at Ellie.

Ellie smiled apologetically. "They told us they'll give us a housekeeper who speaks Italian," she said. "It will be fine while the kids are so little." She was her usual listless self, but she looked as though she was proud of her ambitious husband.

"That's so far away!" said Mother, shocked.

Paul sneaked a cornflake bar to appease his hungry stomach and sat down near Grandma Bakken, who rested in a big, cloth-covered rocker. She smiled at him, her secret, complicit smile, which said, "I'm too old and weak to worry about all of these grandchildren and great-grandchildren. Let them go where they may."

"The company will pay for us to come home once a year," said Bruce. "It isn't like you'll never see us again!"

"I'm glad to hear that!" said Mother, tucking her nose into the soft skin of Rhonda's neck. "We would like to watch you grow up! Yes, we would!" she said to the tiny girl. But there was resignation in Mother's voice too. People were going in six directions and she could not expect to capture them all and hold them under her wing any longer. "We'll be grateful whenever we do get to see you," she said to Ellie.

"So where's that Line?" asked Bruce. A year ago, Line had lived with the Morland family and, despite their differences, Bruce and Line had united in taking care of Ellie during her pregnancies.

"She's in Chicago," said Mother, her delicate eye movements showing exactly what she thought of this. "We're not even sure she'll come to the lake. When she gets home, she'll be heading for Atlanta, Georgia, where she is an exchange student at a Negro girl's college."

"A girl's college?" asked Bruce.

"Line says they are very strict. They lock the girls in at night just as they do at Wittenberg. She wants to find out what it's like to be in a minority."

"There's a college for men right next to them," said Aunt Rose. "They share classes and teachers. They come out of that eastern college tradition of separating the men and women. It's a very good college."

"Sounds like you've done some research," said Bruce.

"Well, you know Line," said Aunt Rose. "And if I were in her shoes, I'd probably be doing the very same thing!"

"Now, maybe," said Mother quietly. "When we were growing up, things were very different."

"Yes," said Aunt Rose. "Of course. We had our responsibilities. But, given the way things are today, I don't blame Line for taking the opportunity!"

"And I guess you can't refuse this trip to Italy, either," said Mother to Bruce. "It's the chance of a lifetime."

Paul listened, hearing Mother's sadness about all this outward movement. Dad had told Paul he refused a pastoral call to Washington state, because he and Mother didn't want to move so far from their own parents. People had so many losses during the Depression and the war. Families stuck together to take care of each other. But, as Mother said, things were different now.

Paul snatched another cornflake bar. They were full of peanuts and held together by a delicious sugar syrup. He was worried that he would never again see Line long enough to become companions. Short visits were hard. He spent so much time trying to understand what his older sisters were doing. There was never time to become what they had been as children, firm friends who shared every thought.

Hanna stood up and came over to complain about Brenda, who was really too little to understand Parcheesi. Hanna was only a year older than Brenda herself, and proud of her abilities. "She's throwing the dice all over the board!" Hanna said angrily, tugging on Mother's skirt and turning her little gamin face up. Hanna herself was schooled by her many older sisters and her brother to play fair or take the consequences!

"Does Brenda want to go swimming?" asked Mother, standing up. "It's too nice to stay in. Let's all go down to the lake, and if the little girls want to go in, we can keep an eye on them. Paul, you'll put on a suit, won't you?"

"Sure!" said Paul. It was his job to watch his little sisters when they were swimming. He couldn't wait for Marty to come. She would be starved for family when she arrived, and would willingly share kid duty.

While Aunt Rose made lunch, Mother sat with Ellie in lawn chairs on the dock platform Dad had built in the shade under the trees. The little girls, in their swimming suits, shrieked at the cold water and the sharp pebbles under their feet, but nothing stopped them. Paul brought out floating inner tubes and helped them paddle about, while Bruce waded out and dandled the baby at the end of the dock. Then he turned Rhonda back over to Ellie, and dived in for a swim.

Paul was something of a fish himself. He loved swimming under water with a pair of goggles over his eyes and nose. But the little girls didn't last long. Soon they were shivering in their towels and rushing up the dirt path to the cabin at the top of the hill in their bare feet. Paul followed. Kristen and Hanna showed Brenda where they slept on the lower floor, with an old iron wood-burning stove to keep them warm on chilly mornings.

A curtain separated Paul's part of the room from that where the little girls' beds were, all of them sleeping under large windows. Aunt Rose and Dad were planning on finishing off the damp lower floor, making bedrooms and a study, with a staircase going up into the cabin. Tools and fishing rods and all sorts of things had begun to collect in the lower level of the cabin. Dad was full of ideas about what could be done.

When Dad wasn't there, the rest of the family relaxed. That day, Bruce and Ellie and their kids napped in the afternoon, and they all spent more time in the cool, breezy shade at the edge of the dock, talking to Mother and Aunt Rose. At 6 p.m., Bruce collected his family and they drove off toward the Twin Cities.

The next day Dad and Marty arrived in time for supper. Everyone talked at once, delighted to see each other. Paul hung at the fringes of the crowd, waiting his turn. As Paul predicted, Marty was overjoyed to see Kristen and Hanna and happy to play with them, while they jumped up and down, dragging her by the hand. Dad walked around the property with Mother, while she told him everything that had happened since he had left ten days previous.

With Dad around, responsibility fell from Paul's shoulders and it felt, once again, as if the Mikkelsons were a family unit. The feeling seemed to depend on Dad and Mother, whose enjoyment of each other was visible to all. Ideas came from Mother and energy from Dad in a flow that sustained the extended family. Paul gratefully fell back into his position on the edge of the family and took advantage of his chance to be outdoors all the time.

Sitting down at the dock after supper, Paul pondered the reality of staying up late at night to see what he could see. Many animals he wanted to see were nocturnal. Bats and moles came out at night, and so did owls, if there were any. At the lake Paul was outdoors so much that he slept heavily. But a scientist, he reasoned, must overcome his sleepiness and learn to stay up and pay attention.

A few animals visible in the North Woods were crepuscular, that is they preferred either dawn or twilight. White-tailed deer, skunks, mink if there were any, swifts and nighthawks could be seen most commonly just before, or just after the sun arrived on the scene.

Paul thought of the creek that ran down beside the Lande cabin and into the lake. Perhaps he could camp on the wooden bridge spanning it at night and see who came down. It was hard to do alone. And the mosquitoes could be formidable. But also, when would he ever get this kind of un-prescribed time except in the summer? Paul felt ashamed. How would he make a scientist if he was dependent on his own comfort?

The skies were very clear at the lake at night, far from the lights so prevalent in places full of people. At the lake, the bright Milky Way lay across the sky like a river of stars, and all the constellations were easy to pick out. Paul used the birding binoculars to look at planets at night.

Most magical of all, the past few nights the aurora borealis hung out across the lake, throwing flames of green and white light into the sky. That would get Marty, Paul thought. She wouldn't be able to resist. He would give her a day to get used to the cabin and then beg her to go out on the lake with him at night.

The next afternoon, after all the Mikkelson kids had come up from swimming and hung out their suits, Paul noticed Marty heading for the lakefront with a book and a notebook. He sauntered down the path after her. It was a warm day and the breeze that came across the lake felt delicious. Marty smiled at Paul and sat down on the bench at the edge of the platform, opening her book of Hemingway stories.

Paul busied himself clearing the dock of wet tee-shirts, swimming goggles and inner tubes, putting things back where they belonged. The blue canoe, pulled up at the edge of the shore and tied to a poplar, felt almost alive to him, pulling him toward it. But the wind took a while to calm down in the afternoon. Right now it was kicking up a few whitecaps and the troughs between them were deep. The lake would be much smoother in a few hours.

"I'll bet you've been loving that canoe," said Marty, looking up.

"It's perfect!" said Paul, emotionally. "The perfect thing for me to get around in easily. There was life before the canoe and now life after it! Life after it is much better!"

"I'm so glad!" said Marty. "I can just see you tooling around these northern lakes for the rest of your life!"

"Yep," said Paul. "You should see Dad shaking his fist at the water skiers who come out and churn up the lake!" The noise of the water washing up on the stony shore was loud behind him.

Marty giggled. "I can see it! He's all about human power, isn't he."

"Yeah," said Paul. "So am I. There are more people here every summer. And motor boats don't help the wildlife population."

Paul sat down beside his sister on the rough wooden bench. "Marty," he began. "Dad says there's still a lot of sunspot activity and that maybe we'll have northern lights again tonight. I've been seeing some the last few nights, but it's hard to stay up! Would you stay up with me? We could take Uncle David's boat out onto the lake so we could be right under the stars." Paul was aware he was pleading, but Marty might just agree.

"Yeah," said Marty. "We could get out past the mosquitoes!" Mosquitoes came out in the evening, when things got still along the shore.

"I know you don't have much vacation," said Paul.

"Well, Paul. I'm always up for an adventure," said Marty laughing. "We don't need Line to have an adventure, do we?"

Paul's face darkened. It was a sore spot. "Do you think she will ever come home?" he asked. "Do you think we'll ever have adventures together again?"

"There is life outside our family," said Marty. "You used to know that, when you were in the hospital so much. Line and I worried about you, but you told us you were fine. Maybe you've forgotten."

"I guess so," said Paul. "I do like it when it's just our family, though."

"Line wants to save the world," said Marty. "And she sees how much there is to do."

"Well it would help if she would at least write," said Paul, gruffly. He was surprising even himself. Line hadn't been home much in years. Perhaps he was just now realizing she was grown up. He stood up by the pine, chinning himself on a branch that stuck out, his muscled arms pulling himself up. "I can't figure out why she wants to live in beastly cities."

"Yeah," sighed Marty. "Cardinal was empty and green and quiet this summer. I doubt if Chicago's that way." She looked up admiring. "Your arms and getting so strong!" she said.

"Lots of canoeing," said Paul. "And something in this body had better get strong," he said darkly, self-deprecating. "You're looking good yourself," he granted.

"I'm happy," said Marty. "I had a great summer. I got to discover lots of literature. Although it all moved too fast! Sometimes I just want to settle into a cabin in the woods and read all the amazing books there are in the world."

"I think that about science," said Paul. "I want to be able to observe things. Like Thoreau on Walden Pond. But then I notice that I'm glad when people call me to supper and that I have to read to the little kids or something. I like people too much. I like the idea of being a hermit, but I don't think I would like it in reality."

"So what branch of science are you settling on?" asked Marty. "I thought you were into plants, but then you start talking astronomy and animals and birds."

"Why choose?" asked Paul. "I like them all."

"In order to be serious!" said Marty. "I don't want to just have hobbies. The idea of hobbies drives me insane! I want to do something seriously. And for that you have to choose." She seemed to warm to her subject. "For instance, in high school, I tried to do everything! Chorus and band and plays and studying. Now I see that if I don't make some choices, I'll never be really good at anything!"

Paul smiled at Marty's vehemence. "Okay, okay," he laughed. "So what are you choosing to be great at?"

Marty looked troubled, her dark eyes turning inward. "I'm not sure. I'm like you, kind of all around. But I want to be serious about something. It will be something about art, about beauty, I think," she said tentatively. "I like photography, but it's expensive. And it's hard to do justice to nature in a photograph."

Paul stood against the tall Norway, looking out across the water. Here they were, dreaming as they always did, their lives ahead of them. "So you'll come out with me tonight, late?" he asked again, looking hard at the sky. "I hope it's clear."

"Sure," said Marty. "I promise."

"Before you start reading," said Paul, "do you want to see the mermaid cabin? It's just down the path."

"Okay," said Marty. "Not very far?"

"No, just a little ways." Paul knew Marty was always intrigued by buildings.

Paul took the narrow path to the west around the lake and Marty followed, leaving her book and notebook. The wind was loud in the trees, rustling the branches, and the waves washed up noisily. Past Uncle David's log cabin which sat high on the hill, they ducked under some trees and picked their way like a couple of deer.

In a moment they came to an A-frame with steep eaves right at the edge of the lake. Only one side of it was built with solid walls. The other side was a screened-in porch. The front of the cabin, looking out to the lake was all windows. The wall which ran down the middle of the cabin was painted with a blue and green landscape showing the little Danish mermaid seated on a rock. It was newly-built by a young pastor, a son of one of the big family clans headquartered on Preacher's Point.

"I hardly ever see anyone here," said Paul as they stood looking in at the open porch. People at the lake were all careful of each other's privacy, but the path along the lake was public, and this cabin sat just off the path.

"So beautiful," said Marty wonderingly. "I wish it was ours."

"Too small," said Paul, practically. "I think they have a couple of small kids, but I bet they spend most of the time at their big family cabin."

"This is where I'd like to hole up and read," said Marty.

"Yeah, I thought you'd like it," said Paul, looking ahead on the path. "I'm going to keep going a while."

"Okay," said Marty. "I'm going back."

That night, Paul and Marty hung around cleaning up dishes and when Mother said it was time for bed, they helped Kristen and Hanna. Marty read a chapter out of the Little House books she loved. But Hanna would not be fooled. She knew something up.

"You're not going to bed," she said sleepily in her three-year-old voice. "I can tell." But Kristen was already asleep, lulled by Marty's voice.

"Good night!" said Paul, and went into his own curtained off space, while Marty started another chapter.

At last, Marty came quietly over to Paul's space against the window where he lay, wide-awake on the bed.

"Dress warm," he whispered. He was wearing a sweatshirt and carrying binoculars. "Dad wants to come too. He thinks we'll see northern lights for sure."

"Okay," said Marty quietly. "I'll get my sweatshirt. I'll meet you outside."

Paul carefully closed the door to the lower part of the cabin, trying to keep the spring on the screen door from making its loud "sprunnnnng" noise.

Lights were still on in the upper cabin, and Marty and Paul slipped down the path. Even before they got to the lake, Paul could see the aurora borealis on the far horizon, glowing and shimmering behind the trees. "See?" he pointed, whispering, to Marty. "It's going to be great!"

"Is it that green haze?" asked Marty.

Dad was down at the dock, putting the oars into Uncle David's boat tied up in the "L" made by the wide piece at the end. "It's spectacular!" he said, excitedly. "I'm not sure I've ever seen them so bright." But his voice too was hushed and quiet in the light-charged night. The wind had gone down and the lake was much calmer than it had been in the afternoon.

"The moon's waning," said Paul. "It won't be up for a while, which is good."

Dad and Paul put lifejackets for all three of them in the boat and Dad settled in at the end, while Paul held the boat for Marty to sit in the little seat in the prow. Last Paul stepped into the seat set up for rowing.

Paul pulled strongly straight out from the dock into the middle of the lake. The sheets of aurora were coming toward them. High in the sky they hung like curtains and veils, shimmering and changing. It felt as if the small boat was surrounded.

Paul stopped and let the boat drift and rock. He hardly knew which direction to look. Above, around, against the horizons, light spread and contracted. Curtains of color hung above them. Most of it was white light, but rays of green and blue shot through. There were even pinkish tones. All they could see was the light, flickering and changing like sheets of mist.

Everyone in the boat was silent, looking up, awed by the display. The water lapped at the boat, pushing it toward the shore. Paul put in the oars and drew it back, moving toward the center of the lake.

"It's amazing," breathed Marty behind Paul.

"To God alone the glory," said Dad. "Soli Deo Gloria."

The shimmering, changing light surrounded their field of vision. Who would go anywhere else, Paul wondered, if they could be here, under this sky, on this lake, in this forest.

19

Line got off the train in Atlanta early in the morning. Warm, moist air greeted her. In the women's rest room, she washed her face and brushed her teeth. Her eyes in the mirror looked tired after a night sitting up on the Dixie Flyer, but excitement thrummed through her. She wore a short-sleeved buttoned shirt and a full skirt, white socks and new penny loafers. Line fluffed up her hair and gave herself a smile. Anticipation would get her through the day.

Line looked hard for evidence of segregation at the train station. But Negroes and white people moved through the space, and Line couldn't see a pattern to it. She began asking people how to get to Spelman College, listening carefully to the soft speech, so different from what she was used to.

Outdoors, the streets were thick with trees and sweet smells hung in the air. Line, eager to know everything, asked the person next to her on the bus what the trees with the big shiny leaves and creamy white flowers were.

"Magnolias," said the older lady, looking askance at her. "Ain't you never seen a magnolia before?"

"No," said Line. "I'm from Iowa and we don't have them."

"You should see 'em in the spring when they're full of flowers! But there's still a few flowers on 'em now," conceded the prim lady, sitting beside her in a hat and gloves, her handbag settled in her lap.

When Line got off the bus, a wall of flowers greeted her at the college entrance gate. Hydrangeas in pinks and purples, and honeysuckle climbing the wall. Just as at Wittenberg, a lawn spread out beyond the gates, encircled by red brick buildings.

"Exchange student?" said the first person Line spoke to. "Go down the hall and talk to Dr. Wolfe. She takes care of exchange students. Room #142."

It was a strange day, with time contracting and expanding and Line half asleep. But she was excited, getting acquainted with a new place and new people. Her roommate, Jane, was a serious girl from a very small town in Georgia. She was a French major and had spent the previous year in Paris. She was excited to be back at college and was anxious to find her friends to tell them about her travels.

Line wanted to find Mae, who had been her roommate at Wittenberg the previous year. She went down to the front lobby of her building and looked over the list of names. Yes! Mae Winkler was in this dorm reserved for juniors and seniors. Being in the same dorm would make it a lot easier to see each other. Line went hunting up the corridor for #304.

Mae wasn't in the room. No one was, but suitcases were open on the bed. Line sat down near the window and looked out on the lawn overhung with trees, busy with students coming and going. Line could now pick out the magnolias with large flat, shiny leaves and a few magnificent blossoms on them. Other trees had smaller, flat shiny leaves with clusters of red berries. It was a lush, wet landscape, utterly unlike Chicago, Line decided.

"Well now, look what the cat dragged in!" came Mae's voice from the doorway.

Line turned around and jumped up to hug her. "How are you! I'm so glad to see you!"

"Glad to be here," said Mae. "It was a tough summer, and Mason's still down there, but, as you can see, I'm pinned!" Mae had taught in a Freedom school in Mississippi that summer, mostly because her boyfriend, Mason was an organizer and she wanted to be near him.

"Congratulations!" said Line. "Let's see!"

Mae pointed to the small gold pin made of Greek letters she wore on her shoulder, a fraternity pin from Mason's college, Morehouse for men, which shared teachers and classes and libraries with Spelman.

"You seem pleased!" said Line. "But is Mason in a fraternity?"

"Sure," said Mae. "He's not very active, because he got so involved in the Movement, but he was a Greek first."

"Hmmm," said Line. "So how was Mississippi?"

"Not as bad as I thought it would be," said Mae. "But it was easier for me than for the white kids. I could blend in better. And I loved the kids. I spent a lot of time teaching reading. The kids loved it!"

"Wow," said Line, ruefully. "I'm sure you accomplished more than I did this summer."

"It was fun!" said Mae. "Amazing meetings. And there were a lot of white students around to get to know. It wasn't so unusual for me, but maybe for them. We have to get used to each other being real! It didn't phase me, of course, after Wittenberg."

"I wish I'd been in Mississippi," said Line.

"Well, how about Chicago?" asked Mae. "You must have felt useful somehow?"

"Working with all kinds of people was the best," said Line. "People so different from me. Working these hard jobs in the heat together. So many poor people there. But it wasn't long enough for me to get to know anyone or get them to trust me. I kept getting shunted around, never got stable."

Line was still assessing her experience in Chicago. She had lived on the South Side, in the attic bedroom of a Lutheran pastor at the edge of the "Berlin wall" between Negroes and whites. Each of the four Wittenberg students got their own job, but, as part of the program, they participated in discussions with the parents, social workers, policemen and church leaders of the neighborhood.

Line worked as a waitress, and then in a peanut butter factory. She enjoyed Chicago and she was good at listening, though she wasn't so sure about the stated mission of the group, "to witness to the fact that Jesus is Lord, even in the cities." She had hoped to just talk to some of the kids on the street, to show them her good intentions. But it wasn't that easy.

"Mississippi reminded me how lucky I am," said Mae softly. "There's a lot of people worse off than me, kids hardly learning to read. So many people not knowing what's due them. We've a long way to go. But I've got one more year here, and I'm going to make the most of it. Get my degree in the spring!"

"I'm so glad you're here!" said Line. "Knowing someone here makes it a lot easier for me."

"You'll be fine," said Mae. "Be sure to try out for chorus. It makes going to chapel every day easier!"

"I will," said Line. "I love singing."

"And how's Henry?" asked Mae.

"I guess he's fine," said Line, noncommittally. "He's in Little Rock, at Philander Smith this semester."

"Good," said Mae. "He'll love it. Arkansas. You're farther south than he is, though. I think." She gave Line conspiratorial look, woman to woman, but didn't get much response.

Line looked around the room. "I bet you want to unpack," she said. "I'll see you later." She felt a little lost, but she didn't want to horn in on Mae's life. She would have to make some life of her own.

Once she got some sleep, Line felt better. The busy round of chapel, meals and classes soon took over. Line looked for sociology and history classes. One social science class was taught by a Negro woman professor who dressed very stylishly. She even wore a hat to class! She had a doctorate, and taught history from the point of view of African Americans. She was encouraging to hard-working students and accepted no excuses. This combination of style and sharpness intrigued Line.

At Morehouse, Line took a class on Christianity and literature which wasn't stimulating. She also found a sociology class on the city. But it turned out not to matter what they read or whether the teachers were stimulating or not. The important thing to Line was hearing a different perspective on life, finding out what Negro students thought.

At first Line tried to make it clear that she herself wasn't racist, but soon found that no one was interested! The students were boiling over with anger. What they wanted was a place at the table, a place from which to speak, places in the democratic process so long denied them. What Line thought or didn't think, didn't matter much to them.

Part of Freedom Summer was the creation of an alternative party, the Mississippi Freedom Democratic Party. At the end of the summer, 68 delegates took buses to Atlantic City, where the Democratic national convention was being held. When this party challenged the white delegates selected in Mississippi from a segregated voting process, the question was sent to a credentials committee where the delegates were allowed to speak. Moving statements showed how they had been prevented from registering to vote.

But Johnson, the incumbent candidate, was afraid to lose southern delegate votes and did not allow the question of whether to seat the delegates to come to the floor. Hubert Humphrey, his running mate from Minnesota, brokered a deal by which two of the Mississippi delegates would be allowed to share the floor, but not vote. The Mississippi group rejected the compromise, and fallout from this failure of Democratic Party nerve was keenly felt among students in the Morehouse class.

"We played by the rules, and had the door slammed in our face," said one of the students. "It's clear that the system doesn't work! We've got to take the power, if they don't want to give us any."

Line's eyes popped open, at this. But it wasn't very surprising. The civil rights movement had been going on for a long time. And here she was, a naïve girl from the Midwest, suddenly showing up in the middle of something she didn't understand. She resolved to keep her mouth shut and listen more.

The general atmosphere at Spelman was nothing like that in Line's sociology class, however. Spelman girls were being educated in morality and gentility. Demure, lady-like behavior was required and the "social graces" were considered more important than "social reform." Line was astounded when the house mother came around to check on the "general tastefulness" of the room she shared with Jane. Even at Wittenberg, which was trying to turn out good Lutheran lasses, this didn't happen.

Line was puzzled. She wondered whether it was because Spelman was a women's college that gentility seemed more important than civil rights. She understood that the families of the students were sharecroppers and sometimes the servants of whites, that the scholarships donated by wealthy patrons which supported them also served to make the women students apolitical. She knew that education led to better jobs, which then led to middle class participation and representation. Perhaps the Spelman girls were right.

But Line was disappointed that most of them spent their time studying, worrying about their hair and clothes, and looking forward to the Friday night mixers, where they met men students from Morehouse.

The two professors Mae had told Line about were no longer there either. Howard Zinn, a fine history professor, had been fired the previous year by Spelman for being an instigator of discontent. Staughnton Lynd, who taught non-violence seminars, had not come back after all the effort of Freedom Summer. Mae told Line she missed them.

Though Line's roommate Jane was nice, and sympathetic to a degree, she found Jane's friends indifferent. Who cared what this privileged white girl felt. Line could hardly have had as much trouble as each of them did. Among other "social graces," Line knew these girls learned how to discriminate from the best, and she didn't take it personally. Generally, though, in choir and in classes, Line found the girls to be warmer and better at sweet talk and flattery than she wished to be. She wondered what Marty would have made of Spelman.

Mae's friends at least, now seniors thinking about their futures, talked openly and freely around Line. One night Mae invited Line up to her room for birthday pie. Her sister, who worked in Atlanta, brought two pies from home on the weekend. One pecan and one sweet potato, made without top crusts.

The pies were beautiful. "Your Mama made these?" Line asked, using the word Mae used to refer to her mother.

"Yes," said Mae. "It's the season. Pecans all over our front yard. They'll be drying them, shelling and cracking them from now until next year."

"Wow," said Line. "I can't imagine a pecan tree."

Vinnie, a tall, thin lightly colored Negro, opened the door, carrying a pitcher of tea she made in the kitchenette. Even though it was evening and cool, she had filled the pitcher full of sugar and ice. Line found that she could get as much sugar as she wanted in the South, just not in the treats she was used to. Everything was different. Vinnie poured tea for each of the five girls into a mismatched collection of glasses.

Ella, Mae's roommate, put tiny colored candles into the sweet potato pie. Ella was usually gruff and silent, but Line saw her warm heart. When 21 candles were placed in the pie, she lit them and they all sang "Happy Birthday." Mae, took a big breath, and blew them out, except for one. A collective "Oooooooh" ran around the room.

"Don't worry," sighed small, plump Corrie Sue, who was a friend of Mae from high school. "You'll get what you wished for anyway. And I think I know what it is."

"Don't think you know everything," teased Mae.

"So are you going to tell us?" asked Vinnie.

"No," said Mae. "I ain't telling nothing. If you tell, you don't get your wish for sure." She cut pieces of pie and handed them round on paper plates. "Now Line here never had pecan pie, isn't that right, Line?"

Line relaxed. "Nope. We have apple pie this time of year. Pumpkin a little later."

"You like it?" asked Mae.

"It's delicious," said Line, chewing on a sweet forkful. "The food's so different here, but I love it."

"Really," said Corrie Sue. "Spelman food ain't half bad. First time in my life I've gotten bacon, eggs and grits every single breakfast if I want. And I do want it! It's worth getting up for!"

"I get up for choir," said Line. "I love singing in the morning. It just gets me going!"

"Oh, Line," said Vinnie. "You don't know the half of it. Wish you'd been here these last few years for the mass meetings. Some singing going on there, I tell you. We had them whenever there were protests, trying to desegregate restaurants, getting people out of jail. You can't imagine how it is to sing together when you're getting your strength up." She took another bite out of her pie and mused, "We've been trying to integrate Lester Maddox' restaurant. And now it's in court and he still won't let us in. It's been kind of quiet this fall, though."

"People are exhausted," said Ella, her dark eyes flashing angrily. "The SNCC staff all went off to Africa. Harry Belafonte thought they needed a rest, and he took them all with him on tour."

"They'll be back," said Mae. "I miss the Hardings. We used to go over to Mennonite House and sit around their table, all of us together. They went to Chicago, I think. And Mennonite House is closed up."

"But Dr. King is here, isn't he?" asked Line. The Southern Christian Leadership Conference was based in Atlanta.

"Yes," said Mae. "We can go to his church. But he's got so many projects going on, he's almost never here."

"Freedom is an uphill road," said the serious Ella. "But if you want some action, Line, we'll find you some. Heck, all we have to do is walk downtown together to get people yelling at us."

"Presents!" cried Corrie Sue. "Enough of your seriousness. Time for presents!" She produced a small package wrapped in tissue paper, as did each of the other girls.

Though Line was stingy with her money, she had spent a few dollars on a pair of leather gloves for Mae. Line could not imagine herself wearing the dyed taupe gloves during the mild winter reported to be coming. But she wanted Mae to have them. She was so grateful for being included among her friends. Eyes shining, she watched Mae unwrap them.

"Oh, Line!" cried Mae. "You shouldn't have!" She smoothed the beautiful gloves over her fingers and held them up to her face. They were a little lighter than Mae's skin color, but the taupe was warm enough to complement it. Mae's delight in the new gloves rewarded Line.

"I've heard they let people like us try on clothes at Rich's department store now," said Vinnie, playfully. "I'd go downtown with you, Line, and try on clothes. See what happens." She looked as if she were ready for trouble.

"Sure," said Line. "I'm not in the market for any new clothes, but I'd go." She didn't want to ask Dad for money for anything any more. She would rather run around in rags.

"Let's!" said Mae, mischievously. "It sounds fun! Have coffee together somewhere. Tomorrow's Saturday."

It sounded quite tame to Line, but she'd been told that only very recently could whites and Negroes walk around safely together as equals.

"I'm going home tomorrow," said Corrie Sue.

"You girls go," said Ella. "I've got a paper to write."

On Saturday, Mae and Vinnie, wearing dresses with full skirts, their sweaters over their shoulders, met Line at lunch. Vinnie was wearing shoes with little heels.

Line wore slacks, her Saturday clothes. "Should I dress up more?" she asked. She could never understand what city girls dressed up for. She felt shabby beside them. Vinnie was from Atlanta, definitely a city girl. Mae grew up near a small town, but it wasn't as small as the towns Line had lived in.

"Well," said Mae, diplomatically. "We're going out, you know. I think you would feel better if you wore a skirt."

Line went back to her room and put on a fresh blouse and skirt. She hung a sweater around her shoulders like her friends and took a handbag. Penny loafers would have to do, though. She was not wearing her best shoes downtown.

The three girls were gay as they walked down the sidewalk towards town. The tree-lined streets felt lush and lovely to Line. The fall sun was warm, but under the big shade trees, there was crispness in air.

"You ought to see the dogwood in the spring," said Vinnie. "It starts blooming early. White flowers turning their faces up. There's nothing like it."

"I guess I won't be here by then," said Line. It seemed a long way off.

The few people walking the streets increased in number as they got closer to town. Line didn't feel strange, walking with her two Negro friends, but at one point a car slowed to a crawl beside them on the road. The driver yelled out the window, "Hey, niggers! Looking pretty!"

The three girls kept on walking, their faces pointed forward. The guy in the driver's seat, who was alone, whistled long and low, trying to get their attention. The girls walked stiffly forward, ignoring him.

"Hey, a nigger lover, too!" the guy yelled. "Hey girl, come for a ride!"

Vinnie and Mae kept walking and Line steeled herself not to respond, to do as they did. At last the guy gunned the motor and took off.

Mae snickered. "Cracker," she said quietly.

Line looked at her. She didn't feel so calm herself.

Rich's Department Store was an imposing six story stone building on a corner with a big clock over the front door. Line bought the gloves for Mae at Rich's, but she was still awed by it.

"We used the Sears Roebuck catalog to buy clothes," she told Mae and Vinnie. "There were no stores like this anywhere near us."

"What about Chicago?" asked Vinnie.

"I didn't go downtown much in Chicago. I'm sure there were big stores there," said Line, "I just never went in them."

The girls loitered in the cosmetics department, looking in the mirrors and spraying perfume on each other, giggling. But Line noticed people staring at them.

They went up to the dress department, and cooed over the dresses. Even though it was fall, Line noticed that the dresses didn't look like they would stand the cold winters she was used to. She picked out a few to try on and so did Vinnie and Mae.

"May I help you, Miss?" asked a sales lady, coming up to Line.

Line looked toward Mae and Vinnie and noticed that no saleslady came up to them. Turning back to the sales lady she asked, "Could you tell us where the dressing room is, please?" But when she said "us," the lady turned away and didn't answer.

The sales lady stepped back and stood whispering to one of her friends. The two of them vied with each other in giving the girls cold, disdainful looks.

Line looked after her, and then at Vinnie and Mae. She giggled, wondering what to do.

194

"Come on, Line," said Mae. "Let's get out of here." She hung her dresses on the nearest rack and walked toward the exit, not looking back. Vinnie did the same and followed.

Line was flustered, but she followed as quickly as she could.

When the girls reached the escalator, they looked back to see if Line was following. Mae and Vinnie both looked angry.

"You see what Southern hospitality has come to," said Vinnie grimly to Line as they rode down to the next floor.

"Would you girls have gotten to try on dresses if I hadn't been with you?" asked Line.

"Maybe," said Mae. "Those sales ladies do want their commission. But they wouldn't have been nice to us. We've been buying clothes there for years, but we couldn't use the dressing rooms. Now they would have to let us."

"Well," said Vinnie smiling. "Let's go try our luck at the coffee shop. Third time's the charm, I've heard!"

Line looked at her, amazed. How quickly she recovered her equanimity. "Okay," she said. "I could use a hot fudge sundae!"

"Don't get your hopes up," said Vinnie, ominously. "Let's see what happens." She led the way to the store's coffee shop, coolly asking for a table for three.

The young, red-headed host smiled and led them to a table near a window. Line breathed a sigh of relief.

"Thank you, sir," said Vinnie pointedly, as he handed around menus.

"Whew!" said Line. "Looks like I get my wish! Anyone want to share a banana split?"

Vinnie and Mae looked at her. "You've got to be kidding, girl," said Vinnie. "At least I hope you are."

Line realized she had once again suggested something tactless. She looked around. No, they weren't her sisters, she realized. Perhaps they didn't want to put their spoons into the same dish as she did.

Mae laughed at her. "Line," she said. "We weren't born in a barn! Let's order some coffee and be civilized."

"All right," said Line, good naturedly. "I see your point."

The waitress was a smiley young coffee-colored woman in a pink dress with a starched white apron. She wrote down their orders and took the menu cards.

"Civilization is worth it," said Vinnie. "Everything I do in public represents me and my people."

"I see," said Line. "There's only one kind of people where I come from. I love seeing different kinds of people." Line spread her fingers on the table and looked down at her hands. "I'm impressed how you girls insist on respect."

"Your mama sounds like she has standards," said Mae, "from what you've told me. She discriminates."

"Yes, she does," said Line. "I guess it's really me. It's me who can't see why we can't all be sisters; why we can't be casual."

"We are sisters," said Mae, quietly, as the waitress came into view bearing a tray of coffee cups. "But a little courtesy towards each other isn't going to hurt. It's like non-violence. You have to practice it."

"Christianity, pure and simple," said Vinnie, stirring sugar and milk into her cup. "Do unto others as you would have them do unto you."

Line smiled. "Exactly," she said. She dipped a spoon into her hot fudge sundae. What a strange and wonderful afternoon, she thought to herself.

20

On a cold October evening, Marty and Ruth, a sweet religious-minded girl, walked up the hill toward Dr. Magnusson's house at the top of town. It was twilight, the crisp air many colors of blue all around them. They smelled dry, burnt fall leaves and wood smoke. Sure enough, smoke rose from a large stone chimney on the brown-shingled house.

Marty was slightly more timid than Ruth, as Mrs. Magnusson greeted them, smiling and exuding warmth in a red woolen skirt and a sage green jersey blouse tied with a sash at her tiny waist. A small daughter, Thea, her long, blonde hair caught up in a red ribbon, stood beside her, wearing a woolen jumper with tights.

The little eight-year-old was eager to help, dancing with excitement, and her mother indulged her. "Thea will take your coats," said Mrs. Magnusson, as Marty and Ruth handed over scarves, coats and handbags.

A wooden staircase led up from the front hall. "Go into the living room and find a seat," Mrs. Magnusson suggested. Dark wainscoting paneled the lower part of the hall and living room.

Around the crackling wood fire were ranged several young men from the college, some on chairs and couches, and some on the floor. Dr. Magnusson, in a crew-necked sweater over a white shirt, sat in a large comfortable chair. Serious, hardbound books on the wooden shelves, a globe and framed art on the walls contributed to a feeling Marty thought must be European. Furniture and drapes were in dark colors of burgundy, forest green and brown, with accents of gold and bright red. The light from low lamps and two candles glowed on the dark colors.

Marty took a mug of fragrant spiced cider from a tray and sat down on the floor. The men were talking, but Marty was having trouble listening, so responsive was she to the fine atmosphere of the house. Thea, pert, self-conscious, stepping carefully around people as if she were an extension of her thoughtful mother, passed a plate of ginger cookies.

"Of course," said Dr. Magnusson, "from the time of the Greeks, philosophers have supported themselves by teaching. And in teaching, one thinks and learns." He looked young and vital, but also as if he came from the "old world" of sophistication and tradition.

"You got your degree at Heidelberg?" asked Erik Lehmann, tall, thin, and one of the most brilliant students in Marty's class.

"Yes, for many years now, Germany has had some of the most influential theological and philosophical thinkers. Even after the war, when I wanted to work on Bultmann, it became clear that I should go to Germany. I was not wrong. Germany was where the action was."

"Why do you think this is true?" asked Mark, another young man Marty barely knew.

"Well, for instance," said Dr. Magnusson, "Bultmann, who was working on the interpretation of the New Testament, was influenced by his colleague Martin Heidegger. They were both at the University of Marburg in the 1920's." He got up and poked the logs in the fire toward each other, the students waiting quietly.

Gesturing as he returned the black iron poker to its rack, Magnusson went on. "Bultmann thought that replacing the traditional supernaturalist interpretations with the temporal and existential categories of Heidegger would make the reality of Jesus' teachings accessible to modern audiences, who were immersed in science and technology."

"And did Bultmann do that?" asked Mark.

"Bultmann raised questions which others, such as Karl Barth addressed," said Dr. Magnusson. "No one was very happy with Bultmann's treatment of the events of the New Testament as myth! But he did open the Gospels to inquiry in a way necessary to the modern world. That was what fascinated me." Magnusson smiled as he placed his hands together under his chin thoughtfully.

The way Magnusson talked held Marty spellbound. Nothing was extraneous, each word was important, leading deeper into the subject. His dramatic lectures for the freshman core courses had been the highlight of the previous school year. She also knew that his modern ideas about religion caused a shakeup when he first arrived at Wittenberg College, though she didn't know what happened or why.

In fact, Marty let the questions Dr. Magnusson raised hang open about her. She wondered how intellectual battles affected Irene Magnusson. Once in a while, at a college gathering, she saw Dr. Magnusson put his arm around his wife in an absent-minded, affectionate gesture. Mrs. Magnusson accepted these gestures, though, of the two of them, she seemed more tuned to how the world might see them. Marty wanted to be the beautiful Mrs. Magnusson, the wife of an exciting, tender, sophisticated man. She did not wish to become any sort of philosopher.

As the evening wore on, the budding philosophers seated at Dr. Magnusson's feet grew more animated. The students had been invited so that he could introduce them to the possibility of work in the field. But as soon as an idea was no longer related to the practical, physical world, Marty was lost. She could not hold a pure idea in her head. "It's why I love literature," she thought to herself. In literature, ideas were embodied. Even when a writer took off on an imaginative bent, they were merely embellishing the real, or holding up an alternative reality replete with physical details.

Shortly after everyone settled into talk, Thea came in to say good night. She smiled widely, her pink cheeks glowing, wished them good evening and went up the stairway to bed, followed by her mother.

Marty looked around. All of the textures in the room looked natural. The thick dark ceramic mugs had been made by hand. The art on the walls was original. The curtains were perhaps home-made, but of beautiful materials. The hardwood floors were softened by a few woolen rugs.

At the root of this conscious home-making must be Mrs. Magnusson, thought Marty. Every detail of the evening made up an aesthetic experience. The Magnussons, their rich and beautiful house, the cider and cookies, the talk of philosophy, even the wood fire, were all of a piece. It felt real to Marty, whole.

As the group of students walked back down the hill to the college in the cold late night, Marty let the others do the talking. She felt uplifted, letting the evening sink to her core and assuring herself that life could be whole and beautiful, the way it was that evening at the Magnussons' home.

But Marty had a long way to go, particularly in the social area. Unlike Line, who felt there were many more important things to do in life, Marty pledged a sorority. To an outsider, the different sisterhoods probably looked exactly the same. But having been at Wittenberg for a year, Marty knew she fit best in Lambda Chi. The girls in Lambda Chi were a bit more intellectual and liberal in their political leanings, unlike the Tau Delts, who would become the leaders of the social sets to which they belonged.

At a dance put on by Lambda Chi's matching brotherhood, the Theta Chi's, Marty talked to Glen Norgaard, a young, pre-seminary student. He was a little taller than she was, slim, with dark hair and pale skin. Glen was funny, with physical antics which matched his quick mind, reminding Marty of Dad. He worked at the radio station, as did Kate, another friend of Marty who emerged out of the welter of things that were happening too fast that year.

Kathryn Ebert was a vivacious, talented farmer's daughter, dark and sociable. She picked Marty out because Marty appeared lonely, even though Marty's many activities made her new roommates declare she was never home. Marty had been placed with two girls she hardly knew when Ann moved in with others. It was hard to feel mismatched, like a third wheel, especially after the intimate summer with April. She welcomed Kate's friendship.

In the hot-house atmosphere of Wittenberg, where even a conversation could lead to an assumption two people were a couple, Marty began going out with Glen, abetted by Kate's fanning of the tiny flame.

Glen asked Marty to go to a concert given by The Four Lads with him. Glen wore a crisp shirt open at the neck, and Marty a soft white blouse. Marty felt like his twin. They were two dark-haired Lutheran kids from small towns. Together they climbed up the backless bleachers at the new field house and looked down at the lighted circle below them on the gym floor where the group, plus a small instrumental ensemble would appear.

Aware she must keep the conversation going, when they were seated Marty asked awkwardly, "How are you faring in Dr. Haatvedt's class?" She was taking two classes of Latin that semester. One was easy, but in Dr. Haatvedt's class, she was trying to translate early church fathers.

"Fine," said Glen. "First thing in the morning. Gets it over with!" He sat beside her easily, close enough but not touching.

"Yeah," said Marty. "That was me last year. Don't you have to take Greek too?"

"That can wait until the seminary," said Glen. "The New Testament was mostly written in Greek. I can't wait to read Paul's original writing!"

"I'm trying to finish in three years," said Marty, sadly. "And I have to take these education classes too." She didn't want to be too negative, however, and scare poor Glen away.

"I'm no scholar," sighed Glen. "I only take what I need as requirements." People were settling themselves around them, and he leaned closer to make himself heard.

"I guess you're more interested in theater and radio," said Marty. Kate had told her about Glen's announcements on the college radio station, KWWC.

"Very important for a pastor," said Glen. "Lots of public speaking involved."

"What makes you want to become one?" asked Marty.

"The pastor in my town was a big influence," said Glen. "He was a lot of fun. I loved Luther League more than any other high school activity! He made me think about it. I'm still thinking about it. Don't have to decide anything yet."

"No," said Marty. "Dad always said that if you weren't absolutely sure about being called, you shouldn't become a pastor."

Below them, the Four Lads warmed up their voices, taking over the responsibility for the evening. Close harmony was the specialty of this group from Toronto, and Marty loved their songs, some silly, some romantic. "Although I may not be the man some girls think of as handsome, to my heart she carries the key." Marty stole a look at Glen, and yes, he was looking at her too.

"Won't you tell her to put on some speed, follow my lead, oh how I need, someone to watch over me." Marty was swept away by the atmosphere. She wondered if, someday, she and Glen would look back and think of this as "their song." It didn't feel like that would ever happen. She hardly knew him. But it might.

Marty tried to let herself go, enjoy the fact that she was going out with a guy. The Four Lads sang a recent hit, "Istanbul (not Constantinople)," hamming it up. How many times must they have sung it?! "Why did Constantinople get the works? It's nooo-body's business but the Turks!" They looked like they were enjoying it.

Marty felt Glen's presence keenly as she sat beside him. His wry, self-deprecating way of speaking made her think he could be a Mikkelson! When they walked back to the dorm, Glen took Marty's hand and gave her a peck on the cheek. She felt as though her feet were not on the ground as she thanked him for the evening. It all felt unreal, but it was exactly what Marty had been led to expect. Perhaps this was romance.

A note from Kate on Marty's desk asked her to stop by when she got home. Marty went down the hall to Kate's room and found her in a blue chenille bathrobe, awake with her lamp on, even though her roommates were trying to sleep in the darker parts of the room.

Marty whispered her report. "That's great!" said Kate, trying to keep her voice low. "He likes you, I'm sure."

"I like him too," said Marty shyly.

A thousand things tried to intervene in the next few days, but Marty felt she was "walking on air." It was so unfamiliar. Friendship with Glen wasn't like her friendship of the summer with April. There was no future to that relationship, and it was thus poignant. But this, the possibility of being in love with Glen, felt momentous. Except that she didn't know him at all! She hoped she would see more of him.

Marty went about classes, chapel choir, sorority meetings, meals and work at the library, keeping her thoughts to herself. But inside, she gave herself free rein. She was imagining becoming a small town pastor's wife, just like Mother. With a sweet guy at her side, who loved her and with whom she could share her thoughts. She wondered all kinds of things about Glen and tried to remember the questions she wanted to ask him the next time she saw him. She wasn't in any of his classes. In fact she was beginning to be in classes with juniors, not her own sophomore class.

In an English class, Mr. Solberg produced a book which introduced English as descriptive, rather than prescriptive. "It's a scientific approach," said Mr. Solberg. "All these years, the old grammarians have been telling us how to write and speak. But linguistics is not a set of man-made rules to the school of thought that regards it as a natural phenomenon."

It was a surprising approach and it captured Marty's imagination. It was quite possible she would be teaching high school English. Perhaps the rules for grammar could be suspended in favor of the study of how people actually spoke.

Young Mr. Solberg was also interested in film. He ordered and presented a series of foreign films for the college. These films fascinated Marty too. Since seeing the Bergman film *The Seventh Seal* the first week she was at Wittenberg, Marty tried not to miss a single one.

It wasn't that she understood them. Quite the opposite. She did not understand them at all. In the case of Bergman's film, the story of a man playing chess with death during the middle of the plague, Marty kept losing track of who was who. Part of the problem was that she must keep watching the English lettering below the photos to find out what the Swedish actors were saying.

The image of Death, ominous and skeletal in a black hood, with the blonde count sitting across the chess table from him, stayed with her. It didn't scare her. Forgiveness and grace were so strong in her own conception of Christianity, that nothing about death or the afterlife scared her. It was just that the image was so intense and memorable.

As with talk of philosophy, Marty had a great capacity to take things in and leave them hanging in her mind, waiting for them to make sense later. When a French film by Robert Bresson was shown, Marty went by herself, slipping into a seat in the science auditorium where the seats stepped down to face a lab desk, with the luminous screen pulled down behind them.

The film, *The Diary of a Country Priest*, depicted a young man who lived on bread and wine while attending to his first parish which scorns him. Marty could not understand why they did so. Where was their human warmth? Everything seemed to go against him. A journal which he kept let the audience know how the young man felt. He was weak and sick and it seemed he was trying to sacrifice himself, as Christ did. But why? As it went along, the story became gripping. All of Marty's empathy went out to the young priest, to the wonder in his eyes, the breath of God flowing through him.

Marty stumbled out of the theater, glad she didn't have to talk to anyone about the film. She hurried out of the hall and into the cold air where she could rest with her feelings for the young priest's death. Marty stood in the cold, under the dark sky, then began to walk slowly, following other people along the lighted paths. The images, so large before her, burned into her brain as if she was being given a key to the intimate life of another person. It was like reading a novel, but deeper. The voice of the young man narrating his thoughts had so much resonance and richness.

Why was it so hard to know people around you, but so easy to see them in films? Marty wondered. The country priest lived in a world Marty could barely imagine, so far away in customs and the cruelty of the people. But the film presented his story whole. No questions as to what happened to him were left. Marty wondered only, why?

When she woke early the next morning, Marty could still see the priest with his bicycle, the hand moving across the page as it wrote in the journal, the face of the priest with his eyes sunk in resignation. She wondered if Glen would have liked the film. He was probably too busy to see it, she thought.

The grey dawn beyond the uncurtained window illuminated the humps of Marty's roommates who were still in bed. The French movie was like a dream, hovering at the edge of her consciousness.

The center was elsewhere, however, looming in color, not black and white. Snow had fallen overnight and the sound of snowplows and shovels could be heard prowling campus. Marty stretched and hugged herself. She was healthy and comfortable, cheerful and full of hope. Breakfast, class and work at the library loomed that morning. Life, possibly Glen, awaited her.

Marty saw a little of Glen that fall, but more of Kate. She and Kate left notes and poems in each other's mailboxes, talked late at night and often met for meals. They were both getting majors in English, and Kate too expected to become a teacher.

One night, Kate castigated Marty for trying to do too much. Marty was fraying at the edges, worn out from studying, working, and trying not to miss any social occasion, spreading herself too thin.

"Just give some of it up!" said Kate.

"Really? Can I do that?" asked Marty.

"Just say no when someone asks you to do something," said Kate. She was not in a sorority. "You can't do it all! You must do what's important to you, not what other people want you to do."

"I suppose not," said Marty sulkily. But she was grateful. It felt like Kate actually saw her, the person she was underneath. And cared about her.

As far as Glen was concerned, Kate kept Marty up-to-date about his doings at the radio station and must also be telling Glen about Marty. Marty rarely saw him. But in November, Glen called and asked Marty to the

Christmas dance. Kate was going with a new boyfriend. The four of them would go together.

A few days later, when Marty entered the dorm, a dozen roses were lying in a box at the front desk. Roses were always an event, leading to speculation about the lucky girl to whom they were addressed. "Marty!" said Ann, who happened to be manning the desk in a navy Lambda Chi sweatshirt, the Greek letters laid on with a white textured ink. "Roses for you!"

Marty stopped in her tracks. "Roses? For me?" She opened the envelope attached to the box. On a little card was written, "Happy Friday, Marty! Glen." It was unbelievable. The roses were deep red buds unfurling their petals, so beautiful. Marty touched the lovely flowers with her finger.

"There's a vase in the kitchenette," said Ann. "I'll get it." She came back with a clear glass round vase, big enough to hold water for all the roses.

"I can't believe it!" said Marty. "I've never gotten roses before in my life!"

"Well, how does it feel?" asked Ann, smiling. "Here's a scissors to cut off the ends."

"Wonderful. Odd!" said Marty. She carefully cut the ends off the roses, put them in the vase and carried them up to her room. The roses lifted her into a different mood. She felt like she was floating, not entirely seeing what was around her.

On her desk, Marty found a little packet from Kate. In it was a tiny book, printed with haiku poems and brush-stroked Oriental paintings. Marty recognized it. She had seen it in the college bookshop herself. She felt blessed. What did she do to deserve these gifts?

When she saw Kate at lunch, she was profuse with her thanks. "I love the little book," she said. "Thank you so much!" She knew she couldn't repay such a gift. She thought about copying out a poem for Kate, and illustrating it. It was the best she could do.

"Did you see the poem about roses?" asked Kate.

"Yes," said Marty. "It was perfect. 'I have bought bread, and I have been given red roses: How happy I am to hold both in my hands!'"

"I knew you'd like it," said Kate. "It's just like you."

Marty felt nonplussed. What did Kate see in her?

Marty did copy out a May Sarton poem for Kate in brown ink, illustrating it with drawings of bees in brown and yellow. But about Glen she was much more confused. The blood red roses lasted a long time, perfuming her room and making Marty feel queer. What on earth did a gift of roses mean? What did Glen expect in return?

Snow fell steadily in December, outlining the leafless trees, piling up along the shoveled paths, and burying the campus in quiet. Kate bought a tiny Christmas tree for her room and decorated it as if she were at home. Small presents accumulated under the tree for Kate and her roommates. She and Marty, with most of the rest of the student body, trooped down to the new field-house for *Messiah* practice.

Glen didn't go. "I have a good voice for announcing," he had told Marty. "But I can't carry a tune." In his quirky but dramatic way of speaking, Glen reminded Marty of Dad. But Dad sang every Lutheran service in his beautiful tenor voice.

"Mr. Duncan says that you don't have to be able to sing," said Marty. But Glen felt too busy. He spent most of his time at the radio station.

Singing the *Messiah* with such a large group of students was wonderful, uplifting. The voices of the Hallelujah chorus played back and forth in Marty's head. "For the Lord omnipotent reigneth, King of kings and Lord of lords," soprano and alto, tenor and bass, one after another in a round. "Forever, and ever, Hallelujah, Hallelujah."

But nothing could stop the Christmas dance from coming. Marty quaked inwardly. Kate bounced around, excited, planning to wear a black velvet top and a gold brocade skirt. Marty had nothing to wear but her Christmas dress from last year, a white wool sac dress, cut like a sailor's tunic with blue satin trim and tie. It didn't look formal, but Marty couldn't imagine spending money on a new dress for the dance.

Even worse, a large pimple was developing on Marty's chin. She tried to open it up with her fingers and let it drain. But that left a red splotch, a scab which no amount of Cover Girl makeup could hide.

When they went down to meet their dates, Glen and Arthur, Marty felt shamed and quiet. The men brought corsages, yellow roses for Kate and red for Marty. Ignominious, Marty posed for photographs in front of a Christmas tree with the others, her black, plastic rimmed glasses, without which she couldn't see, confirming her misery. Glen was gallant and complimented Marty on her dress, but she spoke as little as possible the whole evening.

After the dance, the four of them went to an ice cream shop in Arthur's car. Kate was gay and cheerful. Marty admired her for making the most of the present. But afterwards, when they drove back to campus, Arthur idled the car to keep it warm enough and he and Kate cuddled in the front seat, while Marty and Glen sat primly in the back.

Did a pastor's wife make out? Marty didn't know. She was too miserable to even make conversation. Unlike her high school sweetheart, Jim, Glen didn't put his hands on Marty's waist. He spoke quietly. Perhaps he didn't know what a prospective pastor did either. Most likely it was just too early for this kind of thing, Marty thought. She hardly knew Glen.

They were parked in front of the dorm. "I guess I'll walk you to the door," said Glen, finally, when it didn't seem that Arthur and Kate were going to stop kissing. He opened his door and Marty crawled out on his side. "Good night! Thank you!" they waved to the couple in the car.

Stumbling on her black high heels, Marty grabbed at Glen's arm, who courteously helped her. "Sorry," said Marty.

"You're so sweet," said Glen as they went arm in arm up the shoveled walk.

"It was a beautiful evening," she said, softly. "Thank you. If I don't see you before Christmas, I hope you have a wonderful time at home." She couldn't think of a single interesting thing to say.

"I'm sure I will," said Glen. "But not as much fun as I have here at school." He stood over her, looking down a little.

Marty smiled back, grateful that the evening was almost over. "Me too," she said. "'I have bought bread and I've been given red roses. How happy I am to hold both in my hands,'" she quoted. "When I go home, I'll bake bread!"

"Good!" said Glen. "I will think of you surrounded by your sisters and brother, having a good time." He pecked her on the cheek. "Good night," he said lightly. "Sleep well. Don't let the bedbugs bite."

Marty laughed. "Good night," she said. "Thank you so much for everything." She felt it with all her heart.

Line went to the library in the late afternoon and found Marty filing cards in the blonde wooden card catalog which took up a big space at the top of the marble stairs.

"Line!" whispered Marty. "I'm so glad to see you!"

"I'm going to wait for you," said Line, quietly. "Isn't the library closing soon?"

"Yes," said Marty.

"I'll be in the reading room, reading the newspapers," said Line, smiling and touching Marty on the shoulder.

Line went into the large room with its west-facing windows. The March sun had just set and banks of fluorescent lights were on, lighting the long rows of tables. At the edges of the room were reference shelves, and newspapers hanging on a rack, each threaded into a wooden stick.

Line laid out the two-day old *New York Times* across a table near her. On the front page was a photograph of a man in a white Stetson on a horse, clubbing a Negro freedom marcher in Alabama. In the *Des Moines Register*, she noted that a federal judge had ruled that the state of Alabama must allow and protect the marchers. For months now there had been coverage of brutality against Negroes trying to register to vote in Alabama.

When Marty arrived, turning off lights and clearing the tables in preparation for closing the library, Line showed her the photos. "Henry and Martin Berg are driving down to Alabama tonight, and I'm going with them!" she whispered dramatically.

"You what?" Marty looked shocked.

"Come on," said Line. "Let's have supper together and I'll tell you about it."

Line breathed in the cold air as she walked across campus with Marty in the twilight. Paths were wet and clean. Where snow was still on the ground, it was flecked with dirt and rivulets of water appeared under it. Blue-grey light spread across the sky as lights began to come on in the buildings.

"Isn't it the equinox almost?" asked Marty.

"Must be," said Line.

At a table they picked out near the edge of the dining room, their friends left Line and Marty, who were clearly having a sisterly talk, alone.

"What are you going to sign out to?" asked Marty. Girls at Wittenberg must state where they were going, and that they had permission to leave campus.

"I don't know," sighed Line. "I want to just be honest and say what I'm doing. There isn't time to ask for permission. I can't think of what else to do."

"Maybe just have messy handwriting?" questioned Marty.

"Yeah," said Line. "I'm so frustrated!"

"Didn't you say it was the same at Spelman, though?" asked Marty.

"It was," said Line. "But I'm 21 this year! When is anyone going to start trusting me? And when am I going to be able to do some good in the world?!"

"You're right," said Marty. "Just be honest. You can probably explain how important it is later."

"Henry doesn't have these problems," said Line. "He can do whatever he wants!"

"They're just trying to protect us girls," said Marty gently.

"Oh! Here comes Miss Goody Two-shoes!" said Line sarcastically. "Spare me your platitudes, please."

"It's just that I see both sides of the question," said Marty. "You know I always do."

"Sorry, Marty," said Line less stridently. "I know you support me. And thank you for listening. I'm sure we'll be fine. I just wanted someone to know what I'm up to, just in case."

"I admire you, Line," said Marty. "But I don't think the way you do. I'm kind of blind to what's going on in the world. All I do is study!" She diddled a fork on her empty plate. Resolutely, she looked up. "Line, Glen called me to break up."

"He what?" asked Line.

"He broke up with me, on the phone," said Marty. "I told Mother and Dad I was going out with him, and they wanted to come over and meet him. But they don't have to worry about it now!"

"And how do you feel about that?" asked Line.

"Terrible," admitted Marty. "He was so fun, and quirky, and cute! He was kind of like my twin. But maybe he'll change his mind and come around. I never seem to see him."

"I'm sure there's a better guy waiting out there somewhere for you," said Line loyally. "The perfect guy. Glen didn't say why he wanted to break up?" Marty did look a bit dowdy to her critical eye.

"Glen was the perfect guy!" cried Marty. "No, he didn't say why."

"There's some other girl involved," guessed Line. "Don't worry about it."

"I won't," said Marty, but she looked miserable.

"Don't tell Mother and Dad I'm going to Alabama," cautioned Line. "They'll find out when it's all over."

"I guess I can do that," said Marty. "You'll be back soon. How long does it take to get there?"

"Henry figures 16 or 17 hours. They're going to take turns driving. We're leaving tonight."

"Wow," said Marty. "I guess you'll get your chance to march after all!"

"Hope so! Want some ice cream?" asked Line. "I'll go get it."

"Sure," said Marty. "Why not?"

Line didn't have to ask Marty what flavor she wanted. Marty wanted vanilla with a dollop of chocolate in it. For herself, Line put a coffee cup under the percolator and opened the spigot. She put cream in her cup and took several packets of sugar. Fortifications, she thought. Who knew if she would sleep that night.

In fact, Line was so tired that she did sleep in the back seat of Henry's Chevy. They had brought blankets, and Line the little blue train case that accompanied her everywhere, packed with toothpaste and fresh underwear and blouses. Even nylons. She remembered how proper everyone in Atlanta looked when they went out.

It wasn't hard to find the Old Brown Chapel in Selma. Throngs of people milled about in front of it, many of them singing, while white men in hard hats with batons and sticks stood nearby. Henry parked the car a couple of blocks away and the three walked toward the church, feeling very white, blonde and Norwegian. "Yankee trash, go home," Line heard a man say.

On street corners stood soldiers in olive drab holding rifles with bayonets on them. "Feds," said Henry, low.

Inside the church Line, Henry and Martin struggled to find someone to listen to them. The room was full of people. Organizers sat at tables with packs of cards in front of them, writing, talking, shouting to each other. Line stood in the welter of people, trying to make sense of the scene.

A young white man at a table gestured Line toward him, and she dragged Henry and Martin with her.

"Okay," said the young man, his thin body electric with activity. "You guys are a little late to the party, but no one's going to turn you away." He looked at Line with a steady, deep gaze.

Line smiled back at him. "Just let us know what we can do," she said.

"You can stay at this address," the young man said, writing it down on a card. "Hope you've got blankets. There aren't any beds left. Understand you won't be marching. Only 300 people get to make the whole march through Lowndes County. You can walk at the beginning, and continue with the marchers when they get to Montgomery."

Line noticed his East Coast accent. He wore a blue shirt and his belt was the only thing holding a worn pair of pants up on his thin hips. His hair was curly and a little too long.

"I'm Stephen, by the way," he said and held out a hand.

"I've got a 16mm camera," said Henry, smoothing the wave in his hair nervously. "I just got back from Little Rock, and some of my film work was on television. I was planning on filming things."

"Good," said Stephen. "The press contingent is over there. You can get your assignment from them." He looked at Line, inquiringly.

"Anything you need," said Line sturdily. "I'm good at listening," she smiled.

"Lots of people are working on food. The medical team is based in a van outside. Why don't you ask them if they need help." Stephen pointed out the door.

"Thank you," murmured Line. She stepped back to get out of the way.

Martin, who had been quiet, said ominously as the three of them moved out of the church, "We've got to stick together. This is quite a scene!"

"We're going to stay at the same house!" said Henry, impatiently. "We'll find each other. Stick with me and we'll see if we can help the press group."

"Let's find out where the house will be, and where to park the car and stuff," said Martin, his Midwestern caution getting the better of him.

"Don't worry," said Henry. "We stick out like sore thumbs! Not much blonde hair around here! But maybe we should take our stuff over to the house first and then come back and volunteer."

Line listened to them. But something inside her was sinking like a stone to the bottom of a stream. She felt still in the middle of the milling people, with the sounds of singing all around. She could see the white medical van parked at the corner, MCHR painted in red letters on its side. She was in the right place, where she ought to be.

To confirm this, a magnolia with thick green leaves, crowned with big white blossoms, marked the corner at the Baptist minister's house whose address Stephen had given them. Line stood, looking at it, while Henry and Martin knocked at the door of the white frame house. No one came, but the house was near the Brown Chapel, so they left the car and went back through the crowds, sticking together for safety.

Henry and Line walked the first seven miles of the march the next day, but Martin drove the car, because most of the people were going back to Selma and needed transportation. By the time the march got to the first campsite, it was dark and frightening, impossible to tell friend from foe. Somehow, with a car full of people, Martin made it back to Selma.

That night Line helped out at the Brown Chapel where the Medical Community for Human Rights had left a few nurses. She listened to people's needs and pointed out where they could best get help. She was saddened by the state of people's shoes, and wished she had some to give. But her own shoes, just little flats, weren't in much better shape. She thought of the people who were going to walk 50 miles in broken shoes patched with tape. These people really wanted to register to vote!

For the next three days, while 300 people marched across Lowndes County, Line felt useless. One morning she went with Martin, who drove the car on the dirt side roads, getting into position for Henry to film the marchers. The area was much less well off than the farm counties Line knew in North Dakota and Iowa. Houses were often shacks with tin roofs, outhouses behind them. But the faces of the people who came out and stood along the highway watching the marchers were joyful.

Sentries with rifles stood all along the road and helicopters flew over the route, protecting marchers from the white hecklers with confederate flags cruising the roads. But white students on side roads were not protected. All three of them were amazed at the hatred they heard in the voices of the poor white farmers, who had lived all their lives beside Negroes. Martin was frightened, and after a standoff with a pickup, when someone fired a shotgun, he refused to drive anywhere.

At night, in the pastor's house in Selma where she bedded down in an upstairs hall, Line found herself in line for the bathroom next to Stephen, the young activist who found them places to sleep. Toothbrushes in their hands, they started a conversation.

"I've been down in Mississippi," said Stephen. "Teaching reading to kids and convincing them that they have rights. Nothing more rewarding. But we can't stay there forever either."

"Are you in SNCC?" asked Line, wondering if Stephen was part of the legendary Student Non-violent Coordinating Committee which had planned many demonstrations and was now working, somewhat uncomfortably, with Martin Luther King's Southern Christian Leadership Conference. Gossip swirled about who was getting along with whom and who was doing what.

"Nope," said Stephen. "Students for a Democratic Society. I'm based in Chicago, working on some projects up there and going to school. I'll be going back soon." The bathroom door opened and Stephen gestured graciously to Line, "Your turn!"

But once started, the conversation continued. The next day, at the Brown Chapel, while people milled about, Line sat with Stephen at a table, talking. She learned that he had grown up in Brooklyn, that his parents were Jewish, his mother in public health and his dad an immigration lawyer. They were determined second generation Jews, and Stephen left New York to find out what the rest of the world, outside his insulated neighborhood, was like.

"Me too!" said Line.

In everything else, they were opposites. Stephen was amazed to find that Line had four sisters and a brother. "My mother was hysterical enough about me," he said. "Another one would probably have killed her!"

Line was amazed to hear herself defending Wittenburg College, and Spelman. In Stephen's world, the venerable schools such as Harvard and Yale were the standards by which everything was judged. Even the well-endowed University of Chicago, where he went, didn't have a reputation as solid as the East Coast schools.

Line had never really thought about it. "The point of an education is to get you out of the house and on your way into life. It doesn't really matter where you go. Education is up to you!" she said hotly. "It's what you make of it."

"Maybe," Stephen pulled back a little, looking at her out of the corners of his eyes. "But if you go to a good school they can certainly help you on your way!"

Line was nonplussed. "I guess if you're ambitious," she said. "The most important thing to me is to learn where I can do some good. I really like working with the MCHR people! It feels like I am actually doing something."

"Maybe you should become a doctor," said Stephen. "Like Dr. Howell. She's great!" He mentioned one of the young women on the medical team.

"I do need training," sighed Line. "I thought I'd be in social work, because women can do that kind of thing. Or at least that's what women expect to do. To become teachers and social workers. But there isn't money for me to go to medical school. There are four more kids after me!"

Two students came up to Stephen and asked where they could use a telephone. When they left, Line continued. "I'm not really such a good student either," she said. "My sister Marty is the intellectual in the family. She loves studying, but I don't really care which German philosopher said what!"

Stephen laughed. "Well, why should you." He whispered, "She's not here is she?"

"No," said Line. "I tagged along because Henry had a car, and he talked Martin into coming. While I was at Spelman things were kind of quiet and I never had a chance to demonstrate. I love being around the Movement, but I don't feel like I'm doing much of use."

"SNCC people are beginning to act like they don't need us," said Stephen. "And I think they're right. It was useful for us to be in Mississippi, just for black and white people to see each other and work together. But in SDS, we're setting up projects to work on poverty in the cities. And also we need to fight America's imperialist activity all over the world. SDS is gearing up for a big anti-war march next month in Washington."

"Are you going?" asked Line. "And what's SDS again? There's so many acronyms. I can't keep them all straight!"

"Yes," laughed Stephen. "After King gets to Montgomery, I'm going to New York to work on that march. SDS is Students for a Democratic Society. It's mostly white college students. I've learned a lot from working with SNCC, though. Some really great people," he said musingly.

"But how do you live?" asked Line.

"I'll stay with my parents in Brooklyn," said Stephen. "But there's always people to stay with in the Movement, and money from somewhere. I'm working on a Master's degree too."

For a moment, Line remembered that she too would have to go back to school, to Wittenberg. She hadn't expected to be gone so long. By this time, she really was absent without leave. But I won't think about that now, she told herself.

By the next day, most of the Movement people in Selma had moved on to Montgomery, getting ready to march in the final leg of the journey to the capitol. Henry, Martin and Line packed the car full of people and took off up the highway the marchers had just covered on foot in three days.

When they got to the outskirts of Montgomery, everyone piled out and marched with the protesters the few miles to the City of St. Jude Catholic hospital complex, where they were to camp for the night. They couldn't get close to the original marchers, but freedom songs and chants never stopped as the group's numbers grew.

Line was well rested when they got to St. Jude, wearing the best clothes she could put together. She had saved a fresh blouse and a new pair of nylons. It was chilly in the evening and she was glad to have a coat.

Line found the MCHR tent and again tried to point people in the right direction for help. The stories she heard were tough. Cold, sleet, driving rain and aching feet beleaguered the marchers. The food was cold when it got to them, and the fields they camped in muddy. The athletic field at St. Jude was muddy too, and the tents were falling down! But they were almost there. Spirits, swelled by the huge crowd, were high.

Martin tried to talk some sense into his compatriots. "We've got to get back to school! After this convocation at the capitol, we've got to drive home!" he said. "Now, where will I find you?"

Henry was still bound and determined to get as much onto film as he could. He wanted to rove about, but promised to meet the other two at the edge of the MCHR tent for the march in the morning, and they would all walk together.

Thousands of people were collecting on the spacious, muddy athletic field. After dark, Stephen showed up at the hospital tent, where Line was talking to people. "Come on," he said. "There's not much more you can do here." Amplified voices could be heard in the distance.

Stephen led Line toward a makeshift stage. "Harry Belafonte pulled all these people together for a concert," said Stephen. "I heard the stage is built on coffins borrowed from funeral homes!"

All that evening, Peter, Paul and Mary, Joan Baez, Odetta, Pete Seeger, Dick Gregory and so many others Line had heard of, but never seen live, sang and spoke on behalf of freedom. The power was tremendous and seemed to go on forever. Line and Stephen sat on a blanket, and Stephen put first one arm, and then both around Line while they listened.

"You're going back tomorrow, aren't you," said Stephen.

"Yes," said Line. "After the convocation. It'll be Thursday tomorrow, right?"

"Write me here," he said, giving Line a slip of paper. "It's my parents' house."

"Okay," said Line. She put it in her handbag. "You know where I'll be. I'll be at Wittenberg, facing the music," she smiled sardonically.

"I've never met anyone like you," said Stephen.

"Me either," said Line. "I don't care if I sleep tonight. I don't want this to ever end."

"We'll keep each other warm," said Stephen.

In the morning, Stephen and Line met Henry and Martin at the hospital tent. They could see the jostling for position that was going on at the front as marchers tried to line up. Finally the original 300 marchers, in orange vests, led the procession out, with Dr. King behind them. Much later, the four fell in behind, sticking together, but surrounded by Negroes from all over the South, mostly poor people dressed in their Sunday best.

Line listened to the soft voices, trying to tune in to English she wasn't used to. She could understand when she was spoken to, but the babble of voices all around made it difficult. Singing began up in the front and passed back into the crowd. "Mine eyes have seen the glory of the coming of the Lord. He is trampling out the vintage where the grapes of wrath are stored!" Surging voices accompanied the sounds of feet, thousands of feet shuffling along the road.

A rain shower pattered on people's heads, fast, cold and then went away. Line shivered, walking at the edge of the crowd, looking down the streets at the trees. "Free-Dom! Free-Dom!" cried the marchers. Everywhere trees full of white and pink blossoms lifted flower faces into the rain.

The streets were strangely empty of people. But the trees softened the anger Line was afraid was hidden in the beautiful suburban houses. She couldn't believe everyone was as angry as the people she heard screaming, "Nigger lover" and "I hate niggers!" They should come out and march, thought Line. Open themselves.

Line asked Stephen, walking beside her, "Are those dogwoods?" The trees covered with blossoms were like clouds from a distance.

"Yeah, I think so," said Stephen. "About the right time for them."

Magnolia trees too lined the streets, alive with large, waxy blooms. Line wanted to run up to the flowering trees and look closely at them, touch them, but she felt she must not. Guards in army green carrying rifles lined the streets. The sounds of helicopter rotors beat against the air above them.

Line's feet ached in her little flat shoes which weren't much protection against the road. But she could see the cracks in other people's cheap leather shoes. People were pulling their damp coats around them.

"How far do we go this morning?" she asked Stephen. She was sailing along happily, as if she could go on forever.

"Well, we've come a couple of miles. I think there's another couple of miles to go," he said. He was wearing sturdy boots made for hiking under his ragged trousers.

On and on went the smiling crowds, singing. Young people danced and horsed around as they got close to their destination. Finally they turned on to Dexter Avenue, the main business street. "That's where Rosa Parks got arrested," Line heard someone say as they passed a bus stop. Wave after wave of marchers turned to look as the word went down the line.

"I heard she's up ahead. That was a long time ago!" Henry said. He hung back, holding the camera up to his eye. But no one was at the bus stop and the streets were eerily quiet and empty.

"Think how she must feel," said Line to Stephen. They were in the business district now, with stores lining the streets. Line could see the white capitol building up ahead topped with an arched rotunda. Classical Greek columns lined the front portico.

"This was the first capitol of the Confederacy," said Stephen to Line. "Jefferson Davis was sworn in here."

Lines of state troopers guarded the capitol area. People ahead were stopping and slowing. There wasn't any room to push forward. Up ahead, on a flatbed truck, with huge speakers facing into the crowd, Odetta climbed up to sing. "One more time," she smiled out into the crowd, her cropped black curls topped with a lovely silk scarf. "This little light of mine, I'm gonna let it shine." All around her Line heard the crowd take up the song and she too sang with Odetta's powerful voice coming over the speakers.

At last Dr. King took his place on the truck. The crowd grew very quiet as he spoke and Line could hear every word. Stephen's head was up and alert as Dr. King described the social history which emerged after the civil war, how wages were kept low by the Bourbon interests. How a populist movement which tried to unite poor Negroes and whites was put down by the aristocracy, which spread a belief in white supremacy and made laws which created segregation throughout the South.

It was a long speech and people were tired, but King went on, and on, his words rolling like thunder over the listening crowd.

He went on to honor those who fought and sometimes died for freedom, and insisted that people would continue to march against segregated housing, schools and against poverty. "The only normalcy that we will settle for is the normalcy that allows justice to run down like water, and righteousness like a mighty stream," he said.

"Yes," said Line, to herself, watching Stephen's open, shining face beside her. "Yes."

"I know you are asking today, How long will it take?" Dr. King continued. "I come to say to you this afternoon, however difficult the moment, however frustrating the hour, it will not be long, because 'truth crushed to earth will rise again.'" People murmured in response. "How long? Not long, because the arc of the moral universe is long, but it bends toward justice."

Tears streamed down Line's cheeks as she opened to the promise of the future which Dr. King's words painted in the air, above the people who were making it happen.

22

On Saturday night, Paul was browning hamburger in a big black iron skillet, smashing down the frozen pink clumps with a fork. The rich smell of beef fat rose around him as it heated. Mother was typing up the church bulletin for tomorrow's service on a mimeograph stencil in the study. Hearing a commotion in the front hall, Paul turned off the stove and went out to look. Who should be standing there, but Line!

Flushed and disheveled, she asked Dad whether she could get a ride back to college on Sunday night. When Dad agreed, she raced back out to the car she had arrived in to talk to someone. All five of them, Dad, Mother, Paul and his little sisters, stood in the front hall, letting in the cold March air and watching.

The older Mikkelsons had been wondering about Line's whereabouts all week. When pressed, as the college called Dad to find out, Marty told them Line had gone down to Selma to help Dr. King try to get voting rights for Negroes. Paul, Dad and Mother watched the 10 p.m. news every night on television, knowing that Line was somewhere in the crowd of people marching in Alabama. The news showed the helicopters, the armed guards, the marchers and hecklers, and white celebrities coming out to help.

When Dr. King spoke on Thursday night in his soft Southern accent, Paul could see why Line might take off after him without a backward look. He looked young and inspiring. "I know you are asking today, how long will it take? How long? Not long, because no lie can live forever," he said. "Mine eyes have seen the glory of the coming of the Lord!" he said. "Glory, Hallelujah!" and the camera pulled back to show a photo of the white classical capitol building in Montgomery, and thousands of people shouting their own "Hallelujahs" in front of it.

Paul felt that Line was surely helping the cause of civil rights. Mother and Dad didn't say much, but Paul knew they were weighing the consequences of their restive daughter's leaving without permission with Line's accomplishment. They all hoped she wasn't hurt.

Everyone hugged Line when she came in. Hanna clamored to talk to her. "I can read!" she cried, reaching up her arms for Line to lift her up. "Can I read you a story?" Though she was only five, the Mikkelsons had been surprised to find Hanna reading to Kristen, who was three years older.

Line took off her coat and picked up Hanna. Kissing the little girl's short blonde curls, she said, "I'm so dirty. I haven't had a bath or a shower in a week!" Paul could see that her clothes were wrinkled, her red-gold hair mussed, and the muscles around her eyes drooping, but her face shone as it always did.

"Go ahead," said Mother. "Hanna, let Line take a bath and then you can read to her after supper. Line, when you come down you can tell us all about your trip."

Paul took Hanna from Line's arms and Kristen by the hand. Line went up the wooden staircase, leaning over the banister to say. "I'm so glad to see you all! You have no idea! But it was a wonderful trip!"

That would have to do them until supper. Dad and Mother went back into the study. The little girls went into the living room where they were playing with an ancient set of tattered Author cards, and Paul went back to the kitchen.

That night, after supper, Mother shooed the little girls upstairs to take their baths and Dad said, "The dean of the college called me to ask about you. I'm glad you stopped here on your way, but I think we should go up on Monday and talk to him."

"What do you think might happen?" asked Line, looking chagrined.

"I'm hoping nothing," said Dad. "But you will have to explain yourself."

"I just couldn't pass up the chance," said Line. "Henry was so anxious to go, and we've both been down South and seen how things are." She looked back at Dad. "Do you think Henry and Martin will get in trouble? Or is it just girls who are supposed to obey their 'rules'?" she asked sarcastically.

Paul stood up to clear the table. Conflict made him nervous, but he was glad to be one of the "grownups" in the family, discussing things.

Dad tried to dampen Line's temper. "I don't know," he said evenly. "We'll see on Monday."

"It would have helped if you had told us you were going," said Mother gently.

"I'm sorry you worried. I didn't really think we'd be gone so long!" said Line. She yawned and stretched her long, thin arms high, as if she too had been tense.

"Are you sure this is your fight?" asked Dad. "How do these people feel about someone like you barging into their lives?"

Line looked at him, startled. "No one in Washington seems to pay any attention to the civil rights struggle unless there are white people involved. Alabama doesn't want Negroes to vote. The governor has put up all kinds of resistance, and President Johnson had to get involved."

"Well," said Dad, smiling. "You are your father's daughter, I can tell. I was a hot-head once myself."

Paul watched, glad of this resolution. It sounded as if Line would be able to explain herself and Dad would support her.

But Mother had the last say, as usual. "Line, please don't do anything like this again! We were so worried! You know we support you." She pulled Line toward her, hugging her.

"Oh my goodness," said Line, enveloped in Mother's arms. "I'm so glad to be home!"

Paul was thrilled she was home too. The next day, after Line had gotten some sleep and the Sunday services and dinner were over, he took out his guitar. He wanted to show Line what happened whenever he did. As soon as she heard Paul's hands on the strings, Hanna stood up from playing and came up beside him, waiting for music and ready to sing!

"What shall we do for Line?" Paul asked. He was working on the guitar arpeggios in "The House of the Rising Sun," a song Dennis was determined they learn because he wanted to sing just like the Animals had done it. In fact, after hearing the brash Brit sing, Paul realized that Dennis thought he was Eric Burdon! But the words were too risqué for his little sisters. He didn't want to sing about gambling and drinking in front of them.

Strumming simple minor chords, Paul began, "I am a poor wayfaring stranger," and the bright little blonde girl, standing beside him, turned around to face her audience and began to sing along, "just traveling through this world of woe. But there's no sickness, toil nor danger, in that bright land to which I go." Hanna looked solemn, singing the sorrowful words, but her round pink face looked far too alive.

Line sat on the floor beside Kristen looking up at them, her face opening in disbelief. "Look at you!" she said, when Paul and Hanna had finished. Hanna smiled and dipped her head, as she had seen people do on *Hootenanny*.

"I love that one," said Paul, "because you keep changing from one gloomy chord to another." He laughed, strumming E minor, and then A minor. He listened and reached around to the tuning pegs, twisting them to tighten the strings.

"That's amazing," said Line. "You little sweetheart!" she said to Hanna, who stood there in her play clothes, dark corduroy jeans and a tee-shirt, her eyes dancing.

"Let's do the bucket song," said Paul. The bucket song didn't even really need a guitar, but he struck up simple chords as he sang. "There's a hole in the bucket, dear Liza, dear Liza," he sang, looking at Hanna.

"Then fix it, dear Henry, dear Henry," sang the little girl imperiously. "Fix it!" The song went on and on, and Hanna knew the whole thing, becoming more sardonic as the lazy man singing tried one excuse after another. "Try water, dear Henry, dear Henry," said the little girl.

"In what shall I fetch it, dear Liza, dear Liza," sang Paul to Hanna wickedly.

Hanna slapped Paul's knee, dramatically, "In a bucket, dear Henry, dear Henry, dear Henry."

Paul waited, watching his audience for effect, and then circled back. "There's a hole in the bucket, dear Liza, dear Liza, a hole!"

Line laughed and laughed, and Kristen did too, even though she had heard it many times.

"Can you do 'We shall overcome,'" Line asked Paul. She began singing and Paul struggled for chords to match. It too didn't need much backing. They had all heard it sung by crowds of people a capella.

"Don't start it too high," said Line.

Paul tried a straightforward C chord, which seemed to work.

"Come on Kristen," said Line, standing up. "We can all sing this one." She stood beside the little girls. "We'll walk hand in hand, we'll walk hand in hand, we'll walk hand in hand some day." She was swaying back and forth and the little girls followed. "O-o-o-oh, deep in my heart, I do believe, we'll walk hand in hand some day."

"Oh Paul," said Line. "I wish you had been there. Such hope, such determination and such joy in people's faces!"

Line held the little girls' hands, Kristen reaching almost to her shoulder and little Hanna half a head less. His very own sisters, Paul thought. Kristen was solid and chunky, and Hanna had a lightness about her, flitting variously around like a butterfly. It was wonderful that Line was there!

As twilight fell, Paul and Line snuck out the door together taking Foxy for a walk around the block. Paul always loved getting out of the house. Much as he was fascinated by animals hibernating and trees and plants going dormant in the winter, spring was an unfolding of life that enthralled him. Paul could smell the new green leaves, the blossoming apple trees. The sun did it, going down a little bit later every day. Paul was trying to go out with Foxy at the same time every evening, so he could see the light lengthening.

"We're eating oatmeal on Wednesday nights now, during Lent," Paul said, trying to capture Line's attention, "and we're planning a seder during Easter week."

"A seder? That's interesting," Line said. "I met a Jewish guy this week." But she was also having a strong reaction to the balmy spring air, breathing it in and spinning around with her arms above her head as if she had never been outdoors in her life. "Paul, don't you feel something's about to happen? Something important?" she asked.

"Sure thing!" said Paul. "Spring's here, school's almost out. Dad and I are going to take the canoe out to the slough one of these days."

"More than that," said Line. "Things happening in the world. There's a big march planned for next month, a march in Washington, D.C., against the war in Viet Nam."

Paul looked at her, shocked. "You're not going to it, are you?"

"No," said Line, dampened. "I have to settle down and finish the semester. But I'd like to go. There's a whole student movement happening out there! Not just in the South."

"I hear it in music," said Paul. "Dennis plays all these wild songs, like The Rolling Stones. He really likes the British invasion! Gets these magazines. But I don't tell Mom and Dad about it. I don't think they're so hot on rock and roll."

Line laughed. "To say the least!"

They walked back to the house, close once again, Foxy romping around them. Paul noticed a light in the window of the Sherwoods' house. Mr. Sherwood was probably reading. When they got home, Paul followed Foxy down to the basement to check her water and food.

The next night, when Paul and Mother got home from school, Line wasn't there. Dad said she had apologized to the Dean and pled a good case. Henry and Martin were back in school too. "Do you know who these guys are?" Dad asked Mother.

Mother rolled her eyes, as if to say, do any of us know anything about the wayward Line? But out loud she said, "We have to trust her, Carl.

She's a willful girl, but we've instilled our values in her. She's caught up in something right now, moving too fast. But she'll settle. I'm sure of it." Mother had always been Line's ally. She looked at Paul, "Did Line tell you anything about them?"

"Nope," said Paul. He tried to modify what Line had told him to reassure his parents. "She told me she wanted to settle down, finish the semester. I think she wants to work in Chicago again this summer."

"Yes," said Mother. "I gathered as much. She told me she might have a job in an old people's home as a social worker's assistant. That sounds like our Line."

"Yup," said Dad. "Little pitchers," he said, looking toward Kristen and Hanna, who looked back and forth with big eyes on the other side of the table. Kristen and Hanna were taking it all in. As people often said: "little pitchers have big ears."

"Good!" said Mother. "You'll be Line's age one day, won't you, Kristen. Finish your peas, Hanna!"

Paul practiced his guitar as much as he could that spring. Dennis and Michael, both a year older than he was, were graduating, and they had promised to play a few songs at their senior prom.

At Dennis' house, where they practiced, Dennis pulled out pop songbooks and records he had bought. "You can't dance to folk songs," he said. "But there are some things I think we could do." He popped a small black 45 rpm record on his phonograph and put down the needle.

"We'll sing in the sunshine," went the song. "We'll laugh every day, we'll sing in the sunshine and I'll be on my way," Dennis was singing along loudly and confidently. His feet moved back and forth as if he were dancing. "It's kind of like a farewell to high school," he said when it was over. "Some girl did it."

Paul didn't think it was worth much. "I will never love you, the cost of love's too dear," sang the girl with a jangly pop background. But at Dennis' house, Paul never said much. Usually Michael was the one who chimed in, agreeing or arguing with Dennis. Today Michael wasn't saying much either.

"So I think we could do this one," went on Dennis in the silence, "and 'The House of the Rising Sun' we've been working on. We can't do the Beatles, and I don't want to do too many, because there'll be a disc jockey and he can play the hits. I just want to do maybe one more," said Dennis. "So what do you think, Michael? Got any ideas? Dancing music?"

Michael sat on the daybed, his guitar slung across his shoulder, looking morose. "It's hard for me to think about. I got my letter today. I'm getting drafted."

That stopped Dennis cold. "Drafted?!"

"Well, hell," said Michael. "What'd I expect?! I'm not going to school. They're calling up people left and right. Did I think they weren't gonna call me?"

Dennis sat down beside him. "Drafted!"

"Yep," said Michael. "I have to report to Fort Des Moines by June 10. Sorry, boys. Dennis and the Dots is about over."

Paul watched the two men, who despite their great differences from himself, felt like his friends. It was a shock, though he had wondered if the group would play together after they graduated. Drafted. It was a terrible word, like a prison sentence. But Paul knew they would never take a person who had had polio. He wouldn't have to personally worry about it. It was the only good thing he could think of about polio.

"God!" said Dennis. "Jesus! It makes me wonder what to do. It's coming up so quick! But you'll be fine, man," he said, turning to Michael. "You'll be fine."

"Yep," said Michael. "Take my guitar and get on out. See what happens."

"Guitar's a good thing anywhere," said Dennis. "It'll keep you out of trouble."

"Elvis got to drive around Germany and France when he was a soldier," said Michael. "Had a great time. Funny, I don't think that'll be me. Since we're at war and all."

"That was the marines going to southeast Asia!" said Dennis. "Not the army." The news had been full of the deployment of the first combat troops in Viet Nam.

"Well, anyway," said Michael. "Hard to think about dance music." He slapped his banjo and it shivered into life.

"Yup, you're right," said Dennis. "Be right back." He went upstairs and returned with three beers from the refrigerator.

"Not for me, thanks," said Paul. It was starting to happen. Beers handed to him. But he hadn't tasted beer yet. Didn't want to. He was remembering Dad's story about cigarettes, Dad figuring out that he could save a lot of money if he didn't smoke.

Dennis opened two of them deftly with a church key, and said "Here's to you, mate. Best of luck!" He and Michael clinked their cans against each other and drank.

So that was the end of that afternoon. Paul wandered home, gloomy in spite of the April sunshine that blazed out of the heavens. "I'll sing to you each morning, I'll kiss you every night, but darling don't cling to me, I'll soon be out of sight," ran through his head.

When they drove the Lark out to the high school the next morning, Paul asked Mother, "Why are popular songs so mean?" He loved the fact that he got Mother to himself briefly each day when he drove to school. Mother could now drive herself, and she sometimes drove home if Paul had extra-curricular activities. But they often went home together too.

Mother laughed. "That is a very good question. I don't know," she said. "But I do know that the reason we have such great songs in the church is because of inspiration. Like the scriptures, they inspire us not to be petty and mean."

"Dennis keeps picking these mean songs," said Paul.

"Well, Dennis caters to an audience," said Mother. Dennis was in her English classes. "I don't think badly of him for it. I understand. But I am glad to hear he isn't a role model for you!"

"No," sighed Paul. "Michael's getting drafted. Dennis and the Dots will be over after graduation."

"Hmmmmm," said Mother. "I'm not sorry. I think you've learned something from singing with them, but I'm sure you'll go on to better things, Paul."

It was Mother who came up with the idea for the seder, the Passover meal celebrated by Jews during Holy Week. She had heard that other Lutheran churches were doing it. Paul did a lot of the research, finding books in the school library.

Holy week, the week before Easter, was always full for Dad. There were services all week. At the Good Friday services, the candles would be extinguished and the altars of the two churches Dad served would be covered with black cloths.

On Maundy Thursday night, the Mikkelsons sat down to a Passover meal. The table was laid with Mother's best lace cloth and china. Down the middle of the table were placed four cups of Welch's grape juice, which served as wine, as well as plates of food and a bowl of salt water. Dad, as the leader, lifted the cut glass goblet of grape juice and invoked the

Lord's blessing upon the meal. He passed the glass around and each person had a sip.

Hanna asked the first question, reading carefully from the booklet which Kristen had handwritten in her best printing on photocopy paper from school. Paul had made the half-sized paper booklets to read back to front, as he assumed Hebrew was, and copied them for each family member. "Why is this night different from all other nights?" she began in her small voice.

Dad explained that the Lord had decreed that one day should be set aside each year for the retelling of the story of how the Jews were led out of slavery in Egypt. "Paul, please read us the story," he said. Paul read from the book of Exodus how Moses, hidden by his mother when Hebrew babies were killed, interpreted plagues sent into Egypt by God's hand. Frightened, the Pharaoh allowed the Hebrews to leave. Moses led them out of Egypt and into Palestine, the Promised Land.

"Why do we eat only unleavened bread on this night?" asked Hanna, and Mother explained that there wasn't time for the yeast to rise on the bread, when they were fleeing Egypt. For the traditional matzoh, the Mikkelsons used Norwegian flatbread, thin crisp pieces of unleavened bread.

The questions continued, Kristen struggling with the unfamiliar words in the answers as the family quietly waited.

Finally Hanna asked, "Why do we usually sit at table, but on this night we recline?"

The Mikkelsons were not reclining, but, "We recline at the Seder table because in ancient times, a person who reclined at a meal was a free person, while slaves and servants stood," read Kristen.

"Line's trying to free the slaves," said Hanna, looking around tentatively. Everyone smiled.

Dad lifted another cup of grape juice after this, passing it along. He blessed the flat bread, and passed it. He passed a bowl of salt water and each of them dipped bitter dandelion greens in it, for gratefulness. After that they dipped sharp-tasting radishes in the charoset, which Paul had made from grated apples, walnuts and cinnamon, sweetening the burden of bitterness. Hanna's eyes lit up in surprise, as she tasted the horseradish, the maror.

Hard boiled eggs and venison ribs completed the meal. Dad thought that deer were close to goats or lamb, the main food of the

Israelites, and besides they had little other choice. They certainly couldn't eat the unclean Iowa pigs at a seder!

After every bite of the meal had been eaten, Dad passed around the third cup of wine and gave thanks.

"I'm so glad we did this," said Mother as the solemnity of the meal dissipated. "It helps me understand how many different traditions there are in the world."

"You know," Dad said, "Jesus gave of his body and blood at a Passover meal celebrated with his apostles. It's our tradition too. The Last Supper was a seder."

The Old Testament story of the Israelites being led out of Egypt was well known to all of them, but celebrating the seder felt unusual. Kristen and Hanna were quiet and respectful as each thing they ate was explained. Paul felt uplifted by it. He wasn't Jewish, exactly, but their traditions weren't at all foreign to him.

It was all the more jarring, therefore, when he was called back into the culture of the mean popular songs. Dennis called a few days later. "I got it!" came Dennis' excited voice. "Come on over. Michael's here and we've got the other song we're going to learn for the dance!"

At Dennis' house, Michael seemed to have stopped worrying about being drafted. "Okay," said Dennis when Paul arrived. "I know you've heard this one. It's an old one, but I think it'll work." He put the needle down on the 45 rpm record, and he and Michael listened as if they hadn't played it six times already.

"Now I'm the type of guy that'll never settle down," Paul listened to the scratchy, rowdy, but rhythmic song sung by Dion, trying to understand. "They call me the wanderer, yeah, the wanderer. I roam around and around and around."

"Oh man," said Michael. "That saxophone! We can't do that. That's so great!"

"See," said Dennis, showing them the chords on his guitar. "Here it is. D, and then G, and then A. That's it! It's easy! Listen." He put the needle down on his little record player and played the song again.

Dennis was dancing from foot to foot, and Paul too could tell that it was a great song to move to. Paul knew he'd heard it. He'd just never listened! And now he would have to play it. "And I'm as happy as a clown, with my two fists of iron, but I'm going nowhere!" Luckily, the guys in the background weren't even singing the words, they were just humming along, making music.

Paul laughed. It was such a Dennis song! Like the "The House of the Rising Sun." He knew enough about Dennis now to know. The next time Dennis put the needle down, Paul strummed along and so did Michael.

"What we really need is a drum kit," said Dennis, when they tried playing it by themselves without the record. "It's there, but a drum kit would pull it together."

Paul laughed again, helplessly, unable to keep his mirth to himself.

"What????" asked Dennis, too sharp to miss it. "What are you laughing at?"

"Nothing's going to stop you," blurted Paul. "You're going to get big, and nothing will stop it."

Dennis smiled. "Of course not! That's the idea!"

Nothing did stop him either. Dennis got another friend to put together a drum kit from the high school band, the Dots played their songs at the prom and everyone danced.

After their third song, Dennis announced, "This is a farewell for us, for Dennis and the Dots. We want to thank you for all the support you've given us, and all the fun!" he said. "Michael here is going off into the army, and I'm thinking of the Navy myself. My Daddy did it, I guess I got to do it too! No use waiting until Uncle Sam calls me!" He turned back toward the band, "So, one more time, for all of you! And for Valley High School! And the U.S. of A. Long may she reign!"

The Dots swung into "The Wanderer" again and Dennis sang, "Well, I'm the type of guy that likes to roam around, I'm never in one place, I roam from town to town."

Though he couldn't dance very well, Paul shifted from foot to foot. After the dance, it took him a while to settle down. He had to admit that, outside of canoeing on a spring evening in the twilight, it was as much fun as he could think of.

But then school was over, and the Dots were over.

Paul could hardly believe it. All that stood in front of him was summer at the lake. His own life. Life in the North Woods. He couldn't wait to get back to it.

Marty and Kate sat on the warm concrete of the balcony outside the student union, watching the sun slip behind the trees beyond the river.

"The clouds are so interesting," said Kate. She had followed Marty's lead and was taking summer classes, hoping to finish college early. The two girls were dressed casually in light button-down-the-front shirts and dark Bermuda shorts.

The sun set in a blaze of color beyond the dull green hills. Golden pink clouds tinged with purple were suddenly all that remained. Marty was thinking of Wordsworth, one of the writers in the English Romantic literature class they were taking. The Romantics liked clouds, sunsets, evening color.

Wordsworth described poetry as "powerful emotions recollected in tranquility," and it seemed to Marty that the summer might just be the tranquility she feared. She had only two classes plus working in the library 20 hours a week. She didn't expect to like the Romantic writers and she wasn't very interested in the psych class she was taking for her education minor. The summer did not feel full of possibility.

But she didn't want to tell Kate this. The evening star was growing bright and she pointed it out to Kate, "The evening star," she said. At that moment the carillon in the college chapel began to play the notes for "Beautiful Savior." The notes dropped slowly, resounding in the quiet air. "Fair are the meadows, Fair are the woodlands, Robed in flowers of blooming spring." The words welled up in Marty. She knew them so much better than any Romantic poetry. No one knew who had written them. "Jesus is fairer, Jesus is purer; He makes our sorrowing spirit sing."

At last the notes died away, leaving a peaceful hush. Kate, who was not a tranquil person, stood up and so did Marty. It was usually Kate who wanted to do something and Marty, for lack of a better idea, followed. A little like following Line around, Marty thought.

"The Scandinavians are going to be here next week," said Kate. "Now, we thought that you could move into a room with one of them, and one of them would move in with me."

"Okay," said Marty. Wittenberg was giving a seminar for Scandinavians who wanted to improve their English and study American literature. Kate was helping the Norwegian language teacher organize it.

"So do you want to move your things this weekend?" asked Kate. "I can figure out which room it is going to be."

"Sure," said Marty. It didn't really matter, she thought. Her own inner journey would go on, no matter what was going on in the world. And she was happy to be distracted.

"If you would just say what you are thinking," said Kate irritably as they walked. "I believe in saying what I think, in expressing myself."

Marty sighed, "I know you do." But Marty's thoughts were too jumbled, too confused. "I myself don't know what I think," she said. "I usually see both sides. And I don't really think I have to express all of it anyway."

"But you confuse people," said Kate. "You let them think that you agree with them if you don't state your own mind."

"I'm sorry," said Marty. She was anxious to be alone to sort things out in her head.

Early the next morning, Marty took the camera Aunt Mabel had given her, a simple Brownie camera with a black leather bellows which folded out in front of it, and walked out to the springs near campus where she and April had spent so much time the previous summer. Wordsworth did inspire her to walk. He had walked all over the parts of England where he lived.

Marty rarely had money for film. College was so expensive that money could only be used for books, or maybe shoes if she needed them. Clothes were often hand-me-down from cousins and other people. But that summer she felt daring enough to buy a roll of film.

The morning was wet and misty, the dew lay on the lower vegetation along the road, and droplets hung in the air. The sun made shining rays as it came through the trees. Marty hoped she could get a photograph of the rays. She loved walking by herself, her mind wandering.

Marty was not very interested in the short-lived poets Keats, Shelley and Byron, whose excesses in life produced beautiful poems. She was sure that compression, reality and restraint were just as fine as strong emotion in poetry. She planned to write her senior paper on Robert Frost, insisting he was a Classical poet, and comparing him to Theocritus, a bucolic Greek poet.

No one Marty knew agreed with her. Everyone seemed to prefer passion over reason as a way of living, Dionysian impulses over Apollonian. Marty kept her mouth shut. She didn't know how to defend her ideas anyway. But she found she liked Wordsworth as Mr. Moyer presented him. And she did have strong emotions, it was just that she was scared of expressing them. So far they only got her in trouble!

Who could she tell, for instance, about April? She had never felt so close to a person and been allowed to touch and fondle them. April wrote to her, missed her, was even planning on driving down to see her. But April was a girl. There was no future in their relationship.

And who would listen to how she now felt about Glen? Since he had called to tell Marty he didn't want to go out with her any longer, Marty had conceived a powerful love for him. He was the perfect person for her, an aspiring pastor with a quirky, wonderful sense of humor. Physically too, she thought, they were almost twins. She imagined that he was with her, walking up to Dunnings Springs. She thought about him all the time, but since she never saw him, there was nothing to tell.

Marty took a photograph of the light shining down through the trees by the road, hoping that it would get onto the film. She had taken one of Kate, sitting in a window with ivy growing over it, just Kate's profile, and one of the Martin Luther statue. It excited her to imagine the photographs that would result.

After taking the photograph of the trees, Marty put the camera back in her bag and walked slowly home. The sun was warm on her back as she walked and she already felt sweaty. But walking felt good. She tried to stay under the shade of the trees along the road. It was true, as she had heard, that education made you fit company for yourself. She enjoyed her own thoughts and had lots of time to recollect her feelings in tranquility. She wished they weren't somewhat mournful. It was shameful to be sad when she had so much to be thankful and grateful for.

Marty knew she could have told Line these contradictory feelings. But Line was in her beloved Chicago, working at an old people's home. Marty could write to her, but it wasn't much fun because Line never wrote back. I guess I could try, thought Marty.

Distraction helped, and the arrival of the Scandinavians was certainly that! There were thirty of them, mostly teachers, from Norway, Sweden, Denmark. All of them seemed to speak English well and Marty and Kate spent a lot of time with them, showing them around, picnicking, discussing their differences. The Swedes, the Danes and the Norwegians were quite contentious along nationalist lines, teasing and joking, often in their own languages.

A woman named Berit from Bergen, Norway, took the other bed in Marty's room. She was perhaps ten years older than Marty, but she wasn't a very happy person. In the group she was a leader, speaking for the others. But at night, when she and Marty occasionally talked, she did not indicate much joy or delight in life. It surprised Marty, and depressed her.

What did cheer Marty was babysitting for the Magnussons' daughter Thea. Marty was invited for dinner. It was a hot day and Marty was sweaty after walking up the hill to the house. Mrs. Magnusson, looking cool in a sleeveless dark cotton dress, put ice into glasses of lemonade and set them on a tray.

Marty carried the tray out to the back yard. A picnic table was set out under a big tree on the lawn with a tablecloth. Little Thea, her long blonde hair plaited into braids, helped carry trays of ceramic dishes, bread, salad. Thea wore a simple dress of the same material as Irene Magnusson's. Clearly Irene had made them both.

Thea was quite ready to explain her projects for the summer. "I'm in Brownies," she said. "We're going camping next week. I'm going to learn how to make a fire!"

"Camping!" Marty said. "Where are you going?"

"It's a scout camp. I don't know where it is," Thea explained. She looked to her mother for confirmation.

"It's out near the river, south of town," said Irene Magnusson, watching her daughter fondly. "They're just going for one night, but it's exciting. They have to bring a bedroll. You've never stayed overnight away from home, have you Thea?"

"No," said Thea, her eyes large. "But Becky will be there. And Andrea, our scout leader. I won't be scared."

"No, I'm sure you won't be," said Irene. "Go call Papa for dinner," she said, and Thea went upstairs to the study where Dr. Magnusson was working on a book. Marty had seen the small, wood-paneled room lined with bookcases. The great, brown-shingled house which had felt so European to Marty in the winter, was dark and cool in the summer. Big trees shaded the yard both in front and back.

Dr. Magnusson was relaxed, in a shirt open at the neck. Everyone sat down, talked. Thea too must sit with the grownups and talk. Everything about the meal fit together. The food, the dishes, they way they were dressed. To Marty, it felt like a different way to live.

The Magnusson's were just back from a sabbatical in Europe. Dr. Magnusson consulted with philosophers in Germany on a book he was writing and they had also gone down to Greece.

Marty was still quite shy around Dr. Magnusson, but Mrs. Magnusson put everyone at ease, making her family by knitting them together. As the hostess, she drew out Marty, the guest. She was interested in the Scandinavians who were studying on campus and in Mr. Moyer, the visiting instructor for Marty's class in the Romantic poets. Marty was surprised to find herself talking about the senior paper she would write next year.

Dr. Magnusson talked about his book, which he described as response to the recent rebellion against religion. "What does modern man make of the gospel? That's the question. The gospel tells what happens with Jesus. We need a contemporary way of telling that story," he said.

Marty, as usual, couldn't help but agree. But she didn't have any ability to discuss it. Mrs. Magnusson rescued her, bringing them back to the present. "We're just going to a movie," she said. "We'll be back by 10 p.m. or so. Thea can read to you before she goes to bed, but don't worry too much if it gets late."

"What are you reading?" asked Marty.

"*The Lion, the Witch and the Wardrobe*," said Thea.

"Oh good! I haven't read it," said Marty.

Everyone picked up something from the table and carried it into the kitchen. "You're going to have to call me Irene," said Mrs. Magnusson playfully as they moved into the house, and Marty flashed her a grateful smile.

It was cool enough by this time for Marty and Thea to play indoors. They arranged all the chairs in the family room and covered them with blankets to make a series of tents in which various dolls would live.

Crawling around on the floor with Thea was a way for Marty to get back to her own secure childhood. She suspected that Thea's parents might not think it educational enough, but Marty thought make-believe a good thing for kids. Thea already had enough grownups around her.

On Sunday, the Scandinavians dressed up in their national costumes and Marty went to church with them. The women wore dirndl skirts with aprons, lovely white blouses and vests which were pulled tight with bodice strings to cinch in their waists. Some of them wore the lovely gold jewelry known as solje, delicate filigreed silver work with drops of gold plate. The men wore white shirts and short trousers with woolen socks. The colors and patterns of the outfits differed by region, according to Berit.

At the downtown Lutheran church, the pastor acknowledged the group and they all stood up together and sang a hymn. Marty knew they liked singing together, but she also knew that getting the Swedes, Danes and Norwegians to do anything together wasn't easy!

When they got home, Marty photographed the group in their national costumes and then used the few photographs remaining on her roll to take pictures of the group having a picnic lunch. They were so beautiful together. Marty hoped the photographs would turn out!

Kate was learning hardanger from Mrs. Herseth, the wife of the Norwegian teacher. Marty loved the white work, in which Kate was picking out certain threads and embroidering other parts of the weave with white satin stitches. It was named after the area of Norway it came from, and used in the lovely white blouses of the national costumes, on tablecloths and towels.

At night, when they lay in bed talking after the lights were out, Marty asked Berit about the Scandinavian rivalries. Berit said that in a way it was a friendly, sibling rivalry, but that also, everyone in Scandinavia had long memories. She explained that Norway was once governed by Denmark. "For 400 years!" she said.

When Denmark was on the losing side in the war of 1812, Norway was ceded to Sweden. That was when the Norwegians said, "Enough!" They won their independence from Sweden, not by battle, but by negotiation, and celebrated on May 17. Marty had always heard about "Syttende Mai" but didn't know who Norway had become independent from.

After this, Norway still shared a king with Sweden for almost 100 years, until they chose their own king in 1905, when Sweden and Norway finally separated. Norway had something of a "poor relation" complex. They were conservative and poorer economically, but very proud of their own cultural heroes, Grieg, Hamsun, Munch and Ibsen. "You should read Sigrid Undset," said Berit. "You would like her. She writes historical novels."

Marty took note. Berit didn't seem to be much of a reader, but perhaps Marty should pay more attention to her Norwegian heritage.

"During the war," Berit said. "Norway was invaded and suffered greatly. My own father was on a ship sunk by the German subs. Sweden, by contrast, was supposedly neutral, but they helped the Germans make weapons."

Marty could hear the sarcasm thick in Berit's description of the Swedish "neutrality." Now she understood a little bit of Berit's melancholy temper. Berit had no brothers and sisters and was the major support of her mother. She must have been a child during the war, that bleak, horrible time that Marty could not even imagine, Berit's hopes and zest for life dampened forever.

The talk helped Marty understand the vicious jokes the Scandinavians made about each other, the worst of which they didn't translate! In the post-war world, the Scandinavian countries prospered. From the outside they might appear alike, but among themselves, in deadly earnest, they defended their own lands and histories.

Marty didn't have trouble figuring out where her own sympathies in the Scandinavian conflict lay. Mother's father, the grandfather Marty never knew, had grown up in Denmark. Her other grandparents were all from Norway, born in America. In high school, Marty had learned about the Danish writer, Isak Dinesen, and her wonderful book *Out of Africa*. Marty loved Dinesen's stories and the story of her life.

Even after being at Wittenberg, a thoroughly Norwegian American college, Marty didn't feel she knew much about Norway. But she identified with the Norwegians, and their droll, wry humor, their love of the natural world and their independence. Perhaps the Swedes shared their characteristics, but Marty doubted it. She was perfectly happy to be prejudiced against the Swedes!

The weekend April drove down from the Twin Cities, Marty found her an empty room in the dorm. The two girls had corresponded since the previous summer, but they hadn't seen each other. On Friday, Marty's skin prickled with anticipation, wondering whether April would be the same as before. She couldn't settle down to anything.

When April arrived in the long light of the late afternoon, Marty was sitting on the steps of the dormitory, waiting for her. The old blue Chevy parked briefly in front of the dorm and Marty jumped in on the passenger side. April looked older, just as beautiful, her chiseled face less soft than Marty remembered. She was wearing lots of eye makeup and a sleeveless black shirt. It made Marty shy.

"Do you want to go have pizza?" asked April. She smiled widely.

"Sure," said Marty. "Whatever you like."

At Mabe's, Marty couldn't take her eyes off April. Her hair was very short in a gamin cut. With shadows blushed onto her eyes, long eyelashes and the muscles in her arms chiseled against the tight black shirt, she looked sophisticated, as if she had just come from a European movie set.

"So, what about New York?" Marty managed to ask, trying to get back to some form of intimacy. She felt like a square. She wore no makeup, her usual short curls and a boxy shirt.

"We can't make up our mind to go," said April. "We went for a visit, and even though the city is exciting, Mother and I like where we are. I think Mrs. Houlton is a bit disappointed in me, but I don't want to give my whole life to dance!"

"Yeah," said Marty. "It sounds like a big commitment." Her mouth was dry and she didn't feel like eating at all. She had forgotten how hungry April got and how much she could eat! But April was much more active than Marty.

"My mother has a good job, and I'm still going to the University. I love dancing with Mrs. Houlton. She's so dynamic. She makes new dances all the time. And they aren't strictly ballet. I like the freedom of modern dance, and she does too."

"It sounds like you could stay in the Cities and dance in her company," said Marty.

"Yes," said April, sighing. "I can. It's just that I'll never have much of a reputation. You have to get into a big ballet company to get that. But you know, Marty, I don't care!" April looked more certain as she spoke. "There's more to life than dancing!"

"Your foot's all healed?" asked Marty.

"Yes," said April. "It's fine. But, Marty, what about you?" April's big beautiful eyes looked concerned.

Marty felt terribly flustered. She couldn't get past the fact that she was sitting with this gorgeous, fashionable girl. She felt like a plump hick. "I'm fine," she managed. "But April, you've gotten so beautiful! Or, you always were. It's just that I used to think we were more alike."

April looked at Marty. "It's easy, really," she said. "I don't do anything but some eye makeup. I just get a haircut, stick my hair behind my ears and go!"

"But you look like a model!" Marty blurted.

"I'm still the same inside," said April. "I don't have a lot of friends. I love getting your letters. I'll bet you still love Hemingway, don't you," she leaned back against the mirrored wall of the pizza parlor, smiling.

"You're right," said Marty. "I do. We're reading the Romantic poets this summer, though. Wordsworth, Keats, Shelley."

"I think we're opposites," said April, "and opposites attract! You're more on the inside and I'm more outside. I'm a city girl and you're my little country girl."

"I guess so," said Marty slowly. "What do you want to do while you're here?"

"Oh, I was just thinking we'd go out to the springs, like we did last year, and have a picnic," April smiled. "I've missed you," she said.

Marty melted, finally able to see the April she knew. "That sounds good," she said warmly. She had certainly missed April, though she had tried not to. She did not want to be physical with another girl. She and Kate never even touched each other. Marty had told Kate about April, but she had not invited Kate to go out with them today. She knew Kate would be jealous, in a friendly way.

By the next day, Marty felt closer to April. Without so much dark eye makeup, April looked a little less intimidating. It was a humid day, the sun warm and the air heavy. After their picnic, they lay on a blanket, listening to the water rushing down the rock cliff behind them, close enough so their bare arms and shoulders touched.

"Tell me about the city. What else do you do besides dancing?" asked Marty.

"It's all music," said April, laughing. "Music and dancing. There's a club we go to where folk groups come. I have lots of friends there, and we stay out late and talk. Bob Dylan started out there. You know who he is don't you?"

"No," said Marty. "Maybe I've heard the name, but I don't think so."

"Marty!" said April, turning over on her stomach and looking into Marty's eyes. "You're living in a bubble! Bob Dylan wrote all these great songs, like 'Mr. Tambourine Man' and all these other songs. You've probably heard them, but you just didn't know that a guy from Duluth wrote them."

"Duluth? Nope, I guess not," said Marty.

"Wake up!" said April. "Pay attention to what's going on! You've heard the Beatles, haven't you? The Rolling Stones?"

"I don't listen to pop music," said Marty flatly.

"Well you should," said April. "Mrs. Houlton even pays attention and she's much older than we are! She's excited by it."

Marty lay beside April, wondering what she could tell her. April had never met the Magnussons, didn't know Kate or Glen. Their worlds scarcely overlapped and Marty didn't think she could explain. April hovered above her, full of life. "Dance for me, will you?" Marty asked.

April leapt up. She made herself a small stage on the grass in front of the water falling over the rocks and raised her arms. To invisible music, she danced, gracefully, her feet in ballet positions, jumping, then falling to earth, her hands raised like swaying branches, carving out the space around her.

Marty sat up watching, wishing she had saved some film to take a photograph of April. But she had none. April was receding into the background, into her own life. No one would know how much Marty had loved her, except for April herself. Goodbye, said Marty silently. Goodbye, my love.

When April finished, coming over to flop down on the blanket, Marty clapped delightedly. "Thank you," she said. "That was so lovely."

"Mrs. Houlton says, 'Explode. Make yourself voracious in space!'" said April. "I can't dance without thinking of her."

"She sounds wonderful," said Marty.

"And how's your Dad?" asked April suddenly.

"He's great!" said Marty. "Just the same. They're all just the same. Up at the lake right now."

"I'm going to make a ballet for you," said April. "I'm not sure about the music, but, 'Your eyes have their silence,'" she recited. "Remember? 'Nobody, not even the rain, has such small hands.' That will be the name of it: 'Not Even the Rain.'"

24

Late in June, Paul found himself in northern Minnesota, wandering through the Paul Bunyan State forest on the far side of the gravel road on land that may have belonged to the family. The wilderness went on for 40 miles without habitation and no one really knew or cared whose property it was.

The sun was hot as Paul wandered, fully clothed with a long-sleeved shirt and a hat in the midsummer heat, a vain attempt at protection from mosquitoes. The pungent scents of pine and bracken and grasses baking in the sun rose around him as he tramped. In the shade, wet grass, thistles and tree shoots vied with each other for space. Insects sang in the hot sun, loud and thrumming with various notes. Birds too, if Paul stopped long enough to listen. His steps were loud in the tangle of plants at his feet.

It felt wonderful to be slogging through an uninhabited place, trying to read the natural world like a book of signs in what he saw. Paul followed an old logging road. A boggy place skirted one side of the road, and beside it were low blueberry bushes. Paul picked what he could and tasted them, tiny flavorful berries.

Off the road, Paul followed a thin track, perhaps a deer track, and found himself near a pond. Birch stumps rose near it, one with the recent chew marks of a beaver. Logs on one end of the pond made a natural weir, damming the runoff and keeping the pond full of water. It seemed astonishing that a beaver could have done such a thing, but then who knew how many generations of the beaver's family had maintained it. Paul stood looking down at the debris and rocks that had collected. It looked like a pile of twigs at the edge of the pond, but the mud and stones and larger tree branches probably went far down in order to keep water from draining away.

Rushes and cattails shielded every side of the pond and it looked as if there wasn't an access point. Paul walked around it, climbing the hill on one side. Across the pond he could see the beaver's lodge, another heap of sticks in the middle of the water, in which the beaver would have made a secure, dry nest in which to live, safe from predators.

Paul sat down on the comfy pine needles under the trees at the upper edge of the lake. He pulled a peanut butter sandwich wrapped in a plastic bag out of his pocket. The middle of the day was quite still. Nothing moved. Big puffy clouds sailed across the sky and the air was hot, but it was cool enough under the trees.

It was hard to make himself feel that he was there, in the North Woods, the place he longed to be all the rest of the year. He wanted time to stop, so he could feel it deeply. He marked the edge of a pine trunk's shadow with a stick. But by the time he had finished his sandwich, the shadow had moved. Paul lay down, his arms above his head, listening to the slight movement of tree boughs. "Here I am, where I want to be," he thought.

It hadn't been easy to get there. After school was out, Paul suffered through two weeks of teaching Bible school. Two weeks of mornings in which 13 seven-year-olds had to be occupied with stories, coloring, songs and puzzles. He had known of no way to refuse Dad's gentle insistence that he teach. And they couldn't leave for the lake until after Bible School anyway.

Those two weeks had been agonizing, as the sun lingered in the sky at night and Paul longed to be up north on the lake or in the woods. The only thing that made them bearable was listening to Twins baseball games on the radio. Harmon Killebrew, one of the top batters in the American League, made home runs. Paul identified with Killebrew. Injuries to his knee had kept him from playing and even made him move to the infield.

Mother was just as anxious as Paul to get away after teaching all year at the high school. She loved having days in which she could read and watch birds, and nothing had to be done except feeding her small brood. Dad would go back and forth, as he had only two vacation Sundays.

The car caravan that traveled to the lake took all day, with Paul driving the old Lark, packed to the gills. The blue canoe was tied to the top of the station wagon, so it was easy for Paul to follow Dad's lead.

At the lake, three sections of the dock were gone, washed off the edge of the lake by spring storms and ice breakup. Dad found two of the dock pieces two miles down the lake at the sandy beach and he and Paul dragged them back in the station wagon. They put the dock pieces out, Paul standing shivering in the freezing water holding them up, while Dad stood on the dock and pounded the iron pipes which grounded them into the sand. Usually Line and Marty helped with this task, but this year Dad and Paul managed it themselves.

Grandma Bakken felt poorly, so Aunt Rose stayed home with her. There was no indoor plumbing at the lake, and Grandma didn't think she could manage the primitive conditions. When Dad went back to Montauk to care for his congregation, it was awfully quiet at the cabin. Just Mother, Paul and the two little girls.

Mother was more timid when Dad wasn't around. She wasn't crazy about Paul being gone all day, but he was so anxious to explore, and spend time in the woods she had to agree. He was supposed to be foraging for wild, edible plants. A man named Euell Gibbons had published a book on living off wild plants, and Mother wanted Paul to see what he could find. It was an excuse to loaf about, far from people, spying on the natural world.

Time crept up on him. Paul hated it! He wanted to know he was here, just here, visiting a reclusive beaver. What could pin the day down?

Nothing. It was going to skitter on by like all the other days and he would have to leave. Paul rolled over and pounded on the sunny, pungent-smelling ground with his fist. Then he lay back again, accepting. If I don't leave, I can't come back, he thought.

Paul got up and went down to the edge of the pond. It was very mucky, but he took off his shoes and waded in. Cattails pulled up easily. They were huge, taller than he was. From each brown spike, which looked like a wiener on a stick, protruded a thinner spike covered with pollen. Mother had heard that this golden pollen could be used as flour. The rhizomes under the cattails were also edible.

Paul was under instructions to collect cattails, milkweed pods, rose hips or sumac. It was too late for the fiddleheads of unfolding fern leaves, too early for acorns or pine nuts. Paul had found hardly more than a handful of blueberries. They could eat grass heads. Mushrooms were often edible, but Mother wouldn't eat them without guidance. There were too many that were poisonous.

"Bring some fresh pine boughs," Mother had said. "We'll make tea from the needles!" At least she was adventurous about food.

Soon Paul had so many cattails on his shoulder he couldn't collect anything else. He laid them down and washed the mud off his feet, putting his shoes back on. He was doubtful about the whole operation. At this time of year, what was available was mostly greens. And he didn't like greens. He would rather have gone fishing.

The woodsy area behind the road was dry where it wasn't marshy. Paul kept his eyes open, looking for edible plants while marching along the logging road. Two years ago, Line had gotten lost in these woods. She was gone so long Dad took out a gun no one knew he had, and fired it into the air. Line finally found the road, but she said when she heard the gun, she went in the opposite direction! Paul laughed to himself, remembering.

With strong sun giving him direction, Paul had no problem with getting lost. But he must have looked like a haystack, moving down the road with his load of cattails. When he got home, Mother, Hanna and Kristen met him at the door.

"Don't bring them into the cabin!" Mother said.

Paul put the stack down. Golden pollen covered his clothes, his face and his hair. Hanna jumped up, trying to brush it off. She was like a little cat, Paul thought, while Kristen was a loyal little dog, patiently waiting at one's feet.

Mother came out with paper bags. "We'll put the tops of the cattails in bags, and then shake them to see what dried pollen comes off," she said. "I thought I would try to make pancakes."

"Pancakes!" yelled Hanna.

"Hush," said Mother. But there was no one there to hear her. "Did you find any blueberries, Paul?"

Paul blushed. "Hardly any," he said. He had eaten them all.

"It might be a little late," said Mother. "Or maybe bears found them."

"I'll go out again tomorrow," said Paul. "These got in my way!"

The pancakes Mother made were bright yellow. She had replaced some of the flour with the pollen in her usual buttermilk recipe, and the only thing Paul noticed was a slight appley taste. The pancakes were delicious, especially when doused with Mother's brown sugar syrup.

The next week was pure pleasure, though Paul felt the responsibility of staying close to the cabin to help Mother. He canoed early in the morning, swam with Kristen and Hanna in the afternoons, and once in a while they all drove into town to go to the grocery store and stop at the Dairy Queen for a treat.

It was Kristen who first noticed the dragonflies. She pointed out an ugly, long-legged creature with a large abdomen crawling up the cement blocks at the edge of the cabin. "He's climbing up from the lake!" she said. She thought he had lost his way and put him in the grass, turning him around so that he could go back to the lake.

Paul, Hanna and Kristen watched as the dragonfly nymph turned around, determined to climb up the cabin's foundation. "There's another one!" said Hanna, pointing to a similar ungainly brown creature. It too was determined to climb up the cabin. "I think it's a spider!"

"No," said Paul disdainfully. "It's only got six legs." As he peered closely, the squat back thorax of the nymph split and a thin, green creation began to emerge. "Wow!" said Paul. "Go get Mother!"

Kristen ran to get Mother and the four of them watched, mesmerized, as several of the nymphs split open, unfolding glassy wings to dry. The newly-hatched dragonflies sat still all afternoon, eventually turning from a bright green to a brittle black with transparent wings before they flew off, leaving the dry nymph casing behind.

"It must be their time," said Mother. "They are all facing the same direction!"

Once Paul's eyes were opened, he saw them everywhere. For the next two days, brown nymphs climbed out of the water and headed up the bank. Some were found drying on trees close to the lake, but others had made it up into the sun to dry their wings. Mother dug out nature books and read to them about the dragonfly cycle. They were all excited by the phenomenon.

In the evening, the four of them went down on the dock to watch the sun sink into a bank of pink and purple clouds. A heron flew every evening at the same time from east to west above them. Mother especially looked for it, its huge wingspread sailing across the sky. Paul watched it flap rather lazily, going home to its nest. Rays of light broke out from between the clouds as the sun sank behind the trees at the water's edge.

After sunset, Mother and the girls went up to the cabin. Paul took the canoe out into the bright, soft evening light. Paul paddled softly along the lake, dipping his paddle only when he needed to, listening to the loons' mournful cries as they settled down for the night. He tried to go out just far enough to get some breeze and avoid mosquitoes.

All around the lake Paul could hear domestic sounds and see lights in the cabins. Screen doors closed, people called to each other, fishermen plonked tackle into boats. As Paul sat, someone pulled the cord on his 8-horse motor, which thrummed to life. The boat pulled away from its dock, sending out a rippling wake which made Paul's canoe rock on the still water. The fishing boat, along with another one already there, hung several hundred yards out from shore at the place known as the drop-off, where there were supposed to be big Northern pike.

The sky was full of light still, huge above Paul. Nowhere else, except on a lake, could he see the whole bowl of sky. In most places, trees or buildings obscured it. As Paul craned his neck, a few stars began to appear. The thin crescent of a waxing moon was already sinking into the west, or, as Paul now thought of it, the earth was rolling around its axis, leaving its moon behind.

Paul settled himself in the bottom of the canoe, using a lifejacket as a pillow. He wished he were on one of the pristine lakes he knew were farther north, lakes not ringed with cabins, where the noises of people and motors couldn't be heard. Only birds, chipmunks, maybe a moose coming down to have a drink at the lake's edge. Paul imagined it from photographs. Visiting the beaver lodge on the pond on the far side of the road was the farthest he ever got from people.

Early in June, Ed White, one of the astronauts, had walked in space, attached to his capsule with a tether and using a thruster to move where he wanted to go. It was the first time an American astronaut had done "extra-vehicular activity."

Man was very tiny up in space. It was a wilderness for sure. But only one man got to walk in space. Hundreds, maybe thousands, of men made it possible, and that at great expense. Realistically, and all the science fiction Paul read aside, space didn't look very possible. But, it was easier now to picture the earth in space. Photos from John Glenn's first orbit showed it to be a big blue marble, infinitely beautiful, ringed with atmospheric clouds.

As the sky darkened, Paul began to pick out the brighter stars and planets, Venus in the west, Vega and Deneb. He loved the Milky Way which was a highway strung from east to west across the sky. At home he could hardly see it. But how much better would it look from an uninhabited lake farther north? Paul laughed at himself. His dreaming was getting closer to home! After all, gorgeous dragonflies emerged here, on their very own lake, moving determinedly into the light like explorers.

At last the sky was inky and Paul paddled back to the dock, dragged the canoe up on shore and slunk off to his lair in the bottom of the cabin. It was terribly damp there, so the de-humidifier had to run most of the day. Paul turned it off at night, so the green, wet smells of grass could float in the window. He was the only one sleeping on the lower level now. The little girls slept in Grandma Bakken's room.

On the day Dad was supposed to arrive, Mother grew expectant and watchful. She was hoping he would come at supper, bringing a smoked whitefish from Morey's in Motley, a treat they all loved. It was too far to drive to, but they often stopped on the way to the lake from their home in northern Iowa.

Supper passed and Dad didn't come. After supper Mother and the girls didn't even go down to the lake. They sat in the twilight listening to Mother read *Anne of Green Gables*. Paul went down to the lake to see whether everything was shipshape, but he didn't take the canoe out. He went back up to the cabin and sat in the yellow light, listening to Mother.

At 10 p.m., Dad still hadn't come. Paul listened to the darkness. Insects buzzed around the porch light. A breeze in the birches and pines were all that could be heard.

"I suppose we should go to bed," Mother said finally. Kristen's eyes were drooping.

"No, no!" said Hanna. "We can't go to bed. We want to see Dad when he comes."

"All right," said Mother. "No need to get up in the morning, I guess. I'll read another chapter, if you're not going to fall asleep."

They looked at Kristen, whose head lay on the padded arm of the couch, but Mother kept on reading.

At last, Paul heard a car coming up the rutted driveway and headlights shone into the back windows. He was the first out the door, and there was Dad, getting out of the station wagon, tired after a long day of driving. Mother and Hanna followed. Mother looked girlish as she put her arms around Dad, kissing him.

"I guess you had a hard time getting on the road this morning," said Mother.

"Yup," said Dad. "And I got to Motley too late to pick up some fish. But I got a lot of other things."

When Paul opened the back of the station wagon, there were two hay bales lying there! Dad had brought arrows, bows and the hay bales to make an archery target. Paul carried boxes in from the car, groceries, books, a cooler of frozen meat and vegetables from their freezer at home. Camera equipment Dad was beginning to collect. And there was a burlap bag full of tree seedlings!

Things might be quiet when Dad wasn't around, but when he arrived, the place came to life! Innumerable projects got discussed the next morning as Mother and Dad sat drinking coffee. Paul realized his days of loafing about might be at an end. But he also had a project he wanted to discuss. He bided his time, waiting until Dad had a day to relax.

Of course, relaxing for Dad meant wandering around the cabin property, thinking about all the things he wanted to do. Paul went with him, listening, and showing him the empty dry dragonfly nymphs which he now saw everywhere.

"Wish I'd been here with my camera," said Dad, as Paul explained how beautiful the emerging insects had been.

"I think we need more hay bales," said Dad, tentatively, as they walked out into the bog, which this year was quite dry. "I'd like to make a practice target out here. Or else we could put them on some kind of platform."

"Where'd you get the seedlings?" Paul asked.

"Oh, they were trying to get rid of them at the nursery," said Dad. "So I took them. Can't have too many trees. We better get them in today, get some soil around them before they dry out."

Paul helped Dad plant that morning. Dad never seemed to be in any rush. And he hardly ever badgered Paul to do things. He just worked at his own pace, and in order to spend time with him, Paul joined in.

After lunch, there was plenty of time for Paul to disappear for a while. It was a windy day, and the whitecaps kicked up in rhythmic swells on the lake. The wind was loud in the pines as Paul walked along the lake path. He wondered how to ask Dad to go exploring with him, maybe up north to the boundary waters area between Minnesota and Canada. Lots of virgin forest up there, and wonderful canoeing, he had read. It was real wilderness. He doubted that he would be allowed to go by himself, but he was desperate to get away from domesticity to a place where there were only animals and plants, and the soaring heavens of uninterrupted star light at night.

At dinner, things mumphed along in the civilized way they usually did. Mother and Dad fostered an atmosphere of gratefulness, reminding their kids that as children they had had much less during the Depression. Even the irrepressible Hanna could be subdued by Mother's love and engagement.

Finally Paul could keep his mouth shut no longer. "Dad," he said. "Couldn't we take a canoe trip? Up north? Camping for a few days?"

Dad looked at Mother. Mother knew Paul had been longing to get away. "We'll have to think about that, Paul," she said. "Your Dad doesn't have much time, you know."

"I know," said Paul. "I just want to be somewhere there's no people! Remember when you used to go up on the Rainy River with the men in North Dakota, fishing? Couldn't we do that?"

"We'll have to see," said Dad. But neither of them refused outright.

Paul was relieved. He had gotten his idea out on the table.

After supper when the lake calmed down, Dad took Mother out in the canoe. It was the first time Mother had been out all year. She got gingerly into the canoe, taking her binoculars, and she and Dad pushed off into the sunset.

Paul, Kristen and Hanna hung around on the dock, watching. Hanna and Kristen hung their feet over the edge of the dock and Paul went up and got his guitar. He sat strumming on the dock platform, and Hanna came to sing with him, quietly. On the lake, every noise carried and they didn't want to disturb other people. There were now many cabins on both sides of them along the lake edge.

Late that night, after Kristen and Hanna were in bed, Dad brought out all of the topographical maps he had of the area around Lake Michigami.

"I don't want to leave your Mother alone more than a night," Dad said, spreading out the maps in the lamplight. "And I don't want to spend all our time driving. The boundary waters are pretty far away. But why don't we explore some of these little lakes around here. We could portage between them."

Paul looked at the detailed colored maps, showing hills, wetlands, lakes and waterways. They were beautiful.

"Doesn't that look like a chain of lakes right there?" asked Dad. "Probably not much of a road," he mused.

"We could find it," said Paul, excited. "I'm sure we could!"

"I've seen the spur road, I think," said Dad. "It's off that road to the west of us that they're talking about making into a big highway. All logging roads, of course."

The map thrilled Paul, made the uncarved forest manageable. "I found this beaver pond the other day," Paul said. "I wonder if it's on here. It was just south of us." Sure enough, with his finger he traced his route and found a small lake below the road. The lake on the map looked bigger than the pond he had seen, but maybe.

"Okay, Paul," said Dad. "Friday we'll pack up the canoe and some sleeping bags and some food. Maybe Peter Emstead over next door has a tent. Should be fun!"

In bed that night, dreams of unadulterated wilderness assailed Paul as he tried to fall asleep. Elk, moose and bear hung behind every tree. Lakes smooth as glass reflected the azure, pink and lilac sky as twilight settled. Eagles and herons soared through the sky. At night, a milky river of stars flung across the sky was as bright as the moon path on the lake. Perhaps one place in the North Woods was as good as another, as long as it wasn't settled. Paul was excited.

On Friday, Dad was slow to attend to everything. It was as hard to get him going as it ever was. But finally, after lunch, the canoe was strapped onto the station wagon and the two of them set off up the road.

They turned off onto the marked Spur Road, which was little more than a two-rutted trail. Dad drove while Paul held the map in his hand. Both of them peered into the dark forest ahead, looking for other small roads which led off to the lakes.

All of a sudden, Dad stopped. Ahead was a large round, fuzzy shape followed by two small ones. A mother black bear and two cubs. The cubs were rolling and rollicking ahead in the road, attacking each other and tumbling together. Mother bear paid them no attention. Dad and Paul sat, mesmerized, and slowly rolled up their open windows.

The cubs didn't seem bothered by the car, just curious. One of them climbed on the hood! It didn't seem very heavy. Like a curious teenager, it pawed at the windshield, behind which it probably saw Dad and Paul with its sharp eyes.

When the car yielded nothing of interest, it tumbled off the slick surface, rolling onto its sibling. As Dad and Paul sat watching, stunned into silence, the mother bear, who had been pawing at the ground, finding roots and green shoots to eat, shuffled into the woods and the two cubs followed.

"Wow, that was quite a sight," said Dad. "Wish I'd had a camera with me."

Paul felt odd, as if visited by some unknown presence. He could completely imagine being a cub, hunkering through the woods after his mother, surprised by a big, inedible hunk of metal in the road.

"They were beautiful," Paul said. "They move like liquid. Like something strange, their muscles are so fluid."

"Powerful," said Dad. "They're probably a lot stronger than they look to be at that size. And the mother! I wouldn't want to get between her and those cubs!"

When they could no longer see the cubs, Dad turned the key in the ignition and started again. They drove through the forest, turning onto one road and then another, until they came to a sandy place at the edge of a lake.

"Well," said Dad. "I guess we're not the first here, but I reckon people aren't too prevalent. Let's put in the canoe and try it."

The lake was tiny, no bigger across than the beaver pond, but it was long, and according to the map, another long lake, not accessible by road, was just beyond it. This one wasn't a muddy lake, so ringed by rushes and wild rice you couldn't get at it. A sand bar washed up on its western edge where they could put in the canoe.

Paul was elated as they stroked the canoe and their camping equipment through the small lake. He pretended they weren't only ten miles from Lake Michigami, with its ring of summer cabins all around it. He imagined they were trappers, coming down from Canada to trap and collect furs for trading. The amount of blood and pain shed for the furs didn't enter into it. Dad, who had killed a stag with a bow and arrow, made a good trapping buddy.

That night Dad and Paul camped at the edge of the third lake they found. They had paddled and portaged until it was quite dark. Paul was hardly even hungry. They found dry firewood, made a fire and cooked some wieners over it. That was dinner. It was an exploratory trip, after all.

The moon was gibbous and up late enough that it obscured the stars. Paul was too tired to stay awake until it disappeared. He crawled into the tent after Dad. He could not pin down this longed-for camping trip any more than any other day. They both slept like logs on the hard ground.

For breakfast, there were only peanut butter crackers, but that was fine with Paul. He was thinking of Euell Gibbons. While Dad boiled up some lake water over the embers of the fire and made instant coffee, Paul collected milkweed pods, green and tender, the way they were supposed to be. He would bring a few back to Mother to see what she made of them.

"Euell Gibbons is funny," said Paul, showing the pods to Dad. "He says some writers describe hair-raising adventures of barely surviving in the wilderness, whereas when he goes off into the woods, all he does is lie around getting fat!"

"Well, I have to say," said Dad, "a little butter wouldn't hurt. I'd like a little cream in my coffee, or some toast with butter this morning. Maybe I'm more like your Grandma Mikkelson than I think!" Dad had tried to get his parents to come up to the lake, but his mother told him she wasn't interested in primitive living. She had spent her life trying to get away from it!

"I'd probably eat a lot worse things than peanut butter crackers in order to get away from civilization for a while," said Paul.

"Well, Paul," said Dad, "you're getting to be your own man. Another year and you'll be making your own choices about a lot of things." He pulled the sleeping bags out of the tent and began to roll them up. "So, what do you think? This far enough for one trip?"

All of a sudden Paul felt guilty for dragging Dad away from the cabin. It would take most of the day to get back to the car. "Sure," he said. He was grateful Dad had come out with him. "Thanks so much for taking the time, Dad!" He began folding up the tent and packing it into its intriguing little sack. They had borrowed it from Peter and it was almost new. It had a floor and was mosquito-proof. Paul loved it.

When they were packed up, they put the canoe in the water. Dad took the steering end, and Paul the front. It was a wonderful day, paddling back across the three lakes, portaging between. There was some small talk of what they saw, but mostly they were just silent, listening and looking.

Late in the day, as they lifted the canoe on top of the car, Paul thought of something. Made bold by Dad talking about his future, he blurted, "One thing, Dad. I don't want to go to Wittenberg. I don't want to go somewhere everyone thinks they know me already."

There, he had said it. The words sounded harsh, ungrateful and mean to Paul, changing the atmosphere around them. Dad said nothing. Paul worked his way around the car to Dad, who was wrapping straps around the canoe and pulling them tight.

Dad looked troubled. "I heard you, Paul," he said finally. "Plenty of time to think about all that."

Paul felt bad. He thought about all the times he had been back and forth to Wittenberg with Mother and Dad. About Dad taking Line up to talk to the Dean, about Marty, who seemed to be thriving. About Mother and Dad's hopes for their children. But it couldn't be helped. He was glad he had said it. He wanted to be, yes, he needed to be, his own man.

25

On a warm morning in June, before the sun was even up, Line, wearing Bermuda shorts, a white blouse and tennis shoes, got off the noisy Chicago elevated train at the Hyde Park station and walked nervously down the open stairway. At the foot of the stairs, Stephen's excited face, circled by sandy, curling hair, looking up, was all she saw. Line breathed a sigh of relief. Everything would be okay.

Stephen put his arms around Line, hugging her. "Great to see you!" he said. He too wore casual clothes, his belt tightened to hold up the wrinkled khaki trousers which threatened to fall off his thin frame. "Come on! Shall I take that?" he asked, reaching for her small blue train case.

Line handed it to him and took his warm hand as Stephen walked hurriedly toward a dark, long-finned Chrysler full of people parked on the nearby street. Stephen introduced her and the two of them squeezed into a space for one in the back seat.

Bernie Freeman was driving, and his wife Kay sat beside him. Three other people were also squeezed into the car. The sun came up as they headed east, but soon they turned north, and a hot square of sunshine lay flat on Stephen and Line, pressed up against the back window. They were headed for Camp Maplehurst in Kewadin, six hours away on the other side of Lake Michigan, to a Students for a Democratic Society convention.

Stephen opened the window and warm air rushed at Line, cooling the sweat that dripped down her back. She was quiet, listening to Stephen and his good friends talking. SDS had recently moved its national headquarters to a building on 63rd Street, between the University of Chicago and the notorious Woodlawn ghetto. Stephen had helped find the place, as he studied at the University and knew the area well. He now lived in this building, with seventeen other politically-driven people.

"SDS isn't a single-issue movement," Stephen told Line. "It's willing to work with many groups. It's a broad struggle on many fronts at the same time."

Line wasn't sure what it all meant. She had a summer job at the Lutheran Home for the Aged in the northern part of Chicago, where she lived in a cottage behind the house. She spent her time listening to people's stories and problems, driving them places they wanted to go, and helping them with finances, paperwork and welfare workers.

Line had only been at the Home a couple of weeks and she was nervous about leaving for the weekend. But she was an extra person. The staff had gotten along without her before she came, though she worried that if she was gone too long she might lose her job. She also felt a strong pull toward Stephen Cohen.

Stephen himself didn't seem to be surprised she was in Chicago. "We're a band of brothers, standing in a circle of love," he told Line about SDS on the telephone, "a far-flung network held together by love and work. You've joined us." He seemed to exist in a glow of light. He had helped plan the huge rally against the war in Vietnam in April which drew 25,000 protesters to Washington, DC, and as soon as camp was done, he was heading to the Pentagon, where another rally was planned.

Line had kept in touch with Stephen by letter and telephone since she met him in Alabama a few months earlier. Despite the comfort she felt next to him physically, she didn't know him very well. Beside her in the car, she could feel hard things digging into her side. They turned out to be books Stephen was carrying in a kind of shoulder sack. She turned and pulled the sack onto her lap.

Stephen smiled at her. "It's a map case. I got it at the Army surplus store. Isn't it great?"

It was made of thick, olive green canvas with a webbed shoulder strap. Line felt silly with her little train case at her feet. The army map case was just right for a few shirts, socks and Stephen's books. He pulled them out and spread them in front of Line, Franz Fanon, Camus and *The Autobiography of Malcolm X*. "You need to read these," he urged, low.

When the car pulled into Camp Maplehurst that evening, it was clear to Line that nothing that happened around Stephen would be ordinary. Nothing was organized. There were many more people wandering around than the SDS group was used to, most of whom Stephen didn't even know. Kay took Line under her wing, shared her bedding with her, and found her a bunk in the building the women had selected for their own, though women and men roamed all the buildings freely.

Supper was served in a big camp dining room. Everyone was warned not to take too much of the lasagna, as it might run out. It was cold and not very appetizing to Line anyway. She was sleepy after getting up so early in the morning. After supper the few hundred people gathered in the big fireplace room, sitting on the floor, on the couches and chairs. There was a microphone at one end and speaker after speaker got up to talk and read the papers they had prepared before coming.

"It's a participatory democracy," whispered Stephen between speakers. "It's the organizing principle of SDS, laid out in the Port Huron statement."

Line listened. In fact that was about all she did all weekend. But she learned a great deal. Stephen had met Bernie Freeman, a sociology professor who had helped define SDS, at the University of Chicago. Stephen was seized by SDS' drive towards social change based on non-violence and an inclusive populist democracy. He had jumped in with both feet.

Line noted that Stephen wasn't one of the speakers. He was rather a note-taker and administrator. He kept lists of people's addresses and telephone numbers and wrote up what people said. Because Stephen had been working on big marches, rallies and teach-ins for the last year, he was part of what he called "the old guard." He wondered, privately to Line, where all these new people had come from! Unlike the "old guard" who wore bedraggled, but recognizable button-down shirts and khaki pants, the new people wore jeans, cowboy boots, blue work shirts and had longish hair, with drooping mustaches.

Line wasn't sure what Stephen wanted her to do. She sat by him, listening sleepily as the evening wore on. It seemed no one wanted to go to bed! But finally Line slipped away. In the morning, she noted where Stephen was having breakfast. He must have hardly slept! She sat down at a different table so as not to bother him, but in a few moments, Stephen came over. It seemed that he wanted her with him!

But Stephen did not want to sit by the lake or go for walks in the woods, as Line did. He wanted to participate in the long, long meetings that stretched into the night. He sat by her, put his lanky arms around her often and ate with her, though meals too became long discussions that didn't seem to end.

The discussions were wide ranging. Some thought SDS was spreading itself too thin, that it couldn't continue to maintain the poverty programs it had begun all over the country and also spearhead a powerful anti-war movement. Others wondered whether, when they entered into the fragile world of the oppressed as outsiders, they were not exposing these people to trouble with landlords and police.

Among the group were a few people from SNCC, but after the last summer's failed attempt by the Mississippi Freedom Party to have a say in the Democratic convention, Afro-Americans leaned toward the idea that whites weren't helping, that they must go it alone. Many wanted black nationalism. For whites, the civil rights movement was no longer a place to work.

Earlier that year, Malcolm X, whom Line knew only by name, had been assassinated. Tom Hayden held a moment of silence for Brother Malcolm, who had evolved after a trip to the Middle East and Africa from a radical Afro-American speaking against whites to a compassionate man pointing to solidarity in search of human rights for all people.

All of these things stunned Line. She had herself tried to shed light on some of these things in her quiet little corner of the world, using the Wittenberg College International Relations Club as a place to learn. But these intense young people embraced the word "radical." They went much further than she could imagine, taking on the problems they saw all around them.

Line saw joy in the young speakers. Government was a "machine," an antiquated system run by fearful old war hawks. But people could be educated and empowered to take matters into their own hands. And this group held those who could do it. What if, indeed, they, the New Left, was a bigger movement than they thought, leading students everywhere?

As Line had noticed in Selma, rumors and ideas seemed to swirl around a few visible, vocal people. One of these was a new person, a little older than the rest, but with an articulate, uncompromising set of ideas. In fact Carl Oglesby, whose wife came with him and who was rumored to have three children at home, was elected President of the group. He had grown up poor, then became comfortably bourgeois. But he had sold his red Alfa Romeo and his house and given his life, and family, to the Movement.

After realizing that it was useless to drag Stephen into the woods, Line went for walks by herself, just to let all the ideas filter down into her own, nascent being. One day she saw Kay Freeman sitting in the sun on the sandy beach looking out across the wind-whipped water. She was a warm woman with an accent Line couldn't place. Line walked up to her.

"Do they ever stop talking?" she asked, laughing.

Kay laughed too. "Not that I've noticed. But Bernie and I agree that you have to have balance. He's terribly interested in what's going on here, and I'm not going to drag him away. But at home, we have nice meals, go to movies."

"Thank you, Kay," said Line. "It's all so new!"

"That young man really likes you," said Kay.

Line looked rueful. "We're so different! I can hardly imagine his family, and I'm sure he can't imagine mine!"

"I think he came out of the same tradition I did," said Kay, "though he's a bit younger. Bernie's parents were Russian immigrant Jews. They were fired from their teaching jobs because they belonged to the Communist Party. My parents were born in Russia. After Stalin, Bernie and I don't think much of the Party. But we're thrilled to see an independent political left growing in America."

Line pondered this. She remembered that in North Dakota the farmers discussed politics all the time. Not so much in Iowa. Or maybe she just wasn't paying attention. Her own interests grew from wanting to be a world citizen, wanting to know about other countries, beginning with the missionaries who occasionally came back from the field to speak at her church. The International Relations Club at school opened Line, and so did spending a semester in Atlanta, Georgia at an Afro-American college.

But politics to Line was people, not ideas. Individuals embodying experiences unlike her own. It was too much to explain. "Left, right, center," Line said. "It's all new to me. I just like people," she smiled her bright smile. "And Stephen is attractive!"

"You're like a pair of magnets," said Kay. "Plus and minus coming together wherever I see you. You might be opposites in background, but there's also something about you that looks like twins! Such shining faces!"

Line blushed. "Yeah," she said softly. "It's wonderful." What a lovely, generous woman Kay was.

Finally, the night before the conference was over, Stephen smiled at Line after supper, packed his notes and books into his canvas bag and slipped out the door holding her by the hand. He dragged her with him to his bunkhouse and they lay in the warm, evening heat on top of his sleeping bag. The sun was shining low through the window on the wooden walls of the building. The bare wood smelled like pine.

Line melted, giving in to the powerful attraction between them, letting Stephen kiss and fondle her all over.

"Stephen," Line whispered urgently. "I don't want to get pregnant." She didn't think there was anyone else in the big room full of wooden bunks. At least she hoped not.

"Don't worry," said Stephen, quietly. "I'm not going to get you pregnant." His tongue reached deep into her mouth like a powerful organism, engaging hers. But then he slowed himself down and rolled onto his back beside her.

The two of them lay there, looking up at the sagging mattress above them, not talking. Finally Stephen said, "So what do you think? I love all of these guys so much! Every one of them is extraordinary in his way."

"They are extraordinary," said Line. "And so are you."

"It just feels like I'm living fully," said Stephen, "for the first time!"

"Yes," said Line. "I know what you mean."

"And you're my girl," said Stephen, kissing Line's neck.

Line kissed him back. "I like being your girl," she said.

They lay beside each other, tender and open, talking about their lives.

Finally it was dark at the window. Stephen seemed to wake up all of a sudden. "Jesus Christ," he said, "I've got to get back. It's the last night!"

Line was shocked to her core. Stephen had used Christ's name as a swear word!

Stephen stood up, pulling Line with him. "Can you come with me? Stay up until it's over? It doesn't matter if we sleep in the car on the way back."

"Okay," said Line. The frisson of shock that leapt through her had waked her up too. But he's Jewish, she thought. He doesn't know anything about Christ.

They stumbled back in the dark toward the lights of the main lodge. Line felt as if she had been powerfully used, her tongue sore. Sweet honey dripped through her body and softened her eyes. They crept in to the big room and stood at the back. Surely everyone knew what they had been doing, she thought. Stephen sat down and took out his notebook and Line sat beside him, her hand on the small of his back.

When they got back to Chicago, Stephen took the el with Line up to the Wilson station in north Chicago, to the broad residential street where Line worked. Big elm trees lined the street and cast leafy shadows all down the avenue.

"That's it over there." Line pointed to a large, dark building a ways down the street. "You better not come with me. It will be hard enough to explain myself."

"Sure," said Stephen, casually. He kissed Line. "I'll give you a call."

And that was it. He turned and walked away.

That week Line struggled to come back down to earth, working with the frail older people who lived in the home. Though they were all Lutheran and most were Scandinavian, Line was quite surprised to find that even here, there were great differences. Her favorite people were at both ends of an economic spectrum. Most were somewhat helpless due to minds or bodies which no longer obeyed them. Almost all had lost a spouse.

On a Tuesday, Line wrapped a beautiful green wool shawl around the ancient Mrs. Bergmann and pushed her wheelchair out into the sunroom to have her tea. Mrs. Bergmann let it be known in many ways that she was from an upper class. She dressed carefully, though she needed help, and was slow and ponderous about her movements. Punctuality, an endless round of timely rituals which never varied from day to day, seemed to keep her alive. Her sharp tongue quickened everyone's steps around her. But she liked Line.

Line pushed Mrs. Bergmann up to a table laid with the breakfast plate. "Tea?" she questioned formally. "Jam with your toast?"

Mrs. Bergmann nodded, "Quite," she said. "Marmalade, please."

Line poured hot water over her tea bag and buttered a slice of toast. None of the old people ate much, Line found, but meals reminded everyone they were still alive. She spooned the bitter marmalade over the toast.

"Where did you live in Norway?" Line asked. It always helped to ask questions.

"In Oslo, of course," said Mrs. Bergmann. "It was a lovely place then, when I was a child."

"Not so cold?" asked Line.

"The winter's weren't as bad as they are here," said Mrs. Bergmann. "The sea, even the Baltic, mitigates winter. But it was dark for many months of the year."

"Yes," said Line. "I grew up in North Dakota. But we liked winter. Mother made a big fuss at Christmas. It seemed to last for months, and after that it was spring!"

"Did you have all of the Norwegian cookies? The krumkakke, the sugary rosettes, the sandbakkels?" asked Mrs. Bergmann as she took small bites of the sweet bread.

"Sometimes," said Line. "Neighbors brought them to the parsonage. We made most of our cookies ourselves from recipes in magazines. Mother was too busy with all of us to bake. But at Christmas, Grandma Mikkelson sent us lefse and klub as a treat. Those are the Norwegian foods I know best," said Line.

"Ah," said Mrs. Bergmann. "The food of the poor."

"The poor?" asked Line.

"Blodklubb," said Mrs. Bergmann. "Blood pudding. We never had it at our table."

"We liked it," said Line, loyally. "I put sugar on my lefse. My grandmother made the kind that didn't use potatoes. We liked it better than the common potato lefse."

But it was hard to gainsay Mrs. Bergmann. "Yes," she said. "Peasant food. From the farms. In the city we ate white bread."

Line had never thought of it. She stood up and cleared the breakfast things off to a tray. "Did you bring your needlework with you?" she asked, trying to get Mrs. Bergmann settled so she could take Miss Knutson to the dentist.

"Oh! I think it's in my room," said Mrs. Bergmann. "Thank you, Line," she said graciously.

Line brought the silk embroidery Mrs. Bergmann kept with her, trying to make small stitches with arthritic hands. Then she ran off to find the tiny Miss Knutson, who was proud of being a secretary most of her adult life. City people were so different, thought Line.

Miss Knutson sat in the lounge, doing a crossword puzzle. Older men were reading newspapers and books by lamplight, as the lounge was comfortable, but dark, even in the morning. "Don't you have a dentist appointment today?" Line asked. "It says so on your calendar."

"Oh," said Miss Knutson. "I forgot. What's a word that means 'affected with nausea,' ending in 'y?'"

"I don't know," said Line. "But I think we had better go to the dentist. You don't want to be late."

"All right," said Miss Knutson, struggling to get up out of the deep, upholstered chair. "Let me get my sweater." She was quite ambulatory, but she had no idea what day it was. "Crosswords keep your mind sharp," she said to Line as they left the building. "You should try it."

It was a warm day. Line drove the station wagon someone had given the Home with Miss Knutson sitting beside her. Line felt young, capable and in charge. She had found the dentist's office address on the Chicago map tucked in the glovebox of the car. Miss Knutson sat on the front seat beside her, a biddable child.

Line waited for her outdoors on the steps of the dentist's office. Birds sang in the street trees and an occasional car or person passed. She was trying to put together the surging, potent group of young people at Camp Maplehurst with these sweet old people who were drying up, their skins shriveling on their bones like dry leaves in the fall. She did feel useful at the Home, though, really useful. And happy.

Line thought of Marty, at summer school and working in her precious library, and Paul, probably rowing a canoe around the lake by now. It was a narrow world they lived in. Here in the city she was meeting so many different kinds of people. People whose parents were born in Russia! And Stephen. He was an intellectual, with his papers and notes and books. He said his parents weren't actively Jewish, but it was unlikely they celebrated Christmas! Line smiled internally, remembering his vivid swearing. She herself had begun to say "God!" as an exclamation. Words weren't sacred. They were just words.

What Line and Stephen did have in common was the desire to make the world a better place. Stephen expected to be a teacher and writer, eventually. He was never pointed toward social work. The Vietnam war, however, had opened up a political arena none of them had anticipated.

Thoreau had refused to pay taxes to support war and slavery. Even among Lutherans, civil disobedience was not unknown. Everyone at Wittenberg read Bonhoeffer's *Letters and Papers from Prison*. Bonhoeffer had spent more than a year in prison for plotting against Hitler. He was eventually executed. Line could imagine political dissent as something she should do, but it felt negative. She was more inclined to help poor and uneducated people. It gave her much to think about.

Some evenings that summer, when she quit work, Line took the elevated train down to the South Side. Getting off at 63rd Street, she ran the gauntlet of cruising black teenagers, derelict buildings, boarded-up shops, and fences papered with torn posters, turning up at the SDS national headquarters to see what was going on.

The place was a marathon of office work, telephones ringing, typewriters banging, meals and studying, all in an atmosphere of mild communal chaos. Even in the evening, when the work day was done everywhere else. Music rang through the house from the phonograph albums which collected in the big, common room. Blues, rock, Irish folk music. It was the complete opposite of the staid, traditional institution Line worked at during the day.

Line and Stephen sat on the wooden steps which led down to a small backyard, drinking cream and sugar-laced coffee in the twilight, listening to the music in the background and talking. A black cat came up the steps on soft white feet and curled around their legs. Line ran her hand over its back, enticing it to stay. She leaned her back against the banisters, relaxing. The chaotic flat felt like home.

As Dylan sang "Ain't gonna work on Maggie's farm no more" in the background, Stephen said, "Dylan did this electric set at the Newport Folk Festival. Riled everybody up!"

"Oh?" said Line.

"Want to come to Lansing, Michigan, with me this weekend? I'm doing a teach-in. You could help pass out literature and take names and stuff," Stephen wheedled.

"Okay," said Line. "If you need me."

"I do," said Stephen. "I do need you." He nuzzled her face and neck.

Late at night, Stephen borrowed a car to take her back to the northern part of Chicago. He didn't want her on the trains late at night and walking the dark streets. Line was glad.

That was how the summer went. Line liked the two poles of her life. The regimented life at the home protected her from the chaos of the communal house on 63rd Street, but this house too was a relaxation from the rigid customs which bound the residents of the Lutheran Home for the Aged. Line took weekend trips with Stephen and a couple of friends, helping run teach-ins which instructed students about what was going on in Vietnam, about their chances of being drafted and what they could do about it. Stephen was an effective speaker in small groups.

In August, Mother wrote to ask whether Line would be home in time to go to the lake. Line panicked. She would have to go back to Wittenberg for her final year of school soon, and she couldn't figure out why. What would it get her?

Line felt she was already much more useful in Chicago than she had ever been before. Urgency lay right in front of her, Wittenberg a backwater where she would be stuck studying statistics and moldy old sociological studies which could hardly be meaningful today. Saul Alinsky had organized black voters to challenge Mayor Daly's political machine in the very Woodlawn district where she now spent time with Stephen. She was right there, at ground zero. Could she face going back to Wittenberg?

"You could put it off," suggested Stephen, trying to help. "Get a job here and finish your degree another year."

This hadn't occurred to Line. In the city, there were so many ways of doing things.

"You could work for SDS, but it isn't much of a living," said Stephen.

Line's mind churned. She wondered whether she could stay on in the intern position at the Home. She didn't need much money. She asked Mr. Welch, who ran the Home. "Yes, I think we could keep you in your present position. I can't raise your salary, but you are getting a good deal living in the cottage and eating your meals with us. The residents like you. We can see how it goes," Mr. Welch answered.

"Yes," said Line fervently. "I thank you, Mr. Welch. I would like to stay."

That afternoon, Line sat down at a desk in the bedroom she shared with one of the kitchen workers at the Home. She had hardly written a letter all summer, but now she wrote to Mother and Dad, explaining herself as best she could.

"Dear Dad and Mother," she wrote. Their presences rose up in front of her with poignant clarity. Their desires for her, their sacrifices, their hopes. But she steeled herself. It was her life, after all. "I have decided not to go back to Wittenberg this fall. I'm learning so much here and the Home will keep me in my present position. Mr. Welch supports the idea and there is so much going on here that I would like to continue.

"I've been seeing the person I told you about, Stephen Cohen. Remember, I met him in Selma. He lives in the southern part of Chicago and works for Students for a Democratic Society. He's getting a Masters in Sociology at the University of Chicago. He is very nice, sandy, curly hair, very thin. I don't think the SDS guys eat very well or put much stock in food. They are so anxious to educate everyone, to make their presence felt.

"If it turns out that I need a degree later, I am sure I can go back to school then." Line tried not to imagine the effect this letter would have on her parents. Of course they would have their opinions, but she decided not to ask for them.

"Thank you so much for all of your love and care for me, and for all of us," she wrote. "I think of you often and carry you all with me in my heart. I won't get to the lake this summer, but I will try to come home at Thanksgiving or Christmas.

"Love to all, Line," she finished.

The letter was smudged and a couple of words were crossed out. Line considered whether to send it as it was. She read it over. Normally, she wanted to re-copy letters, make them perfect. It was one of the reasons she didn't get them sent! But, it sounds like me, Line thought. I better just send it as it is. She found an envelope and a stamp, and walked the letter down to the corner post box, as she often had with letters written by her aged people. Free, she thought to herself, as the envelope thudded to the bottom of the blue box. With the stroke of a pen, I have become free.

26

Marty sat typing at a small desk under a window in the corridor between faculty offices for the religion and philosophy department. Dr. Magnusson had given her a book length manuscript to type, but it hardly seemed like work. She was fascinated by what he had to say. The book was a response to a recent crop of books questioning whether God was dead.

Dr. Magnusson wrote that Christianity has always challenged the gods of religion, allowing an intimate relationship between individuals and the Gospel, the story of Jesus Christ.

Marty was so used to Dr. Magnusson's lectures that as she typed the tiny handwriting, she could almost hear him speaking. Small black regular handwriting, "which only you can read," he told her. She had been working as his secretary all year. Handwriting was easy. Marty simply assumed that every loop or movement meant something.

The carriage return whanged against the margin she had set as Marty pushed it to the left after each line. She was careful about typing, because correcting mistakes was a pain. One had to backspace, insert a strip of sticky paper to take up the ink and retype the letter. Marty tried to be accurate. It was like playing the piano, her fingers appropriate to what the machine needed from them.

The offices were empty at lunch-time. It was quite pleasant, the light behind Marty in the tower of Main, with its blonde modern furniture. Marty stacked the finished pages into a stationary box and put it neatly on the shelves in Dr. Magnusson's office. Many days she didn't even see him. They communicated via an out box and sometimes notes.

Marty ran down the stairs and out into the crisp March air, heading to the student union. It was her last spring at Wittenberg and things had begun to take on a conclusive note. Marty would have been happier if she knew what she would be doing next fall, but so far she did not.

Student teaching the previous semester had not gone well. Marty worked with a junior high English teacher who exercised a great deal of control over her class. Only one student stood out for Marty, a dark, morose girl who sat in the middle of class and frowned when Mrs. Albert taught. The girl, the daughter of a mathematics professor at college, was clearly brilliant and when Marty taught, the girl perked up.

Marty simply could not be an unequivocal teacher. At college they studied English in its descriptive, rather than prescriptive mode. But in junior high school, the books treated grammar as if it were dead. Literature too. Marty imagined that if she had been able, she could have turned the class on its head, made it interesting. But, on the other hand, she had to admit that she was probably not a good teacher for that age group. It was not possible to talk only to the few kids who loved language.

At the other end of the scale, Marty found she hated literary criticism. She was auditing a seminar in which the text was called *Theory of Literature* by Wellek and Warren. It was a thick book and Marty could not read it. She was thrilled to attend the seminar full of young teachers just out of graduate school and her most brilliant English major colleagues. It met under casual circumstances, sometimes even in the homes of these faculty members, only a few years older than Marty.

But Marty was glad she was auditing, because she couldn't concentrate on the subject matter. Instead, she found herself thinking about what sort of people the participants were, their surroundings and their relationships.

Marty's English professors thought her an intellectual and supposed she might go on to follow in their footsteps. Each of them was willing to help her. But, getting a Masters in English was about critical analysis. Marty loved literature and had deeply personal responses to writers. She felt so strongly she wasn't sure she would ever be able to be objective. Teaching an established canon of writers deemed "great" would be interesting; there was much she didn't know and it would be worthwhile to have to defend her ideas. But the path of analysis was dreary.

Dr. Haatvedt too thought Marty might want to teach. But Marty knew her intelligence would not support further academic study. The most likely possibility was that she study library science and become a librarian. Marty took the Grad Record Examination. There were scholarships to apply for. She was working on it.

Marty dashed up to her mailbox. She had only a few moments to have a quick lunch before class. Suddenly, in front of her was Glen Norgaard, the young pre-seminary student she had built her romantic fantasies around for the past year. A frisson of fear and delight ran up her spine. She immediately became flustered.

"Glen! I've been meaning to come over to the radio station to see you," she blurted out. It was a plan she had been hatching to go and find Glen in his den. Scary, but it was hard to be in love with someone you never saw.

Glen seemed flustered too. He sidled up to the long bank of mailboxes, trying to stay out of Marty's way. "Yeah," he said. "Jeana is the music librarian there."

It didn't make any sense. "Jeana?" Marty watched as he hurriedly took a letter out of his box.

"Yes," said Glen. "Jeana and I kind of run the place now."

"Okay," said Marty. "Maybe I'll stop by one of these days. I'd like to see it."

"Sure," said Glen, galloping toward the front door.

Marty looked after him, frozen. It was as if she and he were all alone in the busy student union. Sunlight outlined Glen's retreating body. She knew who Jeana was, a small woman with a lisp who played the organ and ate only one meal a day. Was Glen trying to say he was going out with Jeana? All of a sudden the whole thing became clear to Marty.

It was not only Mother and Dad who assumed that the best place to meet your future spouse was at college. At Wittenberg it was hard to go out with someone without being instantly deemed "married." Several guys had tried going out with Marty, but she hadn't found anyone as congenial as Glen. There was even an IBM dance that winter which attempted to match people up. Completed questionnaires were submitted on cards to a computer. The three guys paired with Marty surprised her. But nothing came of that either.

So here she was, all of a sudden free, without even someone to dream about. Marty turned stoically back to the mailboxes. Perhaps it could be worse, she thought. Worse would be being involved with someone she didn't feel strongly about. Or, as she found that night, being in Kate's predicament.

After a busy day, Marty was so sleepy she turned off her lamp and went to bed before Kate got home. Though they shared a room and were the best of friends, Kate seemed as unsure about her life as Marty. It manifested itself in different ways. Kate shared the growing discontent visible on campus.

For one thing, a "new breed" of students now came from cities rather than small towns. These students reflected the unrest which could be seen all over the country in riots over inequality and poverty, resistance to the draft and anger over the imperialist and patriarchal attitudes wielded by those with political power. At Wittenberg, mandatory chapel was challenged and overruled. The curfew for women students was pushed back, but still in place. A double standard still allowed men to roam around all night, but not women.

All of these things bothered Kate, but not Marty. For Marty, internal strictures were more powerful. She put up with the cultural structures around her quite well.

That night, when Kate came home crying, Marty woke up and tried to listen. Kate was involved with a guy named Bob. He was in Men's Senate and prominent in his fraternity. He liked spending time with Kate, but wanted to keep it a secret. Kate was in love with him and it made her miserable.

"What is it?" Marty asked Kate, sitting up in bed in her pajamas, wrapping the blankets around her.

But Kate wouldn't say. She just sat on her bed sobbing and pulling tissues from a box on her desk. "He wants me," she said. "But he doesn't want anyone to know. It's all hidden. Like he pushes me out of the car so that he doesn't have to come up and kiss me in the light." The dorm had a "fishbowl" entrance, brightly lit, where before the doors were locked for the night, men and women stood kissing each other. Established couples were shameless and single people had to run the gauntlet between them if they were late getting home.

"So he's not sure he wants it to be permanent?" said Marty.

"He's sure he doesn't want it to be permanent," sobbed Kate. "I'm not good enough for him."

Marty sighed. "Well what on earth does he want?" she wondered. What could anyone want besides love, friendship, authentic relationship.

"He acts like he loves me. We spend all evening making out, but then, he zooms off!" Kate continued. She pulled tissue after tissue out of the Kleenex box, wiping her eyes and blowing her nose. "Practically shoves me out of the car."

Marty tried to be gentle. "Maybe he's just unsure. Maybe he'll come to his senses and ask you to be his girlfriend." But she wondered if Bob wasn't just a wolf, a guy who wanted physicality, but no deeper commitment.

"He's just like me," Kate blurted. "He comes from a farm in Iowa. I don't know what he thinks he wants!" She was clearly aching inside.

Marty didn't know Bob at all. When she did see him, he said little. He was thin and tall, with acne scars on his face and a slight, sardonic smile. "I'm sorry, Kate," she said. "I just don't know what to say."

"There's nothing to say," said Kate. "I've been letting it happen. I let him get me excited over and over. Maybe I don't want it to be permanent either. I'm not ready to tie myself down to someone either. Forever and ever." Kate blew her nose again. "But it's so painful!"

Marty wrapped the covers tighter. She was glad she didn't have this problem. "Yeah," said Marty. "I hardly know Bob at all." She had seen the furtive maneuverings between Kate and Bob. Probably more people knew than Kate suspected. It had been going on for a while. But if it was a clandestine arrangement, that meant something too.

"Don't worry, Marty," said Kate, beginning to stop snuffling. "I'm sorry I woke you up."

"Oh, it's all right," said Marty. "I saw Glen today. Did you know that he was going out with Jeana?"

"Of course," said Kate. "I tried to tell you. But you wouldn't listen." She took off her coat and scarf and kicked her shoes under the bed.

Marty hung her head. "Yeah, I guess not. Well it's all clear to me now."

"Where did you see him?"

"By the mailboxes. He ran off. Every other sentence had Jeana in it." She giggled. "I'm such an idiot," she said.

"Well as one idiot to another," said Kate, bitterly, with a country stoicism. "I think we had better go to bed. Things may look better in the morning."

"I hope so, for your sake," said Marty. She was thinking of her philosophy of freedom class. There was "freedom to" and "freedom from." She was feeling both kinds of free that day.

Kate began to put on her pajamas. "I guess I'll survive," she said. "But it doesn't seem fair." She grabbed her plastic pail of soaps, shampoos and tooth cleaners. "Good night, Marty," she said quietly as she left the room, heading down the hall to the bathroom.

Marty lay down. What wasn't fair? Life? Men? God? Kate sounded like Line to her. And where was Line? Line had not come back to college that year. She was working in Chicago at an old people's home. But was that what she was really doing? Marty wondered. There must have been more to Line's decision than that. Marty would graduate in a few months, but Line would not.

Marty hoped Line was happy. She must be. It was impossible to get much out of her by letter, but she wasn't that far away. People went to Chicago just for the weekend. One of these days, Marty decided, she would visit. Next year they would all be going different directions, Paul to another college. Carrying each other in our hearts, Marty thought. She was now used to being away from home, but the family was strong in her thoughts. Hanna was in school now, happy as a puppy dog.

Because she had crammed so many requirements for her majors and minor into three years at Wittenberg, Marty was free to take classes she was interested in. This semester she was taking a class called Philosophy of Freedom with Dr. Magnusson. They were reading Martin Luther, Nikolai Berdyaev, and Erich Fromm, each of whom wrote on freedom.

It wasn't as hard as Marty thought it might be. She very much agreed with everything these writers said, but she could not place herself in the positions one must take in order to philosophize. It was like mathematics, using language. She could not keep the equations in her head and she could not see the problem in the first place.

The class met in a corner of the student union like a seminar. Big windows looked out toward the river below the bluff the building was built on. Marty was tense in class because she didn't want to disappoint Dr. Magnusson. She was the only girl with four male philosophy students, but this actually helped. Not much was expected of her. Marty hardly talked in class, though there were short papers to write.

Dr. Magnusson lived and breathed a vibrant philosophy which he had found in the still rarified air of Europe after the war. He had done his doctoral work in Heidelberg and written a dissertation on works by Karl Barth. He had come to Wittenberg College at a time when his ideas contrasted sharply with the conservatism of some of the religion faculty. Some of them had left, since they couldn't get the college to suppress Dr. Magnusson.

Rumors Marty couldn't penetrate surrounded Magnusson's dramatic presence. She could not imagine that anyone would think differently than he did. His presentations were perfectly clear and not in conflict with those of her own father's sermons. Both he and Dad held closely to Martin Luther's teachings and were open to modern science.

Dad's interests were actually more in practical science than in theology, including carpentry, photography and radio communications.

One day in class, discussion was easy around the table. Dr. Magnusson tried to elicit from the class Berdyaev's concept of freedom.

Erik Lehman, thin whispy hair floating over his acknowledged brains, took up the challenge. "I think Berdyaev is saying that God is present only in freedom and acts only through freedom."

"Yes," said Dr. Magnusson. "But does that put God outside of nature? Outside the world of phenomena?"

"I think so," said Erik. "He wants to locate God as a creative force, ruling in 'the kingdom of freedom' as he says, not in determined nature."

"It's rather a different way of thinking about God than we are used to," said Dr. Magnusson. "A God who created the world out of nothing, in freedom, and gave freedom to humans."

"But Berdyaev designated egocentricity 'the Original Sin,'" said Erik. "So he didn't feel our freedom and creativity should be directed towards our own ends."

"Yes," said Dr. Magnusson. "His idea is once again that the world that we live in is merely a phase of an ultimate spiritual reality, the 'kingdom of freedom.' But he is very much a Christian. Do you see it, David?" He turned toward another of the students.

David shifted in his seat, then said slowly, "God became man, came down to earth, making freedom and creativity understandable to us."

"Exactly," said Magnusson, his whole body moving in dramatic agreement. "Redemption through grace overcomes the evil and suffering of the world."

Marty listened in rapt attention to the world of language they had built around themselves. Berdyaev came back to the very point which Martin Luther did.

"Berdyaev was born in 1874 and grew up in that foment of revolution in Russia. But he was an Orthodox Christian. He felt we could create something completely new, something that had not existed before. He wanted us to express our God-given freedom, to make the material world more like the spiritual world within us."

"One thing that has always puzzled me," said Erik. "Not related to Berdyaev, of course. It's just that, how could God expect to become man in one place, as a gift to only one group of people. There are people all over the world. Did He not want to come directly to them as well? Wouldn't it have made more sense?"

Marty did not even hear Dr. Magnusson's answer. The question was so cogent, so compelling. It was the question she wanted to ask, though she didn't even know it. And in a sense, the question precluded an answer. The waters had parted and Marty was walking across to the other side. She was ready. The world fell away. She no longer needed Christ to be her personal savior. She did not need a savior. She was free.

In the next few weeks, Marty walked around with a new sense of inner space. Spring came, "mud luscious and puddle wonderful," with its warm rains, the greening of grass and trees, and the lovely smells of sap and vegetation that the warming sun released. And Marty stopped worrying about the future, due to an unexpected invitation.

As she placed her finished typewritten sheets in the correct box in his office, Dr. Magnusson stopped Marty to say, "My wife and I are accepting an invitation to Mansfield College next year in Oxford, England. We've been trying to decide whether to take someone along as a companion to Thea, so we would have a little more freedom to go out. Would you consider such an invitation for the next school year?"

Marty was shocked. "Oh, yes," she said. "Though I have to ask my parents."

"We couldn't offer you more than board and room, but I think you might find it possible to attend lectures at the university, and of course it would be an opportunity for travel."

"That would be wonderful," said Marty.

"Well, think about it," said Dr. Magnusson, "and let us know."

Marty didn't need to think about it. She wanted to go. But it did mean she wouldn't be making money next year, or even going to a graduate program so as to increase her chances of employment.

Marty called Mother and Dad collect to tell them about the idea.

"I'll be working at the Wittenberg library this summer as long as I can and I might make enough money to cover the plane fare," said Marty doubtfully.

"Maybe you could get some extra work in Oxford," said Dad. "If the Magnussons don't need you all day."

"Thea will be in school during the day," said Marty.

"I can tell from your voice that you really want to go," said Mother. "More than going to library school?"

"Yes," said Marty, yearning sneaking into her voice. "I would love to study at Oxford University. It seems to be sort of open, like I could audit lectures."

"Well, I'm sure we can figure out a way to help you," said Mother. "Perhaps we can meet the Magnussons when we come for graduation. You're a little young to be all on your own in a foreign country."

It was true, Marty thought. She was just 20, graduating from college in a couple of months. "Thank you so much!" said Marty. "I've checked on getting a passport. You just need a birth certificate, or a verification of birth."

"Thief River Falls, Minnesota," said Dad. "Mercy Hospital. I remember it like it was yesterday! Write to them. I'm sure they'll send it to you."

"Me too!" said Mother. "My goodness! Time goes so fast! And you girls are getting away from us!"

"There's Paul and Kristen and Hanna at home," said Marty, reasonably. "But I miss all of you."

"We had a letter from Line," said Mother. "She says she's going to be at Wittenberg for a teach-in on April 20. She says Stephen will lead it and that we should come up and meet him!"

"Wow," said Marty. "I haven't heard from her."

"You will, I think," said Mother. "Have you been to a teach-in before?"

"No," said Marty. "There's some of that going on here, demonstrating and so on, but I'm too busy to pay attention."

"I'm sure you'll want to go if Line's there," said Dad. "Keep an eye on her! It sounds harmless enough."

"Education never hurt anyone," said Mother staunchly. "But save the 20th. It's a Saturday. We'll bring a picnic."

"Oh good!" said Marty. "I can't wait to see you, and we'll have more time to talk."

"Yes," said Mother. "We'll talk more then, Marty. We love and trust you. I think you can go ahead and make your plans."

"I can't thank you enough," said Marty. "You are the most wonderful parents in the whole world!"

"Hope so," said Dad a little ruefully. "Hope the apron strings are long enough so you kids don't forget where you came from."

"Don't worry, Dad," said Marty. "They are. See you soon!"

Marty did get a postcard from Line, who was organizing a teach-in at Wittenberg with friends from the International Relations Club. Apparently Stephen was giving teach-ins at colleges all over the Midwest about the Vietnam war, and Line helped him. Marty couldn't wait to meet him. Line's letter said, "Marty, I think Stephen is the man for me. But you've got to help. He's Jewish, which is probably even worse than Catholic in Mother and Dad's eyes."

Marty considered. Christ was a Jew, after all. And in her new, open state of mind, none of these distinctions mattered at all. She wrote back to Line, offering her help in any way she could. The Vietnam war seemed far away to her, though she knew that friends of Paul's had been drafted and that one of her cousins was in the Air Force. She told Line she would be going to Oxford, and explained how excited she was to be able to attend lectures at one of the oldest institutions of higher learning in the world. It felt like a dream.

As spring progressed, Kate got a job in a small Christian boarding school in South Dakota, teaching high school English. Like Marty, she would graduate in the spring and go to summer school to finish up her credits. Her teaching job would start in the fall.

One windy spring day, Marty and Kate walked down town. Kate was already thinking about furnishings for her new home.

"You'll be a much better teacher than I ever would be," said Marty, as she wrapped her scarf tighter around her ears. The trees had begun to have enough leaves to cast shadows on their path, but seed casings blew around in the wind and lay strewn over the sidewalks and streets.

"I like teaching," said Kate. "I guess the only thing that bothers me is South Dakota. It seems like a step backwards from everything that has been happening here."

Marty looked at her. "Backwards?"

"Well, I guess I will feel more grown up," said Kate. "But I will have to make new friends. Think of all the faculty members we know here. I'll miss Mrs. Herseth so much!" She was still learning hardanger, the lovely white embroidery work, from Mrs. Herseth.

"You'll have all summer," said Marty.

Kate looked at her sarcastically.

"Oh, all right!" said Marty. "Call me Pollyanna, or whatever else you want to. I can't help it!"

"You're just happy," said Kate. "You're a menace," she said, smiling.

"Yes," said Marty, wrapping her arms around herself. "I'm a menace. I don't know what's coming, but it's gonna be great. 'I got a feeling there's a miracle due, gonna come true, coming to me! Who knows, could be.'" She sang the last words softly in the wind.

Kate laughed. "Life in a musical. Might work." She turned away, sighing. "But not for me. I don't think so. It's going to be so tough to leave everyone."

Marty mused privately, wanting to envelope Kate in her own inner expansive space. She was ready to move on. College was brief, it was intense, but it was almost over. Erich Fromm had said, "There is only one meaning of life: the act of living it." At the back of Marty's mind was a picture of Mother and Dad, happily living the life they had made together. Yes, she too was ready.

27

Line jumped out of the car when she saw Marty coming across the Wittenberg campus toward them. She enveloped Marty in a big hug and dragged her toward Stephen's side of the pale Thunderbird he was driving. "This is Stephen," she said. "I can't wait for you two to talk!"

Stephen smiled and took the hand Marty offered through the window. Line and Stephen had come to give a teach-in at the college. Line worked with her old friend Henry to set it up, but Marty was helping them find places to stay.

Watching them, Line was struck by how frumpy Marty looked. She was a little plump, and she was still rolling her short hair to make it curl around her face. She wore cut-off jeans and a Lambda Chi sweatshirt which didn't hide the fact that Marty ate too much and spent most of her time reading. There was nothing athletic about Marty. Line sighed. It would take a while for Marty and Stephen to get to know each other.

"Henry will meet us for dinner," Marty said. "He'll show you where you can sleep," she said to Stephen. "I got you some meal tickets."

"Should we leave the car here?" asked Line.

"Sure," said Marty. "I don't really know anything about parking. Maybe Henry knows."

It was late afternoon, but the sun hung around a little longer on spring evenings. The three of them walked across the grass toward the student union, leaving long shadows behind them. Line felt quite at home, though she hadn't been at the college for almost a year. She felt grown up compared to the students she saw, some her classmates. She did not feel sorry she had left school and gone out into the world. It was so much wider than she even suspected while at Wittenberg.

"Just what is a teach-in?" asked Marty.

Stephen looked at Line and smiled, "Did you call this a teach-in?"

Line nodded, defensively. "Yes, I did. It's sort of a teach-in."

"It's really just a talk," said Stephen. "Teach-ins started at the University of Michigan. Faculty members started these open-ended participatory discussions of politics. Like a seminar. Mostly now we're all thinking about the U.S. presence in Vietnam and the draft."

"Stephen and I go to colleges where they want to discuss the war, because SDS has more information than most people do. A lot about the draft. Certainly more than they are telling us on television!" said Line.

"Sounds interesting," said Marty. She stopped just inside the student union. "We're supposed to meet Henry here."

In a minute, Henry Neering emerged from the crowds of students, holding the hand of his girlfriend, Peggy, a little blonde athlete with a perfectly curled flip. Line had sort of been Henry's girlfriend when they went to Selma, Alabama, the year before. But when Line met Stephen, Henry conceded with good grace.

"Nice to meet you," said Line. Peggy radiated graciousness, almost condescension. Oh, thought Line, giggling inside. She's convinced him he's the cat's pajamas! To Line, there was no one like Stephen for miles in any direction!

"I like the idea of SDS," said Henry as they set their trays down at a table near the big windows looking out across the river where the sun was just setting. "I've been reading about it. Maybe we should have a chapter here at Wittenberg. But I'm graduating in a month. It's really up to someone else."

"I see," said Stephen. "It's a pretty loose group. But you might want someone on the faculty who can advise, can hold it together when people come and go. Do you plan to stick around next year?"

"That's the thing," said Henry. "No one sticks around. Cardinal is a college town, not a city. If you want to go to grad school you have to go elsewhere. We all have to go elsewhere, unless our folks are professors and we grew up here."

Line nodded. "That's why I like the city. There's work everywhere! And it might look big from the outside, but it's full of little communities."

She looked from Stephen to Henry. She had tried to love Henry. But there was no fire there. Henry liked being where the action was, but he was really a small power broker, thought Line. He might very well end up in politics with his perfect little wife. Stephen was a rabble-rouser, an intellectual, a warm and wonderful lover. Line could not even imagine all there was to Stephen.

"Can I get anyone a cup of coffee?" Marty stood up, as people appeared to be finishing.

"Let's go down and get coffee at Dante's!" Line remembered the dark coffeehouse at the bottom of the student union. It purposely had no windows to symbolize the lowest circle of Hell described by Dante. Darkness reigned in the coffeehouse, as well as guitars, coffee, candles dripping over wine bottles on the spool tables.

"We don't have time!" Marty remonstrated. "We have to get over to the auditorium!"

"Oh, all right," said Line. "Maybe tomorrow," she said to Stephen. Their eyes met and Line was stopped for a moment, thinking of the deep interior spaces they had traveled together. But she quickly recovered. There were people all around them, people with needs and claims on their time.

Stephen's speech that night delivered the point of view among the political left opposed to Johnson's escalation of the Vietnam war: It was an un-winnable war. The United States supported dictators in Vietnam and had not learned that freedom cannot be advanced by a military policy that relies on burning villages with napalm and on torturing the villagers for information. He emphasized the long history of foreign aggression against Vietnam and charged that the United States was merely the latest aggressor, and not a savior.

As he spoke, Line remembered when she had first heard of Vietnam at an International Relations Club meeting. Don Claybourne had read a paper on it with views much like that of the left. But Don was nowhere to be seen.

Stephen's speech got a lot of support. Line came up beside him afterwards and passed out the Xeroxed materials she had helped prepare at the SDS office in Chicago. Many people stayed late, asking questions and arguing heatedly with each other. Henry fielded questions and tried to keep order. One group supported US involvement, but another planned to protest against the war the next day outside of chapel.

Line noticed that the women were melting away, slipping off up the stairs to the upper exits. She stood in the aisle with a clipboard, taking the addresses of people who wanted to get the SDS newsletter.

Marty came up beside her, whispering, "We have to go. They'll lock the dorm!"

Line looked at the clock on the wall, which said 11:30 p.m. "Wow," she whispered. "You can stay out to midnight?" She went up to Stephen and handed him the clipboard, whispering low, "I have to go, or I can't get in the dorm. I'll see you tomorrow."

Stephen smirked at her, but he squeezed her hand and let her go. She and Marty put on their coats and rushed out into the fresh spring night.

"Whew!" said Line. "Lots of hot air in there!"

"It was great," said Marty. "Exciting! Or at least I'm excited. How can anyone sleep after talking about all of this stuff?"

"It's the draft which makes it so personal," said Line. "Guys have to decide what they are going to about getting drafted."

"I've been living in my own little world," said Marty. "I didn't realize. Getting drafted wouldn't leave much time for literature or philosophy!"

At the dorm, Marty pulled out a mattress kept for visitors, and put it on the floor beside her bed. After Marty's roommate Kate went to sleep, Line and Marty lay whispering late into the night.

"Just like old times," said Marty.

"Who'd have thought?" said Line. "Do you like him?" It was terribly important to her that Marty like Stephen.

"Sure," said Marty loyally. "He seems to have a lot to say, to have some substance."

"You'll get to know him," said Line. "He has a close family, but no brothers or sisters. His folks are committed to education, just like Mother and Dad."

"That would be strange," said Marty.

"I'm sorry I didn't come to Grandma Bakken's funeral," said Line. "How is Mother doing?" Grandma Bakken had died of cancer a couple of weeks before. Mother was reportedly taking it hard.

"Better," said Marty. "But I guess we'll find out tomorrow. She's not going to say how she feels, you know. She never does."

"I know," said Line. "But I will be able to tell from how she looks. My friend Mrs. Bergmann, from the Home, died. I was the one who found her. I went in to help her get up in the morning and she was dead." Line sobered, remembering. "Her eyes were looking up, her hands folded and stiff. But there was a presence in the room. I felt it."

"How long had she been gone?" asked Marty.

"They thought she had been dead for several hours. She didn't have much family left. But, you know Marty, I like working with older people. People say I'm good at it. It's just paying attention, after all."

"You've always been good in crises."

"I like bodies," said Line, "working with humans. I'm so glad I'm not at school any more. I don't see myself going back either. Unless it's in nursing, or something. I'm just not into books!"

"Hmmmm," said Marty. "Maybe that's what you should be doing."

"But how about you, Marty?" asked Line. "Are you pleased about going to England next year?"

"Pleased is an understatement," said Marty. "I can't imagine anything I'd rather do! It's astonishing. I'm so lucky Mother and Dad are willing to help me. I won't be making money, just board and room. But maybe I'll make some money this summer. I'll work at the library until the end of August."

"That's good," said Line. "Money. I never really thought about it before, but now it's important. I love the city. There are so many different kinds of people there! But you have to have money to do anything! SDS works with all of these poor people who come up from the South looking for jobs. In a way our family was poor, but we had gardens and everything we needed. These people have nothing! And winter in Chicago is freezing!"

There was no answer from Marty. She must not have been as excited as she said she was.

Finally Line drifted off to sleep. But she waked early, surrounded by the hive-like activity of the girl's dorm. A good thing too, as they were meeting the rest of the Mikkelsons for a picnic lunch.

* * *

Marty wasn't sure exactly why Mother and Dad wanted to meet Stephen. It must have been the way Line talked about him. She couldn't see herself why Line was so attached to Stephen. And she couldn't see how being Jewish made him different. In the flesh he looked like any other slightly mocking, earnest student.

They looked nice together, Line glowing with her long red-gold hair waving around her face, Stephen's hair longish also as it curled down onto his forehead, obscuring his steely brown eyes. Stephen was thin as a rail and Line had the small waist Marty always envied, though Line also had Mother's large hips. Something invisible must bind Line and Stephen together.

They met the rest of the family at the Dunning Springs park where Marty had spent many summer afternoons. Dad was energetic and young with his warm hug, wearing a suit coat and a jaunty hat. Mother's face was thinner than usual, but she was gentle and dignified as she greeted Stephen.

Paul must now be the height he was going to be, not tall, only about 5'8", a little lopsided. But as he stood sturdily in his jeans and plaid woolen jacket, one might never have known he had polio.

Marty reached her hands out to the little girls and dragged them over to the waterfall created when springs spurted out of the palisade of steep cliffs, especially now when the snow had recently melted. Marty could never get enough of Kristen and especially of Hanna. But she could also not help but remember April dancing in front of the falls on a warm summer day.

Hanna put her hand in the water, and jumped back. "It's like ice!" she said, putting her hand under her armpit to warm it up. Her very blue eyes were like a cat's, lighting up her fine skin. But the bones of her face could have been those of a little boy. Marty wondered if it contributed to the beauty of this little sister.

Kristen put her hand in too, and touched Marty's face with her cold, wet hand to make her squeal. Kristen wore a kerchief over her ears, as they were prone to earaches. Stocky and freckled, she was constantly overlooked beside Hanna, which made Kristen's bids for attention poignant.

Mother called them back to the table, where Line was helping lay out cold chicken, pickles, mayonnaise and loaves of homemade wheat bread. The men stood aside, talking. Marty heard fragments, trying to make it into something coherent.

"So you do think there could be a just war. But the Vietnam war is not?" asked Dad.

"My parents came out of Russia, you know," said Stephen simply. "They were Jews, so they had no ability to fight. But the White Russians fought for years, trying to hold on in that vast country. Largely without success."

"Ahhh," said Dad. "You're a history student!"

"Yes," said Stephen. "History is full of chaos, but you can take a thread from it and pull that thread, and you will find a pattern somewhere."

Marty all of a sudden liked Stephen. Yes, she thought. Precisely.

"We're all human," said Dad. "No doubt about that."

"History can be seen as a series of conflicts leading slowly, very slowly, to right. My friends and I feel we have to seize some kind of power from the corrupted military industrial complex the United States has become."

Marty saw Paul almost step back from potential conflict! But none came.

"There might be some truth in what you say," said Dad, mildly. "The atmosphere here was very different during the Second World War, you know. You, of all people, must know that was a just war."

Stephen seemed to wilt a little, as if the darkness of that background were passing in front of his face. But Mother was calling them to the table.

When everyone was seated and passing the bread, the salt and pickles, Mother directed the conversation away from war.

"Do you want some milk?" she asked Stephen. The Mikkelsons, even Mother and Dad, all drank milk.

"No thanks," said Stephen. "Water's fine with me. I'm almost tempted to go get some of that spring water over there!"

"Probably fine," said Dad. "It's mostly snow melt."

"Snow gets pretty dirty in Chicago!" said Line. "There's lots of it too!"

Marty was struck by the fact that no one needed help any more. The little girls were now in school and could make their own sandwiches. The family was growing up.

"Our eldest daughter Ellie is in Italy with her family right now," said Mother to Stephen. "Line lived with her several summers, helping her with her small children. But now I expect they're learning Italian!"

"So she's the only one not here?" asked Stephen.

"The only one," echoed Mother. "You've met all of Line's siblings except her."

"Line's lucky," said Stephen. "I don't have any!"

"I can't imagine growing up in New York," said Line, "though I'm learning a lot about cities from Chicago."

"Not so different," said Stephen. "Actually, I grew up in Brooklyn."

"Chicago may not be so different from New York," said Marty. "But you should see the town we grew up in! Four or five square blocks of houses, with farms on every side. I bet you had a real library to go to!"

Everyone laughed. And Paul piped up. "Thoreau didn't need a library."

"Well Marty does," said Line, a bit sarcastically. "I think she's met her match at Wittenberg."

Marty sighed. "I'll never get to read everything I want to. In my whole life!"

"I hear you'll be at Oxford next year," said Stephen. "No shortage of libraries there!"

"Yeah," said Marty softly.

"What's a Jew?" asked Kristen bluntly. "Is it the same as Herod?"

"Yup," said Stephen. "You've hit the nail on the head. But my family was part of the Jewish diaspora, moving first into Russia, and then, quite recently, to America."

"Diaspora?" asked Kristen. Marty was impressed that Stephen didn't try to speak to her as if she was a little kid.

"It just means we were scattered, pushed out of our homeland," said Stephen.

"You know we don't focus much on what happened to the Hebrews," said Dad. "We know much more about the early Christians."

"We had a seder," said Paul.

"You did?" Stephen sounded surprised.

"I researched it and we made the foods and asked the questions," said Paul. "But you're the first Jewish person I've met."

"The last supper of Christ was a celebration of the Passover," said Dad, quietly. "In Galilee."

Mother stood up and brought out an aluminum rectangular cake pan. "Kristen made these bars," she said. She took off the thin sheet of plastic which covered the pan. "I hope they're good!" she smiled at Kristen. "And we do have a thermos of coffee, but it isn't very big."

"Don't worry, Mother," said Line. "We can get coffee back at school. I want to show Stephen Dante's. You'd like it too, Paul," said Line. "Do they still have folk music there, Marty?"

Marty's mouth was full of oatmeal, chocolate and brown sugar. The bars were sweet with caramel and chocolate, her favorite. Finally she said, "Yup, there's music."

"We promised to go to a discussion of the draft tonight," said Line. "Stephen knows more about it than anyone. We should probably get back."

Stephen looked rueful. "Yeah. But it was so great to meet you!" His voice was warm and genuine.

Marty wanted to stay and talk forever, but Dad needed to get home too. He had a sermon to write.

"So where are you going to school next year, Paul?" asked Stephen.

"Astoria College," said Paul diffidently. "It's a junior college."

"So you don't want to get into one of the big eastern colleges?" Stephen seemed to think everyone must want this.

"Education's up to me," said Paul. "I can get it anywhere."

"Wow," said Stephen, as if this were a new idea.

"Paul's probably going to go to the seminary," said Marty loyally. "Become a pastor like Dad." She wanted Stephen to know that they were all well-educated. But Paul gave her a look she didn't expect. A quizzical look, as if to say, I guess you're pretty sure about that, aren't you?

But there was no time to take it up with Paul. Everyone said goodbye. "I'm so glad we got to meet you," said Mother to Stephen. "If only briefly."

Marty felt pulled in two directions. She got into Stephen's car headed back to campus, but in every fiber of her body she wanted to go home with Mother and Dad. She could feel how Mother had graciously pulled the diverse group together around the table, despite feeling the pain of her own mother's death and the pain of all of them growing in different directions. Dad too had reached out to Stephen, finding the connections between them. What wonderful parents they were and how she missed them all.

But she could no longer go back. She must go forward. Into unknown territory. Time, the time of her life, demanded it.

* * *

Paul felt miserable too, as he rode away in the family car, sitting in the back seat with Kristen at the other window and Hanna in the middle. Why did Marty have to bring up the idea that he was going to be a pastor? Couldn't she just keep her big mouth shut? But it had been an interesting day. He had not suspected Mother and Dad could be so welcoming to a Jewish person, someone who did not believe in Christ, the Savior. What was Line doing with him?

The miles crawled by as Paul looked out the window. His mood lightened. The twilight descended, full of promise, a wash of pink fading to darker blue near the horizon. Even if he was set down all of a sudden from some other planet, Paul would have known that it was spring. The fields looked black and soggy, but lawns around farmsteads were starting to green up a little. Deciduous trees still raised bare branches to the sky, but they were thick with small buds. It wouldn't be long now. School would finish and they would go up to the lake.

Hanna stood on the hump in the station wagon that housed the car's drive train, leaning over the seats where Mother and Dad were talking quietly, humming a song from Winnie the Pooh. Kristen looked out the window, lost in a private dream as Paul was.

Finally Hanna got impatient with silence. "Let's sing something," she begged.

Dad turned around and smiled at her. "What would you like to sing?" he asked.

"Supercalifragilisticexpialidocious," said Hanna, her favorite song from the new *Mary Poppins* record.

Mother rolled her eyes and Dad laughed. "Maybe Paul can sing it," he said.

Hanna turned to Paul, who did indeed know the song by heart, much to his chagrin. He sang it ferociously, right into Hanna's laughing face. "Because I was afraid to speak when I was just a lad, my father gave me nose a tweak and told me I was bad; But then one day I learned a word that saved me achin' nose; the biggest word I ever heard, and this is how it goes!" Hanna was delighted, chiming in to sing the chorus of um-diddles and the special, exciting word.

"Again!" she cried when Paul finished. "Sing it again!"

But after a couple of times, Mother said, "Hanna, that's enough. Let Paul alone."

Paul thought of the song he was trying to learn on the guitar, a lovely, solemn song. "Here's one I'm trying to learn," he said to Hanna. "You can sing the chorus with me."

"Oh Shenandoah, I long to hear you. A-a-way, you rolling river. 'Cross the wide and rolling water. Away, we're bound away, 'cross the wide Missouri." He sang more of the verses. He wasn't even sure what it meant, why the Shenandoah was in the same song as the Missouri. The melancholy melody, full of longing, fit his mood.

Paul was thinking about Line and Marty, bound away. Next year he would be too, 'cross the wide Missouri. Astoria was 100 miles from home. About right, he thought. No one knew him there. He could think as he pleased. He was learning from Line and Marty how to leave home, but they could have their old cities and libraries. He preferred rivers, lakes, forests. And sky.

* * *

ACKNOWLEDGEMENTS

The author would like to thank her siblings, cousins and friends who have shared in the experiences of which this is a fictionalized account. She also thanks the many teachers she has had over the years, who have helped her become better company for herself! In addition, she thanks Don Starnes for his wonderful work designing the cover. And for his support throughout this project.

Connie Kronlokken

ABOUT THE AUTHOR

Connie Kronlokken grew up in a large Norwegian/Danish Lutheran family. She spent her childhood in small towns across Minnesota, North Dakota and Iowa. In 1969 she moved to the San Francisco Bay Area and now lives in Los Angeles with her husband Don Starnes. Connie studied filmmaking in Denmark and has been a student of yang style tai chi for more than 25 years. She loves being with her family, the march of the seasons, cooking and gardening. She's been parsing romance from reality for most of her life.

www.ingramcontent.com/pod-product-compliance
Lightning Source LLC
Chambersburg PA
CBHW021335250626
47155CB00002B/713